Praise for The Promise:

Finalist for the 2014 Ohioana Book Awards

"*The Promise* is a gripping drama, at once personal and macrocosmic, a powerful recreation of the hurricane that devastates Galveston in 1900—and the fragile but hopeful life that a young woman is rebuilding there after fleeing from a scandalous past. I was captivated by Weisgarber's deft use of voices, her careful delineation of character, and her ability to pull the reader into a different time and place."
—**Chitra Divakaruni, author of *Mistress of Spices* and *Oleander Girl***

"Excellent use of historical detail and strong character development . . . it should attract wide readership."
—*Library Journal*

"Ann Weisgarber's *The Promise* is set against the backdrop of the worst natural disaster of the 20th century in the U.S., but the weather is no match for [this] story of two women's love for the same man. The coastal isolation of Galveston shows Weisgarber's ability to make a place come alive, and the real storm in the book is the demand of family, the hope of love, and the impossibility of reinvention. Fans of *A Reliable Wife* will find *The Promise* to be a book they can latch onto."
—**Alexi Zentner, author of *Touch* and *The Lobster Kings***

"Based on the true story of one of the deadliest storms in American history, *The Promise* is the work of a skilled storyteller. Weisgarber (*The Personal History of Rachel Dupree*, 2010) has written a beautiful, deeply engaging story about love, loss, and the power of secrets to change our lives."
—*Booklist*

"Set against the worst natural disaster in twentieth century American history, *The Promise* is a riveting tale, told in lean luminous prose, of the power of love and the frailty of the human condition. Weisgarber knows storms, those that devastate the land and those that rage in the human heart. Her characters will live in your imagination long after you've turned the last deeply moving page."
—**Ellen Feldman, author of *Next to Love* and *Scottsboro***

"Full of surprises, impossible to predict."
—*Florida Weekly*

"Weisgarber's conjuring of Galveston Island at the turn of the 20th century is miraculous—a sensory feast. Narrated by a pair of compellingly divergent female voices, *The Promise* is at once an American story of second chances, an achingly felt love triangle, and a psychological tour de force. I am stunned. Rarely do novelists so happily marry depth of insight to unflagging suspense."
     —Lin Enger, author of *Undiscovered Country*

"*The Promise* is a thrilling and heartbreaking novel. Told in alternating voices, with perfect pitch, it brings the past alive with a vivid sense of place and time. This is a story of the enduring bonds between people, of shame and redemption, of promises kept. No one has ever dramatized a cataclysmic storm better, the fury and aftermath. It is a novel of the struggle, the work, and the power of love."
     —Robert Morgan, author of *The Road From Gap Creek*

"*The Promise* takes a historical premise, the Galveston Hurricane of 1900, but makes the story of two women and the way they try to live and love in a hard hard world as affecting and evocative as any storm."
     —Susan Straight, author of *Between Heaven and Here* and
     Highwire Moon

"The narration is split between Catherine and Nan, Weisgarber doing an admirable job in distinguishing between the two, the voice of each ringing out clearly. So, too, her description of the storm itself is wonderfully atmospheric, the fear of her protagonists mounting minute by minute, the tension as thick as the heavy Texan summer air. Combine this with heartbreaking historical details, such as an entire orphanage swept away by the sea, and you have the perfect ingredients for vintage historical fiction."
     —*The Independent (UK)*

"*The Promise* is a gripping, tautly woven story of love, loss, pain and struggle. It is a fascinating hodgepodge of churning emotions and grace (or lack of it) under pressure. It leads readers to wonder if in the wake of nature's supreme power and devastation, any of the characters will ever be what they once were."
     —Judi Sauerbrey, *BookBrowse.com*

"Captivating, enthralling, mesmerizing . . . . Her characters are compelling and fascinating, and combined with a story that is hard to put down, she has created what I consider to be one of the best books of the year so far."
     —*Sharon's Garden of Book Reviews*

"Beautifully written, the characters and story last long beyond the last page."
 —*Roundup Magazine* **(from the Western Writers of America)**

". . . the story is nuanced, psychologically sensitive, detailed and highly visual. The plot moves at a rhythmic pace that constantly tugs at readers. The characters, setting and plot synchronize perfectly . . . . The story brims with themes and conflicts that balance and deepen the novel — man vs. nature, the individual vs. society, struggles with honesty, and colliding religious beliefs and moral standards. This is fiction from a gifted author . . ."
 —*San Antonio Express News*

" . . . once again was startled and drawn in completely by this novel most especially by the voices, exactly as I was with Rachel DuPree, a young African-American pioneer, in the previous novel. With careful and deliberate language and plotting, Weisgarber develops her characters through loaded interactions between Catherine and Oscar, Catherine and Nan, and Nan and Oscar, as well as Catherine's tentative struggle to become a mother to Andre. You'll likely find it impossible to tear yourself away from this story for long until you've finished."
 —**Julie Kibler, author of *Calling Me Home***

"In *The Promise*, Ann Weisgarber has written a graceful and powerful novel about the redeeming strength of love and the struggle to survive against the forces of nature. She's a great storyteller. We need more writers like her."
 —**Thomas Cobb, author of *With Blood in Their Eyes***

"A must read for historical fiction fans, as well as anyone who a love for Texas. This is a wonderfully emotional novel, too, in the vein of women's contemporary fiction, and I think those who aren't sure they like hist fic might want to consider this one for its exploration of love and family. A top ten read for 2014, hands down."
 —*Unabridged Chick*

"Ann Weisgarber has written a fascinating look at life in the 1900's. The reader is caught up in the culture that exists with its strictures placed on women. Yet love finds a way in the harsher environments as individuals strive to find someone they belong to and with. This book is recommended for readers of historical fiction and those who long for a great love story."
 —*Booksie's Blog*

"It's been a long time since a book has caused me to cry and *The Promise* did that more than once with the power of the writing. I was so very involved with these people I hurt for them and felt their joy. I found myself so in place I swear I could feel sand beneath my feet. I love books that draw the reader in the like this. I did not want it to end and when it did I wanted to turn around and read it all over again. Like Ms. Weisgarber's first book, this one will stay in my library so I can savor it again and again."

—Broken Teepee

"The depth of each character, particularly the two women that make up the focus of the story, is phenomenal. The author brings the reader right into the fears and motivations of each woman, and it makes for what is easily the best first-person narrative I've been fortunate enough to read. Not only are the characters detailed, but so is the setting. Weisgarber makes Texas come alive in a way that few authors could."

—City Book Review

"Weisgarber has written a story rich with emotion, detail and history - definitely a recommended read."

—A Book Worm's World

"Quite often I find that second novels never live up to my love of a first one but that is not the case with The Promise. This emotional and haunting novel touched my heart and I know I won't soon forget it . . . .Highly recommended for those who enjoy historical and women's fiction!"

—Peeking Between the Pages

"She wove a great story and created some memorable characters, but it was her prose that really made this book extra-special. She somehow managed to make me think this book was written over 100 years ago, and I loved how she brought Galveston to life! *The Promise* would make an excellent book club pick."

—Booking Mama

The
Promise

Also by Ann Weisgarber

The Personal History of Rachel DuPree

Shortlisted for the Orange Award for New Writers
Longlisted for the Orange Prize

The
Promise

A Novel

ANN WEISGARBER

Skyhorse Publishing
A Herman Graf Book

First published in the United Kingdom by Mantle, an imprint of
Pan Macmillan, a division of Macmillan Publishers Limited

Skyhorse Publishing books may be purchased in bulk at special
discounts for sales promotion, corporate gifts, fund-raising, or
educational purposes. Special editions can also be created to
specifications. For details, contact the Special Sales Department,
Skyhorse Publishing, 307 West 36th Street, 11th Floor, New York,
NY 10018 or info@skyhorsepublishing.com.

Skyhorse® and Skyhorse Publishing® are registered trademarks of
Skyhorse Publishing, Inc.®, a Delaware corporation.

Visit our website at www.skyhorsepublishing.com.

10 9 8 7 6 5 4 3 2

Library of Congress Cataloging-in-Publication Data is available on
file.

Cover design by Georgia Morrissey
Cover photo credit by Trevillion Images

Print ISBN: 978-1-63220-645-9
eBook ISBN: 978-1-63450-629-8

Printed in the United States of America

For Will Atkins

The shore is smooth, the air cool and balmy, the surf sparkling surges upon the sands with the sound of music. Fair ladies with gallant gentlemen in high buggies meet buggies and pass them freighted in kind. It is romance-inspiring, this driving by the sea.

Galveston Daily News
May 24, 1868

Tell all the Truth but tell it slant—

Emily Dickinson

The Vigil

October 1899

There wasn't nothing good about funerals. The very notion of them was a disturbance. I've told my kin, when my time comes, don't lay me out for people to look at. Just close the coffin and bury me quick. But these Catholics had other notions. They stretched a funeral like nobody else could.

That was how it was for Bernadette. She was laid out in the middle of her parlor with three sawhorses holding up the coffin. It was the second day of October, still full daylight and plenty warm, but Sister Camillus had lit three white candles. They were on a tall metal stand near the foot of the coffin. At the other end, a stand held a crucifix. That was what they called it. A crucifix. I didn't like it, Jesus wearing a crown of thorns, His hands and feet nailed to the cross, and His bare ribs showing. It wasn't seemly. I wished someone would move that thing but nobody did.

A few hours before the vigil started, the neighbors showed up in their wagons. That set the dogs barking, and my two brothers had to go out and herd them into the barn. The

1

neighbors came from up and down Galveston Island, and they came wearing black. The women were in their mourning dresses with their corsets pulled extra tight for the occasion. I'd done the same. The men wore suits, and their white collars were starched to stand up even when they took to tugging at them, sweat dribbling down the sides of their faces.

The neighbor women brought baskets of food filled with platters of shrimp and oysters. They brought pans of cornbread, bowls of purple-hull peas, and more cakes than I had room for on Bernadette's kitchen table. They talked in low tones – 'Ain't it sad?' 'Don't it break your heart?' – the feathers on their hats bobbing as we put out the food. It was supper time but nobody ate. It didn't seem right with Oscar standing by the coffin, his green eyes dulled with sorrow. There was no getting away from seeing him, the kitchen being the other half of the front room. Couldn't keep from seeing the neighbor men, either, them clumped around Oscar. They turned their hats in their hands as they mumbled condolences; Daddy kept pinching the crown in his. My brothers weren't much better but the married men were the most skittish. Their gazes skipped around until they found their wives. Don't die, I could see the men think. Don't leave me with our little ones, me not knowing what to do, me having to give them away or remarry quick. Don't let me be like Oscar, widowed with a four-year-old boy.

It was hurtful to watch.

It didn't take long for the men to drift away from Oscar and go out to the front veranda. That was where the neighbor children were. The boys sat on the wide-planked floor with their black-stocking legs poked between the railing posts so that their feet could dangle and swing. The little girls sat on

2

the steps that led up to the veranda, their hair in braids and tied with ribbons. I saw them from the front kitchen windows, and I didn't blame the men and the children for staying outside. There, the breeze whisked away the sweat. Outside, they could look at the sky with its high-riding puffed clouds. The house sat up on five-foot-high stilts and from the veranda, a person could see the rows of tall sand hills that were a quarter of a mile from the front of Bernadette and Oscar's house. The Gulf of Mexico was on the other side of the sand hills and far off, at the horizon, a trail of steamships and schooners waited to come into Galveston's port.

On the veranda, the neighbor men shucked off their high collars and went to the dairy barn, some of them taking their children with them. At the barn, I figured the men did what came natural. They worked. They filled the water troughs, and they cleaned out the stalls. They worked so that Oscar wouldn't worry overly about his milk cows.

Likely Oscar wasn't thinking about nothing else but Bernadette. As Mama said, he wasn't but a shadow of himself since she took sick a week ago.

When the vigil started, the Baptists mostly left and went on home. I wanted to do the same; I wanted to breathe air that wasn't filled up with sadness. But Bernadette had been my friend since she and Oscar got married, and a person didn't run out on friends.

Neither would I run out on Oscar. My family had known him since he came to our end of the island. We were practically next-door neighbors, our house being only a mile and a half away. My brothers, Frank T. and Wiley, worked for Oscar and hauled milk to Oscar's city customers. So I stayed for the vigil, and Mama did, too. Sister Camillus got down on her knees on the braided rug by the coffin, her all swallowed up in nun's clothes so that only part of her face showed. She had her white rosary beads in her hands. Oscar was there, too, kneeling and holding a black rosary, it looking small in his broad hands that were scarred and nicked from hard work.

I could hardly look at him. He was peaked pale, the sun washed out of his cheeks. But his necktie was knotted just so, and he was fresh shaved. Down on his knees, he kept his shoulders back and his bearing upright. He stayed that way all through the rosary praying – 'Hail Mary, full of grace' – each word sliding into the next. There was no end to that rosary; it called for a prayer for each bead and that thing was one bead after the next. But Oscar stayed steady. Likely he did it for Bernadette. It would hurt her hard to see him slump with sorrow.

Leastways, Andre didn't have to suffer through all the praying. The nuns saw to that. The day before Bernadette died, her burning up worse than before with malaria and retching up watery bile, two of the nuns came and took him to St. Mary's. 'He shouldn't be in the house,' Sister Camillus had told Oscar. 'It's worrying Bernadette. She can hear him crying for her.'

I hadn't liked them taking him, not one bit. Andre had cried, I wouldn't say different. He asked for his mama, his little face puckered with puzzlement. But I was there seeing to him while Mama and Sister Camillus took turns nursing Bernadette. I washed his face in the mornings, saying how we had to scrub all them freckles of his. I helped him into his nightshirt at bedtime and made him say his prayers. When I cooked breakfast, dinner, and supper in Bernadette's kitchen, Andre played under the table with his building blocks. 'Miss

4

Nan,' he'd say, his black eyes with long eyelashes fixed on me. 'I made me a fort. See?'

'Ain't that something?' I'd say. When he cried for his mama, wanting to go into the bedroom to see her, I took him to the beach. There, he dug holes in the sand, his four dogs winding around him and dropping sticks for him to throw. When it was about time to go home, me and him picked the yellow sea daisies that grew in the sand hills. They were Bernadette's favorite. We filled up a canning jar with them and when we got home, I'd knock on the closed bedroom door. If Mama or Sister Camillus said it was a good time, Andre took the flowers to his mama. As sick as she was, her eyes lit up when that little boy with his sun-browned cheeks and stand-up-straight cowlick came into the room.

That was how it was during the first four days of Bernadette's sickness. Then she got worse and Andre went to St. Mary's that was down the beach about a half-mile. St. Mary's was an orphanage filled from corner to corner with children. The nuns were good to the orphans, I wouldn't say different. And Bernadette was partial to the nuns. 'They took me in,' she said about them. 'I won't ever forget what they did for me.' But it wasn't the same for Andre. He had a home. I expected Oscar to buck the nuns about taking Andre while Bernadette was sick. Oscar thought the sun rose and set on that little boy, and Andre was the same way about his daddy. But Oscar let the nuns take him.

That was what ran through my mind during the vigil. Andre at the orphanage, waiting for his daddy to come get him. That vigil went on and on, all them beads to be prayed over. When it finally ended, the Catholics weren't ready to quit. The funeral mass was the next day at St. Mary's. The chapel was so crowded with neighbors that the orphans had to sit squashed together. Some city people were there, too, done up in high-quality clothes. The women's hats were showy with big bows and long feathers, and the men had barbershop shaves. I figured they all were Oscar's customers, and I didn't pay them much attention. My mind was on Andre.

I saw him right off when me, Mama and Daddy, and my brothers came into the chapel before the service started. He was with Oscar in the front row, them two sitting pressed as close to each other as they could get. I could have cried if I was given to doing such. Bernadette's coffin wasn't more than a few yards from them.

Daddy made us sit in back, saying how we weren't Catholics. Mama didn't like it. 'We're nearly kin,' she'd whispered.

'Nearly kin ain't the same as being,' Daddy whispered back.

'Well,' Mama said. 'Maybe.' She sat down and the hymn-singing started, but I didn't know the words. Next, the priest showed up and all through the kneeling and praying, I thought how proud Bernadette would be, her little boy being brave, not a peep out of him.

From the day he was born, she fussed over him. She called him *mon cher 'tit chou*. That was Cajun talk for my little sweetheart, Bernadette had told me. She was from the swamps over there in Louisiana. But now Andre was a poor motherless child. That was what the neighbor women called him when the service was finally over and we walked together to our wagons and buggies that were parked off to the side of the chapel. Oscar couldn't raise him alone, they said. No man could. Then somebody said, 'The nuns'll take good care of Andre, least-ways until Oscar remarries.'

I kept my mouth shut. The neighbors didn't know. They

weren't there on the day Bernadette died like I was. I'd been washing her parlor windows, keeping the house up like she would, when Mama came out of the bedroom. 'Nan,' she'd said, 'Bernadette wants to see you.'

It took everything I had to walk down the hall and into the bedroom. The room had a bad sour smell, Sister Camillus and Oscar sat on either side of the bed, and I hardly knew Bernadette. She laid on her side, slick with feverish sweat and pasty-colored. Her lips were cracked and bloody. She was nothing but skin and bones other than her belly, swelled with the baby she was expecting come Christmas. Oscar got up so I could take his place.

I took Bernadette's hand. It was burning hot and her black eyes glittered. 'I'm here,' I said, pressing her hand to my cheek. Across from me, Sister Camillus' brown eyes bored into mine. She didn't like me, plain as day. Bernadette licked her lips. Then she came right out and told me to look after Andre.

'Now you stop that talk,' I told her. 'Ain't nothing all that wrong with you. Just a little fever, that's all.'

Bernadette shook her head. She knew different. The priest had been there that morning. 'Nan,' she said. 'Please.'

'Bernadette,' Sister Camillus said. 'Dear.'

'Forgive me, Sister.' She swallowed hard like her throat wasn't working right. She said, 'Please. Nan.'

'You're going to get better,' I said. 'I just know it.' But Oscar, standing beside me, likely couldn't take it no more. 'Promise,' he said to me; that word coming out hard. 'Say you will,' he said. So I did, squeezing out the words, tears in my voice.

I thought about my promise when we left the chapel. Most of the neighbors went on home – chores were calling – but some of us lined up our buggies and wagons, one after the other, and went up the island to the cemetery in the city. We traveled along the beach road, the tide being low and the sand by the water's edge packed down hard. To our right, the gulf sparkled like cut glass in the afternoon sun. Me, Mama, and Daddy were crowded up in the buggy while my brothers, Frank T. and Wiley, followed behind us in the wagon. The surf was a soft roar, and we didn't say nothing, sadness likely wearing us all down.

The sand crunched under the buggy wheels, and up in the sky, long strings of pelicans floated on currents of air, their wings spread wide. Oscar was partial to pelicans and liked to count them. I hoped that he saw them as he rode with Sister Camillus on the buckboard of the wagon that carried Bernadette. Andre wasn't with them. He'd been left behind at St. Mary's; could be somebody thought he'd had enough. When we got to the cemetery and the priest found more to say before Bernadette was lowered into the grave, I hoped Oscar thought about pelicans, all light and airy up in the sky. Maybe they'd make him remember who Bernadette had been before she took sick.

It'd be easy for him to let the nuns keep Andre. It'd be easy for him to send Andre to his kin up in Ohio. That was where Oscar was from. Most men would do one or the other: a man couldn't raise a child alone. Most would forget the promise I'd made, me not being kin. But when the priest finally ran out of prayers, when it was all over, the gravediggers waiting under the tree for us to leave, Oscar came over to me.

'I'm bringing Andre home,' he said. 'Later today.'

'He'll be purely glad,' I said.

The next morning, well before dawn, I let myself into the dark house and took up caring for Andre.

CHAPTER ONE

Dayton, Ohio

January 1900

Gossip. Breathless whispers. Circles of women in parlors perched on the edges of settees, the pointed gray tips of their shoes showing from beneath their dark skirts, their wide-brimmed hats casting shadows. Teacups in hand, they leaned close to one another. This was how I imagined them.

'Did you hear?' they must have said.

'No. What?'

'Catherine Wainwright was seen with Edward Davis. In Columbus. At the theater.'

'Together? So far from home? Just the two of them?'

'Her hand was on his arm.'

I pictured the women gasping, drawing back, stunned to silence. It was January in Dayton, Ohio. Flames leapt in parlor fireplaces, the burning wood cracked and popped, startling the women. In my mind's eye, I saw them glance at their wedding bands, thinking of their husbands and then thinking of me, Catherine Wainwright.

9

'But Edward Davis' wife?' someone surely said. 'Does she know?'

'The doctor had to be called.'

The women fluttered their hands. They had drawn close again, the circle tightening.

'Poor Alma Davis,' they must have said. 'She's so very frail.'

'And the children, those two sweet little girls.'

Whispers swirled, rushing from house to house. My mother came to the Algonquin Hotel where I lived on the fourth floor, her face covered with a black veil. As soon as she stepped into my sitting room, she raised her hand and slapped me. 'Your cousin's husband,' she said. 'How could you?'

My cheek stinging, I kept my gaze fixed on her dark blue hat, its ostrich feathers seeming to quiver with outrage.

She said, 'Do you know what this is doing to the family? Your uncle is furious. This is his daughter's life you're destroying. As if she hasn't suffered enough. And my husband, the shame is unbearable. No doubt his clients know and as for the clerks, well, one knows how those people can gossip. The humiliation, Catherine. Look at me. Do you know what you have done to your cousin? To me?'

There was nothing to say to that. My mother said, 'Do something. Now.'

Darling Edward, I wrote. *I must see you.*

The surge of gossip condemned me. The women, some of whom had been childhood friends, stopped speaking to me. They were the leading citizens; their fathers and husbands were Dayton's innovators. Their families owned and managed the paper mills, the factories, and the foundries. They were the producers of fine stationery, computing scales, and sewing

10

machines. At the milliner's, these women lifted their chins and looked past me. At the dressmaker's, they turned away, lips pressed tight. Although my father had been a designer of bridges, I had not been part of this circle of women for years. I had moved from Dayton when I was eighteen and returned only a year ago. I had not married; I was a pianist and practiced for hours on end. On those occasions when I did join the circles of women for tea or for discussions about literature, I had little to add when conversation turned to domestic matters and to the rearing of children. Now I had given the women of Dayton cause to rise up against me. In mid-January, the first note arrived in my mailbox at the hotel.

Dear Miss Wainwright,

There has been a change in plans. I regret to inform you that I must cancel your performance at our dinner party. There is one more thing. I regret to inform you that my child no longer requires piano lessons.

Cordially,
Mrs Olive Parker

More notes followed, each one nearly verbatim to the first. The women were not cordial and they showed little regret. No one smiled at me or had a kind word. No one asked for my version of the truth. Instead, behind my back, they whispered, and I did not have to be with them to hear what they said.

'This is what happens when a woman goes to college.'
'And never marries.'
'And works for a living.'

11

'And lives in a hotel.'

January became February. The clouds were gray and low, and the snow was ankle deep. My income dwindled with each canceled performance and lesson, the undercurrent of gossip shattering my life. The family, even distant cousins, all sided with Edward's wife. I stopped attending services at First Presbyterian, and invitations to family occasions ceased. In my sitting room, I turned on every incandescent lamp and tried to read my favorite novels, but the stories that once enthralled now unnerved me. Alone and with time on my hands, I imagined the whispers, rushing and lapping.

'Did you hear?'

'No. What?'

'Catherine Wainwright has been throwing herself at Edward Davis for years. Since Alma first became ill.'

'But she was living in Pennsylvania when that happened to poor Alma. In Pittsburgh, wasn't it?'

'Philadelphia, I believe. Edward Davis traveled there for business, but that wasn't enough, not for Catherine Wainwright. He's the reason she moved back to Dayton.'

Dearest, I wrote to Edward, bills collecting on my desk. *Together we can weather this. But I must see you.*

I dined alone at the hotel dining room. There, crystal chandeliers cast flickering spectrums of blue, yellow, and red onto my white linen tablecloth. Only a few of the residents – elderly widowers and bachelors – acknowledged me with smiles and brief greetings. I was just as restrained: two of the men had slipped notes under my door, their suggestions shocking me. The waiters in their black wool suits and long white aprons ignored me. I was the last to be served, and my meals arrived

12

cold. *It seems there has been an oversight,* the hotel manager wrote at the bottom of my hotel bill. *We have yet to receive payment for the past month.*

I refused to take my meals in my sitting room. I refused to hide. My friendship with Edward was not ugly and vile. We were companions; we enjoyed one another's company. Divorce was out of the question; I had silenced Edward every time he considered it. His wife had suffered a paralyzing stroke minutes after the birth of their second child, and she could not be abandoned.

Now, our secret exposed, I was shunned and forced to dole out my savings, draining the last of my inheritance from my father. I paid bits and pieces of the bills that came from the hotel, the dressmaker, and the milliner. I took walks as though the wind that blew from the river was not cold and brittle. I passed the churches on Third Street and the shops on Main. Wearing my navy wool coat trimmed in fur, my hands in a muffler, I stepped around thin patches of ice, the bare elm trees stark against the gray sky. On First, Wilkinson, and Perry Streets I felt the women watching from their parlor windows. Let them see me, I thought, my shoulders back and my bearing rigid. Through my years as a pianist I had learned never to show dismay at mistakes, never to wince, never to frown, but to continue on as if nothing had happened.

On the first of March, I went to my mother and asked for a loan.

'Marriage,' she said, her eyes hard with disapproval. The etched lines around her lips deepened. 'Do as I had to.'

I heard the accusation in her voice. I was an only child and my father had doted on me. He was proud of my career. Prior

13

to my return to Dayton, I was a pianist with an all-woman ensemble in Philadelphia and on occasion, he sent generous gifts of money to supplement my income. When he died from a weak heart four years ago, my inheritance, small as it was, angered my mother. She considered that money to be hers, not mine. Two years later, her money dwindling, she remarried.

Now, as she wrote a bank check to cover one month's expenses, she said, 'You're twenty-nine, soon to be thirty. You should have married years ago. You should have children by now. You should have a husband to look after you.' She held out the check, and all at once, her voice softened. 'Catherine, please. Find someone to marry. For your sake. Do it quickly.'

I wrote to the other two women in my ensemble telling them that I missed them and the music. *If you need a pianist, I can be there within the week.* They had been furious when I left a year ago. Now, they did not respond.

My thoughts in turmoil, I was unable to sleep, and my complexion turned sallow. I searched through my storage trunks and sorted old correspondence. I wrote letters to former suitors and to friends who lived in the East. *Such good times we had,* I penned in letter after letter. *It would be lovely to see you again.* Every day, I waited for the mail. *I am married,* former suitors wrote. *A visit would be nice,* friends wrote. *But the children keep me so busy these days.*

I considered the elderly sagging widowers and the whiskery rotund bachelors who lived at the hotel. Marriage to any one of them would be the final humiliation and the very idea of it repulsed me.

I wrote to Edward.

14

March 18, 1900

My dear,

    *You and I have spoken often of touring the art museum
in Cincinnati, and I long to see it now. It would be so
lovely to meet you there. We would arrive, of course,
on separate trains.*

    Yours,
    Catherine

His response came five days later. *Catherine. This is impossible. Find a new life for yourself. Go abroad, see the grand concert
halls in Europe.*

Stung, I told myself that these could not be Edward's words.
Someone had dictated his response. He was caught in a maze
of gossip as was I. His hands were tied, he could not see me,
not now. The gossip would fade; it was a matter of time. I
understood that we could not continue our friendship; I knew
it was over. All I wanted was one final hour with Edward to
say goodbye. And then what? I thought, but could not answer.

I kept to my practice schedule as if all were well and as though
I had upcoming engagements. I played mid-mornings and early
afternoons on the Sohmer baby grand in the empty ballroom
at the hotel. My fingers, though, were clumsy and awkward.
Even Beethoven, Mozart, and Chopin had deserted me.

    In the bottom of one of my trunks, I found eleven letters
from Oscar Williams, someone whom I had known since I was
a child. He was a few years older than I, and his father had
delivered coal to our furnace in the basement. After school

and during the summers, Oscar worked with his father, the two of them driving through the alleys of Dayton, their wagon piled high with coal. 'I like how you play the piano,' Oscar told me once, ducking with shyness. He had stopped me on the lawn at Central High School as I was leaving with a few of my classmates. Oscar was tall and lanky, and his eyes were a deep green. My friends teased me and called him the coal man's son but I was flattered by his compliment and by the admiration in his voice. There was something else, too. In spite of his shyness, he was direct and without guile, qualities that set him apart from most of the boys who escorted me home from school or who signed my dance cards at cotillions.

Several months after Oscar had stopped me on the lawn, I realized that I hadn't seen him at school. I made roundabout inquiries. Oscar's father's cough had worsened and he'd died from a lung disease. Oscar was now the coal man and supported his mother and his younger sister and two brothers. During the spring of 1887, though, he found the time to attend my public recital. Just as I had walked out onto the stage at Music Hall, I saw Oscar slip into the back row. After, he waited for me in the lobby. 'Listening to you takes me someplace else,' he said. 'Someplace new.'

The coal man, I reminded myself. He was charming in an unpolished way, but he was not like the young men with whom I kept company. His suit was too small. His white shirt, although clean and pressed, was worn at the cuffs. Coal dust was ground into the skin around his nails.

The summer of 1888, between finishing high school and starting at the music conservatory, I caught glimpses of Oscar at the Saturday evening concerts held at Lakeside Park. He was often alone, while I was usually with other young women, my former classmates from Central High. Alma, my cousin who would marry Edward a few years later, was one of these friends. Oscar would tip his hat to me and I'd nod, my smile faint as my friends teased. 'Unrequited love,' they said about him. 'He's always admired you. But . . .' That one word was enough to dismiss Oscar Williams. We came from homes with pillared entrances and tall arched windows. Our fathers wore starched collars and their shoes were polished to a high gleam. Oscar was not one of us.

That September, I received a letter from him, surprising me.

Dear Miss Wainwright,

I have left Ohio and am Making my Own Way as a Hand at the Circle C Ranch. It is 22 miles south and west of Amarillo, Texas. It is Hot here and Flat. There is Not Much in the way of Trees. Some of the Fellows here are Mexican. They are Teaching Me the Tricks of the Trade. Anything is better than hauling and shoveling Coal.

Sincerely Yours,
Oscar Williams

I had not intended to respond. In five days, I was to leave for Oberlin College in northern Ohio, but out of politeness I wrote him a brief note.

Our correspondence continued for several years with months of silence between letters. I graduated from college and joined the ensemble in Philadelphia. Oscar left Amarillo, moved to Galveston – *There is Water on all Sides,* he wrote –

17

and found work on a dairy farm. Eventually he bought the dairy and when that happened, he proposed marriage. That was six years ago, and my response had ended our correspondence. Now, in a fit of panic and unable to sleep, I wrote to him.

March 30, 1900

Dear Mr Williams,

It is with fond memories that I think of you. My goodness, you have been in Galveston, Texas, for so many years now. Have you forgotten your Dayton friends? I trust that all is well with you and that your dairy business thrives.

I have returned to Dayton to enjoy the company of my mother. She is well, as am I. I do, however, eagerly await the balmy days of summer. Do you recall Lakeside Park? And the concerts by the river? The newspapers report that the concerts will resume in early June. I wonder if the bands will be the same as the ones that once delighted our hearts.

Sincerely yours,
Catherine Wainwright

April, and more bills. I sought distraction and several times a week, I found myself at the public library. There, I wandered the stacks of books or sat in the reading room with a book on my lap. One morning, I rode the trolley that Edward took to his office at Barney & Smith Railcar Works on Keowee Street. I sat in the middle of the trolley car, surrounded by men in business suits, my chin up but my heart turning at the sight of Edward as he boarded, so handsome in his dark blue pinstripe suit, his mustache freshly trimmed. When he saw me, shock, then fear flashed across his face. For a moment, I believed he was going to turn around and get off the trolley but there were people behind him boarding. Without looking again at me, he walked down the aisle and sat somewhere behind me.

I considered moving to Cincinnati or to Columbus. I could place notices in the newspapers seeking pupils who wanted to study the piano. Mothers would invite me to their homes and interview me in their parlors as we sipped tea served in bone china. 'Why did you leave Dayton?' each one would say. 'And what about your references? My husband insists, you understand.' Their smiles would be sweet as if references were not important to them.

A letter came from Oscar Williams. His penmanship was precise even if his grammar was not.

April 22, 1900

Dear Miss Wainwright,

I was Surprised to hear from You. I figured You had Forgotten me. I figured you were Married.

Do You still play the Piano? I recall your Music and how it was like Nothing I Heard before. As for Me, I have 33 Jerseys, most good Milkers. 2 Men work for Me. My farm is a half of a mile from The Gulf Of Mexico Sand hills. A Mile Behind us is Offatts Bayou, big as a lake. West Bay feeds into it.

I have a Good piece of Land and the Saltgrass is Hardy.

19

Fresh Water is Plentiful. I have a Son. He is 5. My Wife died the first of October.

Sincerely Yours,
Oscar Williams

A dairy farmer. A widower with a child. Someone I had not seen in years. I set Oscar's letter aside. Morning after morning during April, I rode the trolley, the oaks and elms along the avenues budding and leafing as the air turned mild. Edward came to expect me, searching for me when he boarded. Our eyes would meet for the briefest of moments but that was enough. Tomorrow, I thought. He'll speak to me tomorrow. But every morning, he looked away.

I reread the letter from Oscar Williams. Six years ago, his marriage proposal had shocked me. Surely he understood that I had maintained the correspondence out of kindness. I had a career. My ensemble played in concert halls and in the homes of Philadelphia's leading citizens.

Now, he was the only person whose letter was not cold or indifferent. I pushed aside the unpaid bills on my desk and composed my next note.

May 1, 1900

Dear Mr Williams,

I am saddened by the news of your wife. Please accept my heartfelt condolences. Surely it is an unspeakable loss, and I fear that my expression of sympathy does little to ease your sorrow. But, Mr Williams, it lightens my heart to hear that you are not alone. You have a son and my goodness, so

20

many cows. However do you manage it all? I greatly admire your many accomplishments.

Yes, I still play the piano. It is kind of you to remember.

With affection,
Catherine Wainwright

His response came three weeks later. It was brief but filled with details about his dairy farm. *The Barn sits on a Raised up bed of Oyster Shells and dirt. It can rain hard here. It is big enough for Five more Cows.* Then, *My boy's name is Andre.*

By the end of May the note from the hotel manager carried a different tone. I was four months in arrears. If I did not settle my account immediately, I was to vacate my rooms by the end of June.

I responded to Oscar's letter and expressed interest in his barn and in his son. I sorted through my jewelry and sold two necklaces and a pair of earrings to a jeweler whose speculating glances further humiliated me. I considered asking my mother for another loan but that would call for begging. It would mean she could dictate what I must do and whom I must marry. I considered again moving to Cincinnati or to Columbus but my courage had slipped. As unforgiving as Dayton was, I could not imagine being alone in an unfamiliar city, my money almost gone. I made arrangements to move to a boarding house where I would share a room with another woman. I wrote again to Oscar. *Whatever is it like to live on an island in Texas?*

Near the end of June, I received the letter I had been waiting for and yet dreading.

Dear Miss Wainwright,

I am not a Rich Man but I am not Poor either. My Dairy is Fair sized and I am free of Debt. Miss Wainwright, will You consider Marrying Me? My Son is in need of a Mother. I am in need of a Wife. I will make You a good Husband and Provider. But there is Something You should know. Galveston is not like Dayton. And there is Something else. Me and my Boy are Catholics. I converted and my Boy was baptized one. But I will not push It on You.

> *Sincerely Yours,*
> *Oscar Williams*

I held the letter, trying to put together the images of a farmhouse, a small child, and a life of rituals far removed from my own. I tried to put shape to Oscar, but with the arrival of his offer his image had blurred, reminding me how little I knew him.

I reread Edward's correspondence, touching his cursive script with my forefinger, tracing each letter on the linen stationery. *I enjoyed our conversation,* he had written two months after we'd met during the Christmas season of 1895. His penmanship was slanted, the *j* and *i* not dotted, but the *t* crossed with a brief dash. *I will be in Philadelphia next month,* he'd written in April of 1897, his wife a confirmed invalid by then. *Perhaps you might accompany me to the art museum there.* Three years ago, that invitation both shocked and thrilled me. Now, I saw his words as his wife might. He had pursued me. Surely, if I reminded him of those letters, he would be willing to provide for me.

The silk drapes at my sitting-room window rustled in the mild summer breeze. Below, the street was busy. Several buggies passed by, and on the sidewalks, women wearing feathered hats carried shopping baskets. At the opposite corner, two men in business suits and derbies stood talking. All of them were going about their day, occupied with their lives, their worries and problems perhaps nibbling at their thoughts as they searched for solutions.

Blackmail. I had fallen to that. Edward would despise me. Just as I would despise myself.

I read Oscar's letter again. He offered escape from my debts, from my mother's rejection, and from certain poverty. He offered escape from myself.

The next morning, I sat at the baby grand in the empty hotel ballroom, the keyboard covered. My face was drawn and my eyes ached from lack of sleep. I had sent my answer in yesterday's late afternoon post. *Yes, Mr Williams,* I responded. *I will marry you.*

CHAPTER TWO

Galveston, Texas

The wind gusted. The train rocked. Sea spray splattered the windows. I gripped the armrests of my seat as we skimmed above choppy white-capped waves. I had understood that Galveston was an island but until now, I had not realized just how unattached it was to the rest of Texas.

The train's ventilation system had stopped and the car was stuffy and warm. The woman who sat across from me opened her silk fan, unfolding a painted picture of snow-covered mountains. 'We're crossing West Bay,' she said to me as she waved her fan before her round, glistening face. Her words were drawn long with a Southern accent. 'Our bridges are the longest in the world. Three miles if they're an inch.'

My father had designed bridges and if this were one of his, I would have faith in its piers and bracings. Instead, I kept my gaze on my lap, unable to look at the other rickety wood train trestles that ran parallel to us, the waves breaking against their thin wood piers.

'Smelling salts,' the woman said. 'That's what I suggest if this is your first crossing.'

'I'm fine,' I said.

The train shimmied. Low murmurs filled the car, the passengers reassuring one another. My seat was second class, and I rode with my back to the front of the car. The woman facing me swayed. The man on the other side of the aisle held himself still as if his least movement might tip the train. Feeling ill, I closed my eyes.

I had left Dayton three days ago with Oscar Williams' last letter in my cloth purse. He had not referred to the wedding nor had he mentioned where I would stay. Instead, there were details of train schedules and railroad routes. The journey from Dayton to Galveston called for changing trains in St. Louis, Little Rock, and Houston. In each station, I was surrounded by strangers while I spent long hours sitting on benches waiting to make my connections. After eight months of being shunned, I was disconcerted by the suddenness of being in such close quarters with so many people. I held a novel open on my lap but the words ran together, and I couldn't recall the sentences I had just read. On board, the trip was a series of frequent stops and delays at small-town depots. Beyond the exchange of brief pleasantries with my fellow passengers, I kept to myself and watched the blur of farmlands, the river crossings, and woods that existed along the railroad tracks. Each mile traveled took me farther west and then south from Dayton. Each one brought me closer to a life so different from what I knew.

I opened my eyes. We were still crossing the bay – three miles, I thought – and now a crowd of steamships, tugboats, and schooners had come into view.

'The last time I crossed the bay, it was storming,' the woman across from me said. She wore a wedding band and her fingers were plump. 'Gracious, that was quite the adventure. But today, we have blue skies and as for this breeze, why it's little more than a puff.'

'How fortunate,' I said. I imagined the train tumbling off of the trestle, the car sinking and filling with water. The window, streaked with grimy water, was locked closed. I'd have to unfasten the locks and pull the window down. I might escape, but I didn't know how to swim. Even if I did, my heavy plum-colored skirt would wrap and drag around my legs.

'Nearly there,' the woman said, putting on her gloves.

The train floated above small islands of tall rippling grass and low dense bushes. We crossed over shallow reedy marshes where long-necked white birds stood motionless. The train sloped down. We bumped off of the trestle and onto land held firm by the occasional grove of listing short bushy trees.

I leaned as far back in my seat as my bustle and the brim of my hat allowed.

The train slowed, passing rows of storage sheds, warehouses, and grain elevators where Negro men unloaded wood crates from unhitched railroad cars. We passed along a wharf, the train running parallel to steamships and sailing ships held secure to the docks with massive ropes. Cranes hoisted containers from these ships, the straining men slick with perspiration.

I was in Galveston, Texas, a thousand miles from home.

The high arched granite walls and the turrets of Union Station shaded the platform, where I stood beside my two traveling trunks and column of hatboxes. People swirled around me, some of them hurrying up the stairs to catch the train on the other side of the platform, while others greeted passengers who had just arrived. Negro porters maneuvered through the

26

crowds pushing dollies weighed down with trunks and bags. Up and down the tracks, trains hissed and black steam poured out of smokestacks. The air was thick and sultry, and smelled of oil, metal, and brine. I searched the faces of the men, but none of them were familiar, not even those whose glances lingered on me. *I will Meet your International and Great Northern Train*, Oscar had written in his last letter. *I will be on the platform at Union Station, Galveston, Texas the Morning of August 29, 1900.* Perhaps it was my hat that confused him, the upper portion of my face hidden in the shadow of the brim. Or perhaps it was the vagueness of memory. It had been twelve years since we'd last seen one another.

I left my trunks and my hatboxes, and walked along the platform looking for any man who was alone, then looking for one accompanied by a small boy. The heat was oppressive and rank from so many unwashed people, their wool clothes splotched dark with perspiration. Black-haired unshaven men in mussed shirts and trousers herded their families around the platform, the women in brown and gray dresses and head-scarves, some of them carrying babies while other children clung to their skirts.

I returned to my trunks and hatboxes.

The crowd on my side of the platform began to thin. A few tracks over, passengers boarded a train from the opposite platform. I straightened my hat; a young man jostled me. 'My apologies, ma'am,' he said without looking at me.

I found Oscar's letter in my cloth bag and checked the date. *August 29, 1900.* Today. I smoothed loose strands of hair into place and pinched each earlobe, securing my black crystal dropped earrings. To my right, a girl with her hair tied back with a yellow ribbon held a child, shifting him from hip to

27

hip. Farther down, a man in a suit and hat stood near the edge of the platform smoking a cigarette while checking his pocket watch, the chain looped from his vest.

My white shirtwaist was damp from the heat, and I longed for a drink of cool water. I found my handkerchief in my cloth purse and patted my forehead. Something must have happened to Oscar; something had delayed him.

The girl with the child left. Two men jumped down from the platform and began to unhitch the engine car from the train I had arrived on. Their faces were red and streaked with perspiration as they worked, the metal hitch screeching, grinding, the bolts loosening.

Oscar had changed his mind. Someone from Dayton had written to him; he had heard the ugly rumors about me. Perhaps his sister or one of his brothers had told him. I had seven dollars, enough for a few nights in a modest hotel. I could find a rooming house and make the money stretch a week. I would have to sell my earrings, a gift from Edward. In Dayton, I could not bear the thought of parting from them, but now, if Oscar had abandoned me, they were all I had.

I dabbed at my forehead with my gloved fingers.

At the far end of the platform, the man with the pocket watch looked my way, the cigarette between his lips and his head tilted slightly as if asking a question. He was cleanshaven and his face was brown from the sun. The brim of his bowler hat was wider than most, but I was able to see that his hair was light brown. Like Oscar Williams'. But this man was bigger than I remembered him to be; this man was broader. He was tall, though, like Oscar.

I looked away, then back. He slid the watch into his vest, dropped his cigarette onto the platform, and put it out with the toe of his boot. He began to walk my way, his footsteps loud on the platform.

Relief rushed through me. I averted my eyes, needing to reclaim my poise, and all at once, I heard the parlor room whispers. 'The coal man.' 'The dairy farmer.' 'Catherine Wainwright has gotten what she deserves.'

He was just a few yards off. A beating sound pulsed in my ears. I felt myself teetering. The instant I spoke to him, the person I was, Catherine Wainwright the pianist, would disappear. Something began to shift and splinter inside of me. I turned away and as I did, I was once again in Dayton. The oaks were leafing and the air was mild. I was on the trolley, and Edward had walked past me.

'Miss Wainwright?'

The dairy farmer. The man who had written that his son was in need of a mother and he was in need of a wife. The man who said he would be a good husband and provider. The man who had once attended my piano recitals.

I turned to face him. He had taken off his hat and held it to his chest. I forced a smile and looked up past the brim of mine. 'Mr Williams,' I said, putting out my gloved hand. 'I am so very pleased to see you once again.'

We stood on the station platform, neither of us saying anything, our glances flickering over and around the other. I had seen the surprise in his eyes when I greeted him. I was thirty now, not a girl of eighteen. Oscar had changed, too. Lines fanned out from around his green eyes. His face was fuller, the gauntness of his boyhood gone. He wasn't handsome, not like the men I was accustomed to with their hair parted just so and who wore their tailor-made suits with ease.

Oscar's jacket was tight through the chest and the cords showed in his neck. The sun had weathered his skin. This man did not earn his living by sitting at a desk. Oscar worked outside, and he worked with animals. He relied on his strength.

'Mighty hot,' he said.

'My yes,' I said. 'I quite agree.'

'How was the trip?'

'Very pleasant, thank you. The scenery was lovely.'

'These here are yours?' he said, referring to my two trunks and stack of hatboxes. His voice did not match my recollection. It was deeper, and there was a draw, his years in Texas telling.

'Yes,' I said. 'All mine.'

'My wagon's at the livery, Mallory's, three blocks up and two over.'

A wagon, not a buggy.

He said, 'I'll have your things sent on. We'll walk to the hotel, it's quicker that way.'

'A stroll would be refreshing after such long days of sitting,' I said. A hotel. I had only seven dollars. I had assumed that Oscar had made arrangements with friends, people who would welcome me to stay in their home while he and I grew accustomed to one another.

Oscar hailed a Negro porter. I ran my gloved fingers along the drawstrings of my purse. Oscar said something to the porter about a hotel on Market Street, then the two of them began to load my trunks and hatboxes onto a dolly. I couldn't afford a hotel past a day or so, and I certainly could not assume that Oscar would finance my stay. The wedding could be weeks

30

from now, perhaps even a month. There would be meals to consider, too. I would have to sell my earrings.

The porter left, wheeling away everything that I owned.

'You hungry?' Oscar said. 'I surely am.'

'A little something would be lovely.'

'We'll have dinner at the hotel.'

'Lunch,' I said, the word seeming to leap out of me.

'Come again?'

'I believe it's close to noon. Lunch, wouldn't it be?'

'Here we call it dinner.' Oscar nodded toward the pair of tall arched doors that led into the station. 'Ready?' he said. He put his hand on the small of my back, and just like that, my concern about my lack of money disappeared.

I came to Galveston expecting Oscar to be an older version of the boy I thought I had known. In my memory of him, I had exaggerated his shyness. He had stood off to the side at Lakeside Park; he had admired me from afar. That may have been true, but he had had the courage to speak and to write to me. Now, as we walked toward the tall arched doors, I realized I had been mistaken to believe that Oscar would stammer with shyness and perhaps be awkward and unsure in my presence. There was nothing unsure about Oscar Williams. Or about the hand on the small of my back.

Union Station was cool, dim, and filled with commotion. Voices ricocheted and echoed off of the high ceiling and the marble floor. Rows of polished wood benches were filled with men, women, and children, their bags at their feet. Oscar steered me around lines of people who waited to purchase tickets. We walked past the shoeshine stands where men read newspapers while Negroes shined and buffed their ankle-high boots. We passed through a high doorway and we were suddenly outside on a city street, the late morning sun blinding me.

'Oh my,' I said.

'That's Texas for you,' Oscar said. He put on his hat and tugged the center of the brim, settling it into place. 'The sun takes some getting used to, but you will.'

'I can't imagine.'

'Five years from now you won't hardly notice.' He smiled as though he had said something amusing but I did not have a smile in me. The wind that had rocked the train as we crossed the bay was little more than a slight stirring here. Heat rose like vapors of steam. Overhangs attached to the buildings covered the sidewalk, but the red and black tiles were so hot that they burned through the soles of my shoes. On the street before us, teams of horses pulled buggies and wagons in all directions. Drivers whistled and shouted, urging on their horses. Piles of dung rotted in the sun. Men crowded the sidewalk, the smell of their wool suits striking me in waves.

'We'll go this way,' Oscar said. 'Show you the sights.' He indicated the street before us. It was lined with three-story buildings, their stone façades shades of cream and red. 'This here's the Strand.'

'Pardon?'

'That's the name of the street. The Strand. Some folks call it the most important street in Texas.'

'Most impressive,' I said as we joined the flow of pedestrians. I felt ill and lightheaded, repulsed by the sight of straining, lathered horses, and the faces of the drivers slick with perspiration. On the sidewalk, there were far more men than women, the women, I believed, having the good sense to stay out of this heat.

'Over there, across the street,' Oscar said, pointing. 'That's the Hutchings-Sealy building. It's just a few years old.'

Squinting against the sun, I looked up to where he directed my attention. That building and all the others had carved cornices and elaborate brickwork that rimmed their flat roofs. Signs identified dry goods stores, the offices of attorneys-at-law, insurance companies, and banks. I tried to see something of Dayton here or of Philadelphia but this was unlike any place I had been before. Sailors stood at corners, talking to one another, their ribboned caps set at angles and their dark trousers flaring below the knees. Painted shutters framed high arched windows on the upper floors of buildings, and at some, white wicker chairs clustered around tables on iron balconies. Draperies fluttered as if there were a breeze. At street level, men and errand boys passed in and out through tall propped-open doors.

We stopped at a corner, the traffic in the intersection a dense knot of delivery wagons and horses. 'Look over there,' Oscar said, pointing to his left. A steamship sat alongside the wharf. Black smoke poured from its stacks, and the deck was as high as a one-story building.

'Sails from Cuba,' he said, raising his voice above the shouts of drivers as they tried to untangle the traffic. 'Carries bananas and suchlike. That flag's a common sight here. Same for the German flag. England's too. We have ships coming and going, day and night. It's the busiest port on the gulf, outshines New Orleans by a mile.'

'Cuba,' I said. 'Good heavens.' I could not place Cuba, not at that moment. It could have been on the other side of the moon.

'It's all rather unexpected,' I said. We were still at the corner, the traffic at a standstill. 'There's so much more to it than I had imagined.'

'It's a little too busy, if you ask me. Suits me just fine to be down the island.'

'Pardon?'

'That's where we are, on down the island.'

'Of course,' I said as if his words made sense.

'Here we go,' Oscar said, the traffic clearing just enough to cross, the pedestrians now flowing into the intersection. He helped me down the three cement steps to street level. 'Sidewalks are raised on account of floods,' he said. 'Newcomers most always are surprised by that.'

His words were part of the city noise. My ankles bowed on the uneven blocks of pavers as we avoided the horse dung. I held up the front of my skirt, sure that my train was sweeping up all manner of filth. We climbed the steps on the opposite corner. 'We're prone to hard-driven rains,' Oscar said. 'Then too, tides can get high when it storms. Can come from the bay or from the gulf. We aren't but nine feet above sea level.'

'Well,' I said. His words took shape in my mind. 'Mr Williams. Are you saying that water from the gulf comes into the city?'

'It's been known to. That's why the houses are up on brick pillars. These overflows give the streets a good washing, that's what most folks say.'

My smile was wooden.

'But where we are, down the island, we have the sand hills. And we're on the ridge.'

A cliff, I thought. I imagined myself on the edge, looking down at the water.

We walked, the sultry air as dense as cotton. My shirtwaist

34

was even damper than before, and my corset and undergarments dug into my skin, chafing. I wished for a cool place where I could sit and think. Things were happening too quickly.

We turned a corner so that the Strand and the wharf were behind us. A hotel, the Washington, was a block up. Its sign was elegant with black curlicue script, and a Negro doorman in red uniform and white gloves stood under the canopied entrance. The brick building was painted white, the sidewalk was covered with a black carpet, and I could not remember the name of the hotel Oscar had given to the porter.

I couldn't stay there, I thought. It was too fine; I could not afford even one night. 'Mr Williams,' I started to say, but before I did, two women came out of the hotel. They were young, perhaps in their very early twenties. Everything about them was fresh and carefree: their pale pink and yellow skirts, crisp white shirtwaists with sleeves that came to their elbows, and straw boater hats. Unlike me, I thought, wilted in my plum-colored skirt and long-sleeved cream shirtwaist.

They didn't notice. It was Oscar who caused their chatter to pause when we drew nearer, the two of them under the canopy, the doorman off to the side now and standing in the sun. It was Oscar who they assessed when he gave the brim of his hat a quick tug, his way of acknowledging them. Oscar nodded to the doorman as well, who then tipped his own hat in return, saying, 'Sir. Ma'am.'

If Oscar noticed the hints of admiration in those women's glances, he didn't show it. We turned at the corner and crossed to the other side. Here, the street was sand and dirt, and buggies were parked face in at the high curbs. We continued on a few more blocks, following other pedestrians as we passed more banks, more merchants, and a three-story building with a clock. Oscar glanced up at the clock. His hand went to his vest pocket as though he might take out his watch to compare the time. Instead, he patted it and nodded toward the building on the corner.

'Here we are,' he said. 'The Central Hotel.'

CHAPTER THREE

Oscar Williams

The Central Hotel was a four-story clapboard building
with a pitched roof. The sign above the open double doors
had a simple black band around the border and the print did
not have the first curlicue. If I kept my meals light – something that would not be difficult since I had lost my appetite
months ago – I believed my seven dollars might cover two
nights.

I nibbled at my lunch, or as Oscar called it, dinner. He and
I were in the hotel's narrow, small dining room. Its ceiling was
high, and the walls were white plaster. Every table was filled,
and the diners, all men, had unbuttoned their suit jackets so
that their vests showed. Their voices competed with the clatter
of cutlery and with the waiters in white shirts and long black
aprons who rushed in and out of the kitchen, the swing door
slapping. They held their trays high as they wove between the
tables, responding to orders, the pungent odors of fish and
steak making me queasy.

Oscar sat across from me with his napkin tucked into his
collar and his elbows on the small square table. Hatless, his
pale forehead contrasted with his sun-browned cheeks and

nose. He picked up a shrimp from a platter. 'Fresh from the gulf,' he said.

I could barely bring myself to look at it. It resembled a pinkish-white worm but with a claw on one end. Oscar twisted the claw and tore it off, then peeled the thin clear shell from what remained.

He put the shrimp on a small plate. 'Give it a try,' he said, passing it to me.

I steeled myself. I pierced it with my fork and swallowed it whole, needing several quick sips of my hot tea to remove the cold spongy texture from my mind.

'How about an oyster?'

'Thank you but no, I couldn't possibly.' They were on a platter next to the shrimp, each oyster in its own half shell. I was accustomed to oysters mixed in stuffing so that their appearance was disguised. These oysters, though, were without pretense. They were slick rubber-like brown sea creatures, raw and primitive. 'I'm afraid I've not acquired a taste for oysters,' I said.

'It can take some doing,' Oscar said. 'But these come from here; they're not store bought.' He picked up a shell and held out to me. 'You sure?'

'Quite.'

His grin was quick. He was laughing at me. 'Well then,' he said. He put the shell to his lips and tipped it. The oyster slid into his mouth.

Only a suggestion of a breeze drifted in through the doors that faced the street. The two men at the table to my left discussed the price of cotton and the recent heavy rains. To my right, the talk centered on the need for more warehouses at the wharf. I once prided myself on being able to hold a conversation with any man. Ask a flattering question – 'My goodness, how did you ever find this charming restaurant?' – and most would talk for ten minutes. Failing that, there was always the weather. But I could not find a thing to say to Oscar.

He cut a piece from his steak and ate it, the muscles along his jaw working. I had a bite of my own. It was tough and stringy.

I should ask about his son. I knew so little about children apart from giving them piano lessons. The boys were often restless, their shirts coming untucked. Lessons were usually their mothers' ideas and many did not like to practice. Some of the boys stared at the keyboard, swinging their legs as I spoke about flats and sharps, measures and beats.

I said, 'I'm looking forward to meeting your son.'

'He's a good boy,' Oscar said. 'For the most part.'

'Oh?'

'Well, he's five.'

'I suppose that can be a rather energetic age.'

Oscar peered at me as though I had just said something peculiar. The two men at the table to my left pushed their chairs away from their table, the shrill scrape of their chair legs against the wood floor heightening my nerves. Oscar ran his forefinger around the rim of his beer mug. Small white scars crisscrossed the backs of his broad hands, and his fingers were long. Calluses ridged the insides of his palm. These were the hands of a farmer, a man who used his hands hard.

Oscar said, 'Well. Now that you're here.'

'Yes,' I said.

He had a little more of his beer, then wiped his upper lip with his forefinger and thumb. His fingernails were clipped and clean, all traces of coal dust were gone. He said, 'Tomorrow afternoon, after I finish up with the chores, I'll come for you, take you to see my boy and the house. I figured you might like to do that.'

'Yes, thank you, I would. But the day is early yet. Perhaps I could see your home this afternoon?'

'I'd like to do that, I would. But I can't. It's a while getting there and then there'd be the trip back to the city. What with chores and all, well, it'd run me late.'

'How far away is your home?'

'From here, three miles. As the crow flies.'

'And if you aren't a crow?'

'Closer to four miles. Takes an hour, give or take, depending on Maud and Mabel, my horses, how cantankerous they are.'

It took me a minute to absorb this. I said, 'I didn't realize Galveston was so big.'

'Twenty-seven miles from end to end.'

'That's quite a city.'

'It's not all city,' he said. 'Just this part here. We're down the island. We're outside of the city limits.'

Oscar drained the last of his beer, and the waiter stood ready with the second one on his tray. Oscar nodded to him and the mugs were switched. A thin layer of white foam bubbled at the rim of the fresh mug, threatening to overflow.

'Miss Wainwright?' Oscar said. 'You all right?'

Nothing was all right. I had stepped off the train just over an hour ago, and I was still stunned by the crowds, the stench, and the heat of Galveston. My sharp awareness of Oscar stunned me, too, seeing for the first time the thin white scar that ran across the bottom of his left cheek, and the crook in his nose. Now there was this discovery that his home was not just down the island, but more specifically, it was outside of the city limits.

I said, 'You have electricity, don't you? There, at your home?'

'It's coming. There's been talk of it.'

Panic fluttered in my chest.

'We have running water,' he said. 'In the kitchen and wash-room.'

'Oh. Goodness. I'm pleased to hear that.'

He had more of his beer, then put the mug down. 'This matter of the wedding,' he said.

I waited.

'There's been a little tangle, you might say.'

'A tangle?'

'A small knot. It came up when I talked to the Presbyterian preacher. I believe that's what you are.'

'Minister,' I said. 'Presbyterians don't have preachers.'

'Is that so? Didn't know that.' He glanced around the dining room. There were only a handful of diners now. His voice low, he said, 'Anyway, this minister, he's not agreeable to marrying us. It's because of me, me being a Catholic. And Father O'Shea, that's my priest, he said that before he'd marry us, you'd have to convert.'

'Mr Williams. That is out of the question.'

'Oscar,' he said. 'Call me Oscar.'

'Yes, of course. Oscar.' I picked up my teacup; I put it back down. My hand had acquired a tremor. In Dayton, I had not allowed myself to dwell on Oscar's religion. The Catholics in Dayton were the Irish and Italians, and my father had considered Catholicism little more than hocus-pocus. It called for the false worship of idols and for blind obedience to the Roman Pope.

41

'Mr Williams,' I said. 'Oscar. I was raised Presbyterian, it is my family's religion.'

'And that's fine by me. So the way I see it, that leaves a judge.'

'You could join the Presbyterian Church.'

'I thought about that, I did. But Miss Wainwright, my boy's a Catholic and I made a promise to his mother and I intend to abide by that.'

I looked off toward the open doors, the sidewalk busy with pedestrians. I had seven dollars and a pair of crystal earrings. I was in no position to bargain. Nor was I in any position to have qualms about the religious sanctity of this wedding. I turned back to him and said, 'Have you spoken to a judge?'

'This morning, before your train got here. He's willing to marry us most any afternoon but Sunday. I figured on Saturday.'

'This coming Saturday?'

'If that's all right with you,' he said.

Three days from now. A few minutes ago, I was concerned about my hotel bill. Now, the solution to that problem at hand, it all felt too sudden. Oscar Williams was not who I had expected him to be.

'Miss Wainwright?'

He waited, the question showing in his green eyes.

I'd come here out of desperation. I'd come here to get married. Whether it was this Saturday or the one after that, the result was the same.

I said, 'You took me by surprise. But yes, Saturday. That's suitable.'

He smiled and in that moment, I saw the boy he had been, shy and sitting in the back row during my recital. The image, though, did not linger. His hands, I thought. Scarred and nicked, and not reluctant to touch me.

The wedding. Three days from now. Three days in which to lose my nerve, three days in which to make an irreparable mistake. 'I don't know you,' I imagined myself saying. 'I cannot marry you.' But I could not afford such a mistake.

Across the table, Oscar assessed me, his head tilted as though he were seeing me for the first time. Perhaps he was noticing the sallowness in my cheeks and the thinness in my neck. He might see that my youth had faded. There were three days for Oscar to think and to reconsider, too.

'Mr Williams,' I said.

'Oscar.'

'Oscar.'

A few rows over, a waiter cleared a table placing dishes and the empty platters on a tray. Oscar drank some of his beer, clear beads of moisture running down the outside of the glass. The waiter left, the tray balanced on the flat of his palm.

I said, 'You're such a busy man. All this going back and forth, tomorrow and then on Saturday. As well as today. I'm keeping you from your work.'

'I don't mind.'

'That's kind of you, but . . .' My voice disappeared.

'Don't you want to see the place? And my boy?'

'Yes. Very much so. But.' My slight smile felt frozen into place. I said, 'Why don't we just get things settled? Tomorrow.'

'Come again?'

'If the judge has the time.'

'Get married tomorrow? Is that what you're saying?'

'Yes.'

'This comes as a surprise. You might say it all comes as a surprise.'

I couldn't meet his eyes.

Oscar picked up his fork and ran it over his plate, collecting a few scraps of gristly meat. We were the last diners. Off to my right, a Negro man swept the floor, his broom making soft whispery sounds. Crockery clattered in the kitchen, and outside, on the sidewalk, a boy selling newspapers called the headline about the rebellion in China. Oscar put his fork back down, the scraps of gristle now in a small tidy pile.

He said, 'I'm going to speak plain here, Miss Wainwright. That's my way. My boy needs a mother. I wrote you that, put my cards on the table fair and square, didn't try to hide it. But there was something I didn't say, not then. Didn't know how to in a letter, but here it is. I want a woman that can give him things I can't. I want better for him, the right way to talk, manners and suchlike. Now, me and you, we don't much know each other anymore, but I recall this about you. You do things right.'

I looked away from him. Framed paintings of ships and seascapes decorated the dining-room walls. Behind several of them, thin cracks zigzagged in the white plaster, some of them running from the floor to the ceiling. Nearby, the man with the broom bent from the waist and swept the droppings of lunch into a dustpan.

Oscar said, 'I believe in fair and square.'

'As do I.'

'Good. So that's why I'm asking. Miss Wainwright, is everything all right with you?'

'Mr Williams. Everything is perfectly all right.'

'You're sure?'

'Of course I'm sure.'

He knew, I thought. The rumors, the whispers. Some-one in Dayton had written to him. Or, at the very least, he suspected that something had happened. Six years of silence, and suddenly I write to him. Suddenly I was ready to marry him but not in Dayton. *How considerate,* I had responded last month to Oscar's suggestion that he come to Ohio. *But I cannot bear the thought of taking you away from your work or from your son. I'd much prefer a quiet wedding there in Galveston, my new home.*

I held his gaze, refusing to flinch, refusing to reveal anything about the past. Those eyes, I thought. He saw right through me. Then, he nodded as though he were satisfied with my answers. He picked up his beer and finished it. I did the same with my tea. Oscar put the mug down onto the table with a soft thump.

'All right then,' he said. 'Tomorrow. I'll come for you around two o'clock. If that's all right with you?'

'I'll be waiting.'

Oscar took his pocket watch out from his vest pocket and sprang open the lid. 'Chores are calling,' he said. 'So I best be getting a move on.' He closed the watch and put it back in his pocket. He smiled, then said, 'We'll honeymoon here tomorrow night. Then we'll go on home Friday morning.'

Eight stories high, Union Train Station was one of the tallest buildings in the city. It was a few blocks from the Central Hotel and in my room on the third floor, I stood at the open windows and watched the station glow in the afternoon sun, the flags on the turrets drooping. Trains arrived and departed, their engines grinding, the whistles shrill and the brakes

45

screeching. On the street below, horse-drawn drays and carriages clopped past. White birds with gray wings swooped and squawked, diving for rubbish near the raised curbs. They were seagulls, similar to the ones at Lake Erie, where my family once had a summer cottage.

I had said goodbye to my mother the day before I left Dayton. In her parlor, the one she had once shared with my father and me, I told her I was engaged to Oscar Williams, formerly of Dayton. Her face had collapsed with relief. She could not remember him, and I did not try to refresh her memory. It was enough that I had solved my problem. 'Perhaps someday you and Mr Williams will come for a visit,' she said. 'Perhaps,' I had said. Now, as I stood at the hotel window, I considered writing to her to let her know of my safe arrival and of my plans.

Dear Mother,

Oscar Williams met my train this morning. We greeted one another with great joy and fell instantly to making plans for the future. We are to be married on the afternoon of August 30, 1900.

I put my hand to my cheek and felt again the sting of her slap. No, I decided. I would not write to her, not yet. Let her wonder.

The washroom was four doors down the hall. There, I filled the claw-foot porcelain tub with lukewarm water. I got into it, ignoring the rusty stain just above the drain, and sank down so that the water was to my shoulders. A hot breeze came in through the awning window near the ceiling. I bathed with the sponge that I had brought from home, washing away the days of travel and the heat of the Galveston sun.

I had met Edward Davis at a family dinner party in Dayton four and a half years ago. I lived in Philadelphia then, but I had come home to spend Christmas with my mother and father. Edward, married to my cousin, sat next to me at my parents' long, oval dining table, the crystal stemware and bone-china dishes glimmering in the candlelight. His father was one of the founders of a company that manufactured railroad cars, and Edward held a position there. He didn't talk about his work, though. Instead, he spoke of art, his eyes shining when he mentioned the artistic genius of Winslow Homer.

'Did he study in Paris?' I said.

'For a very short time,' Edward said. 'But he's an American, one of our own.'

The admiration in his voice surprised me. The professors at Oberlin College scorned American artists and composers who did not study abroad. 'It seems Mr Homer has captured your interest,' I said.

'Indeed he has. First his illustrations, now his paintings. It's his sensitivity to light and color that I most admire. And how he reaches into the heart of his subject and lays it bare for all to see.' Edward glanced at his wife, Alma, who sat across from us, platters of food and a lit candelabra between us. Although no one spoke of it, her waistline was thick with their second child.

Edward turned back to me, and I was pleased that he did. Art was not the usual thing men discussed while dining. The men of Dayton talked about the innovations of the day: electric lights in every home, mechanical cash registers, automobiles, and paved roads.

'Winslow Homer isn't one for portraits, flat and dull,' Edward said. 'Nor does he paint saints ringed in halos. He's better than that. His subject is life, movement.'

'Movement?'

'An oarsman rowing a boat, women repairing a fishing net. Movement.'

'Like music,' I said.

'Precisely,' he said.

Across from us, Alma talked with my mother, who sat beside her. They complained about how difficult it was to keep house-keepers. 'The Irish girls are the worst,' Alma said. 'As soon as they're trained, they run off to get married.'

Edward lifted his crystal flute a few inches above the table, the champagne a soft yellow. He said, his voice low, 'To art. To light and to color. And to those who understand.'

Now, in the bathtub, I wrung the sponge, twisting it. I washed my hair, then drained the tub and huddled near the faucet to rinse it. Back in my room, I dried it with a towel and left it loose. Wearing only my summer robe and slippers, I found my sheet music in one of my trunks. I sat on the spindle chair by one of the windows and read the music for 'Moonlight Sonata', hearing the sad slow notes as if I were playing them. It was said that Beethoven composed it to honor a woman he loved but who did not love him in return. He wrote it to say farewell.

I put the music back in the trunk.

I arranged my hair into a pompadour even though it was still damp. Dressed in a fresh white shirtwaist and my green skirt, I went downstairs and had a light dinner of tomato soup in the dining room. After, I went to the small parlor on the second floor and sat on the pink upholstered settee across

48

from a cluster of horsehair chairs. A gray-haired man sat at a desk in the corner studying what appeared to be blueprints. Long shafts of sunlight came in through the tall open doors. Early evening, I thought, and still so hot. I tried to read the wrinkled newspaper that someone had left on an end table, but the news about the upcoming presidential election blurred before my eyes. I folded it and put it back, and that was when I noticed the brown upright piano near the fireplace.

I had never played an upright. The professors at the music conservatory advised against it. Uprights were inexpensive and their tones were inferior. Play nothing but the best, the professors said. Steinways or Sohmers. But now my hands longed for the cool touch of ivory.

I got up and went to the upright. It was a Mason & Hamlin, and there was sheet music on the rack.

'You play?' the man at the desk said. I looked at him over my shoulder. His spectacles magnified his eyes and showed his curiosity. I turned back to the sheet music. 'The Yellow Rose of Texas.'

'No,' I said.

Upstairs, my room glowed orange from the setting sun. I closed the door and turned the key in the lock. I pulled the tortoiseshell combs from my hair. A train left Union Station, its engine gaining as it slowly picked up speed. I undressed and hung my clothes in the wardrobe, which smelled of cedar. The floorboards creaked beneath my slippered feet as I put on my nightdress. The rose-flowered wallpaper was loose at the seams, and it shimmered with sweat from the dampness in the air. The light faded, and the room eased into darkness.

I pushed aside a panel of mosquito netting that draped from the bed's canopy. The mattress was spongy in the middle

49

and had a musty smell. In the hallway, someone hummed as he walked past, and on the street below, a man called out, 'Robert, I'm coming.' The white linen drapes lifted slightly in the breeze, but the air in the room didn't move and my skin was soon sticky as though covered with salt. In bed, I lay on my side, my black crystal earrings on the nightstand beside me.

It was August 29, 1900, the eve of my wedding day.

CHAPTER FOUR

The Central Hotel

A black silk ribbon dangled from the spine of the worn book that Judge Monagan held open in one hand. Oscar and I stood before him in his wood-paneled office. Two clerks leaned against a side wall with a four-drawer file cabinet between them. The taller of the two had his arms crossed while the other man twisted one end of his dark mustache.

This was my wedding, held in a courthouse office and witnessed by two clerks. For them, this was nothing more than an interruption in their work day. They didn't know that the floor beneath my feet felt slippery or that within minutes, I would step into a world that bore little resemblance to that which I had come from.

The open window behind the judge faced the cream-colored brick wall of another building, and outside, birds cackled. If only there were a breeze, I thought. My navy suit was far too heavy for this climate, but this was my wedding. My pride would not allow me to wear a shirtwaist and skirt. Drops of perspiration ran from the judge's brow, and my own face was damp, my wool hat with its white plumes another choice dictated by pride.

Beside me, Oscar stood with his shoulders back. He was freshly shaved, and his high collar was starched. His suit jacket was buttoned. This was his wedding, too. His second wedding.

He put his hand on the small of my back, his fingers spread wide. My pulse quickened and for a moment, I felt myself lean into his hand.

Judge Monagan cleared his throat. Oscar dropped his hand, and the judge began to read. His voice boomed as if the room lined with shelves of law books and court records were filled with family and friends wishing Oscar and me well. 'We are gathered here on this day, August the 30th, 1900, for the wedding of . . .' He stopped and pulled out a piece of paper he had earlier inserted into the book. He studied it, then started again. 'For the wedding of Miss Catherine Wainwright and Mr Oscar Williams.' He looked at me. 'Are you, Miss Wainwright, here of your own free will, and do you intend to marry this man?'

'Yes,' I said.

'A little louder, Miss Wainwright,' Judge Monagan said. 'So the witnesses can hear.'

'Yes,' I said, and this time it was too loud, my voice startling me.

'And you, Mr Williams,' he said. 'Are you here of your own free will, and do you intend to marry this woman?'

'Yes, sir,' Oscar said. 'I am, and I do.'

One of the clerks laughed. Oscar, his jaw set, gave him a tight look. Both clerks straightened, their smiles gone, and I resisted the sudden urge to take off my crystal earrings. They were a gift from Edward; I should not have worn them.

Judge Monagan continued. 'Is there anyone here who has a reason why this couple may not be lawfully joined?'

He looked up and over his eyeglasses, his gaze going back and forth between Oscar and me, and then to the witnesses. The room was thick with silence.

'Mighty fine,' he said. 'No objections.' He made a twirling motion with his forefinger. 'You two turn and face one another.' We did, my movements jerky, the toes of Oscar's broad boots now just a handful of inches from the tips of my narrow shoes. A thin crack splintered the top of one of his boots, but the leather, I saw, was buffed to a high shine.

I looked up. Our eyes met and all at once, everything – the desk stacked with papers, the judge, the witnesses, the cackling birds outside – fell away. Oscar frightened me, I realized all at once. Not that he would harm me, it wasn't that. It was the way he looked at me, drawing me in, my composure lost.

'Miss Wainwright,' Judge Monagan said.

My thoughts snapped back into place.

'Repeat after me.'

I nodded.

He said, 'I, Catherine Wainwright.'

I echoed the words, my sense of disquiet heightened.

'Take you, Oscar Williams,' I heard myself say, my gaze fixed on Oscar's jacket lapels. They were too wide; the fashion had changed a few years ago. Then, 'To be my lawfully wedded husband.'

'Good,' Judge Monagan said. 'Now you, Mr Williams.'

'Yes, sir,' Oscar said, and again the phrases filled the room, spoken once by the judge and then repeated by Oscar.

I steadied my breathing. The judge licked his finger and turned the page. He said to Oscar, 'Is there a ring?'

'Yes, sir.'

Oscar unfastened the top button of his jacket and took out a wide gold band from his vest pocket. He held it up between his thumb and forefinger. The judge gave him a look of approval and then told me to take off my glove. I did so, my hands all thumbs, my cloth purse with its drawstrings swinging from my right wrist.

Oscar took my left hand. I watched as he slid the wedding band along my ring finger. The band in place but feeling a bit loose, his fingers began to close around mine.

'Good,' Judge Monagan said. 'Very good.'

Oscar released my hand.

'Now then. In front of these witnesses, this couple has declared their intention to join their lives in marriage.'

A declaration, and I belonged to Oscar. As he belonged to me.

'You may kiss the bride.'

Oscar leaned toward me. My breathing turned shallow and fast. Not in this office, I wanted to say. Not with three men watching. He put his hands on my upper arms and all at once, my eyes closed and my chin lifted. He bumped my hat as he kissed me, a light brush against my lips, quick, but long enough for the smell of him to envelop me.

Soap. Tobacco. And fresh-cut hay.

'Ten minutes past four,' Oscar said, the brim of his hat shadowing his eyes. He put the watch back into his vest pocket. We were on a bench in the shade of an oak tree in front of the courthouse. 'More than likely the Jerseys are having themselves a little siesta right about now.'

'Jerseys?'

'My cows.'

I didn't know what to say to this man who was now my husband. I was dazed by the quickness of the wedding ceremony and by the hearty congratulations from the judge. I felt rearranged and marked as though the people walking past us could see by my features that I was a different woman, a married woman.

'All right,' Oscar said. He took out a matchbox and a pack of cigarettes from a pocket in his jacket. 'It's a powerful habit,' he said, referring to the cigarette he held now between his thumb and forefinger.

'My father said much the same about cigars,' I said. My father had never smoked in the presence of ladies but Oscar had no such reservations. The cigarette between his lips, he struck a match. The flame flared. He lit the cigarette; its tip burned red. He flicked the match and the flame went out. His chin raised, he inhaled.

Water bubbled at a nearby marble fountain and splashed into the circular basin. It was a lighthearted melody but it did not soothe my nerves. The Central Hotel was blocks from here. Earlier, Oscar had met me in the parlor and from there, we walked to City Hall for our marriage license and then on to the courthouse. The walk had seemed endless, block after block in the sun. Now, as we sat under the oak tree, a noticeable space between us, I imagined our return to the hotel. His hand would be on the small of my back as we'd step through the open door and into the modest entrance. There'd be arrangements to make with the desk clerk: a change in the registration, a line drawn through my name, and a new combination of names – Mr and Mrs Oscar Williams – written in the narrow space above. The desk clerk, a knowing look in his eye, would hand Oscar the room key.

The leaves of the oak stirred. I should say something but I couldn't think what that might be. Oscar, too, didn't seem to know what to say. The breeze caught at my hem, lifted it and my navy skirt ballooned. I pressed it flat, and on the street that bordered the courthouse park, a trolley slowed to a stop, the sharpness of the clanging bell carrying me to Dayton, the overhead electric wires humming as Edward Davis sat several rows behind me.

'How about we take a ride?' Oscar said. 'Show you the sights?'

'Yes,' I said, the word coming out in a rush. 'I would enjoy that very much.'

'Me too,' Oscar said. He took one last pull on his cigarette and blew out the smoke in a thin stream. He dropped the cigarette on the gravel and ground it with the toe of his boot.

We sat in the middle of the trolley, Oscar on the aisle seat and I at the window. His leg was close to my skirt, and the weave of his trousers was rough and knobby. In front of Oscar a dark-haired woman held a sleeping baby whose cheek was pressed into her shoulder. The trolley, buckling and shuddering, lurched into the traffic.

His hat in his hands, Oscar leaned forward to see around and past me. The trolley creaked as we gained speed, and Oscar's leg came closer.

'We're on Winnie Street, coming up to what we call the East End,' he said. The track dipped and the baby in front of us opened his eyes and then closed them.

'Beautiful homes,' I said. 'And such lovely shade trees.' Block after block of two-story houses with wraparound porches and gingerbread trim slipped by. The houses had complicated roof lines with peaks, dormer windows, and widow's walks. Their staircases were grand, wide and sweeping. In my mind, though, I was at the Central Hotel, Oscar directing me toward the stairs. I'd have to hold on to the banister, the pitch of each scuffed step uneven as he followed with the room key in his hand.

That could happen an hour from now. Perspiration dampened my hairline. Hot wind rushed in through the trolley windows and loosened strands of my hair. I tried to tuck them into place but it was hopeless. Beside me, Oscar swayed with the trolley. His leg crushed my skirt. I blotted my forehead with my gloved fingers.

In front of us, the woman rocked from side to side, and patted the back of her sleeping baby. The voices of passengers floated around me, the trolley stopping at every corner, the bell ringing. People got off and others boarded, a few of the women glancing at Oscar and then at me as they walked past in search of seats.

'Next street up is Ninth,' Oscar said when the trolley started moving.

'Very nice,' I said. I saw myself in the hotel washroom that I had used yesterday. I was in the rusty tub, water to my shoulders, the door locked and Oscar down the hall, waiting in my room. Our room.

We rounded a corner. 'The cross street coming up is Sealy,' Oscar said. 'They're a big family in these parts. They're customers, too. Good ones.'

'Pardon?'

'My milk,' Oscar said. 'The Sealys drink it by the bucket.'

'I see.' With Edward Davis, there had been conversations about literature, artists, and composers. There had been dinners in secluded dining rooms and rides in private cabs, my hand on his arm.

'Broadway Avenue,' Oscar said. 'We're proud of this street.'

'I can well imagine.' Oak trees and bushes with pink flowers trimmed the boulevard in the center of the avenue. The trolley crept across the avenue, the conductor clanging the bell to warn the cross traffic. We stopped and started, the trolley jerking. Finally we were on the other side of Broadway. We gained speed, passing blocks of houses. Here, though, the yards were narrow, as were the small plain one-story clapboard houses, most of them atop brick columns a few feet above street level.

The trolley turned a corner, lurching. I fell against Oscar, my shoulder colliding with his arm, my leg pressing against his. I felt the solidness of him; I heard the quick intake of my breath. He steadied me, his hand gentle on my upper arm. I gathered myself, straightening. The trolley slowed, and Oscar released my arm.

'The Gulf of Mexico,' he said. The city street had given way to sand, and the tracks now ran parallel to a beach. Beyond it, a wide expanse of water shimmered blue and silver in the sun.

'See them?' Oscar said, pointing out the window. 'The Pagoda.' In the water, two round wood buildings stood on top of tall thin posts. Long wood walkways, crowded with people, connected the pagodas to the beach.

'We call them bathhouses,' Oscar said. 'Aren't they something, up on those stilts? Seven feet above the water and some thirty paces from the high-tide line. Folks call them an engineering marvel. Tourists come by the hundreds to see them.'

'I've never seen anything like them,' I said.

'And all this commotion over here is the Midway. See it? Here on the beach? The carnival games, rides, and suchlike? Tourists keep it busy spring, summer, and fall.'

The trolley crawled along the wide, flat beach and took us past the clutter of the Midway. In the surf, children leapt over small waves while others dug barehanded in the sand. Men and women walked along the tide line, the women in belted bathing costumes, their striped bloomers billowing down to their ankles and their hair tucked up under ruffled caps. The men's black costumes were sleek and form-fitting, the shapes of their torsos and thighs unmistakably outlined. Their calves were bare. The straps over their shoulders were narrow so that their upper chests and arms were exposed.

'Murdock's, that's one of the bathhouses out over the water. Can't see it from this angle but it has a restaurant,' Oscar said. 'They're proud of their lemonade. They serve their beer cold, too. I'm a tad thirsty, how about you?'

I forced a smile.

The trolley eased to a stop and began to empty as passengers filed down the aisle and towards the back exit. The woman in front of us with the baby stood up. My pulse rushed. I could have a child by early June. That had been something Edward and I had sought to avoid, although we had never spoken of it. But I was married now, and Oscar was a Catholic. He would expect children. Many children. It was one more thing that I had pushed from my mind when I was in Dayton.

He stood and stepped into the aisle. He thought I had agreed to get off. He didn't know that I couldn't depend on my legs to hold me.

From somewhere, a calliope played, the tinny notes carried on the breeze. The words hummed in my mind.

'It rained all night the day I left.
The weather it was dry.
The sun so hot I froze to death.
Susanna, don't you cry.'

Out in the water, bathers held on to chains looped to staked metal poles, the waves picking the bathers up and setting them down.

This morning I hung my nightgown in the hotel wardrobe that smelled of cedar. Soon, I would take that plain, high-necked gown from the hanger and put it on, my fingers clumsy with the buttons and my knees buckling.

'I can't,' I said.

Oscar said, 'Lots of newcomers say that about the bath-houses. Said it myself when I first got here, the stilts being so thin and sunk down in soft sand. But Murdock's is safe, even if it is high up. It's been here for years.'

The sweating wallpaper on the hotel walls, my crystal earrings on the nightstand, and the bed draped with mosquito netting.

Oscar said, 'Wouldn't take you up there if I didn't think it was safe.' He paused. 'How about it? Willing to give it a try? Catherine?'

The sound of my name startled me. I looked up at him. The scar on his cheek appeared more prominent than it had earlier. The corners of his mouth were turned up in a small smile, and his green eyes carried a steadying calm look. And something else. Disappointment. How could he not feel it? My conversations were stilted, my smiles were frozen, and my bearing was rigid. I found it difficult to be any other way. He was a stranger to me, as was the world he offered. But there was more. There was this sense of disquiet stirred by his very presence.

He put his hand out to me.

The trolley was almost full now. The new passengers slumped in their seats, tired from their day at the beach, faces flushed from the sun. At any moment, the trolley driver would ring the bell and we would begin to move, slow, then faster as we traveled away from the beach and returned to the city and to the Central Hotel.

I reached up and took Oscar's hand.

Hours later, at the hotel, it went much as I had imagined: the speculating glances from the desk clerk, the sinking into the bathtub, my wobbling knees, and Oscar's expectations. What I had not imagined was me. I had not known I would break down into sobs when he finished or that I would say nothing when he apologized. I could not tell him that I loved another man, that Edward's abandonment had hurt me to the quick, and that my mother's had hurt me even worse. I could not tell Oscar that when he embraced me, his arms around me, tender at first and then turning into a quick rush of desire, the pain of the past eight months had unexpectedly welled up inside of me and pierced my very being. Instead, when it was over, I curled away from Oscar, overcome by the turmoil of so many raw and exposed feelings. I wept, Oscar's apologies faint in my ears. I wept, and in that way, I let him think he was the cause of my pain.

CHAPTER FIVE

Down the Island

The wet hard-packed sand crunched beneath the turning wagon wheels. Oscar's horses, Maud and Mabel, plodded as they flicked their tails and shook their heads at the black flies that bit their reddish-brown rumps and gathered in the corners of their eyes. To our left, shallow lacy waves rushed close to the wagon wheels, then fell back and merged with the next oncoming wave. Off to our right by a hundred feet or so, rows of tall sand hills edged the beach. There, bushes with yellow flowers and tall sea grass rippled, swept by the hot breeze.

'We call this the beach road,' Oscar said, breaking the silence between us. He and I sat on the wagon's short buckboard under a canvas canopy. Washed-ashore splintered trees, crates covered with barnacles, and parts of glass bottles littered the flat wide beach that stretched ahead of us for what seemed like miles. I felt small and insignificant. Apart from the steamships and schooners far off on the horizon, there was only Oscar and me.

'Beach works good for the most part,' he said.

'It certainly lacks traffic,' I said.

'That it does.'

The sky was a sharp blue, and the gulf was silver in the morning light. The shallow waves chased small brown-speckled birds that ran and pecked the wet sand. Flocks of seagulls stood near the water's edge and rose in flurries of gray wings as we came upon them.

The slow surf was a soft crash in my ears. The feathering on the legs of the horses was covered with sand, and specks of it flew up from their hooves and splattered the front of the wagon. Oscar's rolled shirt-sleeves flapped in the wind, his suit jacket stored under the buckboard.

'Roads aren't paved on our end,' he said, not looking at me. His hat was low on his forehead. The tendons on the backs of his scarred hands were taut as he held the lines steering the horses around a long tree that lay partially buried in the sand with its bare branches poked up into the air.

I should say something. I should behave as though nothing out of the ordinary had happened last night. That was what Oscar was trying to do with these attempts at conversation.

The wind made hollow beating sounds as it pulled at my shirtwaist and skirt. I said, 'Where do all these dead trees come from?'

'From the rivers, the ones that feed into the gulf.' I felt him glance at me. My straw summer hat hid much of my face. He said, 'Maybe they come from the Brazos south of here or maybe from the Neches at Sabine Pass. Hard to say when it comes to water.'

I nodded as though I were familiar with these names and places. Oscar said, 'Sailors dump the crates overboard, most of it's trash and such. Once in a while, passengers lose things, leastways that's what we figure. A year ago in June, Andre found a baseball, and that, I can tell you, was a big day for him.'

'A baseball, of all things,' I said. Andre. My stepson. I couldn't begin to picture this child with a French name.

The wagon wheels ground in the sand. The sun bore down. Perspiration ran from under my arms and into my corset.

Oscar said, 'We have the ridge road; it's inland over a half of a mile from the sand hills.' He inclined his head toward the right. 'That's where the house and dairy are, on the ridge.'

'Here?' I said. 'We've arrived?'

'We're on down a ways.'

I nodded.

The muscles in his forearms flexed as he navigated the horses around a barrel crusted with barnacles. 'We use the ridge road when the tide comes up too high on the beach,' he said. 'The ridge is rough going, it not being much more than tracks – and plenty hot. But here we get the breeze.' He paused and gave me a sideways look. 'Thought you might appreciate that.'

'A breeze is most welcome,' I said.

'It surely is.'

The horses plodded on, the wheels turning, but the scenery didn't change. Just more sand hills, the water, and the long beach before us.

'There used to be a narrow-gauge train,' Oscar said after a while. 'It ran from the city to the lace factory.'

'A lace factory? Here?'

'Had been. By Offatts Bayou. Building's still there but it's empty. It was called Nottingham, and I didn't like the idea of it, women cooped up and doing that kind of work with machines. And in this heat. Wasn't right, and I wasn't altogether sorry when it closed down.'

The three layers of lace on my shirtwaist ruffled in the wind. I'm not prone to hysterics, I wanted to say to Oscar. But last night . . . To say this, though, called for an explanation that would shock him and humiliate me. I couldn't tell him that I cared for someone else. I couldn't tell Oscar that last evening when he held me, his heartbeat in my ear, I felt myself give way to raw feelings. During the night, we had stayed on our own sides of the saggy bed. Spent from weeping but my nerves pulled tight, I listened to Oscar's breathing settle as he eventually fell asleep. Around dawn, I felt the mattress give when he got up. The floorboards creaked while he dressed, the rustling of his clothes loud in my ears. He whispered that he was stepping out for a while. He wanted to check on his horses at the livery, and after that, he'd stop by the barber's for a shave. I lay still, feigning sleep. As soon as his footsteps faded in the hallway, I got up, my legs shaky and my eyes puffy. I hurried, desperate to be washed, dressed, and to have my hair arranged before Oscar's return.

I waited for him in the hotel parlor, my composure somewhat in place. We had breakfast in the dining room where I managed a piece of toast while Oscar had eggs and bacon between quick cups of coffee. Our conversation about what time to leave and about the loading of my trunks in the wagon was short and choppy. I was unable to meet his eyes. Yesterday, while riding the trolley, I believed I had seen disappointment in his eyes. This morning there must be regret that he had married me.

Now, we rode in the wagon, the beach stretched before us without end. It was all endless: the water, the sky, and the need to cover my past and my feelings.

'See that on up ahead?' Oscar said. 'Those two big houses

on the landward side of the sand hills, can you make them out? That's St. Mary's. It's a home for orphans.'

I needed to stop thinking about last night. Oscar was trying to do so. I said, 'Those poor little children.'

'The sisters do their best.'

'Who's looking after your son? Or is he in school?'

'Nan Ogden's looking after him; school doesn't start until the first of October. She's a neighbor woman. Her brothers are the two that work for me. She's been a big help, knows her way around a kitchen. She's willing to stay on. If that suits.'

'Thank you. I'd like that very much.' I paused. 'Nan Ogden and her brothers. Are they next door?'

'Well,' he said. 'They live nearby, but not like how people do in town. The Ogdens are on down a ways.' He gave me a quick look. 'They're a mile and a half wagon ride from us, give or take a few feet.'

'But you called them neighbors.'

'It's different here, most of us spread out like we are. They're the closest to us and that makes them neighbors.'

We fell back into silence. Waves lapped and receded, and the sun was a hard light. Coated in a fine layer of salt, my skin prickled. It was impossible to imagine how I would manage on this remote part of the island. Yesterday's bath-houses and crowds of bathers could have been figments of my overwrought imagination. Nor could I think what I would say to Andre, who must be waiting for us.

'Look,' Oscar said. 'Pelicans. There, offshore.'

I drew in my breath. A flock of brown birds with long beaks coasted on a current of air only they could feel, one after the other, their wings spread wide and their shadows skimming the surface of the water.

'Ten of them,' he said. 'I admire them, have ever since I got here. Folks say their wingspan is five feet across.'

'Nearly my height,' I said. 'And so graceful.'

'Surely are.' He clicked his tongue and turned the horses away from the surf. My traveling trunks and hatboxes in the bed shifted and slid. Now, I thought. Allow yourself to lean toward him. Put your hand on his arm. In that way, apologize for your aloofness and for your frozen smiles. But I didn't. The horses had picked up their pace and we headed toward the sand hills. There, boards formed what appeared to be a makeshift road over the soft sand and between the hills. On the far side, three rooftops were visible.

'We're home,' Oscar said.

Four dogs shot out from nowhere, barking and yapping as they streaked toward us. The wagon wheels creaked as we bumped off of the warped sand hill road and onto a pitted trail that led inland toward three buildings. My stomach roiled. A sharp pungent odor had hit like a slap. Dung. Wave after wave. I held on to the side of the wagon and fought the urge to be ill. My eyes watered as the stench filled my nose and mouth.

'Catherine,' Oscar said. 'You all right?'

I shook my head, my hand to my nose. 'That smell,' I said.

'It's the barn. Frank T. and Wiley didn't have time to clean it. I'll get to it this afternoon.'

His hands, I thought. And the things they touched.

'Settle down,' Oscar called out, the dogs darting around the horses and the wagon. Flies and mosquitoes swarmed and whined. Still covering my nose, I saw his home in fragments as though I could absorb only one thing at a time: the flat, rough scrubland, a small grove of short bushy trees; the stable, the barn, and the house, all in a row and facing the beach.

'Here we go,' he said when we got to a split in the trail. 'This'll help.' We turned east, my trunks and hatboxes sliding again in the wagon bed, the stable and the barn now behind us and the house up ahead.

'Better?' he said.

'Much.'

I breathed through my mouth, now seeing the details of Oscar's home. It was a small one-story clapboard perched on top of thin wood stilts. The only solid thing that secured the house to the ground was the base of the red brick chimney that ran up one side.

Do not fall apart, I told myself. Not in front of Oscar, not before the little boy who stood on the covered porch watching our arrival. Oscar's son. His hair was dark, and he wore brown short pants and a white shirt. A young woman – the house-keeper, I thought – was with him, her hand on his shoulder.

We stopped just before reaching the foot of the porch steps. Oscar pulled up the brake handle, and as if its grinding screech was a signal, the boy leapt down the steps and ran toward us with his arms spread open. 'Daddy! Daddy!' Oscar jumped down, rocking the wagon. Andre flung himself around Oscar's knees.

'It's only been one night,' Oscar said, but with his back to me, he squatted and pressed the child to him as though it had been months. 'Andre,' he said, and in that one word spoken so softly that I almost didn't hear it, I understood what his son meant to him. They held on to one another, Andre's arms around his father's neck. The dogs circled them, their tails a blur of movement.

Andre raised his head just enough to look over Oscar's shoulder and up at me where I sat on the buckboard. His face was brown from the sun, and freckles dashed across his nose and cheeks. Black hair flopped over his forehead. He was so young, I thought. So little.

He frowned, his dark eyes wide and unblinking. 'Who's she?'

'You know,' Oscar said, his voice low. 'I told you yesterday. Remember?'

He ducked his head, his small fingers curling into Oscar's shirt.

Andre didn't want me here, I understood. He had his father, and that was enough. Until now, Oscar's son had been a shadowy figure in the back of my mind. So, too, was Oscar's first wife, the woman who was this child's mother. But here, at Oscar's home with this small boy clinging to his father, I was pierced by one more truth about this marriage. With barely a thought to it, I had intruded into a child's life and changed the balance of his existence.

Oscar feathered the cowlick at the back of Andre's head, then straightened and stood up. Andre's arm went around his father's leg.

'Miss Ogden,' Oscar said to the woman who stood at the top of the porch steps.

'Mr Williams.' Her tone was flat as though our arrival was of little consequence. She wore a plain blue dress, and its white collar was unbuttoned at her throat. She'd crossed her arms, and her sleeves were rolled to the elbows. Her gaze drifted off toward the sand hills, then wandered back, finding me.

'Ma'am,' she said.

Her coolness startled me. So did the touch of Oscar's hand

as he held mine and helped me down from the wagon. My feet on the ground, the dogs pushed their noses into my skirt, driving me toward the wagon. Oscar whistled, sharp and curt, and they backed off.

'You're not scared of dogs, are you?' he said.

'Only when there are so many.'

Andre said, 'There's just four,' and that started the introductions. 'This is my boy,' Oscar said to me. 'Andre Emile Williams.'

'I'm so very pleased to meet you,' I said, but the sentiment was not acknowledged. Andre wouldn't look at me. Instead, he studied the polished tips of his laced-up boots.

'Young man,' Oscar said.

Andre looked up.

'What do you say?'

He wrinkled his nose, the freckles blending. 'Thank you?'

Oscar hesitated, then, 'Thank you, what?'

'Thank you, ma'am.'

Oscar nodded. 'Andre, this is . . .' Oscar glanced at me and then away. He didn't know what to call me. He cleared his throat and said, 'My wife.' Andre's eyes widened again but Oscar ignored him and turned toward me. 'Let's get out of this sun,' his hand now on my elbow.

'House is five feet up,' Oscar said as we mounted the steps, Andre behind us. 'Never had a drop of floodwater inside.'

I heard the pride in his voice. I said something foolish about the comfort of living in a house that did not flood. It was the best I could do. We were on the covered porch now and Oscar had begun the next set of introductions. The woman was Miss Nan Ogden, and I was Mrs Catherine Williams. She and I exchanged greetings, my 'How do you do?' hollow in

70

my ears and her 'Pleased to make your acquaintance' equally hollow but spoken with a drawl that stretched each syllable. She was thin and bony with knobbly wrists and high cheekbones. Andre leaned against her, one foot on top of the other, and clutched a fistful of her skirt. I had to look up past the brim of my hat to meet Nan Ogden's eyes. They were gray and remote, and her eyebrows were full. Her skin was smooth; she was younger than I. She'd tied her brown hair at the nape of her neck and with her arms still crossed, she stood with most of her weight on one foot, her hip out at the side. It occurred to me that she did not wear a corset. Her gaze skimmed over the daisies on my hat, dropped to the rows of lace on my collar and shirtwaist and then, finally, moved on to Oscar, lingering there.

'I've got something for you,' he said to Andre.

'You do?' Andre said.

'Yep.' Oscar pulled out a small paper sack from the pocket in his trousers. He crouched down so that he and Andre were eye level. Andre put his hands behind his back and grinned with excitement. He bent his knees a little and peered into the sack that Oscar held open. Astonished, Andre sucked in his cheeks and rounded his mouth. His eyes sparkled as he looked at his father and then up at Nan. 'Candy,' he said.

'Lemon drops,' Oscar said. 'Your favorite.'

I'd made a terrible faux pas, I realized. I should have brought Andre a book, a spinning top, or a ball. A gift would have smoothed the way for both of us but it had never entered my mind.

'One piece,' Nan said to him. 'Or you'll spoil your dinner.'

There must be something I could give Andre. I opened my cloth purse. My mirror. My comb. The torn halves of train

71

tickets. I fumbled with the purse, trying to find something suitable without anyone noticing.

'Give you a bellyache, too,' Nan was saying, a thread of sternness beneath her lazy drawl. 'One piece. You hear me?'

'Yes, Miss Nan.' Andre held up a yellow drop of hardened sugar between two fingers, twisting his wrist as he studied the candy. I found my coin purse inside of my bag.

Oscar said to Nan, 'Did Frank T. and Wiley get off on time this morning? Everything all right around here?'

'Maisie's leg's still swelled up. Frank T. couldn't get much milk out of her, her not taking her feed.'

'Can't say I'm overly surprised,' Oscar said, his attention on the barnyard. 'Course I'd hoped otherwise.'

Andre might like a penny, I thought. The coin purse still deep inside of my bag, I opened it. Andre was studying my face now as he popped the candy into his mouth. His gaze dropped to my purse, my hand inside of it. His eyebrows drawn, he squinted as if pondering. He knew, I thought. This five-year-old child understood that I was desperately trying to find something that might pass as a gift. Still studying me, Andre picked at a brown crusty scab on his right knee, the skin around the sore a tender pink. A small shudder crawled down my spine.

Oscar took off his hat and used it to point toward the front door. 'I'll show you the house,' he said. 'Let you get situated. Then I'll see about Maisie.'

'I'd like that very much,' I replied. I closed the coin purse. Timing was vital in music, and the same was true about the giving of a gift. I'd find another opportunity to give Andre a penny.

The floor shook as we walked, and the thought of the thin

stilts that held up the house unnerved me all the more. Andre came in with us but Nan stayed outside. The front room served two functions. A small parlor was on the left side and the kitchen was on the right. There was a coffeepot and a skillet on the stove, and the house smelled of onions cooked in butter. Pots and pans hung from the kitchen wall. A nail tacked a calendar to the wall by the icebox. A long table with two benches filled much of the kitchen, and on the cooking table, flies crawled over the red and white checkered dishcloths that covered dishes and platters.

Oscar said, 'It's nothing fancy.'

'But it's pleasant with all the windows. It's bright and cheerful.'

He tilted his head toward the parlor end of the room. 'Some of the keys stick,' he said. 'I've noticed that.'

I followed his gaze. An upright piano was up against the wall by the fireplace.

Oscar said, 'It's all this salt in the air. Some days are better than others.'

An upright, scorned by my professors. I walked over to it. The floorboards trembled beneath my feet, but the blue and green braided rug in the parlor dulled the sensation. Embossed scrolls decorated the upright's front board, and the music rack was bare. The name of the manufacturer, Behning, was ornately scripted in gold leaf across the keyboard lid. Nicks and dents marred its cabinet, but the mahogany wood shone with polish.

I opened the lid, then pulled off my right glove, one finger at a time. I touched the surface of middle C and felt the grain in the ivory. In Dayton, my ability to lose myself in music had deserted me. Now, this keyboard was the one familiar thing on this island.

Without turning to look at Oscar, I said, 'Do you play?'

'Me? No.'

I put my hand on top of the cabinet. The upright must have been his wife's, his first wife. I ran my finger over a long, thin gash in the wood. To my left, two long windows looked out past the porch. Beyond the sand hills, the water glistened, the ships at sea little more than black dashes. The beach strewn with debris could not be seen from here. Framed by the windows, the immensity of the gulf was diminished and felt less overbearing.

Oscar said, 'I expect you were hoping for better.'

I turned around and saw him again as the young man who had watched me from afar in Dayton. The distance between us was immeasurable. Our backgrounds were worlds apart, and we had little in common. Now, there was the unspeakable thing that had happened between us last night at the hotel.

Andre's arm was wrapped around Oscar's leg. His dark eyes stared up at me, his cheeks drawing on the hard candy.

I said, 'I believed I might never play again.'

'It's not like what you had. I know that.'

Oscar glanced down at Andre and then back at me. He said, his voice low, 'You'll get used to things.'

His words hovered in the air, the sound of the surf on the other side of the sand hills a soft steady whisper. A breeze rustled my skirt. The windows were open. I felt Nan on the porch, listening.

I said, 'I'd like to see the rest of the house. If I may.'

Oscar's house was plain but clean. The bare walls were painted white, and the floor was laid with wide boards of oak. He had sent Andre outside and as Oscar showed me his home, we used care to step around one another, each room feeling small and tight. In the parlor, two black-upholstered chairs faced the fireplace. A red-bound book and newspapers were on the white marble-top table between the chairs.

'These are the stairs to the attic, for storage and such,' Oscar said, referring to a closed door on the back wall.

'Very convenient,' I said. A small roll-top desk and chair were on one side of the door. A clock encased in a square block of pink marble was on the fireplace mantle, and in the kitchen there were kerosene lanterns on the table and a hand pump at the dish wash basin.

We went down a short hall. Andre's room was on the right-hand side. There, seashells and rocks lined the three windowsills. The braided rug by Andre's bed was shades of green, and the mosquito netting that hung from the canopy was looped back and tied to the wood bedposts. His clothes hung on wall pegs, and a shelf held a box of dominos. Wood building blocks with painted letters and numbers on their sides were stacked on the floor. A framed picture was on a small table, and over Andre's bed, a figure of Jesus nailed to a crucifix dripped painted blood from its head, hands, and feet. What I believed to be a rosary hung from the crucifix, the white beads and silver cross twirling in the breeze that came from the open windows.

In the bedroom across the hall, the crucifix was bigger, and the figure's crown of thorns was even bloodier. I looked past it. This was Oscar's religion, not mine. He stood in the center of the small room while I stayed in the doorway. This was his room.

'Settle in to suit you,' he said. 'Change it any way you want.'

Our room. In Dayton I had convinced myself that we would have separate bedrooms.

'Thank you,' I said. 'But I'm sure it's fine as it is.'

The oval rug in the middle of the bedroom was a blur of blue. The rocking chair, the wardrobe, and the dressing table were heavy pieces of dark furniture, none of it mine, all of it Oscar's. And his first wife's.

'This over here goes out to the back veranda,' he said, pointing to a door at the back wall.

'What a lovely idea.'

'We can see the bayou from there, Offatts. It's about a mile from here.'

'I don't believe that I'm familiar with bayous.'

'It's water that cuts into the island. Like a river, you might say, but marshy and slow-moving. Offatts looks like a lake; West Bay feeds into it. Nights it comes alive with frogs calling to their mates. The bayou's good fishing, too, and in the winter, the goose hunting can't be beat.'

'You're a hunter?' I said, but I didn't hear his answer.

The bed, I thought, letting myself see it for the first time. Tonight the mosquito netting will be released from the tiebacks on the posts. The summer quilt with its yellow, blue, and green squares will be turned down. Hours from now. Or sooner.

Oscar left the center of the room and came toward me where I stood on the threshold. Heat rushed to my face. The light was dim here, we were only inches apart, and I found myself looking up into his eyes, drawn.

'No, sir,' I heard Nan Ogden say from the front porch. 'No more candy, won't have it.'

I stepped back. Oscar did the same.

76

'And this room?' I said, gesturing toward another door in the hallway as though my cheeks did not burn.

'The washroom,' Oscar said. 'The tub and washstand. Cistern's in there too. Having lived up in the Panhandle those years back, I've learned to catch water any way I can.'

'You're a practical man,' I managed.

'Try to be. The outhouse is between here and the barn. A path leads directly to it. You can't—'

I put my hand up to stop him. It wasn't the kind of thing people talked about. Nor was I accustomed to outhouses. In Dayton, we had indoor plumbing. 'Well then,' Oscar said, his color deepening. 'Yes, all right. Your trunks. They're cooking out there in the sun. I'll get them, that way you can get settled.'

'I'd like that.'

'Dinner's at noon.'

Lunch, I thought.

'Frank T. and Wiley'll be back mid-afternoon. Those are Nan's brothers. They help with the milking and run the deliveries into town. Nan'll go home with them but she'll leave supper for us. It's how we've been doing of late.'

'I see,' I said.

'But we can do different. You can do the cooking, if that suits better.'

'No, no. This arrangement is fine.' I paused. 'I must admit that I don't have much experience in the kitchen.'

'You weren't brought up to it,' he said. 'It's why I asked Nan to stay on. I don't expect you to run this house by yourself, and she's glad for the work.' He hesitated. 'About Nan,' he said.

'Yes?'

77

'She's a good woman. Strong in her opinions, but a good woman.'

And one who did not like me, I thought, remembering her cool assessment. 'I'll try to remember that,' I said.

CHAPTER SIX

The Wardrobe

I tried to remember Oscar's words about Nan Ogden when the four of us sat down for lunch on the benches at the kitchen table. Oscar had changed out of his suit and it was as if he were a different man. He was at ease in his collarless faded blue shirt and dark trousers held in place by braces. These clothes did not strain and constrict as his suit had, but were loose, the material worn soft. This was the true Oscar Williams, I understood as I sat to his left while Nan and Andre were across from us.

His napkin tucked in at his throat, he prayed, both he and Andre touching their foreheads, chests and shoulders with their right hands as they squeezed their eyes closed. Nan watched me while they prayed, her gray eyes widening when she saw that I wasn't a Catholic.

'Amen, let's eat,' Oscar said and with that, he and Nan sprang into motion. She poured milk from a pitcher into four canning jars. Oscar passed a platter of fried fish to me. 'Help yourself,' he said. 'And there's gravy.'

'Thank you,' I said, but there was little here that was familiar to me: the bowls of rice, the yellow beans mixed with onion, the fried flat biscuits, and Andre on the other side of the table, a bewildered look in his eyes.

'Is there tea?' I said.

'Huh?' Nan said.

'I'm sorry, Catherine,' Oscar said. 'Should have thought of that, you being a tea drinker. None of us here are. I'll have Frank T. and Wiley pick up some from town.'

'If it's not too much of a bother.'

'It's not.'

Nan pursed her lips as if I had made an unreasonable demand. I had a bite of the fish, the fried coating heavy with cooking oil.

'Delicious,' I said.

'Tasty,' Oscar said.

'Just redfish,' Nan said. 'Nothing extra about that.'

'Perhaps,' I said. 'But it's very good.'

'Nothing like home cooking,' Oscar said.

Color rose in Nan's cheeks. Andre scooted his rice around on his plate. Oscar drank his milk in two long swallows. Nan refilled his jar.

From behind Nan and Andre, heat rose from the stove. Flies crawled on the mesh that covered the kitchen window. I dabbed my upper lip with my napkin that I kept on my lap. I imagined opening the icebox and letting its cool air wash over me. Beside me, Oscar held up the bowl of biscuits. 'More corn pone, anybody?'

I declined. 'Wouldn't overly mind one,' Nan said, helping herself, then Oscar taking two.

'We saw a ship from Cuba,' he told Andre.

Andre stared down at his plate.

'It was most impressive,' I said.

80

He looked up, his eyebrows drawn.

'That means big,' Oscar said. 'Impressive.'

Andre's lips moved as if he were trying to say the word.

'Young man,' Nan said. 'Your dinner's getting cold.'

'Yes, ma'am,' he said. He stabbed at a piece of fish with his fork, and under Nan's watchful eye, he ate it.

Her gaze skipped from Andre to Oscar's plate and over to mine. I waved away the flies and had another bite of fish. Apparently satisfied with that, Nan bent over her plate as though she were eating her only meal of the day. Oscar had second helpings of beans and rice, and at the wall, the stove ticked, unmeasured beats in contrast to the constant muffled whisper of the gulf.

Oscar ran the back of his fork through a pool of thick white gravy. He said, 'It's mighty good to see the sun after all the rain we've had.'

'Ain't that the truth,' Nan said. 'But the sun surely did bring out a fresh crop of skeeters.'

Mosquitoes, I took that to mean.

'Big enough to carry you off,' Andre said, looking at me, his mouth full. Oscar went still, his fork over his plate. Nan turned away, but not before I saw the smile in her eyes.

Lunch ended when Oscar stood and thanked Miss Ogden, as he called her, for the fine cooking. He told me to make myself at home. 'I've got some catching up to do,' he said. 'I'll be in the barn.' He paused. 'You doing all right?'

'I'm fine,' and he took me at my word. He left, the door closing behind him. The three of us still at the table, Nan told Andre it was time for his nap. 'Awww,' Andre wailed, but she put up a finger and said, 'No, sir, none of that.' She stood and he did too, looking at me from the corner of his eye.

'Sweet dreams,' I said.

A smile showed around the edges of his mouth. Nan took his hand. 'Day's not getting any younger,' she said, taking him out to the front porch. This surprised me. I had expected them to go to Andre's room. Unsure what to do, I stayed at the table and through the long open windows. I watched her unfurl a red blanket that had been folded on the seat of one of the brown wicker porch chairs, and put it on the floor. Andre climbed up onto a chair and sat with his legs straight out.

Nan untied the shoelace of one of his boots and plucked at the long laces with her fingers to loosen them. The pack of dogs must be on the porch. I heard the click of their toenails and their loud pants. 'Ain't it good to have your daddy home?' she said.

'Yeah, but that lady, I don't—'

'None of that, honey boy,' Nan said. 'Won't have it.' She glanced through one of the windows and our eyes locked. I held her gaze. She turned her attention back to Andre, busy again with his boots, dropping them to the floor with a thud. He slid off of the chair and disappeared from my sight. 'Now close them little eyes of yours,' Nan said. 'Go to sleep.'

On the porch floor, I thought. Outside. With flies and mosquitoes.

She came back in and without a word, she began to clear the table. On the porch, the dogs scratched at the flooring, then thumped down. Nan's hands, red and chapped, were quick and steady, accustomed to this work. She carried the dishes, platters, and bowls from the table to the counter with a silent grace as if she had been in this kitchen all of her life.

82

I folded my napkin and placed it on the table. 'Thank you for lunch,' I said.

'Dinner.'

'Yes. Well. Regardless, it was delicious.'

She came to a standstill, a dirty dish and canning jar in her hands. She said, 'You didn't eat but a speck.'

'Well, yes. But it was all very good.'

She put the dishes on the counter. I scooted the bench away from the table. I said, 'If you'll excuse me, I believe I'll unpack and then have a little rest.'

'You all right?'

'Pardon?'

Nan surveyed me as though recording my sallow coloring to her memory. She said, 'It's the heat, that's what's making you need a rest most likely.' Her accent made each word drip as though coated in boiled sugar. She said, 'And the excitement and all. Mr Williams said how you come from up north. Ohio.'

'That's correct. Dayton, Ohio.'

'His hometown. When Mr Williams first came here, we took him for being from the Panhandle. But that weren't so, he told us.' The table was cleared now, and all of the dishes were on the counter. Flies gathered but Nan didn't seem to notice. She said, 'He told us how you all grew up together.'

'I suppose you could say that. We attended the same school.'

Nan picked up a bucket kept in the corner by the stove and put it on the cooking table. I started to stand. She said, 'Mr Williams told me you play the piano, said you play good.'

'That was very kind of him to say.' I sat back down. If she and I were going to be in this house together, we needed to become acquainted. This, I supposed, was as good a time as any.

Her back to me, Nan scraped a dirty plate with a knife, the bits of leftover food going into the bucket. She said, 'You play for your church back home?'

'No.'

'Dance tunes maybe?'

'Waltzes have never been favorites of mine. But yes, there were occasions when patrons specifically made such requests. I performed, you see, at concerts and at private gatherings.'

For the briefest of moments her hands stopped and then she was back at work, the sound of her knife shrill against the plate. 'Mr Williams, he's been all stirred up,' she said. 'Last week he had me clean this house from top to bottom. Not that it needed it, I've been keeping it up good. But Mr Williams, his mind was made up. All last week I scrubbed floors and washed windows. I beat every rug like I hadn't just done it last spring. Polished the stove, too.'

'You've worked hard,' I said. 'And it shows.'

She rubbed at a piece of dried food on one of the plates with her thumbnail.

'There are few things more pleasant than a clean house,' I said.

'That's so.' She paused. 'He had me clean out the wardrobe.' Her tone had changed. The drawl was still there but now there was a hard edge. A feeling of dread came over me. 'He hadn't been able to do it before,' Nan said. 'Wouldn't let me touch Bernadette's things. Wouldn't let nobody, not even Sister Camillus. But last week he told me it was time. Told me to do what I thought best with her clothes, said I could keep them or take them to St. Mary's. But if I was to keep them, he didn't want me wearing her things here.'

I didn't know what to say.

Nan said, 'I didn't keep them, couldn't. I gave them to the orphans. Figured Bernadette would want that.'

Pressure tightened in my chest.

'That's how I came to find out. How we all did.'

'Pardon?'

She ignored my question and ran the knife over a serving platter. Bits of fish fell into the bucket. Her back still to me, she said, 'Saw you go to the outhouse.'

'You were watching me?'

She shrugged. 'Didn't Mr Williams tell you to bang hard on the door? To call out before going in?'

'No.'

'There's rattlers in that outhouse.'

'Rattlers?'

'Rattlesnakes.'

The hair rose on my arms.

'Bang on the door, let them know you're coming, wake them up. That gives them time to slide on out.'

'Dear God.'

Nan took the lid off of one of the pots still on the stove and stirred whatever was inside it. Finished, she thumped the wood spoon a few times on the side of the pot, clumps of food dropping into it. She put the lid back on and put the spoon on its rest. She faced me. Her hands trembled. She crossed her arms and held her elbows. She said, 'I saw how you didn't bang on the door. I said to myself, If that ain't just like Mr Williams, trying to spare you, not wanting to tell you

85

something that might unsettle you.' She regarded me. 'All the same, a person appreciates knowing.'

I stood up. 'If you'll excuse me, I have my trunks to unpack.'

I worked the pump in the washroom by the two bedrooms, the handle squeaking as water trickled into the small porcelain basin. In my mind, I heard Nan's voice with that slow, irritating accent, the meaning behind her words designed to put me in my place. Until last week, Oscar hadn't been able to part with his first wife's clothes.

I pulled the pump handle up and pushed it back down again. It upset me that I allowed Nan to rattle me to this extent. I pumped the handle again and tried to remember the name of Andre's mother. The water was still a trickle and the puddle in the basin barely covered the plug. Oscar's straight razor and shaving mug were on a small shelf off to the side. The bathtub was spotted with red rust. The cistern, a large wood barrel with a lid, was in the corner. A pipe ran from the lid up to the ceiling close to the awning window.

Bernadette. That was her name.

'Saw you go to the outhouse.' Nan had watched me as I opened the door to the outhouse, my nose pinched against the smell of the barn. Inside, bitter fumes of lime burned my eyes. The outhouse was hot and dim. The mesh-covered window on the door was too high for the light to reach the corners. Flies bit my hands and face, and wind whistled through chinks in the walls and from around the door. The seat had two openings, one small for a child.

Rattlesnakes. Oscar should have told me. I pushed and pulled the pump handle harder. Water gushed out and splashed into the basin.

Texas. The heat, the beach road, and the flies. And now the household help in the form of Nan Ogden. 'Do something,' my mother had said when she first heard the rumors about Edward and me. *Go abroad*, Edward had written in a brief note. 'You'll get used to things,' Oscar said.

I rolled up my sleeves and lathered the soap, my fingers brushing over the wedding band. I washed my wrists and forearms, scrubbing. From somewhere a fly buzzed. It landed and bit my neck. I let go of the soap and swatted at it, the wedding band flashing before my eyes. The fly flew off, and landed on the opposite wall.

Texas. Backward and primitive. I held up my left hand. Married. I tugged at the band. It was tight. I put my hands in the water and pulled it off. It sank to the bottom of the basin and landed near the plug. The soap floated on the surface, and all of a sudden, I inhaled the sweet scent of home.

Ivory soap. It was what I used in Dayton, everyone there did. It was made in Ohio. I scooped it up with both hands and held it to my nose. Water dripped from my hands and onto my lacy shirtwaist. Ivory soap, here in Texas, here in this house. It was the faint flowery fragrance of my home. And more. Beneath the tobacco and fresh-cut hay, it was the scent of Oscar.

Last night, his embrace had unleashed my sorrow. For eight months no one had had a kind word for me, no one had consoled me, and no one had held me. Only Oscar, a man I had not seen in twelve years.

It had been different with Edward. He and I corresponded for over a year, slowly becoming acquainted. His first letter arrived at my apartment in Philadelphia during February of 1896, almost two months since he and I had talked about art during Christmas dinner. A letter from my cousin's husband,

I'd thought as I opened the envelope. How peculiar. I waited a month before responding. *I, too, enjoyed our conversation about Winslow Homer's works.* Five weeks later, his next letter came. *Homer's* Fox Hunt *is on display at the Academy of Fine Arts in Philadelphia,* he wrote. *Have you seen it?*

There's so little time, I wrote to him four weeks later. *My music consumes me. Last Saturday my ensemble performed before an audience of three hundred. The mayor was there.* Edward's response had been one of congratulations and admiration of my success. It would be impolite to ignore his kind remarks, I decided, and so I responded within the week. Our letters continued, the time narrowing between each one. In the spring of 1897, Edward came to Philadelphia.

The wedding band in the bottom of the basin was a faint gleam of gold beneath the sudsy water. I put the soap back on the washstand where it formed a milky puddle. I dried my hands and arms with the thin white towel that had hung from a nail. I patted the damp towel to my neck to ease the fly's sting. Then I pressed it to my cheeks and forehead.

Near the ceiling, the glass in the awning window was propped open and pushed out. Flies clung to the mesh that covered the opening. Mesh was nailed to all of the window frames in the house. Perhaps it was meant to keep out rattlesnakes. It certainly didn't deter flies.

I hung up the towel, reached into the basin, felt the wedding ring, and found the short metal chain attached to the plug. For months, while the whispered rumors drove me to despair, Oscar had so mourned the death of his wife that he had been unwilling to part with her clothes. Nan had cleaned this house, she'd cooked Oscar's meals, and she'd taken care of his son. Perhaps she'd expected him to marry her. Oscar might have given her that impression. Then, this spring, my first letter arrived.

I almost felt sorry for her.

'Strong in her opinions,' Oscar had said about Nan, 'but a good woman.' He didn't see her as I did. In her unrefined way, she was patronizing and cutting. If I could, I would tell her to leave. But beyond making tea and toast, I knew nothing about running a household. I needed Nan.

I let go of the chain, found the wedding band again, and dried it on the towel. I held the band up toward the window. Until this moment, I had avoided looking at it. Now I angled it so that it caught the light. It was wide, plain, and unmarred. The gold glowed, and inside there was an inscription. *Galveston 1900.*

Two days ago, during our lunch at the Central Hotel dining room, Oscar must have sized my hand. That afternoon, he must have gone to a jeweler's and selected this band. He must have waited while the jeweler inscribed it. That might have been when he bought the lemon drops for Andre.

I held the ring in the palm of my left hand. Oscar could have married Nan but he wanted better for Andre. 'The right way to talk,' he had told me, 'manners and suchlike. You do things right.'

Yesterday, the wedding band was too big, but today my fingers were puffy. From the salt air, I believed. I slid the band past my fingernail and down my finger. Oscar must have predicted the swelling. Today, the band fit.

In Oscar's bedroom – our bedroom – the gray weathered barn was visible from the west windows. I opened the back door and went out to the narrow porch where there were two wicker

89

chairs. In the distance, a wide body of water shimmered in the sun. The bayou, I thought. Between it and the house, reddish-brown and beige cows grazed, a few of them in the shade cast by a stunted tree that leaned toward the bayou, its lower branches touching the ground. Other cows were knee deep in the small ponds scattered throughout the rough, bushy land. At one, a tall white bird with a long neck stood at the marshy edge. There was no sign of Oscar. Nor were there any signs of houses.

I went back inside. My traveling trunks and the stack of hatboxes were next to the wardrobe. From the kitchen, I heard the clinking of pots and crockery as Nan washed the dishes.

The wardrobe was tall and imposing in this small room. Its two doors were plain and so too was the crown molding that trimmed the top. For months, this wardrobe held the memory of Bernadette for Oscar. I was not the only one to hold on to the past.

I opened the doors.

There was no sign of Bernadette, not even a stray button. Instead, there were bare hangers, and Oscar's clothes.

So few things, I thought. He had two coats: one was wool for winter, and the other was made of canvas and waxed for rain. Near the coats were a pair of dark trousers, a gray shirt, a vest, and the suit and white shirt Oscar had worn to the city.

I touched the sleeve of the white shirt and rubbed it between my thumb and fingers. It was mussed from wear but the cotton fabric had body. It was new. He'd bought it for the wedding, I imagined, with the hope that I would think well of him.

Oscar's other shirt – the gray one – was faded and the cuffs were frayed. *I have left Ohio and am Making my Own Way as a Hand at the Circle C Ranch,* he had written in one of his early letters. He had been young and alone, and I couldn't begin to fathom what it had been like for him when he came to Texas. Nor when his wife died, leaving him with a child.

One of the lower drawers in the bottom of the wardrobe was empty but in the other, I found a small wood box the size of a cigar case. It was smooth and looked to be made of walnut with light streaks running through the grain. In the center of the lid was an inlaid *W*. I started to open it, then stopped. It was not mine. I returned it to the drawer.

'Settle in,' Oscar had told me. From one of my trunks, I took out the navy skirt that I had worn yesterday for the wedding. I shook it, then folded it lengthwise and draped it over a hanger. I hung it in the wardrobe and all at once, I was overcome by the intimacy of my skirt so close to Oscar's clothes.

Flushing, I closed the doors and stepped away. I touched my earrings; I thought of Edward but in my mind, I saw him as if he were in a distant haze.

A different image filled my thoughts. I was on a stage with the two other women in my ensemble. My evening gown was a deep blue, and I was seated before a Steinway. My hands poised above the keyboard, I looked to Helen Christopher, the violinist. Her bow hovered over the strings. The audience was quiet, and a feeling of anticipation filled the concert hall. I waited for Helen's nod.

Pain squeezed my chest. I had given up everything I had known for a man whose face was slipping from my memory.

Outside the house, dogs barked, a wild confusion of noise. Someone whistled, quick and sharp. The barking stopped

91

and was replaced by the creak and groan of moving wagons. Through the window, I saw Oscar, wearing boots to his knees, come out of the barn.

Unwanted memories rose to the surface: Edward's delayed written response when I wrote him that I planned to return to Dayton, his occasional failure to meet me as planned, and his half-hearted talk of divorce.

A cad. Edward was a cad. And I had been a fool.

A fool. How had I not known?

The words I'd used to describe our arrangement – friendship, companionship – were veils meant to ease my conscience. All of the excuses for the time we spent together – our mutual admiration of the arts, the desire for intelligent conversation and debate – justified nothing. Edward was married. Our liaison was disreputable. He was disreputable. And so was I.

The crucifix over the bed loomed, the slumped Jesus bearing down. *Thou shalt not commit adultery*. I had pushed that from my mind and disregarded every moral objection. Edward and I were the exception. He and I belonged together. Edward's wife was no longer a wife, not in the truest sense of the word. She was an invalid, bitter and quarrelsome. Edward loved me. I loved him.

But there had never been love. Only weakness.

Adulterer. The word ricocheted through my mind.

A married man with children. I had wounded Edward's wife. I'd disgraced my family. I'd left Dayton with my bills unpaid. I had ignored the ugly truth about myself and worst of all, I had deceived others.

It is with fond memories that I think of you, I had written in one of my letters to Oscar this spring.

Two days ago, I told Oscar I wished to be married immediately. 'Is everything all right with you?' he had asked, wariness showing in his eyes. 'Mr Williams,' I had snapped, as if he had been the one who had insulted my honor.

I had held myself so high; I considered Oscar beneath me. I believed I could fool him, but he was not a stupid man. Alone, he had left Ohio. Alone, he had built a farm. And now he had married me, taking me in, too much of a gentleman to ask further questions.

Through the window, I watched Oscar walk across the barnyard, his stride long and sure, and his hand up in greeting. Two wagons, each driven by a man, came to a stop side by side. These must be Nan's brothers. They were due to return mid-afternoon after delivering milk in the city. They sat on the buckboards with their hats pulled low and their braces off of their shoulders. The dogs sniffed at the wagon wheels and one lifted his leg. Oscar said something and gestured toward the house. The brothers turned and looked my way.

I backed away from the window, sure that the mark of adultery was visible on my features. Galveston was a thousand miles from Dayton, I told myself. And here, down the island, Dayton could be on the other side of the moon. Oscar might suspect I was in some kind of trouble but he couldn't know the details. If he did, he would not have married me.

Someone still might tell him the truth. His mother might write to him. Or his younger sister or brothers. Oscar's sister had been three years behind me in school. I couldn't remember her name and I didn't know what had become of her. But if she still lived in Dayton, if Oscar had written to his family about our engagement, if his sister had heard the rumors, she would warn him. A letter from her might arrive any day.

I went cold inside.

I must admit to it; I must confess to Oscar. Better to hear it from me than from his sister. I imagined telling him – 'I found myself entangled with the wrong man, a married man.' I pictured the shock on his face; I imagined him backing away from me.

The Ogden men had climbed down from their wagons and were walking this way, pulling up their braces. Oscar was with them. Andre ran to them and one of the men caught him and swung him in a circle. Andre laughed. Back on the ground, the little boy skipped, flinging his arms as the men walked with long strides. Oscar intended to introduce them to me, I realized.

No. I couldn't bear for Oscar to see me, my disgrace exposed. 'You do things right,' he'd said about me. If he discovered the truth, what then?

The house began to shake. The men had come up the front steps. I went to the bedroom door to close it. 'Don't you all be tracking dirt on my floors,' I heard Nan say.

'Shoot,' one of the Ogdens said. 'You're near as bad as Ma.'

'Hush up,' Nan said, and it was as if she were speaking to me. Say nothing, keep still. Oscar's family might not know. His mother might not be living. His sister might have married and left Dayton years ago. His brothers could be the kind of men who did not write letters. Oscar might have lost touch with all of them.

On the crucifix nailed to the wall, painted blood dripped from the crown of thorns. Should Oscar learn the truth, he would turn me out of his home.

'She's having herself a rest,' I heard Nan say.

'She poorly?' This was one of the Ogden men.

'I asked her. Told me she wasn't.'

'Worn thin from the trip,' Oscar said. 'That's what it is.'

Gratitude rushed through me. He'd made my excuses.

I closed the door and sat down at the dressing table. My face, pale and gaunt, stared back at me from the mirror. The voices of Oscar and the Ogdens in the parlor were distant and faint.

My hands trembling, I took off the black crystal earrings. Trinkets, I thought. For Edward's mistress. I had worn them every day, even for my wedding. Now I couldn't bear the sight of them. I went to the open trunk and pushed the earrings into a side pocket beneath my handkerchiefs and sachets. Tomorrow I'd bury them. Or throw them into the gulf.

Through the closed bedroom door, Oscar's voice was a soft mumble. He'd wanted the men to meet me, his wife. As if I were a spoiled child, I had placed him in a position where he had to make excuses to his employees for my absence.

I deserved everything that had happened to me. I couldn't repair the damage I'd done to Edward's family. I couldn't make amends to Oscar for my letters that were one deception after the next. But I would not shame him before his employees.

I put my hand on the doorknob and opened the door.

'I'm ready to get on home,' I heard Nan say.

'You don't look ready,' one of the Ogdens said.

'That's 'cause I'm waiting for you to get the ice. Guess you all are just going to let it melt out there in the sun.'

I raised my chin and began the walk down the short dim hall to the parlor to meet the Ogdens.

CHAPTER SEVEN

Mrs Williams

I saw how the new Mrs Williams looked at the house when Oscar brought her here. Her face was pinched like she was on the windward side of meat left out to rot in the sun. Oscar's own face was streaked with worry as he helped her down from the wagon, then helped her up the veranda steps, doing his best to please her. For pity's sake, I thought as he stumbled through the 'howdy do's, me and her taking our measure of each other. Oscar should stand proud of his house. It was painted and the veranda went all the way around it. There was running water in the kitchen and washroom, and the floors weren't pine but oak, sanded smooth as could be. It wasn't patched together like my family's house was, Daddy adding on a room now and again, the floors not altogether even. Oscar had the finest fireplace on our end of the island, other than the Fultons', but they were city people. The Fultons' house by the bay was all about show, them able to have a big house in the city and one here, too. But Oscar's fireplace was red brick, and if Mrs Williams noticed, she kept that to herself.

Then there was Oscar himself. A finer man couldn't be

found nowhere, and everybody on the island knew it. Everybody but him, that was.

My own brothers, Frank T. and Wiley, were nearly struck dumb when they met the new Mrs Williams. Oscar brought them up to the house as soon as they got back from their milk deliveries. At first I didn't think she'd leave the bedroom, but there she was, her chin high. 'Ain't you all never seen a pretty woman before?' I nearly said. I was that ashamed. Them two shuffled their feet on the parlor floor like they were ignorant schoolboys, not grown men. Frank T. put his hat to his heart like he wasn't promised to Maggie Mandora. Wiley did the same, but he kept his mouth shut so as to hide where a cow had kicked out a few of his front teeth. They called her 'ma'am', and when she smiled that narrow smile of hers, both of them turned beet red. Frank T. took to patting down his brown hair like it could be tamed, and Wiley's hand went to the back of his pants to make sure his shirt hadn't come untucked.

It was plain to see that Mrs Williams cast a spell over men. Maybe it was that neck of hers, nearly as white as all the lace on her collar and shirtwaist. Or maybe it was her figure, buxom full but narrow at the waist. Her eyes were blue and her eyelids drooped just a tad, lending her a sleepy look. Her complexion wouldn't win no prizes, though – it had a washed-out color – but all in all, she added up in a way that turned men silly.

'Supper's laid out on the stove,' I told her when the men finally clomped off to the barn, Frank T. having told her she was mighty welcome to Texas. It was nearly time for me to go home, and if she knew about tomorrow's dance set up just so folks could meet her, she hadn't let on.

'Pardon?' she said. She was looking at the piano in the parlor, her long fingers tapping the sides of her yellow skirt.

Earlier, she'd told me she was going to rest and I took that to mean she'd change from her Sunday best into something more everyday. But there she was, close to four o'clock in the afternoon and still dressed up. She'd taken off her black glass earrings, though, and I was glad for it. Nobody wore earrings that dangled, not during the day they didn't.

'I'll be going on home directly,' I said. 'All you've got to do is heat up supper. It's mostly what's left over from dinner, fish and rice, it being Friday.' Puzzlement showed on her face. I said, 'Catholics don't eat meat on Fridays.'

'Oh yes,' she said like she knew that.

'Mr Williams likes his supper at five. Shortly, stoke up the stove, get it good and hot.' Now another question showed on her face. I said, 'Maybe you're not overly familiar with a wood stove. What do you all have up there in Ohio? Gas?'

'I'm afraid I can't say,' she said. 'I've lived in a hotel for the past few years.'

Oh good Lord, what on earth had Oscar gone and done? I knew of only one kind of woman that lived in hotels. Tears burned the backs of my eyes and a sick feeling settled in the bottom of my belly. I turned away from Mrs Williams, just as I had resolved to turn away from Oscar and bury my feelings for him. I had to; I was a curse to the men that took up with me. When I was sixteen, Oakley Hill drowned five days before our wedding, his fishing boat found overturned and him all tangled up in rope. I was twenty-one when Joe Pete Conley, a man who had been courting me for five months, got lockjaw and died. That was June of last summer.

I was a danger to men, anybody could see it. When I told Mama and Daddy that, they sat me down. Mama said, 'There's women like that,' and Daddy said, 'Best you never marry. Best

98

you just plan on taking care of us during our coming old age.'

Ever since Bernadette died, I had stepped around Oscar, telling myself I couldn't care for him, not overly. I had to keep him safe. Not that he'd tried to court me. Likely he hadn't even thought about it, mourning Bernadette the way he had. And if he had thought of it, could be he figured I was still grieving for Joe Pete Conley. But now there was Catherine Williams, come from out of the blue, a woman that had lived in a hotel and cast spells over men.

I kept all of that to myself when I went home and Mama asked about her. 'She's a Yankee,' was how I put it.

'Same as Oscar,' Mama said. 'Wouldn't surprise me if that's why he married her. Likely he wanted somebody that knew him when he was a boy, somebody that knows his kin.' I was washing the supper dishes and she was drying, a little bent over, the arthritis kicked up bad in her back. Daddy and the boys were on the veranda with their feet propped up on the railing, puffing on pipes as they watched the day shift into evening, their bellies filled with oyster stew.

'Well, she's old,' I said. 'And she's nothing like Bernadette.'

'Don't talk to me about being old,' Mama said. She was gray-haired and sorrowful about it.

'Yes, ma'am.'

'And nobody's like Bernadette. But we're going to welcome Oscar's new wife tomorrow night because that's how we do.'

'She's not overly fond of waltzes, told me that herself.'

'That's something Oscar will have to sort out. She's his choice, not yours.'

I held Mama's words in my mind early the next morning as I rode in the wagon to Oscar's. I sat with Wiley on the buckboard. He drove the horses while Frank T. was in the wagon bed, likely dozing some. Overhead, the stars started to fade as they gave way to dawn. We lived on the bayou, and as the crow flies, it wasn't all that far from Oscar's. But we weren't crows. It was a mile from our place to the ridge road, the trail rough in places. There was the fence gate that marked Oscar's western boundary to open and close. After that, it was a half-mile of ridge road, us going east, a speck of light up ahead.

That came from Oscar's barn. He was at work, like always, but the house was as dark as a tomb. The boys dropped me off at the veranda steps, and when I let myself into the house, Mrs Williams' bedroom door was closed. It was coming up on four-thirty, and there wasn't even a sliver of light to be seen from around the edges of her door.

The very notion of it was a disturbance. Dairy farm people didn't laze about in bed unless they were sick or feeble, and Mrs Williams wasn't either. Leastways, I didn't think so. I lit a few kerosene lamps in the kitchen, got a fire going in the stove, and went to work cooking breakfast. About the time I put the biscuits in the oven, Andre stumbled out of his room in his nightshirt. His hair stood up in little spikes, and his eyes were puffy.

'Honey boy,' I said, pressing him to me.

'She gone?' he said.

'Hush that talk, she's your daddy's wife.'

'I don't like her.'

'Well, your daddy does and that's what counts.'

'She said I ain't allowed to say ain't.'

Acting like a schoolteacher was no way to start with a child. I held him to me, feeling the smallness of his back and liking how he put his face against my shoulder.

'She's your daddy's wife,' I said. 'Now get your britches on and go on to the outhouse. Bang on the door and holler in.'

I had biscuits in the oven. I'd cooked the grits, cracked the eggs, fried slices of ham and there still wasn't the first sign of Mrs Williams. The men came in from the barn and ate, Andre ate too. My brothers looked all woeful that she wasn't sitting there for them to gawk at while Oscar made excuses for her. 'This heat,' he said. 'It takes the starch out of a person when you first get here.'

The sun had risen bright when I heard Mrs Williams open the bedroom door. I scrambled a few eggs for her while she was in the washroom. It was the Christian thing to do even if she was lazy. Lazy was something this house had never seen before. It was after seven o'clock, and I had the breakfast dishes washed, Oscar was cleaning out stalls with Andre helping some, and Frank T. and Wiley were in the city, dropping off bottles of milk at people's doors. When Mrs Williams sat down at the table, I put some biscuits and slices of ham on a plate along with the eggs and grits.

'Thank you,' she said. Then, 'Coffee, please.'

'It's warming on the stove,' I said. 'Help yourself.'

It took her a while to understand that I didn't intend to wait on her hand and foot. She got up and poured herself a cup. Her clothes were a notch down from yesterday's. Her skirt was dark green, and her shirtwaist had only half the lace, but these were still Sunday clothes and finer than anything I'd ever hope to own. She was showing off, I thought. Then I told myself that was envy talking, an ugly quality if there ever was one.

She ate, and I scrubbed the frying pan, my back to her. I'd

done nothing but wash dishes this morning. Mrs Williams had done a poor job in the kitchen last night. I couldn't find half what I needed. She'd put the forks where the spoons belonged, and the dishes were stacked wrong on the shelf. Every pot was speckled with stuck-on dried food. Some of the plates were, too.

She said, 'The scrambled eggs are very good. As are the biscuits.'

'Thank you,' I said.

'There is, however, something that you've served which is new for me.'

I looked over my shoulder. Her fork hovered above her plate. I said, 'Grits. Those are grits.'

'I see. A Southern dish.'

I didn't know what she was talking about. Grits was food, not a dish. I said, 'You all don't eat grits up there in Ohio?'

'No. Nor, I must say, am I accustomed to so much fish.'

'What do you all mostly eat up there in Ohio? Only meat and 'tators?'

She clicked her tongue. 'Yes. Meat and potatoes.'

She talked prissy in that Yankee voice of hers, her words coming fast and like she was talking through her nose. I went back to scrubbing the frying pan. I said, 'My daddy's a fisherman, flounder, redfish, and snapper mainly. He traps crab in the bay and rakes oysters. He carries them into the city when he's of a mind to. He has his steady customers here, too, Mr Williams being one of them.'

'Your father has customers on this end of the island? I haven't seen any other houses. Where is everyone?'

I heard the insult in her questions like she thought this was the ends of the earth. People in the city most always

102

thought that. But they didn't know. Some of us liked having room to move about; we wanted to look out the windows and not see piles of buildings. I wouldn't trade our end of the island for nothing. We had plenty of neighbors. Some of them were relations: aunts, uncles, and cousins by the handful. Mrs Williams would know that if Oscar had told her about tonight's dance given in her honor. But if Oscar wanted to keep the dance a secret, that was his business. I wasn't about to tell her. I'd seen how she'd looked at me when I'd told her about rattlers in the outhouse.

I said, 'There're all kinds of folks here, cattle ranchers mainly. The Fultons have a fine house; they've got China rugs and a room filled with books from top to bottom.' Now I was the one showing off. I said, 'Course there're the nuns and orphans at St. Mary's, and a few Italians way down by the pass.'

'The pass?'

'The western end of the island.'

'And these people with the library, where is their home?'

'Near the bay. A handful of miles on down the island. But they ain't here right now. Mrs Fulton and her littlest children are in Colorado for the air.'

At that, she sank into herself, going quiet. We stayed quiet all morning. I washed her dishes and wiped down the top of the stove, then swept the kitchen floor. She just wandered about. First she went outside to the front veranda and then she came in and looked through Oscar's red book about the stars. I never could see the need for that book of his, not when the stars were right overhead, night after night, easier to look at than all that bitty print in a book. But that was Oscar for you, he liked to read. Mrs Williams must be the same way

103

because she took up shuffling through the newspapers that Oscar made Frank T. and Wiley buy when they were in the city. She told me she thought she'd look at them out on the porch.

'You mean the veranda?' I said.

She mashed that around in her mind for a short time. 'It is a beautiful word, isn't it?' she said.

Well, for Pete's sake, I thought. Who had time to sort through words and call them beautiful?

She fussed around the piano, too. She opened the keyboard cover but didn't play a thing; she just sat there with her hands in her lap. When she got tired of that, she brought out an armload of books from the bedroom and put them on the parlor table. She propped them up with bookends made of pink marble, and that made me think, Well, how do you like that? They went with the clock on the mantle except these bookends were rough and unpolished. She didn't put Oscar's book with hers; she left it on top of the newspapers.

I'd never been around a woman that had so little to do. I wanted to say, 'Here's the broom, the veranda needs sweeping.' Or, 'How about lending a hand with dinner?' Women up and down the beach, Mama one of them, were cooking for tonight's dance and here was Mrs Williams with not one worthwhile thing to do. But I held my tongue. Leastways she knew enough to make her own bed. I had looked when she'd gone off to the outhouse, expecting to find it a rumpled mess. But it wasn't. She had tucked the corners tight, pulled the quilt neat, and laid the pillows just so. Like how she held herself, I thought. Stiff-necked and cold.

A little later, I walked down the hall and came across her in Andre's room. She was holding the photograph that Andre

104

had on the table by his bed. It was a picture of Oscar and Bernadette, made on their wedding day. I had studied it myself more times than I could count. It helped me to remember Bernadette as an alive person. In the photograph, Oscar sat on a chair and Bernadette stood behind him with her hand on his shoulder. They were in their finest, him all handsome in his suit and her looking like somebody from a magazine in her white linen dress. The sisters at St. Mary's had made it for her. Last October, Oscar buried Bernadette in that dress even though Mama told him it wouldn't look right. 'I'll have to rip out the seams to get it to fit,' she told him. 'I'll have to put in a panel of material in the back. Even then it won't lay right.'

'It was her favorite,' he'd said.

'But, Oscar, to take it apart? Would she want that?'

Oscar's jaw firmed up.

'You're one bull-headed man,' she'd said. So Mama did what was needed to make the dress fit around Bernadette's swelled-up belly. At the funeral, folks remarked on it. 'Bernadette looks good laid out in her dress,' they'd said. 'So pretty.' None of that was true. She was dead, and there weren't nothing good or pretty about that.

It would hurt Andre hard if he knew Mrs Williams held the photograph of his mama, but I didn't say so. I just nodded to her from the hallway and kept on with my chores.

It was the piano that broke the quiet. I was tidying up the washroom when I heard the first note, then the second and the third. She went at it slow, like her fingers were trying to find their way on the keys. She added more notes and picked up speed as she went up and down the keyboard, the notes going from deep to high-pitched. Warming up, I thought. She was getting a feel for it like how I did with my fiddle. I tried not to listen as I cleaned the washroom floor, sweeping sand and dirt into the dustpan. Music was for evenings when chores were finished, not for mornings when things needed doing. When she stopped and everything went quiet, I thought, There. That was all she knew. I heard her come down the hall and go into Oscar's room. Something metal sprang open. The clasp on one of her black leather traveling trunks, I figured. Then she came out with some papers and walked past the washroom. Before I knew it, she was playing again but this time it had a melody. This time it was music, each note clear and deep and pretty and sorrowful.

It was like nothing I'd ever heard before. This music clutched at my heart; it made everything around me fall away. Without knowing how I got there, I found myself in the parlor but off to the side. Mrs Williams sat on the bench, there were sheets of paper spread out on the front of the piano. She played, leaning into the music, swaying a little. Each note bore down. Each note pulled at me and stirred up everything I thought I was done with – the boys I had intended to marry, the loss of Bernadette, and the wanting of Oscar.

He stood in the doorway, I hadn't heard the door open. Andre was with him, his little eyes wide with surprise. The music, carried by the breeze, must have found Oscar in the barnyard, the notes must have pulled him, too. He watched her, this new wife of his, her fingers casting a spell, the muscles tugging around his mouth.

Mrs Williams played on and on, laying bare the thing that hurt the most: Oscar picking a woman so different from me. I had my hands to my chest; my heart was near to busting wide open. Then she played the last two chords, deep and somber. The music hung in the air before it slipped away, overcome by the low crashing sound of the surf. Mrs Williams put her hands on her lap and folded them, that graceful neck of hers bowed.

'Catherine,' Oscar said after a while.

She turned around on the bench. Her face was wet.

He said, 'You used to play that. When I delivered coal.'

'I remember.'

'I'd stand outside your window and listen. When I left Ohio, I figured I'd never hear it again.' He paused. 'I never knew what it was called.'

'"Moonlight Sonata." Beethoven.'

Oscar's eyes were fixed on Mrs Williams. Like hers were fixed on him. He said, 'It's graver than I recalled.'

'Are you disappointed?'

'No.'

A small smile played around her lips and that was when I backed away and went into the washroom, latching the door behind me. Something had passed between them just now. It was like there wasn't nobody else in the world but them two. It wasn't love, this thing between them. It looked too unsettled for that. It was a wanting. Him wanting to carry her off but too awestruck to do it. Her wanting to be carried off but too stiff-necked to give way to it.

I leaned over the wash basin, a heavy feeling in my belly. Nobody had ever looked at me like Oscar had looked at Mrs Williams. Not Oakley Hill, not Joe Pete Conley. Not nobody.

The heavy feeling stayed with me for the rest of day. It made me wish I could quit all this housework and go sit in the shade

107

of the sand hills so I could watch the push and the pull of the tide. Doing that would clear my mind of what had passed between Oscar and Mrs Williams. It'd get rid of that music of hers, that mournful tune about the moonlight that kept playing over and over in my head. But a person didn't sit in the shade when there were things needed doing. Unless that person was Mrs Williams.

I cooked noon dinner and got through eating with them two and Andre, the air nearly snapping with things not said, that feeling between them jumping like sudden flashes of lightning. The thought of tonight's dance sunk me even lower. Everybody was going to fuss over Mrs Williams, and I didn't want no part of it. But if I didn't go, Mama would look at me funny, speculating. If I didn't go, neighbors would likely talk, saying it was peculiar since I worked for Oscar. So, I hung my apron on the nail by the icebox, went home, and got myself ready. Late afternoon, I climbed up on our wagon with Mama and Daddy, and we took off for the pavilion. I carried something with me, though, and not just the three baskets filled up with all of the food Mama had cooked. I had my fiddle.

Me showing up with my fiddle turned Biff McCartey and Camp Lawrence narrow-eyed with surprise. 'What's this?' Biff said, pointing at it, those wiry brows of his all scrunched together.

'Thought maybe I'd try my hand,' I said. 'Maybe play the first waltz, if you all don't much mind.'

'Ain't I been saying it all along?' he said. He had his mandolin. 'Ain't that so, Camp?'

'That's surely so,' Camp said. His face was pitted with deep scars. He most usually didn't have much to say for himself, but he played the fiddle good. Those fingers of his traveled up and down the neck like nothing I'd ever seen before.

Biff and Camp had been after me to play with them at dances ever since word got out that I was done with courting and all that went with it. Biff ran cattle on down the island and Camp was one of his hands, even though he was older than Biff. They had a habit of coming by our house now and again on a Friday evening with their wives, Alice and Nelly, along with their packs of children. Biff and Alice had the most with seven, the oldest a fourteen-year-old girl. Camp and Nelly had a married daughter but they still had four children at home. The youngest was a baby. Sometimes my aunt Mattie and uncle Lew came by. We'd all sit on our front veranda, the bayou before us.

Me and Camp fiddled, and Biff played his mandolin as he sang some of the tunes. Everyone tapped their toes while the children danced like they were all grown up. Before Bernadette took sick, her, Oscar, and Andre would drift over. We played everybody's favorites as the night sky turned a blue-black color, the moon throwing long shadows over the land. Daddy always wanted 'Clementine' and Bernadette would say, 'Nan, play "Jolie Blon." Please.'

'I'm mighty sorry you taught Nan that old Cajun song,' Biff would say to her but I played it anyway. We all liked it even if it was swamp music. We liked the shine on Bernadette's face as she sang in French, taking her back to when she lived in Louisiana.

When Biff and Camp took up pestering me about playing at dances, I shushed away the idea. 'Ain't seemly,' I said to them. 'A woman sitting before folks with a fiddle pressed to her chin.' It was my granny, Mama's mama, that told me that.

She'd taught me how to play and when she passed her fiddle on to me before she died, she'd said, 'Never play music for money. It ain't becoming.'

Hearing Mrs Williams play the piano changed that. She had brought Ohio into Oscar's house. She'd brought city ways with her fine clothes and her high-handed manners. This here was Texas. This was down the island, miles from the city. I wanted her to see where she was. Our ways were different. But mostly, for reasons I couldn't put shape to, I brought my fiddle to the dance to show Oscar's new wife that when the dishes were washed and put away, when I took off my apron, there was something else to me.

The pavilion was next to St. Mary's, it being a place for the orphans to play out of the sun. It was just on the other side of the sand hills, and the surf was loud here. I sat on a stool by myself in the cleared-off place where Biff and Camp usually played. Wagons and buggies, the horses hitched to them, were parked by the inland side of the pavilion. I fixed my brown skirt, laying it so my ankles didn't show overly much. I had on my Sunday best, my shirtwaist wasn't fancy like Mrs Williams', but it was what I had.

I settled the fiddle on my shoulder. Folks milled about, the men going off toward the hills to pass the whiskey bottle while the women calmed fussy babies and put away the food that was still on the long tables. Boys had lit the kerosene lamps on the tables, getting ready for dark. Sweat rolled down my sides even though the sun was sinking fast, the pavilion didn't have walls, and the breeze stirred the air. I had never played before so many; there must be two hundred people, maybe more, a fair number kin. The aunts and uncles were here, so were all the cousins, leastways the ones that lived in Galveston. There were the ranchers and their wives, the ranch hands, too, some of them with the women they courted, them women strangers to me for the most part. They were from the city, I thought, and that added to my nerves.

Everybody was in their Sunday clothes. The women were corseted with brooches fastened to their collars. A fair number of the men had shaved their chins clean and trimmed their mustaches. Daddy had nearly outdone himself. He'd slicked back his wavy gray hair, wore a collar, and had polished his boots to a high shine. Mama looked pretty; she'd pinned up her hair with her tortoiseshell combs. Even the children looked Sunday good, the boys with their shirts tucked in and the little girls wearing ribbons. The ten St. Mary's nuns were here – they admired Oscar, he was always doing for them – and so were the orphans, all ninety-three of them. Those children were easy to pick out. They were dressed alike wearing white on the top and black on the bottom, the girls in skirts and the boys in short pants, their black stockings held up by garters.

So many people, I thought. They'd come for Oscar and Mrs Williams, they'd come for the dancing. I pulled the bow, hardly touching the strings, trying to get the rust out of my fingers without making a sound.

The crowd in the pavilion got tighter around me. Any other time these folks were family and neighbors but tonight, with them all looking at me, I didn't know nobody. They were just swirls of eyes. Maybe that was why Mrs Williams was frozed up good when she and Oscar first got to the pavilion, Andre dragging behind them with his bottom lip poked out. Their arrival had caused a stir; most everybody was curious about this woman from Ohio. They looked her over as Oscar made

111

the 'howdy do's, the men tripping over themselves and the women smiling at her but not knowing what to say.

Mama, wanting to do right by Oscar, kept to Mrs Williams' side and filled in the gaps. She told her that Bumps Ogden was Daddy's brother, and that Mattie Anderson was her sister. She told her who baked the best cakes and who was known for her quilting abilities. I figured Mama was wasting her time thinking any of that mattered to Mrs Williams. She had a reared-back look on her face, her smile fixed like somebody had stepped on her foot and she was trying to act like it hadn't hurt. The women mostly stood off a ways, taking note of the rows of lace on Mrs Williams' shirtwaist and how it showed off the shape of her bosom. The women looked at the tips of her shoes, too. Them shoes were a soft kid, the color of butter, a color that would dirty real quick around here. I could have told the women something about them shoes that they couldn't see. The buttons that ran from the anklebone to the top were also covered in kid.

Oscar saw to Mrs Williams, everybody noticed that, too. He squired her around the pavilion before taking her to one of the long planked tables propped up on sawhorses. He set her down with Mama, Kate Irvin, Aunt Mattie, and Daisy Calloum, then went off to the sand hills likely for a drop or two of whiskey before sitting down at the men's table. When he left her, Mrs Williams drew into herself like she'd just been tossed into a barrel of winter rainwater.

She didn't pay a bit of attention to Andre. It was me that made sure he was settled with the orphans at one of the children's tables, him being friends with them. It was me that made sure he had food on his plate and not just slices of pie or cake. And when everybody was done eating, I made sure Andre's mouth was wiped clean.

Now, holding my fiddle and sitting on the stool, I got my handkerchief out from the sleeve of my shirtwaist and wiped the chin pad. I was sweating bad. Frank T., that foolish brother of mine, hollered out, 'Oscar? Where's Oscar and that pretty little bride of his?' The crowd gave way and there Oscar was, bringing Mrs Williams to the cleared dance floor close to where I sat. Her eyes went wide when she saw me, my fiddle likely coming as a surprise. Andre clung to his daddy, a fistful of Oscar's pants in his hand. He looked like he was fixing to cry but there wasn't nothing I could do about that because now folks were clapping. Oscar grinned, and Mrs Williams' cheeks were pink, making her even prettier. Mama reached out, caught Andre by the arm and brought him back with her into the crowd. He buried his face into her skirt, and more than anything I wanted to put my fiddle down and hold him tight.

I touched the bow to the strings but my hand was unsteady and the strings screeched. Somebody laughed, it sounded like my cousin James Robert. Mrs Williams was in the middle of the empty dance floor with Oscar, and now the pink in her cheeks was gone, and she was ghost white. She gave me a begging look, and I guessed what she was thinking because I was thinking it too. All these people. Hurry up and play. Fill up this quiet.

I did the oddest thing then, I could hardly account for it. I nodded at Mrs Williams. It was the kind of thing I did when I played with Biff and Camp, us all nodding at the others, our way of saying, Yep, I'm ready to start. I don't know why I did it, Mrs Williams wasn't playing, but something made me do it, and I was glad I did. Her shoulders eased just a tad and the corners of her mouth lifted. She returned my nod, a slow bob of her chin. Without knowing why, a touch of calm took ahold of me.

I drew the bow again and this time I did it right. This time it was the first notes of 'Sweet Evelina.' Oscar, his smile gone now, bowed to Mrs Williams. She put one hand up on the broad crest of his shoulder and he took the other, swallowing it up inside of his. They stood straight as could be, her looking up at him, and him looking at her. I played on but them two were stuck, that spark shooting between them. Around them, people gave each other high-eyebrow looks. Mrs Williams whispered something and all at once, her and Oscar lurched into the waltz, their steps small. They stumbled but they kept with it, and I saw that Oscar was counting. One, two, three; one, two, three. His steps smoothed out. He gathered her up like he was sure of himself, his steps longer, almost gliding as they circled the floor.

Biff sang the refrain, shoring me up.

'Sweet Evelina, dear Evelina,
My love for thee will never, never die.'

Oscar and Mrs Williams waltzed, his grin back and her close to smiling.

'In the most graceful curls hangs her raven-black hair,
And she never requires 'fumery there.'

There were other folks on the floor now, and my playing evened out. So did my nerves. The waltz ended but I played on with Biff and Camp, our fiddles and mandolin going from one tune to the next. The candlelight from the lanterns that hung from nails on the support pillars made every woman pretty. The hollows and lines that came from hard work had eased into shadows. Folks stomped their feet to 'Cotton-Eyed Joe,' and they whooped when we shifted to 'Bonnie Blue Flag.' Mrs Williams' lips tightened at that one, it being a Rebel tune, I figured, and her being a Yankee. Oscar wouldn't let her sit it out, though. Him and her danced, sometimes together, other times her with the neighbor men.

Frank T. was one of those she danced with, him grinning like it didn't matter a whit what Maggie Mandora thought, even though he was promised to her. Like a rooster, that brother of mine two-stepped Mrs Williams around the floor, not caring that she held herself back and away. He didn't even see how she kept Oscar in her sights as Oscar danced with some of the women, including Mama. Oscar even got Sister Camillus to polka with him, her face nothing but a circle of pink surrounded by that starched white headdress of hers.

I didn't know how those nuns stood them things bearing down on their foreheads and coming up to their chins. It was hot at the pavilion, all those people and all that dancing. But nobody seemed to mind. The old people sat at the tables, tapping toes. On the dance floor, the courting couples held fast to each other, and the ones that had been married a long time danced and smiled like they were newlyweds. The children danced, too, the girls snagging a few of the boys. Andre was in the middle of all that dancing, grinning wide like he had forgotten about his daddy's new wife, him chasing a few of the orphan boys, them chasing him back, all of them slipping and sometimes spilling off of the pavilion floor and out onto the sand.

115

Me and Biff and Camp went from the polka to 'Arkansas Traveler'. That set Sister Finbar and Sister Evangelist jigging like they weren't weighed down in black dresses and them belts of beads with silver crosses hanging at the ends.

'It was raining hard but the fiddler didn't care.
He sawed away at the popular air,
Tho' his rooftree leaked like a waterfall
That didn't seem to bother the man at all.'

It was a refreshing sight, the nuns dancing as everybody clapped time for them, somebody letting out a whoop now and again, all worries set to the side. Biff pushed the jig faster, and I stayed with him, sweat running down my face. The nuns kept up too, their circled faces red, those silver crosses flashing and their black shoes nothing but blurs of toe-to-heel jigging.

Oscar and Mrs Williams were part of the crowd watching the nuns. She didn't clap like everybody else; that wasn't something she seemed to know how to do. Instead, she tapped her fingers against her dark blue skirt keeping time like she couldn't help herself. The music had caught hold of her. And Oscar, he didn't hold back. He clapped and the size of his grin was something I hadn't seen since before Bernadette took sick. Just that quick, my bow stopped and my fingers on the neck of the fiddle went still. Oscar had forgotten all about her, I thought. Everybody here had forgotten Bernadette.

Camp shot me a questioning look and I caught up with him and Biff, finishing up the jig, the two nuns breathing hard and near to collapse. We played 'Buffalo Gals' and then it was time for 'Sweet Evelina', the waltz that had started the dance. This time it said something different. It told everybody that if they hadn't danced with their sweethearts, they best do it now: the night was wearing down.

'Altho' I am fated to marry her never,
I'm sure it will last for ever and ever.'

Over at the long tables, children laid stretched out on benches, their eyes slits as they tried to keep them open. Near them, babies slept in baskets on the floor. The married folks danced, the women letting their husbands press them close. Frank T. danced with Maggie, him trying to pull her to him but her putting up a little fight. Likely she was thinking about how he'd made a fool of himself with Mrs Williams. Wiley paired off with April Burnett, a woman he admired, not that he could come out and say it, him being shy due to those kicked-out teeth of his. Daddy, a little tipsy from drink, waltzed Mama around the floor.

It was Oscar and Mrs Williams that stood out. He took her in slow sweeps, a noticeable amount of air between them but both so fixed on the other that I had to turn my head. This ache high up in my chest had nothing to do with Oscar, I told myself, my bow moving slow across the strings. It was because of the boys I had been promised to, Oakley Hill and Joe Pete Conley. They had been cut short, and that had cut me short too, and I missed them both but Oakley most of all.

The last note drifted away, swallowed up by the whispering surf. A kind of clumsiness came over the dancers as they broke apart, the swell of the music still in their blood but the planked floor flat under their feet. In hushed whispers, the women packed up the empty platters and the cake dishes and put them in baskets. The men went off to the sand hills likely to kick sand over the whiskey bottles, not wanting wives and mothers to know how much they'd drunk. The nuns made the orphans stand in lines of ten so they could count heads, and when they left, it made a sizable hole in the crowd. I wrapped my fiddle in the old pillowcase that I used for such. 'You did just fine,' Biff told me. Camp said, 'Surely did.' I was still pinking up from that when Oscar came by, a lit cigarette going, and me pulling in that good smell. He took my hand and said, 'You outshined the boys by a mile.'

It turned me airy, those fingers of his closing over mine. It was just me and Oscar Williams, our hands together. Them green eyes of his, I thought. They carried me to a place I didn't ever want to leave.

He let go of my hand. There was a coin in my palm. I stared at that coin, warm from his hand but cold and hard all the same. It made me want to say, 'It ain't money I'm needing. It ain't,' but he had moved on, shaking Biff's and Camp's hands just like he'd done mine, likely palming coins. Wages, that was what this was.

Across the pavilion, Mama looked at me. I righted myself, and that was when I saw Mrs Williams. She was by one of the tables where Andre laid on a bench, flat on his belly, an arm dangling over the side. She eyed me, her head tilted like she had just got wind of a secret and was puzzled by it, trying to make the jagged pieces fit. She looked over at Oscar. He was saying something to Camp. She turned back to me and when she did, her face was shadowed up with green.

I didn't need sunlight to see that or to sort out what was behind it. I could guess what she was thinking. Mrs Williams believed something laid between me and her husband.

It weren't so. I held her gaze and willed her to hear what I was thinking: I ain't that kind of woman, don't you go that way. And Oscar ain't that kind of man. You should know that about him; you shouldn't need me to tell you.

Her shoulders slumped. A tiredness came over her. It wasn't me she was looking at, not now. Mrs Williams was fixed on my wrapped-up fiddle, pressed to my bosom. Yesterday she told me that she performed at concerts. Saying that had made her puff up with pride. But tonight, she wasn't the one that had played in front of folks. It was me.

Oscar went over to her, the cigarette smoke trailing behind him. I put his coin in my skirt pocket. Other folks came up to me saying, 'You did good,' and, 'You added something pretty,' and, 'You did the family proud.' Frank T. left with Maggie, aiming to see her home, I figured. Wiley was gone too, and so was April Burnett. Across the way, Mama and Daddy waited. Daddy inclined his head at me, his way of saying, Hurry up, girl, don't have all night. At the table, Oscar stooped and pried Andre from the bench. He gathered that child up like he was a bag of shifting oats, hoisting him to his shoulder. Andre's arms went around his daddy's neck. Oscar said something and Mrs Williams got the lantern that was on the table.

Past the pavilion, lanterns were moving specks of light that poked holes in the darkness. Wagons and buggies creaked as people got into them, the horses blowing and shaking their heads, their harnesses clinking. Near the edge of the pavilion and in the shadows, Oscar and Mrs Williams were nothing but dark shapes, air between them. Just before they stepped down from the planked floor and onto the sand, Oscar put his arm

119

out like he was helping her down. For a moment, their shapes blended. Then they pulled apart, air between them again.

If he were mine, I'd lean right into him, nothing would stop me. Nothing had held Bernadette back. Her hands went to Oscar every chance she got, touching his arms, his shoulders, and his hands. She called him *mon cher*, and she didn't care who heard her say it. This new Mrs Williams was different. She was cold and stiff-necked but it didn't seem to much matter to Oscar. The way he looked at her, it was like the sun rose and set on her.

She could play the piano to make a person want to fall right down and cry. But tonight, I'd been the one sitting on the stool playing music with Biff and Camp. We were the ones that raised folks to their feet and got them to dance. We were the ones that set hands clapping. Tonight, I'd stepped right up to the curse that I laid over the men that cared for me and decided I could still find my pleasures. I didn't sit with the old people; I didn't spend the evening fussing over the food. Tonight, with everybody watching, I put my bow to the fiddle strings and showed another side of me.

CHAPTER EIGHT

The Sea Daisies

It was mighty hot the next morning, me taking the path that went alongside of the bayou, dew and cockleburs catching hold of my hem. The air didn't move, not one little bit, and purely hissed with steam. It was plenty dark too, my lantern throwing just a patch of light, the thread of pink dawn at the horizon along the gulf not doing much good.

The bayou's low tide was a soft whish as it lapped into the marshy salt grass. A few toads croaked, and from time to time, something plopped into the water. Mud turtles, I figured, them sliding off of pieces of driftwood.

I wasn't given to walking, not if there was a wagon or a horse to ride. But this was Sunday, and Oscar gave Frank T. and Wiley the day off. That meant I had to walk to Oscar's. It meant I had to carry the basket that was heavy with eggs and food from our garden, onions and okra and suchlike. Everything was different on Sundays. Mama and Wiley took the wagon to the Baptist church on the west side of town while Frank T. went in his buggy so as to court Maggie Mandora. But Daddy didn't go. He couldn't sit still, not even to hear a preacher preach.

Last week when Oscar got around to telling me he was fixing to get married, I was so taken aback that I couldn't think straight. 'Leastways you can take up coming to church with me,' Mama had said when I'd told her. But that was before Mrs Williams showed up, before I found out Oscar had married a woman that didn't know one thing about a kitchen. I could let him starve on Sundays; he was a grown man and knew what he was getting with her. And Mrs Williams didn't eat but a speck; she'd get by fine. But I couldn't let Andre go hungry. Neither could I let the three orphan boys that worked for Oscar on Sundays go without. I couldn't live with myself, sitting in church knowing little bellies rumbled at the Williams' house.

I high-stepped over the rusty train tracks that went to the boarded-up lace factory on down the island, and I opened and closed the gate to Oscar's back pasture. I held the lantern high so I could step around cow patties. Up ahead by a mile, a light came on at Oscar's barn. Things ran an hour late on Sundays, him going to Mass. That was what he called church. Mass. It didn't make sense to me, but I wasn't a Catholic and glad of it. I couldn't sleep with a crucifix over my bed but it didn't seem to bother Mrs Williams. The house was dark. She wasn't no dairy farmer's wife, that was one thing I knew for sure.

Skeeters whined in my ears. My hands were full and I couldn't wave them off, but nothing was going to spoil the lightness in my feet, not this morning. I might be carrying a lantern and a basket of food, but I could still feel my bow riding the strings of my fiddle.

'It was raining hard but the fiddler didn't care.
He sawed away at the popular air.'

I could feel the strings under my fingertips; I could feel the music inside of me. This was what I wanted to think about, not how Oscar and Mrs Williams looked when they danced, their want for the other showing. Neither was I going to think about her mournful piano tune about the moonlight. That woman was nothing but an aggravation. She stirred things up; she woke up hurts. Or put them there. But I wasn't going to let her do that. Not today.

I let myself into Oscar's house, and there, I put my mind to my work and rolled out biscuits, boiled the grits, and fried the bacon while Mrs Williams laid in bed. Andre was asleep, too. The dance had worn him out. When the coffee was perking strong, I woke him up. 'Honey boy,' I said, my hands cupped around both sides of his little head there on his pillow. 'Breakfast is nearly on the table.'

He nodded, his eyes all puffy and his hair standing high in every direction.

'The orphans'll be here,' I said.

That got him to his feet, and it wasn't long after that when a light showed up around the edges of Mrs Williams' bedroom door. She didn't move quick in the morning, no one could say that about her. When she finally came looking for breakfast wearing her white shirtwaist and green skirt, there was a lively crowd at the table. Oscar, collarless but his shirt buttoned up all proper-like, was on one bench with Andre. Me and the three orphan boys were crowded up on the other.

'Oh my,' she said, taking us all in.

Real quick, Oscar pulled out the napkin he'd tucked in at his neck. He got to his feet and said, 'Catherine, these are my Sunday employees. James, Bill, and Joe. Likely you saw them

123

at the dance. They were the ones surrounded by all the pretty girls.'

That turned the orphans red.

'Boys,' he said. 'This is Mrs Williams.' He might have been talking to the orphans but his gaze was fixed on her. It made her heartbeat show in her neck. It made her fumble as she sat down beside Oscar, an empty plate waiting there for her.

'How do you do?' she finally said to the orphans.

The orphans mumbled their 'ma'am's. Even though they were alongside of me, I felt their glances skipping from her to Andre and then landing back on her. Her spell, I thought. She'd cast it over these three boys as young as they were, the oldest being thirteen, them gawking at her blue eyes and dainty lips. But this was different than it was with grown men. The way those orphan boys looked at Andre made me think they wished they were him. They'd give anything to shuck off their charity-box shirts and patched-over pants that marked them as orphans. They'd give anything for a mama, even one that didn't know the first thing about taking care of children.

Oscar said to Mrs Williams, 'The boys are letting Frank T. and Wiley have the day off.' He passed what was left of the scrambled eggs to her. I saw her look at her empty cup and then at the coffee pot over on the stove. There wasn't any tea; Oscar had forgotten to tell my brothers to get some. She must have figured that out because she got up and poured herself some coffee, saying, 'Would anyone else care for some?' We all said no, this being our second pot. When she sat down, Oscar said, 'The boys here rode back with me after Mass.'

'Mass?' she said. 'You've been to church and back? It's not quite seven o'clock.'

'Went to five-thirty Mass.'

'Good heavens. So early. I heard you get up but . . .' She stopped herself like she had just said something shameful. Maybe she had. Something crossed over Oscar's face, the kind of look a person gets when he tries to make sense of things that don't make sense. The color, what there was, dropped right out of Mrs Williams' cheeks. Right quick, she busied herself with a swallow of coffee. Then it hit me. For all their wanting of the other, things weren't right in their bedroom.

Oscar stepped around it. 'That's dairy farming for you,' he said. 'We're up with the cows. Those gals of mine weren't listening when God declared Sunday a day of rest.'

Mrs Williams patted her mouth with her napkin like she'd been eating and had made a mess somehow. I told myself to stop thinking about their bedroom. It wasn't none of my business. She put her napkin on her lap, spread it out, then fixed her attention on the orphans and said, 'And where do you boys live?'

'St. Mary's, ma'am,' Bill said.

'We're orphans,' James said. 'We don't have any folks.'

'Oh dear,' she said. 'Oh dear.'

'That's all right, ma'am,' Bill said. 'We know what we are.'

She nearly buckled at that. 'I'm so very sorry. I didn't know.'

A person would have thought she'd made the orphans lay a secret out on the table for everybody to look at. That wasn't so. We knew their stories. James was a foundling. Thirteen years ago, he'd been left on the doorstep at St. Mary's. It was January and cold. He was wrapped in a tattered blanket with a note pinned to it. *Please. He is better off with you than me.* The nuns at St. Mary's didn't take newborns, those went to the orphanage in the city. But they wanted this baby boy that had a tuft of red hair. They said it was God's will. God had whispered into the mama's ear and led her to St. Mary's. Folks up and down the island thought different. Most figured the daddy was somebody nearby, a ranch hand maybe, the mama leaving the baby here as a reminder to that man. But that didn't much matter to the nuns. They held on to that child. They gave him a name, a birthday, and a home, proving his mama right about him being better off with them.

Things weren't so foggy with Bill and Joe. They were brothers, a few years apart. Bill, the older one, was twelve. They were brown-haired, and when Joe smiled, dimples showed up. Bill and Joe's last name was Murney. Five years ago, their mama died from consumption. The very next day, her barely cold, their daddy's heart seized up and killed him. The boys' older sisters brought them to St. Mary's, the girls crying and telling the nuns they couldn't raise Bill and Joe, not on their own. The girls had to hire out as household help; their folks had left them close to penniless.

'Hard workers,' Oscar said. 'That's what I say about these good men from St. Mary's. Couldn't run the dairy without them, not on Sundays I couldn't.'

'My, yes,' Mrs Williams said, her words coming in big puffs. 'I can well imagine.' She said that like she knew something about dairy farming. Then I was thinking that this was how it was going to be between her and Oscar. She'd say or do something to embarrass herself, and he'd come in behind her making things right.

She picked up her fork and that made the orphans gawk for the second time in a handful of minutes. This time, though, they were shooting each other sideways looks, the kind that said they could hardly believe their eyes. Mrs Williams was fixing to eat and she hadn't prayed. That was what I figured

126

they were thinking. Them St. Mary's boys couldn't pop nothing into their mouths without praying about it first. But here she was, taking bitty bites of egg. Joe was so surprised that his jaw hung open. Andre's new mama was a heathen. I saw that thought dash across his face.

Oscar got himself another biscuit out of the bread basket. That made James do the same, so did Bill and Joe, their skinny wrists showing as they reached into the basket, the cuffs of their sleeves frayed some. Oscar poured honey from the jar over his biscuit, so did the orphans. Honey was a Sunday treat. Andre ran the flat side of his fork through a puddle of it on his plate, then licked it. Mrs Williams shook her head a little and frowned at him. His face clouded up. Her frown deepened. He put his fork down.

'We'll be done in the barn in an hour or so,' Oscar said to Mrs Williams. 'We'll get the milk on over to St. Mary's, leaving just enough time to get you to church services in the city.'

'Oscar,' she said. 'I'd like that very much.'

'But, Daddy,' Andre said. 'What about seeing Mama?'

A bolt of lightning, that was what them words were. Mrs Williams went straight as a ruler. So did Oscar, the orphans, too. Going to the cemetery was what Oscar and Andre did every Sunday. But Oscar had forgotten, and now the shock of forgetting gave way to something else. Misery. His green eyes were dark with it. He'd hurt Andre.

'Son,' Oscar said. His voice was low. 'Not today.'

'But, Daddy? We always—'

'Son.'

'I want to see Mama.'

'I know.' His voice had gone lower. 'But not today.'

'I want to see Mama.'

Oscar's jaw firmed up. 'Andre. No. No more of this.'

Andre started to open his mouth.

'Young man.'

The two of them glared at each other, Andre from under his scrunched-up eyebrows.

'Oscar?' Mrs Williams said. 'What—'

'Not now,' he said. 'Not here.'

She clamped her mouth shut; her glance darted from Oscar to Andre. Their faces were storm clouds. Oscar bolted down the last of his coffee and got up, the bench scraping loud on the floor and jostling Andre and Mrs Williams.

'Men,' Oscar said to the orphans. There was gravel in his voice. 'Time's wasting,' and that set the orphans moving. The three boys scuffled, getting themselves untangled from the bench, hurrying to catch up with him.

'Ladies,' he said when he got to the door. He shot Andre one last look, one filled with warning, and then Oscar was out the door, the orphans nearly riding his heels, pushing and shoving each other, them always having a contest about who got to the barn first. All the ruckus set the dogs to barking. They'd been asleep under the house but they were stirred up good, the pounding of feet on the veranda doing that to them.

At the table, Andre slumped. His face puckered, tears ready to spout.

He'd shamed Oscar, it was plain as day. And he had done it before the crowd at the table. Andre wanted his mama even if Oscar thought the sun rose and set on Catherine Williams, her sitting where Bernadette used to with her hand on her cheek like she'd just been slapped. Oscar might have forgotten Bernadette, but Andre hadn't.

'Ah, honey boy,' I said.

'I just want to see Mama,' he said. 'That's all.' Tears were building, pooling in his eyes.

Or maybe, I thought, Oscar hadn't forgotten. Maybe he figured Andre would forget, what with the excitement of last night's dance. Keep still and Andre might not notice. After all, a visit to the first wife's grave might not sit too well with the second wife.

Tears dripped down Andre's face. 'Come here,' I said to him but he didn't move. His head down, his shoulders shuddered, him fighting the tears but the tears winning. He put his hands to his eyes, mashing them like he could hold back the flood but it was too late for that. A sob bubbled up and then he buckled, crying.

Mrs Williams sat right there beside him, but it was me that went to him. It was me that got down on my knees so I could turn him around. Still sitting on the bench, he wrapped his arms around my neck and pressed his face to my shoulder. 'Honey boy,' I said, letting him cry, even if he was five years old. I rocked him back and forth. 'Andre. Honey boy,' and there sat Mrs Williams, stiff as a board, not doing nothing, not saying a word.

'Daddy's put out with me,' he blubbered.

I rubbed his back, feeling the sobs and those bony ribs of his. I counted to thirty and took my time about it. A child allowed to cry any longer was a spoiled child, that was what Mama always said. When I got to thirty, I added another five. I walked two fingers up the back of Andre's neck, tickling him. His back twitched. He rolled his face from side to side against my collarbone.

'Now,' I said. 'Be a man.'

He nodded into my shoulder. I put my hand on the back

of his head and allowed him to stay close. I said, 'Your daddy's got a lot on his mind.' I let that settle on Mrs Williams. When I figured it had, I said, 'And he's wanting to get the milk to St. Mary's before the day gets any hotter. But there's something else that daddy of yours is turning over in his mind. He's wondering where you are, his top hand.'

Andre sniffled and mumbled something I couldn't make out. But maybe I wasn't trying all that hard since my mind was on Mrs Williams. She had gotten up and was heading down the hall without one look back. Well, I thought. If that didn't say it all. She didn't care one little bit about this child. It'd break Bernadette's heart to see her boy in the hands of this woman.

I gave Andre a quick hug and let go, rocking back on my heels. His face was swelled up and his little eyes were red. 'What's the first rule for top hands?' I said.

He shook his head. 'I just wanted to do like always. Why can't we?'

'No whining, I won't have it. Now then. What's the first rule for top hands?'

He looked down at his knees and pushed at a worn spot in his pants with his fingers. He said, 'Don't let the boss down.'

'That's right. Them are words your daddy lives by, through and through. So you go splash a little water on your face and then you can go help the boss. But wait, hold up. That nose of yours is running bad.' I fumbled for the handkerchief I carried in the sleeve of my dress, but before I could get it, I heard Mrs Williams say, 'Andre. Here.'

She held out a handkerchief. It had more lace to it than solid cloth with a fancy C embroidered in blue. Andre looked at it and then up at her, thick streams running from his nose to his upper lip. Her own lips were mashed together and I thought she was going to turn tail again, but she didn't. She sat down on the other side of Andre. Before I knew it, Mrs Williams, her hands a little unsteady, dabbed at his cheeks and then took up wiping his nose with that pretty handkerchief. Her ministering took Andre so by surprise that he let her.

She held the handkerchief to his nose. 'Blow,' she said. He did, dirtying that pretty cloth, the kind not meant for nose blowing. When he was done, she folded it into squares like it had just come out fresh from the wash. She left it in the middle of her lap.

'Better?' she said.

He pulled his shoulders up to his ears and then dropped them. He wouldn't look at her. Maybe he was ashamed she'd seen him cry. Or maybe he was blaming her for changing everything. Could be he wasn't ready to stop thinking about wanting to go to the cemetery. He had a stubborn streak as wide as his daddy's.

'Good,' Mrs Williams said. 'I'm glad because I have something very important that I must ask. Are you ready?'

He didn't say anything, but that didn't bother her. 'Have you ever been to a place that is new for you?' she said. 'A place where you've never been?'

He still wouldn't look at her, his chin was riding on his chest. She tried again. 'Have you, Andre?' She was a coaxer, her words were rolled in sugar. 'Houston, perhaps? Have you been there?'

He poked out his bottom lip, but he slipped her a sideways glance.

'Well,' she said. 'You can't imagine such a thing, not today, not when you're so young. But someday you'll travel. You'll board a train and go to a new place.'

He pursed his lips, considering, his eyebrows pulled together. Mrs Williams waited. After a while, Andre said, 'I will?'

'I have no doubt of it.'

Andre squinted his eyes like he was trying to see that train, him riding on it and crossing over the bay.

Mrs Williams said, 'You might visit this new place for a day or for a week. Or you might move there, taking everything you own.' She stopped. Her mouth had gone all trembly-like. I didn't know what I'd do if she took up crying. She didn't, though. She got herself some air and started up again. 'That was what your father did when he was a young man. He boarded a train and left his home in Dayton. And now, that is what I've done.'

'Daddy rode a train?'

'He did. He left Ohio and came all the way to Texas. Just as I have.'

Andre eyed her, his nose scrunched up, those freckles of his changing shape. She said, 'This house and how you and your father do things are new for me. But it won't always be this way. I'll learn. But until that happens, I'll need your patience. And your help.'

And there it was: me feeling sorry for her. I didn't want to, but sorryness washed right over me. I couldn't do like she had. I couldn't go live someplace new, not even for a man. Galveston was my home. But if I had to leave, and I couldn't think why I would, I'd likely freeze up in a new place, over-come by the strangeness of not knowing where I was. Maybe being here froze up Mrs Williams, and it was no wonder. She

132

and Oscar had courted only through letters. I'd seen the ones she wrote to him; he kept them in the roll-top desk. The envelopes were fancy, the color of cream, and the penmanship had so many curves and curls that I could only make out a few words in the address, Galveston and Texas being two of them. I'd seen the letters Oscar tried to write to her, too, the ones with mistakes on them, I figured. More than once I'd found bits of paper with black-curled edges inside of the oven.

But letters were nothing more than flat words scratched on paper. Mrs Williams might know that on Sundays Oscar carried all his milk to St. Mary's. But I was willing to bet my last dollar that she didn't know he gave it to the nuns, him not taking a penny, them having only one milk cow for all those children. Likely she didn't know either that I packed a picnic lunch on Sundays for Oscar and Andre, and how they went into the city carrying that picnic along with yellow sea daisies kept fresh in a bucket of water. They laid those flowers on Bernadette's grave. They did it so Andre would know his mama hadn't just disappeared and flown off to heaven to be with the angels. His mama had a place that marked her; her particulars were carved on a tombstone made of gray granite. 'Miss Nan,' Andre had said more than once, 'I touched Mama's name. And mine and Daddy's.' I'd done the same when I'd gone by myself a few times. I knew my letters good enough to guess some of the words on the stone. *Bernadette M. Williams. B. April 5, 1874. D. October 1, 1899.*

After laying the flowers on the grave, Oscar and Andre most always went to the sand hills for their picnic unless it was winter and too cold. And there were other things Mrs Williams wouldn't know, her not being from here. In the city, Hendley's on the Strand carried the freshest coffee beans on the island,

and over on Mechanic Street, Mistrot's had a fine selection of fabrics ranging from cotton to silk. Here, down the island, my aunt Mattie made the worst potato salad but folks ate it anyway when she brought it to gatherings. And old Chancy Nelson had a foot missing because he'd been shot at Chickamauga, but he'd kept on fighting anyway, doing General Bragg proud. I was born on the island, I knew these things. But Mrs Williams just got here; she couldn't know.

'Might I count on your patience?' she said to Andre. He didn't say nothing; he just studied her like he was pressing her features to his memory. 'Andre? Might I?'

'Yes, ma'am.'

'Thank you.' She gathered up some air and said, 'There's one more thing, something important, something I want you to remember.' She looked right into his eyes. She said, 'I won't take your father from you. I didn't come here to do that.'

That nearly knocked the wind right out of me. But not her. She smiled at Andre. It was a new smile, one I hadn't seen from her before. It made everything that was tight and high and mighty about her just slide on away. It turned her soft, making her prettier if such a thing could be. Right then and there, I saw another reason why Oscar married her. He'd likely done it just for the chance to step into the warmth of that smile.

Her fingers tapped over the back of Andre's hand. I took that to be her idea of affection but whatever it was, he was wide-eyed with wonderment, him likely feeling this new-found warmth of hers. He looked right up at her, his head back a little. It was like he'd forgotten about going to the cemetery, like he'd forgotten all about his mama. And maybe he had. Maybe he only knew Bernadette's picture, the one made on her wedding day. That, and the carved letters on her tombstone.

Mrs Williams said to Andre, 'Your father is expecting you. I don't imagine that you want to disappoint him, do you?'

'No, ma'am.'

'Good.' She nodded, and so did Andre, his head bobbing up and down like she held a string with him tied to the other end of it.

He got up, the leather in his boots squeaking just a tad. They were eye level to one another, him with his hands behind his back. She set that smile of hers on him again. His eyes lit up, then a sly look came over him. He hunched down a little. His hand darted out and he touched Mrs Williams, right on her wrist. Then quick as can be, like he knew he'd done something brave, Andre ran to the front door, grinning big as he flung it open. Without a look back, he shot outside, his footsteps clattering across the veranda and thumping down the steps.

Well, I thought. Well.

I got up off of my knees. One pretty smile from Mrs Williams, that was all it took. Not that I was his mother, I knew that. But Andre touching her, it punched a hole in my chest. It made me a little put out with him, too. He had forgotten it was me that rocked him when he cried.

'A sweet boy,' Mrs Williams said.

'Mostly,' I said. Now I was put out with myself. I had felt sorry for her and there was no need for such. This woman got everything she wanted.

I started clearing the table, not caring that she hadn't eaten more than a few bites. This woman had Oscar and now she was roping in Andre. She had pretty clothes, and she could play the piano like nobody else. She had this house, and she had me cooking and cleaning for her. Men gawked at her. Frank T. was the worst of all, dancing with her while Maggie Mandora watched, fighting back tears. Not that Mrs Williams had noticed; she hadn't even bothered to say the first thing about me playing the fiddle. Not her. She was too busy being the belle of the ball.

I plunked the dirty dishes down harder on the counter than what was called for. I said, 'Folks sure did give you a mighty big welcome last night.'

'They did indeed. They were very kind. But of course you were the one whom everyone admired. You played beautifully.'

'Oh,' I said.

'But yes, the community did turn out. People were curious, I suppose. Oscar Williams' new wife. They must have wondered what I was like.'

I hunched over one of the dishes, working at a spot of dried-up food with my thumbnail. She said, 'I recognize that I might be seen as an oddity.'

She didn't know the half of it. She'd showed up from nowhere, nobody knowing one thing about her, the wedding happening in a flash. I put the dish on the counter. I said, 'It's 'cause you come from up North.'

'Is that it?'

'Like you said. You're new to these parts.'

'Yes. I'm the stranger.'

I worked the pump, filling the wash basin, glad for once that Oscar hadn't gotten around to oiling away its wheezy squeak. I wished she'd get up and leave me be. Calling herself a stranger was her way of getting me to feel sorry for her again.

The wash basin filled now, I got a bar of soap and lathered

up, ready to put breakfast behind me. I picked up a plate. It had a dab of butter on it and leftover grits. She had me so rattled that I'd forgotten to scrape the dishes.

'Miss Ogden,' she said. 'Would you sit down for a moment?'

I turned and looked at her.

'Please.'

I had dishes to wash and floors to sweep. It was Sunday, my half-day off, the day I had to pack all of my chores into the morning.

She said, 'I know you're busy. I won't take much of your time.'

Mama would tell me to sit down with this woman. Mrs Williams was in need of a spot of company, she'd say. 'Well, all right,' I said, but I was talking to Mama, not Mrs Williams. I shook out my hands, and dried them on my apron. I pulled out the bench across from her, sat down, and folded my arms on the table.

'Tell me how she died,' she said. 'Please.'

That came as a surprise; I hardly knew what to make of it.

'Andre's mother,' Mrs Williams said. 'Had she been ill? Or perhaps there had been an accident.'

'That's not mine to tell. That's for Mr Williams.'

'Yes. I understand. But you see, I find myself in rather an awkward position. It's as if I've arrived in the middle of a play and must try to make sense of it all. I could ask Oscar – Mr Williams – but that might open wounds.'

She said that like wounds could heal. Wounds stayed wounds. A person just got so they knew that; they just got to where they put one foot in front of the other. But I figured Mrs Williams didn't know much about sorrow.

Across from me, she pinned me with them blue eyes of

137

hers. She might not know anything about sorrow, but she did know a little something about coming into another woman's house. It'd haunt me, if I had to do such, thinking about somebody I couldn't give shape to. I'd want to know. But if somebody was to ask me about Oakley Hill's drowning, about the waiting for him to be found, and then how he looked, I wouldn't want to say it. I wouldn't want to say it about Joe Pete Conley either, how he'd suffered with lockjaw, getting all stiff, and then that burning fever and him likely knowing what was bound to come. I couldn't put words to none of that, somebody else would have to do it for me.

I said, 'Malaria took her.'

'Oh dear.' Mrs Williams brushed the side of her hand over her part of the table, gathering up a little hill of crumbs. She said, 'This was last October? Was she in the hospital? Or here?'

'Here.'

A tight look came over her face, and I guessed what she was thinking. I said, 'Mr Williams and Daddy burned the mattress. Burned the bedclothes, the netting too. There wasn't no need for that: folks say it ain't catching that way. Skeeters carry it; most of us have a touch of it now and again. But Mr Williams had it fixed otherwise in his mind so Daddy went on and helped him.'

'You have malaria?'

'A touch.'

'And Oscar? Andre?'

'Not Andre. He don't sit still long enough for skeeters to light on him.'

The corners of her mouth lifted, then she got all serious again. She said, 'Where is Andre's mother buried?'

'In the city cemetery. On Broadway.'

'Oscar takes Andre to see her grave?'

'Every Sunday if it ain't raining. They lay flowers.'

Mrs Williams looked off, her blue eyes going all dim. Her forehead was beaded up with sweat, and her shirtwaist stuck to her skin just above her bosom. She didn't know that in the summer, nobody cinched their corsets tight or wore high collars. Leastways we didn't on our end of the island.

She said, 'Last night at the dance I thought I might meet her family. Her parents or brothers and sisters, if she had any.'

'There's only her mama and Mr Williams has nothing to do with her.'

'That sounds rather ominous.'

I wished she'd talk regular so a person could understand her on the first try. I combed through her words, then said, 'Her mama lives on Post Office Street. Leastways she did last any of us heard. She drifts over to Louisiana from time to time, her being a Cajun.'

'Cajun?'

'She's a Frenchy. They come from Louisiana mainly. They're swamp people.'

Mrs Williams' lips pursed up at that. After a while, she said, 'I'm not familiar with this Post Office Street.'

'There's a stretch of it that ain't proper, let's just leave it at that. It ain't no place to raise a child, especially a girl. The nuns got ahold of Bernadette before it was too late; they got her out of that place and raised her up.'

A kind of quaky look came over Mrs Williams like she had just gotten a mouthful of something bad, and I figured she had. Bernadette's mother was no good. As for her father, there was no telling who he was, but I didn't say that. It'd shame Bernadette. Not that she came from bad blood, not all the way. She had a grandma over there in Louisiana, and when Bernadette was little, her mama would leave her there from time to time. 'Grandmère cooked like nobody else,' Bernadette would say. 'And she had a garden like your mama's, raising carrots, greens, and melons. I used to help her, holding the stakes and patting the ground when she'd put in the seedlings. And Grandpère, he made pirogues, his boats so light they were like herons skimming the Atchafalaya.'

Mrs Williams said, 'You and she were friends?'

Me and Bernadette were more than friends; we saw eye-to-eye on most things. Once in a while, I'd come by to see her after I'd finished helping Mama at home. I'd be walking through the back pasture and there'd be Bernadette, coming to meet me. 'I was just now thinking of you, Nan,' she'd say, that curly black hair of hers coming loose from her ribbon. 'Just now. And here you are.' I'd roll up my sleeves, and me and her would scrub clothes or I'd help out with the cooking. She was a little thing. Mama said that was because Bernadette was nothing but a half-starved shadow of a girl when the nuns found her. But she wasn't scared of hard work. She made this house of hers shine, she was that proud of it. Sometimes she'd sing while we'd do the chores, her calling up swamp songs. For a while, she made me sit at the table so she could teach me my letters. The nuns had taught her to read and write, and she thought everybody needed to know how. But I didn't like school and how the schoolteachers looked down their noses at me and my brothers, us coming from down the island. 'It ain't in me,' I'd tell Bernadette. 'I don't like sitting still. My hand's fighting this pencil.' But Bernadette wouldn't listen. 'Try again,' she'd say as she guided my hand.

Other times me and Bernadette talked about the oddness

of the world and how there were just enough good times to make the rough patches easier. When Bernadette took to thinking about her mama and worrying about the life she was living, I'd listen, not passing on one ounce of judgment. When I'd get to missing Oakley Hill, she'd say, 'Tell me about him, me not ever knowing him. Say his name, say it right out loud.'

'That's right,' I said to Mrs Williams. 'Me and Bernadette were friends.' She looked to be turning that over in her mind. I said, 'She was expecting. That's why malaria took her.'

'Dear heavens.'

'Expecting at Christmas or thereabouts.'

Mrs Williams closed her eyes. This house was a-swirl with things not said, Oscar sheltering her from anything that was a few shades off of being pretty. She opened her eyes and when she did, she laid her hands flat on the table. Her skin was white and soft, not red and roughed up like mine. The ends of her nails had been filed smooth and curved a tad on the sides. Her wedding band was nothing like Bernadette's. Bernadette's had been thin, Oscar having just bought four Jerseys to add to his farm. But Mrs Williams' was wide. He'd been willing to spend whatever it took to claim her.

I said, 'He got you that piano, you know.'

'Pardon?'

'Mr Williams went to the city just last week, got it for you then. Had it delivered the very next day.'

'He did?' she said, her eyes going wide some. 'I thought it had always been here. I assumed that Andre's mother played.'

'He got it for you.' Along with that pretty wedding band, I thought. Then, plain as day, I recalled what Oscar told Mrs Williams after she played that moonlight song of hers. It was like he was right here, saying them words again: 'I'd stand outside your window and listen.'

When Bernadette died, Oscar kept away from other women. But from out of nowhere, letters started flying from here to Ohio. Maybe he'd carried Catherine Williams in his mind for years. Maybe when him and Bernadette sat out at night looking up at the stars, he'd been thinking of this woman with that smile of hers and her figure that turned men silly.

I stood up. 'I've got dishes to wash.'

I washed and she dried the dishes. I didn't want her help. I didn't want her standing so close to me, the two of us looking out the same kitchen window. I didn't like thinking this woman might have flooded Oscar's thoughts when he was married to Bernadette. Mrs Williams hadn't asked if she could help, she just took up the dish towel like it was the most natural thing in the world. I kept my mouth shut, saying only what I had to about where the frying pan went and how the spoons and forks had their own places in the drawer. I wanted to be left alone. I wanted to figure out that it wasn't true about Oscar, him thinking about her for years. I wanted to be able to tell myself that my imagination had gone in the wrong direction. Most of all, I didn't want Catherine Williams handling Bernadette's things.

She didn't wear an apron and that didn't sit well either. It'd be me scrubbing the dirty spots from her skirts, me washing and ironing her shirtwaists. I heard Mama's voice in my head telling me that Oscar was paying me to do such work. If the new Mrs Williams wanted to dry dishes, that was her right. This was her house, not mine. Maybe so, I argued back in my head. Didn't mean I had to like it. Didn't mean I had to talk to her. Not that Mrs Williams noticed the argument I was waging with Mama. She looked out the window like there was something at the sand hills that only she could see.

It was eight o'clock when Oscar, Andre, and the orphans left for St. Mary's in the two wagons, the beds packed with containers of milk. As soon as they were on the other side of the sand hills, taking the beach road with the dogs trotting along with them, Mrs Williams sat down at the piano. She had sheet music spread out in front of her but she didn't play that moonlight song, and I was glad for it. I hurt bad enough as it was.

Mrs Williams didn't seem to care when some of the piano keys stuck. She just kept on and made the music flow through the house. It flowed through me, too, like it had yesterday, but I didn't let on. I kept to my chores.

When Oscar and the boys got back around nine, St. Mary's being nothing but a quick trip, Mrs Williams stopped right in the middle of a tune and went outside. She stood on the edge of the veranda and watched them unload the empty metal containers from the two wagons.

I fried slices of ham and boiled a dozen eggs. Oscar's cows might not know it, but Sunday was a day of rest calling for a light dinner and an even lighter supper. I had just turned the ham slices in the skillet when Mrs Williams came in from the veranda and went to the bedroom. When she showed up again, she had on one of her fancy hats with feathers and bows. This one was wide-brimmed and made of straw. Without a word, she left the house and took the narrow path that went to the outhouse, holding her skirt above her ankles.

I didn't know what to make of it when she went on by the

outhouse and headed toward the barn. The orphan boys had unhitched the horses and were taking them to the stables on the other side of the barn. Andre was with them, and so were the four dogs. Maybe she took the unhitching of the horses to mean that Oscar wasn't going to carry her to church, her not knowing the horses needed water and they won't lower themselves to drink out of the cow trough. It wasn't like her to pay a visit to the barn, I didn't know if she'd ever been there. But there she was at the barnyard gate, having all kinds of trouble with the wood latch. More than likely it was swelled up from the sea air.

After some doing, she got it open and knew enough to close the gate behind her. She picked her way through the yard and held her skirt so high that her white stockings showed. When she got close to the trough where Maisie was, she hurried up like she was scared. She didn't know that milkers weren't given to chasing women, especially a milker with a swelled leg.

A handful of minutes went by before Oscar and Mrs Williams came out of the barn. Oscar held a bucket. By then, the boys and dogs had left the stables and were on their way to the barn. Oscar and Mrs Williams met them outside of the barnyard gate and they had themselves a big meeting with her in the thick of it. Oscar gave the bucket to Andre and then Oscar put his hand on Joe's shoulder. See you next Sunday, I guessed they were saying. The orphans were finished for the day and would walk home now. That was how they did, Sunday after Sunday, taking the path from the barn to the sand hills and on down the beach to St. Mary's. But this weren't the usual Sunday. No, sir. The orphans headed for the hills but not alone. Andre went with them and so did Mrs Williams.

144

I could hardly believe my own eyes. She waved the boys to go ahead of her since the path was too narrow to walk any other way but one behind the other. James, being the oldest, led the way. Andre marched behind the orphans, holding on to the bucket, knocking it against his knees. Mrs Williams took little steps in them fancy shoes of hers. She held back some like she didn't want to get too close to the dogs. She didn't know they were herders and that they'd keep to her heels no matter what.

Closer to the hills now where the breeze was strong, Mrs Williams' skirt mashed against her legs. She plodded and sank in the soft, deep sand. Her hand on her hat, she followed the boys. At the pass between the hills, they waited for her to catch up. Once she got there, they took off again, the walking easier since they were on the planks. Straining my eyes, I watched as they slipped out of sight, Mrs Williams the last to round the hills.

The orphans were going home. Like always. But that bucket of Andre's, I knew what it meant. Andre and Mrs Williams were getting sand hill sea daisies for Bernadette, and Oscar had watched it all. He was at the barnyard fence, standing there like he didn't want to do nothing but wait for her to get back home.

I turned the ham slices one last time. The butter popped loud in my ears. I took off my apron and hung it on a nail by the icebox. I moved the skillet off the stove and covered the ham with a lid. I got my bonnet and tied the strings under my chin, then started for home, taking the path through the back pasture and stirring up a crop of skeeters. Oscar wasn't nowhere in sight now. His good sense must have gotten ahold of him and told him to get back to work. I didn't stop at the barn to tell him I was heading on home and how I'd see him bright and early in the morning. I didn't feel like it, not one little bit. Not with Andre going off with Mrs Williams.

High up, the clouds were puffy but flat bottomed, and the breeze blew from the gulf. Some of Oscar's cows stood in the ponds to escape the skeeters. Others were clumped up in the side shade of the salt cedar tree. They watched me as I passed by, my unlit lantern in one hand and the empty basket in my other. I opened and closed the back gate, and stepped over the rusty lace-factory train tracks.

At the bayou now, I stood at the place where the land thinned down into mud and marsh with salt grass poked up in the shallows. Dragonflies darted, flashes of shiny green. Seashells were scattered every which way. Oscar called them whelks, him liking to know the fancy names for such things. He had a skiff here; it was tied loose to the dock, rocking a little as the water lapped. Daddy had helped him build the dock when Oscar bought the dairy. 'If I'm going to live on an island,' Oscar had said, 'I'm going to have me a boat.'

Him and Bernadette used to take the skiff out on Sunday afternoons if it wasn't overly hot. After Andre was born, he went too. 'Just for the doing of it,' Bernadette said. Now the skiff looked like something that nobody cared about. The keel needed to be scraped. It was covered with thin-shelled barnacles at the water line. The latches that locked the oars in place were crusted with rust. And nobody'd want to get in that skiff, not with rainwater pooling in the bottom and white bird droppings dirtying the seats.

Daddy had wanted to pull it out of the water: it bothered him to see it this way. But Mama told him no. 'That's Oscar's doing,' she'd said. 'Maybe it'd hurt him worse to have it on

146

dry land. It's a lonesome thing, an upside-down skiff with grass growing around it.'

I looked past the skiff to where the mud flats glimmered. The bayou was smooth and sparkled under the morning sun. There were other skiffs out there. Packs of seagulls circled behind them like the fishermen might go soft in their heads and share their catches. Pelican Island showed from here and so did the mainland. A good ways off to my right, a train crossed over West Bay. It was going to Virginia Point on the mainland, its black smoke leaving behind a dirty trail like it wanted to let folks know where it'd come from. There were people on that train; they were leaving Galveston. Maybe some of them were going to places they'd never been before.

My family's house was the other way, to the west. It was close to the bayou and was raised up on stilts a few feet higher than Oscar's. From here, the house looked old and rickety, Daddy not believing in paint. He was partial to trees, though, and had planted a few extra salt cedars around it just because he thought it gave the place a cooling appearance. I grew up with those cedars and I figured I'd be looking at them same wind-bent trees when I was old and rickety myself.

I put down my lantern and basket, and edged closer to the marsh. Mud sucked at my boots. I hitched up my skirt to my knees and tucked it around me so I could squat down without dragging the hem. The bayou looked different from here, me low to the ground. It was wider, the stretch from here to the mainland longer. I reached out and tore off a blade of salt grass, then got up and went back to drier land, slipping a little in the mud. I turned around and watched water rise up where I'd been standing and fill my shoe prints.

When I was a girl in braids, there was nothing I liked better than the smell of salt grass. Now, I put that thick blade of grass I'd torn off right up to my nose, smelling its greenness and smelling the sun. And mud, its sour smell was part of it, too.

I wouldn't be staying on much longer at Oscar's. I saw that as plain as I saw this bayou. I couldn't stay to watch Andre turn away from me. And I couldn't watch that unsettled thing brewing between Oscar and Mrs Williams. He was going to have to find somebody else to cook and clean for them. I didn't know who but that wasn't my worry. No, sir.

Tomorrow I'd come right out and tell him to start looking for somebody new. One week, I'd give him one week. And if he asked why I was leaving, I'd tell him the truth. Leastways I'd tell him part of the truth. I wouldn't say that me and Mrs Williams didn't get on. I wouldn't tell him that I saw him in a different light, him being with this new woman. Or that as hard as it'd be to leave Andre, it'd be a harder hurt to stay. I wouldn't say none of that. But should Oscar ask, this part of the truth I'd lay right out flat. There was no room for me in his house. I'd run my course.

CHAPTER NINE

The Cemetery

I felt Nan Ogden watching from the house as I fumbled with the latch on the barnyard gate. The soft soil in the yard was churned with hoof prints, and flies buzzed around a pile of dung. Water streamed from the chin of the cow that stood at the trough, her unblinking eyes taking note of my every move as I closed the gate and walked toward the barn door. I'd never been so close to a cow, and her size was alarming. So, too, was her udder. It resembled a balloon but one that was lined with swollen blood vessels. I hurried past her.

Andre's request at the breakfast table to see his mother had chilled me. So had Oscar's temper. I thought him to be a man of endless patience, but I heard the clipped anger in his voice when Andre insisted on going to the cemetery. I saw, too, the collapse of Andre and at that moment, he was very small and very young. It reminded me again how my presence had upset the balance of this household. When I pressed Nan Ogden to tell me about Andre's mother, she was sullen and stubborn. She told me only fragments but that had been enough. Bernadette had died of malaria, and she had been expecting a child. Upon hearing this, I felt a sudden ache in my heart for Oscar.

There was pain in Nan's eyes, too, as she spoke about Bernadette. They had been friends, and I had taken her friend's place.

During meals, Nan wouldn't look at me. When I played the upright, she stomped around the house as she went about her duties. I heard the mocking scorn in her voice when I didn't know that the skillet hung on the peg by the cookstove rather than by the cupboard. But if Nan thought she could unnerve me, she was mistaken. I had faced the women of Dayton. I had held my head high as I took walks past their homes, knowing they shunned me and that they called me harsh names.

Names that I deserved, I thought now, as I stood just inside of the wide doorway and waited for my eyes to adjust to the barn's dimness after the sun's glare. I heard a soft whishing sound before I saw Oscar in one of the empty stalls. His back to me, he pitched straw from a wheelbarrow onto the floor, his movements rhythmic and smooth.

I took a few steps into the barn. Its coolness surprised me and so did the smell of fresh hay with a slight undercurrent of dung. The three rows of stalls were empty. Other than the cow at the trough, the rest were in the pasture behind the house. For a moment, I watched Oscar work, his back bending and straightening as he lifted and threw the straw.

He had lost his wife eleven months ago. He might have expected that our marriage would help him to forget her. I imagined, though, that it made him miss her all the more. On Friday, my first day in his home, the evening meal had been awkward, the memory of the Central Hotel magnifying in my

150

mind. Neither Oscar nor I seemed to know what to say. I had managed to burn the fried fish that Nan had left, and the rice had solidified into thick clumps. Andre complained but with good cause, I had thought. When dinner was finally over, Oscar left, explaining that he had his evening chores. 'If you'd see to Andre, I'd appreciate it,' he'd said. 'He's to wash good, say his prayers and be tucked in by seven-thirty.' Without looking at me, he'd said, 'I'll likely be late, Maisie being poorly with that leg of hers and me being gone these few days. No need to wait up, most likely you're plenty tired.'

I washed the dinner dishes, my hands stinging from the sharpness of the soap. Under the kitchen table, Andre played with his building blocks but I felt him watching me. This would be a good time to give him my gift, a shiny penny, I thought. Then no. I'd wait until I had him settled. That would end his day on a high note.

I had never put a child to bed before, and I depended on him to tell me what to do. In the washroom, which felt too small for the two of us, Andre stiffened when I cleaned his face with a washcloth. Soap got into his eye and he yelped, hopping up and down. In my hurry to rinse his eye, water splashed over the side of the basin, soaked his shirt, and pooled on the floor.

In Andre's bedroom, I asked him what he wore to bed. 'My nightshirt,' he said, his tone a mix of wonder and disbelief that I didn't know such a thing. The eyes of Jesus on the crucifix followed me as I turned down the bed. I couldn't give Andre the penny, I realized. Not here. I imagined him peering at it as I held it out to him, his nose wrinkling, then looking at the photograph of his mother on the nightstand. I'd find a better time, I decided. And a better place.

Once Andre was in bed, I told him to say his prayers. 'I don't say them in bed,' he said. He got up and knelt by the side, the hem of his bed shirt under his knees and his hands pressed together. The bottoms of his feet were dirty. He looked up at me as though waiting for me to begin. When I did – 'Now I lay me down to sleep' – he shook his head from side to side, saying, 'That ain't right, you're saying it wrong. I want Daddy.'

'That *isn't* right,' I said.

'What isn't?'

I resisted the urge to snap. It had been a long day beginning with the Central Hotel, then the beach road, the house, Nan Ogden, dinner to prepare and dishes to wash. Now grammar lessons. 'Please don't say the word ain't,' I said. 'Now let's say your prayers. Your father is working in the barn, he's busy.'

After Andre's prayers, one that was unfamiliar to me, I made him sit on the bed so I could wash his feet with a washcloth. That finished, he asked for a drink of water and after I brought him that, he needed to visit the outhouse. 'How about the chamber pot?' I said.

'But I ain't sick and it ain't raining.'

'You *aren't* sick and it's *not* raining,' I said.

'Huh?'

'Please don't use the word ain't.'

'Why not?'

'It's incorrect grammar.'

'What's that?'

'Grammar refers to the correct way to speak.'

He poked out his lower lip and looked up at me from under his eyebrows.

152

'Now then. You may use the outhouse. But knock on the door first.'

'Huh?'

'In case there are snakes.'

'Miss Nan says to bang on the door. Bang real loud and holler in.'

Oscar was wrong, I had thought. Andre was not in need of a mother. He had Nan.

Now, though, as I watched Oscar pitch hay, I remembered the pain behind Andre's words when he'd said he wanted to see his mother.

I walked farther into the barn. Along the dirt floor, small drifts of straw were caught against the stall posts, and a cat, sitting on a railing, watched without moving. 'Oscar,' I said.

His pitchfork came to a standstill midair, straw caught in the prongs. He turned.

'I'd like to speak to you,' I said. 'About what happened at the table.'

'Here? Now?'

'Yes,' I said.

I walked up the aisle toward him. He tossed the straw onto the floor and propped the pitchfork against the railing. Inside the stall, Oscar waited for me, saying nothing as he wiped his face with a handkerchief. I felt his wariness but wariness was nothing new between us. The memory of what had happened at the Central Hotel – his passion, my hysterical sobs – was a rift that lay between us, seeming to grow with each passing hour.

We stood with the stall railing between us. The top four or five buttons of his blue shirt were unfastened, and on one side, the worn material had fallen back and open. In the barn's dull light, there were pockets of shadow along his collarbone.

I said, 'Nan told me about the cemetery.'

He didn't say anything.

'Andre's a child,' I said. 'And there have been so many changes. If he's accustomed to visiting his mother's grave, then perhaps today is not the time to break from tradition.'

'My mind's made up. I told him no.'

'I understand that. But he wants to put flowers on her grave.'

'Things are different now.'

'Very much so. And that's why you need to take him. He misses her.'

'He was four. It's been eleven months. He stopped asking for her a while back. By now, I figure he might not much remember her.'

'That could be, but you've been taking him every Sunday.'

Oscar looked away, his eyes clouding. He took a cigarette from his breast pocket and put it to his lips. He drew in his cheeks as though it were lit. Along the wall behind him, coiled ropes and odd-shaped tools hung from pegs, only the hammers and the saws somewhat familiar.

Oscar put the cigarette back into his pocket. 'We need to leave soon. Get you to church in time for eleven o'clock services.'

'Thank you, but I'd rather go to the cemetery with you and Andre.'

He looked at me, his head tilted.

'If I'm welcome.'

A smile inched across his face.

*

154

We made the three-mile trip to the cemetery, the horses and wagon scattering seagulls as we traveled the beach road. Andre rode beneath the buckboard and from time to time he made popping sounds as though he were playing some kind of game. Once, he touched the buttons on my shoes, pressing them with his fingers. Startled, I drew in my feet. Then I moved them back to where they had been, close to Andre, waiting for his touch.

It didn't come. Perhaps the heat turned him as sluggish as I was. I had forgotten to loosen the stays in my corset, and I was lightheaded from the sun. While Oscar steered the horses around the strewn driftwood, I conjured up images of a pastoral cemetery with rolling hills and expansive shade trees.

This, however, was Galveston. City Cemetery was flat, and although it was large, the number of trees could be counted on one hand. Sunken gravel walkways with curbs cut the cemetery into squares. Marble domed vaults and above-the-ground crypts glittered in the sun, hurting my eyes. Monuments with columns and spires, winged angels, and saints with hands clasped in prayer soared, while other graves were marked by small headstones of thin marble. Bernadette had been laid to rest in the Catholic section. Her grave was marked by a gray rectangular stone of granite centered on the top of a one-tiered foundation.

I stood off to the side under my parasol's small circle of shade. Oscar removed the dried, brittle flowers from the vase attached to Bernadette's stone. Some of the other graves had fresh flowers but in the heat of the day, we were the only mourners.

Together, Oscar and Andre filled the vase with the daisies we'd brought in the bucket. Sandy water dripped from the flowers' stems and splattered Andre's shirt and short pants. His hat was too big, I thought. The tops of his ears were folded over, and one of his black stockings had collapsed into wrinkles above his ankle. He must have taken his garters off while we were in the wagon.

The flowers now in the vase, Andre stood on the foundation of his mother's marker. He ran his fingers over the carved wreath of ivy at the top of the stone.

Loving Wife to Oscar and *Devoted Mother to Andre*. Bernadette was from Louisiana, Nan had told me. A Frenchy. That had made me think of Longfellow's poem about the exiles from Canada. My high-school classmates and I had thought the story about Evangeline and her lost groom was romantic. We thought the exiles were brave and noble. Nan called them swamp people.

Bernadette's mother lived on Post Office Street. 'There's a stretch of it that ain't proper, let's just leave it at that,' Nan had said, her gray eyes hard with disgust. As she spoke of Bernadette's mother, I'd felt ill. Five days ago when I arrived, swaggering sailors gathered on the corners of downtown Galveston. At the wharves, dockworkers wet with perspiration hoisted cargo from the ships. Although such things were not spoken of in polite society, it was common knowledge that there were houses of entertainment for such men.

Bernadette's origins were sordid and shameful, and it had stunned me to think that I followed in the footsteps of such a woman. Then I remembered. I was in no position to have qualms about such things.

B. April 5, 1874. She was younger than me by four years. Andre traced the eight over and over, humming to himself.

Oscar studied the sky, his head tilted back so he could see past the brim of his hat.

In the photograph in Andre's room, Bernadette wore a white dress and a small floral headpiece with a short veil. Her hand was on Oscar's shoulder. Her hair was dark and looked to be unruly. A few curly strands had fallen around her face. She had the figure of a young girl and taken feature by feature, she was ordinary. Her nose was too thin, and her chin was pointed. There was a softness, though, in her eyes, and the corners of her lips were slightly turned up, and this made her pretty.

Andre, standing on the foundation of his mother's stone, teetered on the edge, then jumped. His knees dipped as he stumbled on the uneven ground. 'Steady,' Oscar said, putting his hand on the boy's shoulder. Andre looked up at him and grinned.

'Son, is there anything you want to tell your mama, while we're here?'

Andre squinted and twisted his mouth as he considered. I waited, sure that he would say something about my arrival. He said, 'There was a dance, and Miss Nan played the fiddle.'

'Your mother will be glad to hear that.'

'And everybody came.'

Last night, before we arrived at the pavilion, Oscar told me that his neighbors were good people, hard-working people, and I understood that he was defending them. He expected me to dislike them and to hold myself above them. The women's thin faces were etched with weariness, and their hands were large from the years of housework. Most wore their hair parted in the center and pulled back into tight buns. The men were long-hipped, bowlegged, and weathered brown. They loosened their neckties, and some of them took off their collars. Nan's father

157

was tall and angular with curly gray hair and sunken cheeks. Her mother, a thin gray-haired woman whose back was stooped, clung to me as she recounted details about the neighbors that were meant to impress but only made me feel all the more displaced. 'Loretta Ellis here has nothing but boys,' Mrs Ogden said. 'Eight of them.' Mrs Ellis smiled with pride. Mrs Ogden said, 'Come meet Bessie Gerloff. Her kin were some of the first here. They came when Texas was part of Mexico.'

The men and women ate at separate tables with the children's table near the women's. The ten nuns sat apart, their faces made narrow by their white headpieces that covered the sides of their faces and their foreheads.

'Your purple-hull peas are mighty pleasing,' Mrs Ogden said to Mrs Irvin, who sat across from us.

'It's the bacon fat,' Mrs Irvin said, waving off a swarm of flies around her plate. Deep lines ran from her nose to the corners of her mouth. She said, 'I had some extra, and don't it do something nice for peas?'

'Surely does,' Mrs Ogden said.

Mrs Irvin picked up one of the shrimp from her plate and pointed it at Mrs Ogden. 'This batch is extra good. You boiled it just right.'

'Why, thank you,' Mrs Ogden said. 'Though I weren't overly happy with the seasoning, thought the cloves didn't stand up and do what they should.' She looked at my plate. I didn't have any shrimp, only potato salad, corn pone, and Mrs Irvin's peas that were slick with grease. She said, 'Mrs Williams, is all your kin up there in Ioway?'

It took me a moment to decipher her accent. 'I'm from Ohio,' I said. 'Not Iowa. But yes. My mother and her husband, my aunts and uncles, they're all in Dayton.'

158

'What about your brothers and sisters? Whereabouts might they be?'

'I'm an only child.'

'Oh, your poor mother,' someone said. At that, Mrs Anderson, the woman on my right, made a disapproving click with her tongue. She said, 'Your Mr Williams is one fine man; we think the world of him.'

'Good Lord, yes.' This came from the woman directly across from Mrs Anderson. I believed her name was Mrs Calloum. She was younger than the others, and her brown hair was swept up into a pompadour. She said, 'When Everett was laid up a few years back with a broke leg, and me with those two babies of ours, Mr Williams was forever coming by and helping out. He told Everett how it'd give him a mighty pleasure to patch that little hole up there on the barn roof. Had him a few spare minutes with not a thing to do.'

'Ain't that just like him,' Mrs Anderson said. 'One time he brought milk when our cow was poorly. Said how those gals of his were in a spry mood, giving more than usual and I'd be doing him a kindness by relieving him of the extra.'

'Always lending a hand,' Mrs Ogden said. 'And doing it like you'd done him a favor, letting him help out and all.'

'You've got yourself a good one,' Mrs Calloum said to me.

I said something, agreeing, my smile feeling lopsided. The conversation turned to quilts, the women's voices floating around me. Across the pavilion and at the men's table, Oscar talked, waving his fork as he did, grinning. *Have you forgotten your Dayton friends,* I had written in one of my letters to him. *Whatever is it like to live on an island in Texas?* I inquired in another. I spent hours composing those letters. I tried to strike the right tone, wanting my curiosity about Galveston to show

159

my interest. I had phrased my questions so that he was compelled to respond.

Oscar had seen through that. He had sensed my desperation. He might think that I'd been abandoned at the altar. Or that I was fearful of living the rest of my life as a spinster. *My Son is in need of a Mother,* Oscar had written. *I am in need of a Wife.* His marriage proposal was designed to make me think I was doing him a favor by accepting.

Across the way, the men boomed with laughter as though someone had told a joke. Oscar leaned forward, his attention on someone farther down the table.

Around me, the women talked about okra, something I'd never heard of. 'Fresh from the garden, cut into thin pieces, and cooked with 'maters and rice,' Mrs Irvin said. 'That's the only way Henry'll eat okra.' I nodded, but it was difficult to breathe and my skin had turned clammy. On the other side of the table, Mrs Calloum peered at me.

I gathered myself. 'The air's a bit close,' I said. 'So damp and heavy.' I picked up my drinking glass, a canning jar. Its thick lip bumped up against my front teeth. The suddenness of our marriage must have shocked these women. I had appeared from nowhere. I imagined the gossip traveling along the hard-packed beach road, the wind carrying the whispers. The details would be provided by Nan Ogden. First, there had been the removal of Bernadette's clothes from the wardrobe and then the delivery of the upright. Next was my arrival on Wednesday. We married on Thursday and were at Oscar's home by Friday noon. 'She don't know how to cook, and she didn't bang on the outhouse door before going in,' I imagined Nan telling her mother.

Worse things had been said about me.

I held my head high when the neighbors called Oscar and me to the dance floor. However I came to be his wife, regardless of the distance between us, I was here, he and I standing before the neighbors as though museum pieces on display. From somewhere I heard an off-note squeak. A man laughed and I saw Nan Ogden with her violin. I was surprised; she hadn't said a word that day about the dance. Our eyes met. I expected to see sullen resentment on her face but instead, she acknowledged me with a nod. I returned her acknowledgment. She took a deep breath and in that moment, I understood that she was nervous to play before so many. She drew her bow across the strings. Oscar took my hand and put his other hand on my back.

His touch was a spark of electricity. He felt it too; I saw the sudden shock of it in his eyes. My cheeks flushed. The neighbors were watching. I put my hand on his shoulder. Fixed in position, he stood as though suddenly paralyzed, his gaze skipping from me to the people who surrounded us, Nan's waltz going on without us. 'One, two, three,' I whispered to help him find the rhythm. 'One, two, three.' Oscar didn't move. He was shy, I thought. And unaccustomed to being the center of attention. I kept counting, nodding on the downbeat, and then he counted with me, his lips forming the words. All at once we lurched, stumbling more than dancing, the awkwardness between us showing.

'*Sweet Evelina, dear Evelina,*
My love for thee will never, never die.'

I gave his hand a quick squeeze of reassurance. His steps began to smooth out and so did mine. He smiled with relief,

161

and then we were dancing, circling the pavilion, everyone and everything around us a blur, the kerosene lamps flashes of light.

'Evelina and I, one fine evening in June,
Took a walk all alone by the light of the moon.'

The dance, the music, drew us together.

'The plants all shone for the heavens were clear,
And I felt round the heart, oh! mightily queer.'

We waltzed, the breeze and the whooshing of the surf all part of the music, our nerves slipping away. I smiled and as I did, a lightness came over me as though I were suddenly free of the past.

This lightness stayed with me when our waltz ended and I danced with the men, one after the other, their faces slick from the heat as they shuffled me around the pavilion, the music and the steps unfamiliar. It held me when the crowd whooped and clapped for the two nuns who jigged, the tune too loud and too fast. As long as there was music, even unrefined music, I was light, and there were only the violins, the mandolin, and Oscar. The music filled our silence, neither of us needing to be careful, neither of us measuring each word or watching every step. We danced, together and with others, our eyes meeting, smiling.

Then the last waltz ended and in the silence, Oscar turned cautious. He stepped back and dropped my hand as though he thought his good fortune had run its course, and I would splinter at any moment.

Now, at the foot of his first wife's grave, Oscar crouched and pulled up a spiky weed with his bare hand, the soil tearing. Andre fingered the daisies in the vase and rubbed a petal between his thumb and forefinger. He pulled the petal loose and put it into his pocket.

Straightening, Oscar said, 'That it, son? Ready to go?'

'I'm hungry,' Andre said.

'Me too,' Oscar said. He glanced at me. I nodded. He said, 'Time to find us some shade.'

We took the wagon to the beach and found that shade in the base of the tall sand hills, a mile or so from the cemetery. Among the sea grass and flowers, Oscar unfurled the red wool blanket that Andre used for his naps. It rippled in the wind and I caught the opposite end. Andre pounced onto it to keep it from blowing away.

We sat on the blanket, Andre between Oscar and I. Oscar filled our jars with the bottled mineral water that he had brought while I passed out the boiled eggs and the fried ham sandwiches I'd wrapped in dish towels. Earlier, when I had returned to the house with the flowers, Nan was gone. Oscar told me that she worked a short day on Sundays. 'But it isn't like her to leave without saying so,' he'd said. 'Or without making our picnic. Looks like you'll have to fix it.'

I hadn't known what to do with fried ham. 'Sandwiches,' Oscar said. 'That's mainly what Nan packs. That and boiled eggs. Cookies if there're any left.' I made our lunch, clumsy and unsure, burning my fingers on the skillet and spilling hot grease onto the kitchen floor.

I unwrapped one of the sandwiches I had made and battled the dish towel to keep it from blowing away as I spread it out

163

on my lap. To the east, the bathhouses were distant shapes in the haze. The gulf water was streaked with green, and at the horizon, the sky curved down and blended into the water. Close to the tide line, a few buggies passed by going in both directions, the drivers steering the horses around the driftwood. An older man ambled near the surf with his head down. He wore his trousers rolled mid-calf and carried a small bucket. A collector of seashells, I thought.

Oscar said the Catholic prayer – 'Bless us, o Lord, and these Thy gifts' – the words now familiar. The seating arrangements were not. The sand under the blanket was lumpy, and my corset cut into my skin beneath my arms. I sat with my legs bent at my knees and angled toward my side, my skirt tucked in. Barefoot, Oscar and Andre were cross-legged with their dish towels bunched under their feet. Oscar's sleeves were rolled to his elbows, his jacket, vest, and collar in a small pile by the edge of the blanket.

Andre held up his sandwich and squinted at it as though it were an exotic creature from the bottom of the sea.

'This looks funny,' he said. He poked his finger into the middle of the bread. It left a deep dent. 'This here is all mushy and Miss Nan, she don't cut off the crusts.'

'She *doesn't* cut off the crusts,' I said.

'I know. This looks funny.'

'Indeed,' I said.

'Son,' Oscar said, 'eat your food.'

'But it's all mushy,' Andre said. 'Miss Nan pats it dry. She puts the ham on a towel and pats it.'

Just a few hours ago, I had wiped his tears. He had touched my wrist as though he no longer resented my presence. Apparently, a five-year-old's memory was fleeting.

164

Andre lifted a corner of his sandwich and studied the ham. A drop of juice landed on his pants.

'Please, if you would, spread out your dish towel and eat over it,' I said.

'Why?'

'To spare your clothes.'

'So Miss Nan won't holler at me for making a mess?'

'Yes and because it's good manners.'

'Look up there,' Oscar said, getting his towel out from under his foot. 'Pelicans. And that schooner way over there. See it? It could be the kind that sails from Cuba. Andre. What do you think it's carrying?'

Andre frowned at his sandwich, then at me. He put his sandwich down on the blanket and wiped his hands on his pants, leaving dark streaks.

'That schooner,' Oscar said. His voice was tight. 'What comes from Cuba, Andre?'

'Bananas,' he said, the word flat.

'And if it comes from Brazil?'

'Coffee beans.'

'Mexico?'

'Lemons.'

'England?'

'Kings and queens!' His heart was in the game now and the tension eased. Oscar asked about Spain and Andre answered, 'Christopher Columbus,' the rhythmic pattern of it telling me that they had played this many times before. His eyes on the ships, Oscar peeled a boiled egg, turning it, the small pieces of brown eggshell falling onto the blanket. The breeze ruffled his hair and did the same to mine. A few loose strands caught at my mouth. I brushed them away. The man

165

who had been collecting shells was farther up the beach. There were only the three of us, Andre nibbling now on his sandwich as he guessed the cargo on the ships.

I had grown up in a household of three. A second child, an infant boy, had died when I was four. 'My Catherine,' my father called me. 'My little pianist.' He came from a family with tin ears and off-tune voices but had been determined to marry my mother, he once told me, the moment he heard her play the piano at a social. My mother was eighteen and had just had her debut. My father was older by eleven years and his career as an engineer was well established. 'His proposal was the only one that came with the promise of a piano,' my mother was fond of saying when I was young. My earliest memories were of her in the parlor at the piano, her fingers skimming the keyboard; and of my father at his drawing board in the study, hunched over sheets of paper, a pencil in his hand.

I begged my mother to allow me to sit with her as she played. 'For twenty minutes,' she'd say. 'If you're quiet.' She wore her hair in ringlets then and always had a brooch pinned at the collar. I watched her hands, the scent of her lavender water enveloping me. Before either of us knew it, she was guiding my fingers on the keyboard and showing me how to read music.

By the time I was eight, I played simple renditions of Chopin's and Mozart's concertos. This pleased my mother but it staggered my father. 'A child prodigy,' he'd say. His confidence that I could master complex techniques made me believe that I could, too. 'Just as I do with my bridges,' he once told me, the part in his graying hair as precise as the creases in his trousers. 'The first design that I did on my own was simple, the span a mere eighty-two feet. It was during the war, General Sherman was massing troops in Tennessee, in what would be called Shiloh, and we needed that bridge. It had to bear the weight of wagons and cannons. I had designed others but this time I was the only engineer. I put myself to the task; the Ohioans were counting on me.'

I thought his bridges were beautiful with their patterns of triangular framework and high cross bracing. My mother, too, was proud of his work and kept newspaper articles on his accomplishments pressed between the pages of her journal. 'Your father is an important man,' she told me. When I was small, he was gone for days on end supervising the building of his bridges, and if his absences made her unhappy, I didn't notice. I had the piano and my mother's lessons.

I loved the feel of the keys beneath my fingertips. I heard music in the jangling bells worn by the horses hitched to the delivery wagons that traveled our back alley. It was in the hiss of the hot iron as our maid pressed my father's shirts. At school, I memorized poems, hearing harmony and tone more than the words. Long columns of arithmetic were musical notes, each one influencing the next. When I turned ten, my father believed I needed more than what my mother could teach me. He arranged for the pianist with the orchestra in Cincinnati to come to our home on Monday afternoons as my tutor. My mother argued against it. 'She's my pupil,' she told my father. 'I know her strengths and her weaknesses. This Mr Brand, he knows nothing about her.'

'She has a gift, it needs to be fostered,' my father said.

'And I can't do that?'

For days after, my mother's smile was set in place. My parents' conversations became increasingly polite and distant.

167

My father spent more time at his drawing board, and my mother criticized all the hours I spent practicing. 'Your needle-work is suffering,' she'd say. 'And so too is your china painting.' As my father's reputation soared, his trips lengthened in dura-tion. My mother found even more women's clubs to join, attending lectures about literature, art, and music. When my father was home, he consulted with Mr Brand, my tutor, about my progress. A few months after my fourteenth birthday, my father arranged for me to spend the summer boarding with Mr Brand's family in Cincinnati. 'Catherine will have lessons every day,' he said to my mother, the two of them in the parlor. I listened through a closed door. 'Hours of lessons,' he said. 'Just think of the progress she'll make.'

'And not summer at Lake Erie?' my mother said. 'But it's what we always do. The picnics, the games of badminton, croquet. Albert, please. You can't ask Catherine to forgo her summer.'

I was thrilled about going to Cincinnati. 'Only for this year,' I told my mother before I boarded the train. 'Just for Father.' She went alone to our Lake Erie cottage, my father's work keeping him busy during the warmer months. At the Brands' home, a small two-story house on Mount Adams with a view of the Ohio River, I lived in a world of music, the tempo of that household so different from the well-mannered routine of my home. 'You're rushing,' Mr Brand would shout to me from wherever he was in the house as I practiced in the narrow parlor. He was a thin man, and although I understood he was close to my father's age, he moved like a boy, quick and agile. 'It's music, not a gallop,' he'd say. He'd be in the parlor by then, pounding on his chest. 'Reach into your heart, Catherine. Feel it there, hear it there. You can. I know you can.'

I reached for it all, working hard, the days flying by. The Cincinnati Orchestra practiced during the summers for the upcoming season and on Wednesday afternoons, Mr Brand allowed me to attend those practices. I sat off to the side, observing, enthralled by the passion of each musician and marveling at the conductor's ability to control those passions, blending each instrument into a unified symphony. At dinner-time, some of the musicians showed up on Mr Brand's doorstep. Mrs Brand, a robust, red-cheeked woman who spoke with a German accent, was known for her cheerful willing-ness to set extra places at the dining-room table. 'This is why God did not give us children,' she told me. 'He wants me to feed musicians.' She served meats of the cheapest cuts but no one seemed to mind. Meals lasted for hours. The men spoke of Prague and Vienna as though they had studied there. They talked about the brilliance of Liszt and the tragedy of Beethoven's deafness, preventing him from hearing his own compositions. 'Do not forget the Vienna Damen Orchestra,' Mrs Brand said from time to time, winking at me. 'Times are changing. Soon you men will have women in your orchestra.'

I listened to it all, my heart flooded with the desire to be a musician. It was then that I realized I cared little about marriage or about motherhood. Such a life would be stilted and dull. Six years later, when I finished my studies at Oberlin College and joined the ensemble in Philadelphia, I was alive with the excitement of performing. Music, I believed, would carry me for the rest of my life. It was my fulfillment.

'Catherine?' Oscar said. He held out the peeled egg in his callused palm. The game he and Andre had played about the ships and their cargo had drawn to an end, and Andre had wandered off. He was a handful of yards in front of us, squatting with his hands on his knees as he studied something in the sand. I thanked Oscar and told him no. I had had plenty. He shrugged as if he had expected me to refuse his offer. He bit the egg in half, then ate the rest.

The last two evenings Oscar had worked late in the barn, returning to the house long after I'd gone to bed. Both nights, I held myself still while he undressed in the dark. I waited, not moving, as he parted the mosquito netting, and the feather bed gave way under his weight. My back to him, he did not touch me. He was not going to risk another scene of hysterics.

The silence between us was unbearable. A few dances and a trip to the cemetery were not enough. I needed to apologize for what had happened at the Central Hotel.

Oscar lit a cigarette, then flicked the match into the sand and leaned back on both elbows with his legs stretched out before him, one bare ankle on top of the other. Propped on his elbows, he looked off to where he had staked the horses in the shade of the sand hills.

I was overwrought, I imagined saying. The trip, the wedding, and a new city.

The surf rushed forward, then fell back, over and over, a dull roar. The salt air prickled my skin. The sun crept closer to my side of the blanket. The heat was unrelenting. I poured more mineral water into our jars. The muscles in Oscar's forearm flexed as he tapped his cigarette, the ashes falling into the sand beside him. I unfastened the top cloth-covered button on my high collar. Farther from us, Andre scooped sand with a seashell he had found, his shadow a dark patch beside him.

It was nothing you did, I imagined saying to Oscar. But that, of course, was not quite true.

His gaze on Andre, Oscar tapped the side of his foot against the blanket. His trousers had hitched up a few inches. The lower curve of his calf muscle tightened and released with each tap.

I'd like to start anew, I could say. That might be all that I needed to say. Or it might call for more, an explanation of something that couldn't be explained.

I straightened my bent legs; they were numb. I tucked my skirt around them. Like Oscar, I crossed one ankle over the other. The breeze ruffled my hem. A few inches of my white silk stockings flashed just above my ankle-high shoes. Oscar drew on his cigarette and then blew out the smoke, glancing at my stockings, then away.

The breeze was hot, but it stirred the air. Out past the tide line, a fish leapt, a flashing arc of silver. I unfastened the second button on my collar, then the third. I pulled the sides of my collar apart so that the air reached the base of my throat. Nearby, the long sea grasses and daisies rustled as they bent and tangled.

'Oscar,' I said.

He looked at me, his eyebrows raised.

'I . . . The other night . . .'

Oscar waited, saying nothing.

'What happened. On Thursday.'

He laid his cigarette in the sand and turned toward me, his weight now on his left elbow.

'I was—'

'Catherine.'

I stopped. Oscar's glance flickered toward my ankles, skimming over my stockings, and then he was looking at me, his green eyes taking me in, lingering at my throat, my mouth, and then my eyes.

I felt myself slipping. Oscar put his fingertips on the center of my lips as if to keep me from speaking. His touch light, he traced my upper lip, a few grains of sand on his fingers. I leaned toward him, inhaled his scent of tobacco, then salt and hay. He brushed back strands of my hair, his palm cupping my face.

He kissed me, his hand at the nape of my neck, and mine on the broad curve of his shoulder.

All at once, he pulled away, startling me, his hat tumbling off. He sprang up onto his feet, his gaze searching the beach, his face tight with worry. Andre. He was gone. A two-horse buggy clipped along the tide line. Andre, all that water. I tried to get up. I knocked over my canning jar, then Oscar's, my feet tangled in my skirt. The buggy passed on, the wheels spinning, and there he was, a little boy digging near the edge of the surf.

Oscar turned to me. His smile was crooked with relief and in that moment, I saw the worries and the responsibilities of raising a child. Andre came first; I had to think of him. Not my mistakes, not my disappointments. Not the distraction of Oscar's eyes, his touch, and my response that took me by surprise and now embarrassed me.

I stood, fumbling as I fastened my collar buttons, then straightened my hat and brushed sand from my skirt. I glanced at Oscar. His smile was gone, and I saw myself as he might, my posture straight, my clothes just so, my reserve back in place.

A muscle ticked near the corner of his mouth. 'Likely it's time to get on home,' he said.

'It's been a long day.'

He nodded, then whistled for Andre, calling him in

172

before going off to retrieve his hat, which was caught in a stand of sea grass farther down the beach. I put on my gloves and by the time Oscar returned, slapping his hat against his leg to shake off the sand, it was as if we were acquaintances who happened to be in the same place at the same time. I packed the picnic basket while he and Andre unrolled their stockings, put them on, and laced up their boots. Oscar helped me up onto the wagon but his touch on my waist was brief. He called to the horses and we lurched out of the soft sand of the hills.

CHAPTER TEN

The Yacht

Monday. Laundry day. Pots of water simmered on the stove. The kitchen walls glistened with moisture. Garments, under-clothing, and bed linens soaked in tubs of hot soapy water. At the kitchen table, Nan raked Oscar's and Andre's shirts over the metal slats of the washboard. Perspiration beaded on her forehead and upper lip, and damp circles darkened her bodice. She'd pushed her sleeves up so that her knobby wrists showed. Her hands were red from the harsh laundry soap and nicked from the washboard. She scowled when she came across Andre's pants that were stained from yesterday's picnic and clicked her tongue as she held up one of my shirt-waists, the layers of lace apparently adding to the burden of her work. Laundry, I was given to understand without Nan saying a word, was an onerous task. When I asked what I might do to be of help, she looked at me as though I had spoken Greek.

She snapped at Andre and told him that he was in her way, she didn't have time for him to follow her around. 'You're too big for such,' she said. 'Five years old. Go get your spade and play under the house. Go on.' He scurried away. 'Looking for buried treasure,' Nan said when I asked what he was doing with a spade.

'I see. Like *Treasure Island*,' I said.

'Huh?'

'Robert Louis Stevenson's novel,' I said. 'There are buccaneers, and a quest for a map that marks the location of a buried chest. It's a great favorite among little boys.'

'Never heard of it.'

I busied myself in the bedroom and at the dressing table; I rearranged my jars of cream, my brush and comb, and my bottle of lavender water as if the exact placement of each object was important and gave purpose to my day. Next, I straightened my skirts in the wardrobe. I could play the upright or read a book on the veranda, but both were unthinkable while Nan labored in the kitchen. When I was a child, my mother's maids, usually young women from Wales or from Ireland, were trained to work without being seen. Laundry was done in the kitchen, a room with a door, a room that was not the other half of the parlor. Floors were scrubbed and furniture was dusted while I was at school and my mother called on friends.

I unfolded and refolded my embroidered handkerchiefs. In the washroom, I pumped water and cooled my face and neck with a damp washcloth. I considered writing a letter to my mother to announce my marriage but beyond a salutation, I could not think what to say. I certainly could not write the truth. *My new home is rustic, to say the least. The housekeeper resents my presence, and my stepson questions everything I do and say. My husband is a man who so unnerves me that I do not know what to make of him. Or of myself.*

Lunch, a thick stew of red beans and rice, was on the front veranda since the kitchen was cluttered with laundry tubs.

The breeze shifted the air from time to time as Oscar, Nan, Andre, and I crowded around the small round veranda table. The floorboards were warped from the sea air, and the table wobbled so much that Oscar had to slide yesterday's newspaper under one of its legs. Flies buzzed and landed on our food. We waved them off but they didn't go far. The space between Oscar and me was narrow and when his knee bumped mine, we both angled away from the other.

It was what we did so well. Last night, after our visit to the cemetery and the picnic in the sand hills, Oscar again worked in the barn until well after dark. In bed, he stayed on his side, and I kept to mine. I should be relieved, I told myself while we had our lunch, Oscar just inches from me. I should be grateful.

Lunch ended, and when Oscar got up to leave, giving Andre a quick smile and a nod to Nan, his gaze settled on me. In that instant, I felt yesterday's caresses – his hand on the nape of my neck, his kiss. 'Catherine,' he said, tipping the brim of his hat. He left, and I was all at once warm and not just from the heat of the day.

Nan stood up, bumping the table, the dishes rattling. 'Well,' she said. 'Well.' She began to gather up the spoons, knives, and forks. 'Young man,' she said to Andre. 'It's nap time. Go get your blanket.'

'But, Miss Nan, I'm not tired. Do I have to?'

'We all have to do things we don't like. That's the way it is, the good with the bad.' She gave me a sideways look. I patted my mouth with my napkin, composing myself. She turned back to Andre. 'Go on, get your blanket. I've got laundry to do and it ain't doing itself, I can tell you that.'

He did as he was told. This was their routine: commands

and protests. Everyone here had a routine, doing things that must be done. For years, my life had revolved around music, the hours of practice with the ensemble seeming to pass by as mere minutes. But now, the only thing I had to do today was put dinner on the table and even that would be prepared by Nan. My life stretched before me, one vacant hour after the other.

The comfort of routine, I thought as Nan began to stack the lunch dishes. It was what Oscar turned to, seeming to escape to the barn every chance he had.

I picked up his drinking glass, then Andre's. 'I'll wash the dishes,' I said to Nan.

Nan and her brothers had left for the day, and I was bent over the open oven door trying to stoke the fire with bellows when Andre ran into the house. 'Ma'am!' he shouted. 'Come see. Daddy said to come get you. Hurry!'

'Is something wrong?'

He shook his head, his eyes bright with excitement. 'Come see!' he said and then he pointed at me. 'Your face is all red.' Before I could tell him that it was impolite to point or to tell a woman that she was in a state of disarray, he was off, running out the door.

I closed the oven and went out onto the veranda. At the foot of the steps, the dogs and Andre circled around Oscar. 'A yacht,' Oscar said to me, grinning. He pointed to farther down the beach. Near St. Mary's, a small ship was just past the breakers, closer to the shore than any I had seen before. Black smoke poured from its stack, and it moved so slow that at first glance, it appeared to be stationary.

'Get your hat,' Oscar said. 'We're going to the beach to get a good look. Hurry. Before it's gone.'

'But dinner. I need to heat the oven. And this sun. It's still so terribly hot.'

'It's a yacht, Catherine. When was the last time you saw a yacht?'

'Daddy,' Andre said, pulling Oscar's hand. 'Can we go? Can we? Now?'

'Andre, enough,' Oscar said, his words sharp with impatience and exasperation. And not just because of Andre. His grin was gone as he looked up at me where I stood at the top of the steps. The ship was moving closer, its smoke a black plume against the sky.

'My hat,' I said. 'I'll only be a minute.'

'Hurry,' Oscar said, and I did. I'd heard the surprise in his voice; I saw it in his eyes. I had not pulled away.

The yacht was long but narrow, and the American flag at the back end – the stern, I recalled from my summers at Lake Erie – rippled as the ship steamed toward us. The sails on the three masts were rolled and tied, and toward the bow there was a small cabin with windows. In the middle of the yacht, a canopy shaded part of the deck. Barefoot, Oscar and Andre stood in the tide to get as close to it as possible, Oscar's trousers rolled to just below his knees. I watched from farther back on the beach where I sat on a long piece of rough driftwood that bowed up a few feet above the soft sand. Oscar and Andre waved to the yacht, their arms raised high and sweeping back and forth, Oscar's hat in his hand.

'Hello,' Andre called, the pitch in his voice high. It went all the higher when three people left the shade of the yacht's canopy and came to the railing. One was a woman. Her skirt whipped around her legs. They waved, shouting, but their words were lost in the surf and in the rumbling hum of the ship's engine.

They must be surprised to see us here on this isolated stretch of the island, I thought. We might look as exotic to them as they did to us. A farm family, they might think, the rooftop of the barn visible above the sand hills. To them, I imagined, we were common people with uncomplicated lives and few desires.

The yacht became smaller and smaller, its smoke a dark trail as it steamed up the island toward the city with its paved streets and buildings with wrought-iron balconies. 'Goodbye,' Andre called, the word stretched long. 'Come back again.'

Oscar put his hand on the top of Andre's head, then turned around toward me. I drew in some air, startled. A moment ago, he and Andre had been calling to the yacht. Now, there was something sharp about the way he looked at me. It was as though he was seeing how far back on the beach I sat, how my skirt was tucked around my legs, how tightly I had tied the ribbons of my sun hat. He began to walk toward me, leaving Andre in the ankle-deep tide.

Invite him to sit down, I thought. We can talk about the yacht, about the sweetness of Andre calling to it and the kindness of the passengers who returned his waves.

'Catherine,' Oscar said when he reached me. His hat in his hand, the wind blew through his brown hair. The sun was in his eyes and he squinted against it. For a moment, he looked past me as if searching for something. An odd expression, one that I couldn't read, crossed over his face.

'It's been six days,' he said, his gaze on me now.

179

'Pardon?'

'You've been here six days. Since Wednesday. And you haven't felt the sand. Or the water. Haven't even said you wanted to.'

The thought had never crossed my mind. 'I—'

'No, Catherine.' He stood over me. The breeze caught at his clothes, and his shirt-sleeves and trousers beat against his skin. 'You live here now. It's time. Take off your shoes and stockings.'

'Oscar.'

He didn't say anything.

I struggled with the buttons on my shoes, unnerved by his abruptness. He watched as I pushed down first one stocking and then the other, trying to do this without raising my skirt and showing my legs. When I'd finished, I stood. The sand was deep and soft, and hot from the sun. Without saying anything, Oscar turned and headed toward the water. I walked behind him, my feet tender. I had not been barefoot in years.

Sand sprayed up from his heels as I followed him around driftwood, broken pieces of bottles and seashells, and orange seaweed that smelled of fish. Then we were on the hard-packed sand that was cool and wet but solid. He went to the tide line where Andre crouched, studying tiny holes in the sand that bubbled around the edges.

Oscar walked into the tide, the water coursing around his bare ankles. He turned around and faced me.

He was testing me, I understood. I could walk into the water and become part of this place. Or I could stay behind and the silence between us would only deepen.

He stood, waiting, his jaw set. He was prepared for me to turn back, I thought. He expected to be disappointed.

I gathered up my skirt and, bracing myself, I walked into the water. It rushed over my feet. It was warm, almost hot, not like the sharp coldness of Lake Erie. Oscar turned and walked a few more paces into the tide. I followed, the water above my ankles, and stood beside him.

He glanced down at me. The force of the water unbalanced me; my feet sank into the eroding sand. It was gritty against my skin and I curled my toes, gripping. The tide rushed out. I staggered, letting go of my skirt, reaching for Oscar and catching his arm. Lacy spindrift whirled around my legs and dragged my hem. I tightened my hold on his arm.

'Take a step,' he said. 'There's nothing to be afraid of.'

I did, still holding on to him, the tide rushing in and out, everything off kilter, everything sinking.

'Oscar,' I said, 'I'm sorry. For what happened on Thursday. I'm so very sorry.'

He stared at the horizon. He hadn't heard, I thought. Or didn't want to. The tide whirled around us, pulling and pushing. Before I could think twice, I let go of his arm and took his hand. I worked my fingers between his so that our palms were together. He looked at me, a small smile at the corners of his mouth, and nodded.

A sense of lightness swept over me, a release, a forgiveness. On the other side of Oscar, Andre jumped over a rippling shallow wave, swinging his arms and landing flat-footed.

'Look,' he said. 'Pelicans. Four of them.'

They glided just a few feet above the waves and all at once, Oscar laughed. It was deep and hearty, and infectious. I laughed too, something that I had not done in months, something that took me by surprise, both of us stumbling and falling against one another, but now holding on, not letting go as the sand washed out from beneath us.

That evening, I went to the back veranda while Oscar finished his work in the barn. Long streaks of orange, red, and purple lit the wide sunset sky, and the bayou glowed a silvery pink. Seagulls skimmed over the ponds in the pasture, their wings iridescent as the sun sank into the bayou.

It was all so vast, I thought. The sky, the water, and my life that lay before me. As though I were still on the beach, I felt the tide around my ankles, the sand eroding. I gripped the railing and watched Oscar leave the barn and take the path that led to the house. When he saw me, he slowed as if surprised.

I again felt the tide but this time my hand was in Oscar's. 'There's nothing to be afraid of.' I let go of the railing and walked to the top of the veranda stairs. There, I took the first step down.

CHAPTER ELEVEN

The Crystal Earrings

I played the upright the next morning, the music expressing what words could not.

I played concerto after concerto, believing that Oscar could hear each note while he worked in the barn. Andre was with him, and Nan was in the kitchen at the ironing board, one iron heating on the stove while the other one thumped as she pressed bed linens and shirts inch by inch. Yesterday it had been unimaginable to play the upright while she labored. Today, I was driven to do so, hearing the music as I had not heard it before.

It stayed with me after I'd closed the lid over the keys and sat on the front veranda, mesmerized by the gulf and by the rain showers that came in quick bursts, drumming on the roof, then stopping as suddenly as they had started. When Oscar and Andre came to the house for dinner – as Oscar called it – I went to him, our hands meeting for the briefest of moments, both of us understanding the need to maintain a façade of formality in the presence of Nan and Andre.

In the afternoon, the rain was dense and heavy, and the gulf had turned the color of pewter. I was on the veranda, an unopened book on my lap, and Andre was sprawled near my feet, napping on the blanket, when lightning splintered the sky. He bolted awake, his eyes wide with fright. 'Andre,' I said, reaching for him. Thunder boomed. He ran into the house and flung himself at Nan where she stood at the ironing board.

'Don't you start up crying,' she said. I was in the doorway. Andre was wrapped around Nan's legs, but her face was set and she held herself rigid, the iron in her hand. 'Ain't nothing but a little storm,' she said. 'Now you let go of me.'

Lightning cracked the air. Andre clutched Nan tighter and pressed his face into her skirt. 'A storm,' she said. 'That's all. Be a man.' She put the iron down and gave him a little push. 'I've got work to do.'

'Miss Nan,' he pleaded.

She shook her head. He edged away from her, his chin down, and she returned to her work, her iron thumping over the small shirt spread out on the board. Something was wrong with Nan, I thought. This coldness toward Andre wasn't like her. There were shadows under her eyes, and she was pale as if she were ill. I went into the kitchen and put my hand out to Andre. 'Come with me,' I said. 'I have a treat for you.'

'You do?' he said.

'Most certainly.' I glanced at Nan as Andre took my hand, and if she appreciated my help, she hid it well. Her attention was fixed on her work as if I were not in the room. 'How about a piano lesson?' I said to Andre.

'Daddy said I couldn't touch it. He said it's not a toy.'

'And he's right. But this will be a lesson and that's different.'

184

'Like school?'

'Like school. Except the upright is our desk. Now. Let's give it a try.'

That evening Oscar and I lay together and talked, our voices low. 'You'll get used to it here,' he said. 'Just give it time. It took me a while, the heat and all. But then again maybe it was different for me. I hadn't figured on staying. I came by accident, you might say.' My head was on his shoulder and beneath the palm of my hand, I felt the beat of his heart.

'By accident?' I said.

'Hadn't meant to come here. I was on my way to south Texas, looking to hire on at a ranch down there. Had two winters up in the Panhandle and that was enough.'

The slight drawl in his voice was smooth, and the mosquito netting rippled, the night air cooling us. The rain had stopped hours ago. 'Took the train over to Dallas and then on down to Houston,' he said. 'Met all kinds of folks along the way. One fellow talked about Galveston, about the cotton exchange, and how ships came here from all over the world. I'd never seen an ocean, couldn't even get an angle on it. When I got to Houston, I figured I'd come to Galveston just for the doing of it.'

'And then you stayed.'

'Didn't mean to, but it was the gulf, how it was never the same. I wanted to see what it would do next. In the morning it might be flat, but by mid-afternoon, the waves could be riding high and coming in a slant, other times face on. Just one more day, I told myself. Then I'd head on down to south Texas. But I got to studying the night sky. I took to watching the moon and the tide. I wanted to see how high it'd come and how far back it'd fall.'

185

My fingers skimmed his collarbone, then the hollow at the base of his throat. The gulf must have been a wondrous thing to a man who once drove a slow-moving wagon heavy with coal through narrow alleys lined with carriage houses. The scrape of his shovel, the tumbling of coal down chutes, and the air thick with black dust must have felt far away when he first saw the wide, flat beach, the curling waves, and the curve of the horizon.

'Watching the tides put a hole in my pocket,' Oscar said. 'So I found a job here at the dairy. The wages were low, but the work came with a bed and meals, and I got so I liked it. When Old Man Tarver died, he left the dairy to his daughter over in Houston. She didn't want the life, said ten cows were ten too many for her. She set a fair price and I bought it from her.' He paused. 'Cleared my debt three years ago.'

A point of pride, I thought. 'You're a self-made man.'

'That's the shined-up version of stubborn.'

I laughed.

He said, 'But you, a college woman.' He played with my hair, running strands of it between his fingers. 'What was it like, college?'

'There's little to tell,' I said, forcing my voice to be light. I felt Oscar's question leading to others about Philadelphia, about the ensemble, and about my return to Dayton. 'If I wasn't at the piano, I was in the classroom or studying in the library,' I said. I kissed him then, distracting him, bringing us back to the present where there was only the two of us, a place I wanted to stay.

Such a thing was not possible. There were the constant demands of the dairy, Oscar's concern for the cow with the swollen leg, and the rustic conditions at the small plain house

186

on stilts. There was Andre, a little boy who needed his shirt tucked into his short pants, his grammar corrected, and piano lessons. And there was Nan Ogden.

Wednesday was cleaning day. Nan's face was pinched as she worked with a fierce determination, scouring the tub and the basin in the washroom, scrubbing the floors and washing the kitchen walls. Outside it rained off and on, but instead of cooling the house as it had yesterday, the air was so thick and oppressive that I was forced to loosen the stays in my corset and to open the top buttons on my high collar.

The few times Nan did speak, her words snapped. 'Them building blocks of yours are scattered every which way in the hall,' she said to Andre after his nap. 'You put them back where they belong. Right now.' She glared at her brothers, Frank T. and Wiley, when they returned from their milk deliveries and came to the veranda where I sat with a book, Wiley carrying the block ice for the icebox, and Frank T. holding the newspapers.

'For pity's sake,' Nan said. 'Never known it to take two grown men to carry in a bitty block of ice. And don't you track mud all over my floors.'

'What's wrong with you?' Frank T. said. 'You've been scratchy all week. Somebody's got to carry in Oscar's newspapers, don't they? Wiley can't do it all.'

'Yes,' I said. 'Someone certainly must.' I smiled at Frank T. and took the papers from him. Frank T. grinned and that caused Nan to mutter something that I couldn't hear. I thanked her for her hard work, and finally they left, evening just a few hours away.

That night, Oscar sprinkled water on the bed linens to keep us cool. The sky had cleared and the room was silver in the moonlight. 'Moon's working its way to full,' Oscar said later. On our sides, we faced one another, his hand resting on my hip. 'Let's you and me go have a look.'

'Now?' I said. 'But we're not dressed.'

'No one'll see.'

'But—'

He got up, put on his trousers, and pulled his braces over his bare shoulders. He found my hands and lifted me to my feet. Wearing only my nightdress and leaving my slippers behind, I went with him past Andre's room and on through the parlor to the front veranda. Beyond the sand hills, white-caps glimmered in the moon's light as they crested. We left the veranda, the breeze ruffling my nightdress against my bare skin. The dirt was wet from the rain, and I walked slowly, the soil much rougher than the beach had been.

'We won't go far,' Oscar said. 'Just enough to clear the house. That way we can see the stars better.'

Wagging tails thumped against my legs, startling me. The dogs had come out from under the veranda. Oscar backed them off, and then he pointed up at the night sky with its thin wispy clouds. 'She's a beaut,' he said about the moon. 'And over there, that's the North Star.' He crouched down a little and had me put my cheek beside his raised arm so I could follow his finger. 'It's the one that's fixed; it guides the sailors. It's part of the Little Dipper. Now, over here, follow my aim. That's the Great Bear. Those three stars, they make the tail. They form the handle of the Big Dipper, too. Once those clouds pass, we'll see the body of the bear.' We waited, the clouds drifting, the moon's light dimming, then brightening. Beneath the sky's vastness, I felt free, all restraints gone. 'There,' Oscar said. 'Right there. That's the Great Bear, plain as day.'

'You see things that I do not,' I said. 'It's all a maze to me.'
I reached for him, running my fingers up his arms and
breathing in his scent of hay and soap.

'Cathy,' he said.

I embraced him. I wanted this moment never to end.

The night seemed to last only minutes with Oscar up hours
before sunrise. If he was exhausted, it didn't show. His smile
came as easily as did his caresses, our hands touching when
mid-morning he came back to the house. 'Just to see how
you're getting on,' he told me. He stayed only a few minutes
but it was long enough to put Nan out of sorts. She was short
with Andre when, a little later, he brought her a rock he'd
found in the pasture. 'I'm busy,' I heard her say. 'Dinner won't
make itself and I can hardly do it with you on my heels every
time I turn around.' He slunk off to the veranda where I was,
his head down and his shoulders slumped.

'I'd like to see it,' I said. 'If I may?'

He opened his hand. It was an ordinary gray rock and even
Andre now seemed to see it as such, drooping all the more.

'Tell me again the names of your dogs,' I thought to say.
'I didn't have a pet when I was a child.'

He wrinkled his freckled nose, his dark eyes puzzled. 'Why
not?' he said.

'My mother wouldn't allow it.'

'Why not?'

'She believed dogs and cats were dirty.'

'How come?'

'She had strict rules about hygiene.'

'What's that?'

'Cleanliness,' I said. I stood. 'Now, no more questions. Let's go see your dogs.'

He grinned. I'd surprised him, I thought as we stood in the yard with Bob, Streak, Bear, and Tracker. They smelled and were in need of baths, but all the same I felt a measure of pride. This was what a mother did, I told myself. She distracted her child when he was upset. I was learning.

That afternoon, I took Oscar's book, *The Milky Way*, and went outside to the front veranda where Andre played on the floor with his set of dominos. The long-haired brown dog that Andre called Bob lay on the second step down with his back legs kicked out and his chin between his mud-flecked paws. Inside, Nan prepared the evening meal, the clanking of crockery and skillets telling me that she was hard at work.

I opened Oscar's book and looked at the illustrations of star clusters as if this would tell me something about the man who showed me the North Star and the Great Bear. I skimmed over the text but stopped when I came across a passage underlined with pencil.

> Night is, in truth, the hour of solitude, in which
> the contemplative soul is regenerated in the universal
> peace. We become ourselves; we are separated from
> the factitious life of the world, and placed in the closest
> communion with nature and with truth.

I had expected it to refer to the names of stars and planets. I read it again: *the hour of solitude*. The phrase turned in my mind.

The past eight months in Dayton had been my hour of solitude. My income almost gone, I had examined all of my choices. A possibility had been marriage to one of the elderly widowers who lived in the hotel. Another was employment in a shop and certain poverty. I had even considered using Edward's letters against him. Instead, I chose Oscar.

I read the passage again. *We become ourselves; we are separated from the factitious life of the world.* Five nights ago at the pavilion, Oscar ate with the neighbor men and danced with the women, rural unrefined people, but that hadn't mattered to him. He enjoyed their company. The music was simple and sentimental but for Oscar, it could have been a symphony. He found pleasure in the stars and admired the grace of pelicans. He was without pretense and this, I realized, was what drew me to him.

I found another underlined passage.

Fiction can never be superior to truth; the latter is
a source of inspiration to us, richer and more fruitful
than the former.

The truth. Not fiction. I went back to the first underlined passage: *closest communion with nature and with truth.*

I put the book on the small table beside me and got up.

'Ma'am?' Andre said. 'Where you going?'

'Nowhere. Just thinking.'

I stepped around Andre and his dominos and went to the western edge of the veranda. All was still at the barnyard, and farther down the island, the rooftops of St. Mary's were visible in a haze of salt.

The truth. It was important to Oscar.

The truth. My past. Something that must stay buried. If Oscar should find out, he'd never forgive me. But he wouldn't find out. Unless someone from Dayton would write to him.

Don't think about it, I told myself. I was finished with the past.

The black crystal earrings, I thought. The ones from Edward Davis. Last Friday, I had tucked them into a side pocket of one of the trunks. I had resolved to bury them in the sand or to throw them into the gulf. Before I'd had a chance to do so, Oscar had taken the trunks to the attic.

Perspiration broke out along my hairline. I couldn't bear the thought of the earrings being anywhere in the house. I stepped back around Andre and went inside. At the cooking table, Nan chopped an onion with her back to me. She disliked me, I thought. She considered me unworthy of Oscar and of Andre. I could not cook, and I did not keep house. She watched my every move and passed judgment. I saw her disdain in the way she looked at me, and I heard it in her tone. I could not begin to imagine what she would do or say if she knew the truth about me.

Nan's movements were jerky, stopping and starting in fits as she handled the knife. The door that opened to the attic stairwell was at the back parlor wall. I walked toward it. A floorboard popped and Nan turned around. Her eyes were red and tears ran down her cheeks.

'Why, you're crying,' I said.

'Am not,' Nan said. 'Don't know why you'd say that.' She put the knife down on the cutting board. 'It's the onion. I'd like to know the woman that can chop an onion and not bawl.' She wiped her cheeks with the backs of her hands. 'I ain't no crybaby, can't nobody say that about me.'

'Of course not.' I couldn't go up to the attic, I thought. Not with Nan watching.

'Oh, all right,' she said. 'Might as well tell you now. Might as well just come out with it. Since you're asking. Sunday's my last day.'

'Pardon?'

'I'm needing a change, let's just you and me let it go at that.'

'I don't understand.'

She didn't say anything.

I said, 'You're leaving us? Quitting?'

'I don't quit nothing, never have. I'm making a change, that's what this is.' She turned around to the counter, her knife a sharp staccato on the cutting board again. Her back to me, she said, 'But I won't have it said that I didn't give fair notice. I was fixing to tell you, this being just Thursday. There's others out there. Maybe one of the older girls at St. Mary's. Or somebody in town that's looking for a change. Someone tired of working in a big, overly fancy house.' Nan's knife stopped; she turned to face me. 'Mr Williams'll have to ask around. There's other women that cook good. I won't have it said that I left you all in a fix.'

'No one will say that about you, Miss Ogden.'

'Good,' she said. 'Because I won't have talk going around. And Frank T. and Wiley'll bring the peas and eggs and such-like, fish and all, that won't change: nobody's going to starve.' She ran the palms of her hands along the sides of her apron, then did it again. 'Let's just leave it at that.'

'Of course.'

'I'll tell Andre on Sunday. Not a minute before. I won't have a fuss made.'

'I understand. We don't want him upset.' He would be upset, though. He was attached to her, but as difficult as the

193

parting would be, I felt a great sense of relief. This house was too small for Nan and me. Soon I'd be free of her judgmental glances and her knowing tone of voice. Just as she would be free of me.

She picked up the cutting board and brushed the diced onion into a skillet.

'Andre will miss you,' I said. 'We all will.'

'Don't want to talk about it.'

'And so we won't.' Some things, I understood, could not bear the weight of words.

As soon as Nan left for the day with her brothers, I put on my sun hat. In the parlor, I opened the door to the attic. Hot air rushed out in waves, and at the top of the staircase, thin slivers of light pierced the darkness.

I hurried up the narrow stairs, the air becoming denser with each step. Support beams held up the roof, and in the gloom it took a few moments before I saw the trunks that were near a side wall between two rafters. I opened one of them, slid my hand into the side pocket and found the black crystal earrings. Struggling to breathe in the dense air, my corset compressing my lungs, I put them in my skirt pocket and closed the trunk. I left the attic, then the house, taking the front veranda steps.

'Where you going?'

I started. It was Andre. He was under the house on his hands and knees holding his spade.

'I'm taking a walk.'

'Now? In the middle of the day? Can I come?'

'No.' My tone was sharp. I gathered myself. 'I'll only be a few minutes. When I return, we'll play the upright before I start dinner.'

194

'"Mary Had a Little Lamb"?'

'Yes.'

He grinned, and before he could say more, I was on the path that led to the sand hills. Should Oscar happen to see me, I would tell him that I'd had a sudden desire to see the beach. The dog with the bushy tail, Bear, came with me and although I told him to go back, he was undeterred and stayed close. The path was muddy from Tuesday's and Wednesday's rain and it was a mistake to have worn my better shoes but I would not turn back.

At the hills, a wispy layer of sand covered the planked road, and in places, hoof prints and the narrow tracks of the wagon wheels were visible. I followed the road, winding through the hills. When I was sure that I couldn't be seen from the house or from the barn, I stopped and took the black crystal earrings out from my skirt pocket.

Each dropped earring had three linked beads and their facets caught the light just as they had when Edward gave them to me two years ago. He had come to Philadelphia, and we were dining in a small restaurant located on a side street off of Delancey Place. 'Happy birthday, my dear,' he'd said as I opened the box. My birthday had been the previous month but I smiled as though it didn't matter. Our liaison had begun a year before, and I had quickly learned to make excuses and allowances for the three- or four-month gaps between visits. I pushed Edward's family from my thoughts and convinced myself that the whims of his business dealings with the Pennsylvania Railroad dictated his trips.

Should we happen to encounter someone he knew, I was introduced as his cousin. 'Friends since we were children,' he'd say. In public, we walked with a respectable distance between us as cousins would do. I maintained this same façade with my friends and said little about Edward. The earrings, though, were something that I could touch, a reminder, along with his weekly letters, that he cared deeply for me and that I was never far from his thoughts.

In the restaurant, I held them to the light. The facets sparkled with shades of pink, lavender, and blue. 'They're exquisite,' I said to Edward across from me at the small table.

'They are, aren't they?' he said. He laid his hand flat on the white linen tablecloth and inched it across the table until it met mine. 'They're from Austria,' he said. He caressed my fingers for a moment, a promise of what would happen later that evening when we were alone. Then, with a quick glance around the room, he withdrew his hand.

On the sand hill road, the wind gusted and my skirt wrapped around my legs. Bear ran on ahead and disappeared from my sight. I couldn't throw the earrings into the surf. They might wash ashore along with the splintered trees torn from river banks and the bottles thrown from ships. I imagined them weeks from today, months even, shining in the sand, drawing attention and someone – Oscar, Andre, Nan, or the Ogden men – finding them.

I got down onto my knees. The planks were warped and uneven, and in some places along the sides, small drifts of sand had formed while in others the wind had scooped out deep hollows. The surface planks were held fast, I saw, nailed to two perpendicular boards below.

I pushed one earring, then the other, through a space between two planks. They fell onto the sand beneath the road. This was the one place where I could bury them and not leave deep footprints in the hills or signs of digging. Here, they would stay covered. The sand might shift, but the road would not.

I rocked back onto my heels. Bear had returned. His brown fur was spiky with water. He looked at me, panting, his head cocked. I got up and followed the road toward the beach. I wanted to be able to tell Oscar at least part of the truth should he ask what I had been doing. Ahead of me, the dog shot off, chasing seagulls near the tide line. At the end of the road, I stopped.

Without Oscar or Andre, the beach was a lonely place, eerie in its vastness with not a soul in sight. 'Bear,' I called, but he didn't hear me. He kept running, scattering the birds.

The tide was high and washed closer to the hills than I had seen before. 'It was the gulf,' Oscar had told me on Tuesday night as we lay together, my hand on his chest. 'How it was never the same.' Unexpected tears filled my eyes. Oscar shoveling coal outside my window as I practiced the piano, his decision to leave Dayton, his letters, the tides pulling him to Galveston, the death of his wife, my liaison, my desperation, all these things had brought me to this place and to him. To change one was to change it all.

Past the breakers five pelicans sat on the water, bobbing on soft swells, their wings folded and their long beaks pointed down as though they were resting. Up the beach, the dog was a distant figure. 'Bear,' I called, blotting my tears with my fingertips.

Oscar will not discover the truth about my past, I told myself. No one will write to him; I will never breathe a word about it.

'I'm leaving,' I called out to Bear. He raised his head, and all at once he started to lope toward me, ignoring the birds, sure of his way.

I turned around and there, on the other side of the sand hills, were three rooftops. Andre was waiting for me, I thought. I had promised him a lesson. I began to walk, the light layer of sand crunching beneath my shoes, the earrings lost beneath the road.

A few minutes before five o'clock, I sent Andre to wash for dinner. 'Your face, too,' I told him. 'There's a bit of dirt on your cheek.' Then, I left the house, went beneath the veranda, and took out a penny from my pocket. It was dull and its rim was flattened in one place as though it were old. I tossed it close to where Andre had been digging. It landed with a soft plop. Treasure, I thought. For him to find someday.

After that, I met Oscar on the path between the house and the barn, and told him Nan had given notice and Sunday was her last day.

'This Sunday?' he said. 'Why? What happened?'

'Nothing. Or at least nothing that I'm aware of. It surprised me, too.'

'And she didn't say why?'

'It seems she wants a change.'

'A change? That's what she said? She's not one for such.'

'She didn't want to talk about it.'

'But she's part of this family. All of the Ogdens are. Have been since I bought the dairy.' He paused. 'I'll talk to her.'

'Oscar, she wants to leave. She was quite emphatic about that. Perhaps you should let her.'

'No,' he said. 'Things are different now, I see that. But we can hardly do without her. Nan knows her way around here.

No, there's something more to this. Likely it's that foolish notion she has about a curse.'

'A curse?'

'That's what she calls it. Thinks she's bad luck for the men that care about her, two of them dying just before she was to marry them.'

'Oh, Oscar.'

'Could be she sees herself as a curse to Andre. I don't know. She's superstitious. Some of the people down in these parts have peculiar notions. Nan's given up the idea of ever marrying.'

'She's told you this?'

'Not me, Bernadette.'

I flinched. Misery crossed his face; he couldn't meet my eyes. Even at the cemetery, her name had not been said. But now it was as though he had given life to her, the woman with whom he had lived, who had borne his son, and who had died carrying his next child.

I was the second wife and always would be. Oscar and Bernadette had shared a life; they had shared confidences. Perhaps Bernadette would have told him the truth about Nan. Perhaps she would have told him that Nan's need to leave had nothing to do with a curse but everything to do with her feelings for Oscar. At the pavilion last Saturday evening, a mix of pain and longing showed in Nan's eyes each time she looked at him. I had seen, too, how she'd held on to his hand when he thanked her for playing the violin. She'd bowed her head when he left to speak to the other musicians and for a moment, I thought she was crying. Then, she raised her head and our eyes met. Although I was on the other side of the pavilion, I felt her resentment. Nan cared for Oscar, but he had chosen a woman very different than she. That was an insult that cut to the quick.

I didn't say this to Oscar. I would not expose Nan in such a way.

I took his hand. 'Talk to her,' I said. 'But, Oscar, you left home and I have done the same.' I paused. 'You and I, we both know what it means to have a fresh start.'

He rubbed his thumb along the back of my hand.

I said, 'If she wants to leave, let her.'

He brought my hand to his lips and kissed my palm.

That evening, while Oscar was in the barn finishing his work, I played Schumann's 'Reverie', wanting its tenderness to send Andre to sleep. Just minutes ago, I had put him to bed and when I said goodnight, he told me that I smelled good. For an instant, I hadn't known where I was, the crucifix over the bed and the photograph of Oscar and Bernadette blurring and falling away. The purity of Andre's few words had astonished me. This was why women smiled at the mention of their children's names, I thought. Mothers carried the memories of sweet words spoken from the heart.

Years ago, Mr Brand, my piano teacher, pounded on his chest and told me to reach into my heart and feel the music. Now I played Chopin's 'Raindrop Prelude' for Oscar, believing he could hear it in the barn. The notes began as the soft tapping of a rain shower, innocent but with a hint of passion that grew, gathered, and rose until it was a storm of passion. The music thundered, a crescendo, then diminished as the notes returned to a soft tap but with the passion still an undercurrent. By the time I played the last chords, Oscar was in the doorway.

Later, the bedroom in darkness and the two of us content,

Oscar told me he wanted to have our picture made. 'We'll go to Harper's on Market Street,' he said. 'We should have done it last week, you looking so pretty in that blue suit of yours. And the hat with all the feathers. We'll go Saturday.'

He didn't mention the earrings that I had worn. Perhaps he hadn't noticed them on our wedding day. 'A photograph,' I said. 'I'd like that very much.' I ran my finger along his cheek and over the stubble of his beard. 'But not in this heat, I couldn't bear that wool suit. Let's wait. As soon as the weather cools, why don't we go then?'

'That'll be the middle of October. Won't hardly count as a wedding picture.'

'Mr Williams,' I said, 'a woman is a bride for longer than a day.'

He laughed, an easy rumble that started in his chest. The sound of it filled me with pleasure. Happiness. Not derived from playing with my ensemble, or from tickets to the theatre, nor from dining at a fine hotel. But from this: being with Oscar and making plans for the future.

CHAPTER TWELVE

Storm Warning

Oscar, he tried talking me out of making a change. He went on about how the house could hardly get along without me, how nobody cooked like me, and that Andre would miss me sorely. That was this morning, Friday. He'd left the barn and got to the house not more than a handful of minutes after Wiley and Frank T. had dropped me off at the steps. I didn't even have the stove lit, only the kerosene lamps. It was like he'd been waiting for me with his arguments all laid out ahead of time. Likely he had been, Mrs Williams telling him my news. He asked me to come out on the veranda and that was where we did our talking. I said I needed a change, but he didn't listen to none of that. 'Nan,' he said. 'Is it your wages? Is that it?'

That made me head for the door. Them questions were an insult and I had breakfast to cook. He took hold of my arm, stopping me. 'Didn't mean it that way,' he said. 'I'm just looking for some kind of reason.'

Well, I thought. If he couldn't see how him and Mrs Williams mooning for each other during the light of day was enough to turn a person's belly, then he was just going to have to stay in the dark. If he couldn't figure out that water and oil, meaning me and her, didn't mix, he was just going to have to stumble along in ignorance. But the hardest thing for me to take was Andre, his little face lighting up as big as a bonfire every time she threw him the bittiest nod of affection.

I said to Oscar, 'A person needs a change once in a while, and that's me at this particular time. Now let's leave it at that, there's not another word to say.' I made a point of looking at his hand on my arm. He let go, and when he did, a wave of sadness came over me. As wrong as it was, I wanted him to hold on to me. I wanted him to tell me he'd be the one to miss me most. There was even a part of me that wanted him to tell me he'd married the wrong woman.

He didn't say none of that. Instead, he did as I asked, not saying a word more, and I did the same. I cooked and tidied the house, all the while studying the clock on the fireplace mantle, wanting the hands to turn fast so that it'd hurry up and get to Sunday afternoon, ending this. Instead, it was like the clock was broke, the second hand taking deep, long breaths before deciding to lurch forward. All week I could hardly bear the idea of telling Andre I was leaving. I just knew he'd cry and that I would too. The idea of not seeing him every morning and feeling his arms around my neck put an even bigger hole in my heart. Without knowing why I did it, I fussed at him and told him he was in my way. I saw the puzzlement in his eyes; I saw how I stepped hard on his feelings. But I couldn't stop it. My misery turned me into a sharp-tongued woman.

Mrs Williams, on the other hand, was like a thorny weed that surprised the world when it sprouted a soft-petal flower. She was finally climbing down from her mountain top and seeing Oscar for the fine man he was. For the life of me, I didn't know how it happened, but as soon as Oscar and the boys came in for breakfast on Tuesday morning, her still in bed, I knew things were different. Oscar looked plenty worn out like he hadn't done much sleeping, but his eyes shined, his gladness showing. Later, Mrs Williams drifted out to the table long after the men had had their breakfast, the dishes washed and me at the ironing board. She took up playing the piano, the music saying things about the doings between a man and a woman that shouldn't be aired. The thing that simmered between them had finally bubbled up, taking them both. If it hadn't been for Andre, I would have walked out the door right then.

And Oscar thought it had to do with wages. That was a hurt I'd be a long time forgetting. I played them words of his over and over as I did my chores, that clock on the mantle tormenting me. I thought the day would never end. The air was heavy with a wet heat, the kind that made my skin itch. It didn't help none that the surf made a pounding sound with pauses in between, like the beat of a drum for a funeral march. Bernadette had told me about these marches. Processions, she called them. The Negroes over in Louisiana did such things. Someone beat on a drum real slow with all the mourners following behind the wagon that carried the coffin.

'For pity's sake,' I'd told her. 'A drum? That don't hardly seem fitting, not to me it don't.'

'Ah, Nan,' she said, them dark eyes of hers all cloudy from remembering her childhood. 'It isn't like that. That drum reaches right here.' Bernadette put her hand on her chest and thumped on it slow. 'It untangles the knots and helps people cry,' she said.

Maybe for people in Louisiana, but this was Texas and the sound of the surf rubbed my nerves. The wind did, too. It came from the mainland, blowing through the house. Andre's clothes that hung on pegs fell on the floor, the lid on the stove's chimney clinked up and down, and the fireplace hooted, the wind coming down it. I dropped a cooking spoon two times and when I poured a glass of milk for Andre after his nap, I misjudged and slopped some of it over the side. It took me for ever to get supper cooked even though it wasn't nothing more than beans and rice, boiled shrimp, bread, and a vanilla cake. It came as a relief when Frank T. and Wiley finally came clunking up the veranda steps. Friday was nearly over. I took off my apron and hung it up. Come Sunday, I'd be taking my apron home with me. Come Monday, somebody else would be doing the laundry, and that I had to admit, I wasn't overly sorry about.

'How do?' I heard Frank T. say to Mrs Williams. She was sitting on the front veranda with one of her books. A novel, she'd called it like I'd asked. The wind wasn't all that much out front since it still came from the back and the house blocked it. Andre was with her, playing with his building blocks on the floor. I heard Wiley say, 'Howdy, ma'am.'

She said her niceties, like only she could, saying how it was a pleasure to see them and how very kind it was of them to bring the ice, the newspapers, and the box of groceries. I stayed in the kitchen and tied my bonnet. I didn't care to watch them two make fools of themselves, gawking at Mrs Williams. She had taken to loosening her corset some and instead of that spoiling her figure, it improved it, giving her a softness and making her bosom fuller somehow.

'Tide's running high,' Frank T. said now. He was dawdling,

just to stretch out the time to be with her. 'Thought we was going to have to take the ridge road but we got through.'

'Oh my,' Mrs Williams said.

'Can we go to the beach and look?' Andre said.

'Wiley,' I called out from the kitchen. 'You dripping all over everything?'

He came in with the ice, ducking his head like he figured I'd light into him but I didn't say a word. All I wanted was to get on home. I gave the kitchen one last look to make sure I hadn't left anything undone. I hadn't. I went outside and right then and there, I nearly stopped breathing.

The gulf was nothing but a mass of high-rising swells, pushing forward like there was a giant rippling sea snake just below the top, the kind of monster Daddy used to tell us about when me and the boys was little and had misbehaved. But these swells were real, like nothing I'd seen before. This past July, we'd had us a bad storm. The water had been all churned up, the waves curled up as tall as a grown man, and the tide came close to the foot of the sand hills. I hadn't liked that, not one little bit. But these here were swells, not waves. They made the gulf look raised up like it was higher than the land.

'A big blow's out there,' Wiley said. He was on the veranda now.

'Good Lord,' I said.

He didn't say nothing. He was fixed on them swells out there, his eyes all squinted up. I said, 'You sure?'

'Yep.'

'But the wind,' I said. 'It's coming from the other way. From the mainland. And these here clouds, they're as white as can be. There ain't the first sign of rain.'

'It'll change.'

'But—'

'It'll change.'

My lungs squeezed up.

'Are you talking about a tornado?' Mrs Williams said. She had gone straight as a ruler. Andre was on his feet now with his head back, looking directly up at Wiley.

'No, ma'am,' Wiley said. 'Don't much get 'em here. We ain't like the Panhandle.' He tried to look at her, but I could tell she made him nervous. He had taken to tugging on one end of his mustache. 'A big blow's in the gulf,' he said. 'A hurricane.'

'Good heavens.'

Frank T. said, 'Wiley's got a feel for weather, always has, him being born in the middle of the '75 storm. He's got an eye for clouds and waves, knows their meaning. He can sniff the air and tell what's going to happen. Wiley knew it first thing this morning.'

'Nobody told me,' I said.

'That's 'cause you're scared of storms.'

There was no call for Frank T. to say that, not in front of Mrs Williams. He said, 'By the time we left the city, folks were talking, saying how the warning flags were up at the weather station.'

'Warning flags?' Mrs Williams said.

'For the ships. Rough seas and all.'

'Does Oscar know?' she said. She was on her feet now, her hand to her bosom like her heart was leaping. 'Mr Ogden,' she said. She was talking to Wiley. 'Did you tell him?'

'Andre,' I said. 'You go on now and play in the yard.' He didn't need to hear none of this.

'But, Miss Nan—'

'You heard her, bud,' Frank T. said. 'Go on.'

Andre muttered something but shuffled off, us all watching as he went down the steps, one at a time. Close to the bottom, he threw his arms back and jumped. The dogs that had been under the house took up with him as he meandered toward the barn. Likely he could still hear us when Mrs Williams said to Wiley, 'Mr Ogden. Does Oscar know?'

She was scared, anybody could tell that, her blue eyes were all wide. She was impatient too. Her hands balled up like it took everything she had to keep from shaking the words out of Wiley. But talking had changed for Wiley when the cow kicked out some of his teeth. He'd become a man that picked his words, trying to stay clear of the ones that made him lisp extra bad.

Frank T. stepped in for Wiley. 'Yep, we surely did,' he said. 'Told Oscar how it'll be here tomorrow night, maybe after dark. That gives us plenty of time. We'll get the milk delivered tomorrow long before the wind starts up. Ain't a thing to worry about. Especially up here on this ridge.'

'Everyone refers to this ridge, but I don't see it,' Mrs Williams said. 'It all feels flat and low to me.'

'Begging your pardon, Mrs Williams, but it's here all right. Might be a gradual slope, might not leave you winded to climb but it's the highest point on the island. Eight feet up. So don't you worry none. This ain't the first big blow to come our way, I can tell you that. We're old hands at this, us being from here. We know what to do, these things being mostly rain and a hard wind.'

Doubt spread over Mrs Williams' face. 'That's all?' she said. 'Rain and wind?'

'Yes, ma'am,' Frank T. said. 'That's about the size of it.'

I could hardly believe my ears. Frank T. was flat-out lying. He was near as bad as Oscar, sheltering this woman. Big blows could take off roofs. People like us that didn't live on the ridge might get a flood, waist deep and with a current so strong it could knock down a grown man. We didn't call them big blows for nothing. But could be she needed sheltering, her not being from here. A scared-silly woman didn't do nobody no favors, and right now the doubt and fear on Mrs Williams' face had eased up some. She'd fastened her gaze on the barn like she was thinking of Oscar and how he made everything all right.

'Tomorrow night,' she said. 'Over a day's notice. Unlike a tornado.' She was talking to Frank T. now. 'Those, I can tell you, are frightening. They appear from nowhere.'

'You all get them up there in Ohio?'

'We can. Particularly in the spring. During the summer months we have electrical storms. They can be quite violent. Windows vibrate from the impact of thunder, and when I was a child, a lightning strike split our neighbors' tree in half and burned down part of their carriage house. I don't care for storms but in Ohio, well, one can expect them during the warm months.'

Frank T.'s face knotted up like he was trying to sort through her fast-talking Yankee words. Wiley stepped over Andre's blocks and went to the west side of the veranda. There, he looked toward the bayou that was a mile behind the house.

'Yes, ma'am,' Frank T. finally said. 'If there's one thing you can count on, it's summer storms.'

'You two fixing to lallygag all day?' I said to my brothers. This talk about bad weather was working on my nerves but that wasn't the only thing. I was going home, and I'd sent Andre off before telling him goodbye. I wanted to tell him I

209

was sorry I'd been peevish with him. More than anything, I wanted to put my arms around him and hold him.

'Wagon's hitched, ain't it?' Frank T. said. 'We're waiting on you.'

'Then why's this box of groceries still sitting out here instead of sitting in the house?'

He picked up the box and took it inside. Two more days, that was all I had left. Come Sunday, I'd walk down these steps knowing I wouldn't be back. I could hardly picture it, didn't want to. But maybe this storm would make it easier. If it came in tomorrow night, by Sunday morning there'd be nothing to it but the mess it'd left behind. There might be fences to mend, and roofs to fix. If there were leaks, there'd be floors to mop. Could be it'd turn everyone so busy, maybe even Mrs Williams, that Sunday would be over before I knew it. Not that I wanted a storm, I didn't. But if there was to be one, it'd take my mind off of the hurt in my chest.

'Mrs Williams,' I said, nodding my goodbye.

'Miss Ogden,' she said. And then I went on down the steps. Two more days. And a storm to help me get through them.

Us Ogdens weren't ones to talk while eating; we didn't do like Oscar did. Most usually we just ate, me and the boys on one side of the table and Mama and Daddy on the other. Talking came later when the men were on the veranda with their pipes, and me and Mama washed the dishes. But tonight, with Wiley's storm fixed in our minds, Mama couldn't hold back. She saw everything that needed doing to get ready. There were the hog and piglets to think about, and there were the hens in the chicken coop. 'Need to be ready to move them,' Mama said. 'If the water comes up. Don't relish the idea of keeping them on the veranda but if that's what we have to do, that's what we'll do.' She directed this to Daddy. She wanted to live on the ridge but Daddy said no, he had to be close to his dock and fishing boat. We were two hundred feet from the bayou, and for him, that was too far.

Mama said, 'Have to bring in all them trays of seedlings from under the house, and I don't even want to think what the wind'll do to my garden.'

'Yep,' Daddy said. 'Fishing won't be worth a dang for a day or two after the storm is over, not even in the bay.'

'We'll get by,' Mama said, putting aside her laments. 'Always have.'

That was true. We were island people, all of us, but Daddy was born and bred here. Mama's roots went way back, her grandparents on both sides being island people. Daddy's people got here when he was five. Andre's age.

I scooted my food around the plate. My throat was tight and not only because of the storm. I hadn't told Mama and Daddy about my intention to make a change, and here it was, Friday. All week it worked at me. I wanted to say, 'Come Monday, I won't be working for Oscar.' But every time I tried, the words stuck, me knowing it'd kick up a fuss. If there was one thing I didn't like, it was a fuss.

At the table, Daddy ran his chunk of bread through the grease that pooled around his beans, and beside me, Frank T. worked on his flounder. Wiley poured himself some milk from the pitcher and downed it in one long gulp. And there was Mama directly across, her eyes boring into me. She had put her worries to the side and was speculating, I could tell, her just now noticing my puny appetite.

I took a bite of flounder. The carrying of a secret was a

211

burdensome thing. Daddy said something about letting out the line on his boat and checking the knot. Frank T. said he might ride up the island a ways, just to let folks know about the weather. I felt Mama looking at me, seeing clear through. I dabbed at my mouth with my napkin like I was Mrs Williams. All this table talk, it was throwing me. 'I'm making a change,' I blurted out. 'Come Monday.'

'How's that?' Frank T. said.

In a hurry to get it out, I said, 'I've already told Oscar, Mrs Williams, too. I'm in need of a change, and that's what I intend to do. Make a change.'

That kicked up a fuss all right, nobody getting my meaning at first, everybody saying, 'What?' and me having to lay it out flat on the table. 'I ain't quitting, just leaving,' I said, trying to make that part clear.

'I'd call that quitting,' Daddy said. 'And Oscar nearly being family. You don't walk out on family, leastways the Ogdens don't.' From there the fuss took a new direction, Daddy asking if this change of mine would pay me ten dollars a week.

'There're others out there that pay good,' I said, but these were just words meant to make me feel better. No other place would be like working at Oscar's. I knew my way around there good. I didn't like the idea of going into the city, knocking on the doors of strangers and asking if they were in need of help. I'd never had to do such before. But I liked having money of my own. It gave me a solid feeling. I saved most of it but spent some, buying buttons to spruce up an old dress and picking out high-quality material for a new one. Three months ago, I had a pair of shoes made. I bought for Mama, too, extra coffee because she had a taste for it and bottled remedies for her back pains, her needing it by the spoonful.

Frank T. made some sassy remark about how the sweet-natured, pretty Mrs Williams would surely miss my bossy ways.

'Leave Nan alone,' Wiley said.

'I'm only saying what's true,' Frank T. said.

'Boys,' Mama said. 'Stop it, won't have bickering, not at my table. Bad enough there's a storm coming. Supper's over and there's things that need doing. Now out. Everybody. Out.' I started to get up. 'Not you,' she said. 'Sit down – the dishes can wait.'

I did, me and her not saying anything, just listening as the men left, their footsteps making the floor shake. I knew what was coming. Mama would remind me about my promise to Bernadette as she'd laid sweating on her deathbed, Bernadette holding my hand until I said I'd look after Andre. After refreshing my memory about that, Mama likely would point out how Andre might have a new mother but Mrs Williams was still getting her bearings, her and Oscar being married just eight days. She ain't like us, I figured Mama would say and then she'd recommend the merits of me living up to my responsibilities.

She said, 'This notion of making a change. Whose idea was it first?'

'Mine.'

She gave me a long look. I held it, not backing down because what I said was true. Then all at once, a kind of sadness settled over Mama. Her shoulders slumped as she took to studying the white dishes on the table. It wasn't like she was thinking they were dishes that needed washing, but more like she was seeing the scratches made from all the years of scrubbing. There were chips too, mostly on the edges. The dishes were older

213

than Frank T. by a year, and he was twenty-six. Mama bought them a week before her and Daddy got married. Daddy had given her the money.

She said, 'Nan, you're a grown woman. Twenty-two years old. When I was that, I was married, had me a baby and was thinking about the next one. But you, you've had more than your share of hard times, losing Oakley, then Joe Pete, and now, well, now this.' Mama stopped. She knew, I thought. Without me ever saying a word, she knew there was a powerful ache inside of me from wanting Oscar Williams.

She slid her hand across the table toward me, working her way past the empty platters and bowls. I did the same with mine, meeting hers, feeling the swelled-up knuckles and knobs on each finger, and knowing my hands would get the same way, hard work doing that.

'Honey,' Mama said. 'There are times when leaving is called for. That's how I see it. So you go on with this. You've given enough to that man.'

I went to bed, Mama's words running through my head. I would have given more, but things had a way of not working out, leastways not like how I wanted. I was a curse to the men that cared for me. As for Oscar, he'd never carried such thoughts about me, not with Catherine Williams likely fixed in his mind since he was a boy.

I wasn't the only one restless that night. Everybody got up early. Three-thirty in the morning and Daddy was moving the wood pile up to the veranda. The coffee not even perked yet and there was Mama, using that wood to build a makeshift holding pen for the hog and her piglets. 'Nan, honey, the bayou's overflowing a tad,' Mama told me when I came out on the veranda. I held up the lantern and there it was, water glistening in the salt grass, not more than a handful of yards from the front of the house.

This storm of Wiley's, it was on its way. Storms pushed the tides in, that was the first sign. Overhead, there wasn't the first hint of the moon or even the bittiest flicker of a star, the night sky was that clouded. The wind had picked up but it still blew in from the mainland instead of from the gulf. I hurried off to the chicken coop to gather eggs, and them birds were a flutter of nerves, squawking and pecking at my hand. When I left the coop, I stepped into a thin layer of bayou water, it had come up that fast. By the time I got to the house, my boots were muddy and water had seeped in through the seams along the soles. My stockings were wet but there was no time to change, the boys were waiting for me in the wagon. My poncho folded up over my left arm, I handed Frank T. the basket of eggs and climbed up. We were in a mighty hurry, nobody had to tell the other that. The boys wanted to get the milking done, the wagons loaded, and the deliveries made before the weather turned rough.

Leastways the ground was dry once we got a little ways from our place, but that didn't make the horses, Blaze and Mike, feel much better. They tossed their heads like they wanted to shake off the wind, but there was no getting rid of it. It was a nervous wind, jumpy and jerky.

It made me the same way. At Oscar's, I burned my fingers when I lit the second lamp. I boiled the grits and cracked over a dozen eggs, getting ready to scramble them before I thought to start the coffee. It didn't help that I had to cook in my bare feet. My muddy boots were on the veranda, and my stockings were drying in the oven. Oscar and my brothers came in

215

and sat down at the table, and nobody said nothing about my nakedness. Any other time Frank T. would call me a wild Indian or other such nonsense. But not today. In the lamplight, the men were shadowed up with worry and nearly too twitchy to eat.

'Tide's high at the beach,' Oscar told me between mouthfuls. That meant the boys would have to take the ridge road into Galveston. I didn't even think about eating with them, I got busy making sack lunches. They had just downed the last of their coffee when the rain started up, coming in a fit and drumming on the tin roof. It made us look up at the ceiling like we could see through it, and then Frank T. said to me, 'Tide's more than high. It's clear to the sand hills. Beach is swamped.'

That made my belly flutter; it made the island feel like nothing but a narrow spit of land. Wiley shot Frank T. a look that said, Don't you say one more thing. That made me wonder what else they weren't telling me. We'd had high tides and overflows before, plenty of them, the wind doing that. Or sometimes the overflows happened when we had hard rains, the soil the kind that didn't hold water. But this was different, and everybody knew it. There was something in the air, something big and alive. But folks in the city needed their milk, that didn't ever change.

The boys left for the city wearing their ponchos. Daylight finally showed itself, puny and thin. It quit raining, and by the time Andre got up, the sky had brightened some with a few patches of blue over the gulf. But there were still dark clouds piled up, and yesterday's swells had turned into tall, gray waves. Mean waves. They roared as they fought against the north wind from the mainland.

216

Them waves was the reason I gave Andre an extra-long good-morning hug. I needed to take in that little-boy smell of his, sweetness with a bit of mustiness right below that. 'Miss Nan,' he said. He nuzzled close, his words slurred from sleep, His hair poked up in every direction. I made big circles on his back with my hand, taking in the feel of his ribs and his knobby backbone. Then all at once, I had to push back tears, the idea of leaving him hitting me hard. He pulled away from me. 'Ma'am!' he said.

There she was, dressed in her green skirt and shirtwaist with layers of lace, and me in my bare feet. This was early for Mrs Williams. I hadn't heard her stirring in the washroom, but the rain had started up again and was plenty loud. Andre went to her. She put her hand on his head and cupped the back of it. He scooted closer.

'Good morning, Andre,' she said, like he was a grown person. Then she said good morning to me, her eyebrows shooting high when she saw my bare feet.

'The bayou's overflowing,' I said. I didn't know why I felt the need to explain myself but I did. I had to raise my voice to do it, the rain came down that loud. 'My boots and stockings took a soaking.'

'Pardon?'

'The ground's covered at home.'

'From the rain?'

'It wasn't raining then. It's from the bayou. Like I said. It's overflowing and going where it don't belong. It's clear to my house.'

The color dropped right out of her cheeks. 'Is it deep?' she said. 'What about your home? Will it get inside? And here? Will it reach us here?'

'Just covering the ground, like I said. Maybe an inch or two. And we're up on stilts. Six feet. As for here, this ridge is plenty high. Same for the house.'

'Miss Nan,' Andre said. He was still propped up against Mrs Williams, and her hand played with his cowlick, trying to pat it down. 'Can we go look?'

'No, sir, not in this rain. Now you go on and get yourself dressed. Use the chamber pot, but, young man, I won't have any fancy tricks, you hear me? Aim. Aim good. Now scoot.'

Mrs Williams pressed her lips, and at first I thought it was because of what I'd said about Andre's aim, but that weren't so. She had just gotten a look at the waves out the windows. Andre scampered off, his fingers trailing along the wall likely leaving smudge marks, but she didn't take no notice. She was at the middle window now, blinking those blue eyes of hers. Maybe she was trying to make them tall waves out there fit with her notion of Ohio storms.

'Miss Ogden,' she said. Her voice was low. I had to get close to hear her over the rain. 'Have your brothers left for the city?'

'A good while ago. They should be making their deliveries by now.'

'And no one was alarmed by these waves? Or the rain? They weren't concerned about this sky?'

'They remarked on it,' I said. 'Said how the tide's clear to the sand hills. But children need their milk. Don't much matter if the beach is swamped and they have to take the ridge road. Folks count on my brothers just like they count on Mr Williams and his cows. Especially on Saturday, milk not being delivered again until Monday.'

'I see.' Mrs Williams pulled in some air. 'So no one is all

that concerned. At least not enough to cancel the deliveries. And what you said about the bayou. How it's out of its banks. Is anyone alarmed about that?'

I could tell what she wanted. Mrs Williams wanted me to say that there were laid-out rules for storms and that this one was doing just like it should. She wanted me to be like Frank T. and tell her we were old hands at this. We were, nobody could say different. But that didn't mean we turned a blind eye to high tides and riled-up waves. It didn't mean I liked storms, even if yesterday I thought it might keep me from thinking about Sunday being my last day. I was sorry I'd had that notion. I didn't like the feel of this air. I didn't like seeing the bayou sloshing close to my house, and I didn't like that the beach was swamped. But that didn't mean I was scared, because I wasn't.

'Ain't nothing new about this storm,' I said. 'Not for us. And like I said, what's happening at the bayou, we call that an overflow.'

'Oh yes,' Mrs Williams said. 'An overflow. I remember now.' Her tone had lifted around the edges. 'Oscar mentioned that on the day I arrived in Galveston. Overflows cleanse the city. They're the reason the sidewalks are elevated and the houses are on brick pillars. It's a common occurrence in the city, it seems, when it storms. All the more true since the beach there doesn't have sand hills.' She looked again toward the gulf and then at me. 'Not that this appears to be a storm. Not in the true sense. There isn't any lightning or thunder, and see, it's stopped raining. Perhaps this is the worst.' She was close to smiling now. 'Miss Ogden, to be frank, an Ohio electrical storm is far more frightening than this.'

219

'Then I'm purely glad I don't live up there,' I said. Her smile went away and that suited me fine. She didn't know one bitty thing about hurricanes, and I wasn't going to say another word. She didn't want to know. And there was another reason for clamping my mouth shut. It could be she was right. This might be all we'd get. Storms were known to play themselves out or maybe they went somewhere else, on down south to Corpus Christi or east to New Orleans. So I went back to the kitchen and did like I'd been doing since Oscar had married this woman. I scrambled more eggs and got the second round of breakfast on the table. When Mrs Williams wasn't looking, I pulled my stockings out of the oven and stuck them into my apron pocket.

The rain came in squalls, starting and stopping. At the table, Andre chirped away about playing out in the rain, the fun of puddles and making mud pies. 'But you'll get so dirty,' Mrs Williams said, and I said that was what little boys did best. 'They play in the mud and come into the house to shake it all off.' She didn't say nothing after that but went back to eating, taking tiny bites and prissy sips of tea. I got busy washing the skillet.

Out the window, the blue patches in the sky had been overtaken by fast-moving dark clouds. It made the house gloomy. I watched them clouds as I scrubbed, my hands in the dishwater. The wind whipped around the house and the floorboards shook under my feet. Most usually Oscar had turned the cows out in the pasture by now, but not today. He'd kept them in and that meant he was filling their feed troughs. By now the bayou could be washing over the bottom veranda step at my house. Mama and Daddy, I figured, were pumping fresh water before the well flooded. I thought about Mrs Williams, too, my back to her as she ate. She arranged things to make them suit her. Her story about an Ohio storm that split open one tree and burned down a carriage house was nothing, not to me. I didn't know where Ohio sat but I figured it didn't have water on all sides.

Galveston was my home and you won't catch me saying one bad word against it. But I remembered from my school-going days the map of the United States. It was pinned up on the wall by the chalkboard. Texas was big, like it deserved to be. It outshined every other state by a mile. But a person had to look hard to find Galveston. It was off to the side of Texas, just a sliver of land in the Gulf of Mexico. From that, a person wouldn't know it was twenty-seven miles long and up to three miles wide in the middle. They wouldn't know it held buildings and people. Sitting at my desk in the back row, I'd raised my hand and after a while the schoolteacher, Miss Marquart, called on me.

'What's keeping us from floating away?' I said.

'God's will.'

'That's all?'

I got a whipping for asking a disrespectful question about God, and I figured I deserved it since what I'd said came out wrong. After that, I didn't raise my hand no more. I tried to quit looking at that map: it was a disturbance. But I was drawn to it. Mama told me later that Galveston had long roots and at the time, I took that to mean it was attached to the bottom of the gulf. That had eased my mind, but we were still a low-lying island with water on all sides. Maybe Mrs Williams didn't understand that, her not being from here. But ignorance didn't change nothing. The bayou and the gulf were high, and Wiley said a big blow was coming. It might not hit us directly but somebody was in for it. What was out there in the gulf wasn't no Ohio storm.

This rain, it worked on my nerves and made my skin stand up. Twenty men banging away on the tin roof with hammers couldn't be louder, and it didn't help none that the air steamed more than ever. The clock on the mantle showed half past ten so I put my hands to work and made corn pone for noon dinner. I took care as I measured out the cornmeal and baking powder but when I mixed in the lard, I couldn't remember if I'd added salt. Mrs Williams didn't know nothing about cooking but I was glad she wasn't here to see me nibble the dry mixture, tasting for salt. She was on the front veranda, the house still blocking the wind. She probably hoped to catch sight of Oscar, that being her favorite thing to do of late. Andre, barefoot and his short pants rolled up above his knees, played in the rain. He was jumping off the veranda steps and landing in puddles, making a mess but having a grand time.

I added a half-measure of salt, stirred in the milk, patted the dough into cakes, and laid them in greased baking pans. I'd bake them, I decided, instead of frying. I didn't have it in me to stand over a hot skillet with sizzling butter popping every which way. I worked the kitchen pump to rinse my hands, its squeak setting my teeth on edge, adding to the rain, the wind whistling around the corners of the house, and the drafty sound in the chimney. I didn't know how many times I'd told Oscar the pump needed a good dose of oil but them ears of his plugged up when it suited him. I'd have to tell him again. Then it came back to me, how I wouldn't be here after tomorrow.

It startled me, this forgetting. But it wasn't a real forgetting, not with this ache fixed in my chest. It was like I was between two places: what used to be and how it was now. Maybe this was because I never thought it would end like this, me packing my apron and turning this house over to another woman. Not after all that had happened, not after all I had seen.

Nearly a year ago, on the first day of October, Sister Camillus and Sister Vincent from St. Mary's washed Bernadette in the bedroom while Mama tried to talk Oscar out of burying her in her wedding dress. 'Oscar honey,' she'd said, 'Bernadette wouldn't want you seeing her in it, not this way.' Neighbor women from all directions were here and had gathered on the veranda. They'd brought platters of ham, cakes, and pies, and I'd laid the food out on the kitchen table. 'It's a mighty grievous thing,' I heard Aunt Mattie say. I was inside, and her words came to me through the windows. 'Especially when there was a baby on the way. And Mr Williams, well, that man carries a shine for Bernadette, marriage hasn't dulled that one bit.' They all agreed and said how it broke their hearts to think of it. That wasn't the only thing that broke their hearts. There was Andre, motherless at four years old. All that sadness, and in the hallway, I heard Oscar say to Mama, 'If I have to do it myself, I want Bernadette in her wedding dress.'

Leastways, Andre didn't hear none of them, him staying at St. Mary's. But them words of Oscar's stuck in my mind as I polished the cookstove from top to bottom. When I finished that, I washed down the walls and then the windows.

Without Oscar coming right out and asking, the morning after Bernadette was laid to rest, I rode with my brothers to this house and at the foot of the veranda steps, I climbed down from the wagon and let myself in. I cooked and cleaned, and saw to Andre. After two weeks, I found an envelope on the kitchen table. There were ten dollar bills in it. That money surprised me; I'd been helping out, not working for pay. But the big surprise was what was printed on the envelope. I didn't care nothing about reading but I knew what the letters spelled. Miss Ogden. Until then, I was Nan. I put the envelope in my pocket and that night I showed it to Mama. 'Bernadette's gone and won't be coming back,' she said when she opened it and saw all the bills. 'But Oscar can't say them words, not yet. But he knows it, knows he needs you. This is his way of saying it.' Mama pointed to the printing on the envelope. 'And this here is his way of setting the terms. You understand what he's saying, don't you, you being a young woman and him a widower. He don't want no gossip. That's why you're Miss Ogden and honey, he's Mr Williams now.'

Oscar was hollow-eyed and unshaven during the first three months. He didn't sleep good. I made up the bed in the mornings and them scratchy-new sheets were a tangled mess. I figured he sat up most nights, because every morning I found an old coffee can on the back veranda with the burned-down ends of cigarettes in it. Every day I threw out the cigarettes and put back the can. Oscar had Frank T. and Wiley bring home bottles of beer along with the usual supplies, but I never found the empty bottles. Likely, Oscar buried them somewhere. At noon, him, me, and Andre ate dinner with nobody saying much. But when it was just me and Andre, I kept up a chatter. That little boy needed to hear a lively voice. Me, too. Without Bernadette, this house had lost its heart.

I guessed it was the nuns at St. Mary's that reminded Oscar he had a child to see to. I didn't know what happened but on the second Sunday in January, he came home from church and it was like he started to try again. Somebody at St. Mary's had trimmed his brown hair so that it didn't hang over the back of his collar no more. He had a smile for Andre and one for me. He told the three orphan boys he'd brought back with him that he'd see them in the barn; he had something he had to do first. Oscar went into the washroom and shaved his face and neck clear down to bare skin. He even shaved off his mustache that he'd had for as long as I'd known him. Without it, he was a different man, younger somehow. When it was time to load Andre in the wagon for their trip to the cemetery, Oscar swung that little boy so high that it set Andre laughing. It was such a pleasing sound that Oscar laughed too, a rusty sound at first. I was on the veranda and he glanced my way. There was a lightness in his eyes but when he saw it was me, that light dimmed. I wasn't Bernadette. I thought he'd fall back into his sorrowfulness but Andre, sitting on the buckboard, wouldn't let him. 'Daddy!' he said, and that word was a bubble of shiny happiness. It lifted Oscar, I saw that. He gathered himself a lopsided smile and got up on the wagon.

Now, outside the window, the gulf was riled and the dark clouds moved fast. Things could get bad. But this time tomorrow, it'd be over. Storms did that; they moved on and went someplace else. Like I had to do.

I shook off my low feeling and put the corn pone into the oven. I gritted my teeth against the squeak in the pump, filled pots with water, and hauled the pots to the stove. Andre was still outside having himself a high time in the rain. Noon dinner wasn't too far off and he was going to need a bath whether he liked it or not. And he wasn't having it in the washroom;

he'd track mud all over this house if I allowed that. No, sir, he was going to have his bath right here in the kitchen and he'd take it in the laundry washtub. I had just emptied the first pot of hot water into the tub when Mrs Williams came in from the veranda.

She got herself a cup from the shelf and poured some tea from the teakettle, my brother finally bringing her some from the city. She'd made this pot earlier but likely it was lukewarm. I'd set it off the stove a good while ago. She didn't say nothing about it, though. Neither was there the first question about all the water simmering on the stove, she didn't ask about the laundry washtub on the floor by the table. Her mind looked to be elsewhere; her plucked-thin eyebrows were all knotted up. It was like she didn't even know I was there. A tight feeling started up in my belly.

Mrs Williams put the teakettle back on the counter, and got the milk pitcher out of the icebox. She gussied up her tea with the milk, then added a teaspoon of sugar from the sugar bowl on the table, some of the sugar spilling around the cup. She didn't look to notice that circle of splattered sugar. Her gaze was fixed on the front windows.

Something told me I should look out the window too. Something bad was happening out there. But I couldn't get myself to look.

Mrs Williams didn't sit down. She kept standing, stirring the tea, her spoon clinking from side to side. 'From what I understand,' she said after a while, 'the house is on stilts as a precaution.' Her voice was flat; it gave me the shivers. She said, 'The ridge has never flooded.'

'Other than the time it did,' I said.

She gave me a sharp look.

226

'It came up in the storm of '71.' My mouth had gone as dry as a rock. I swallowed. 'Mama and Daddy, they saw it.'

'But you never have?'

'No.' I needed to look out the windows but I couldn't get my head to turn. My neck was froze up.

Mrs Williams kept stirring her tea. She said, 'I just saw a rather unusual thing. Or at least it is for me. It happened while I was on the veranda. At first I thought my eyes were playing tricks; I couldn't believe what I was seeing. But it wasn't a trick.' She tapped her spoon two times on the lip of the cup. She said, 'Streams of rushing water are coming through the sand hills. Through the passes, I mean. From the beach.' She put her spoon on the counter. 'Miss Ogden? Should we be concerned?'

My neck came unstuck. Out the window, through the rain and past Andre stomping in mud puddles, I saw water from the gulf fan out on our side of the sand hills. It mashed down the grass, coming this way.

'Miss Ogden?'

I opened my mouth but nothing came out.

'I see,' Mrs Williams said. 'I'll let Oscar know.'

All that water streaming through the sand hill passes made my heart gallop right up into my throat. Wiley's big blow, it was closing in. Didn't matter that the wind still came from the mainland. Didn't matter that the wind should push the gulf back and that the tide should be low. Big blows did what they wanted; we weren't nothing to them. On a map, we weren't but a sliver of land.

Wiley said it would hit tonight. Hours and hours from now. There was time to get home; there was time to get ready. I

227

smothered the racing in my chest, and if Mrs Williams' heart was knocking hard, it didn't show. She went off to the barn wearing a fancy pearl-colored raincoat with three shiny black buttons. That coat didn't even come close to covering the bottom part of her skirt. She had on a rain hat, too, or what I took to be her idea of one since it didn't have feathers on it. Mrs Williams wore my boots too, them already being muddy. That had been my idea. I'd figured she'd turn down my offer, my boots not being pretty, but she took right to it. Probably she wanted to spare her shoes.

She'd laced my boots tight, them being too big for her. That done, she held up her skirt and turned her feet from side to side. She studied my square-toed boots with clumps of mud stuck on the sides and laughed. It was a raggedy laugh. Then she sobered up and thumped down the veranda steps with her white umbrella held to shield her backside. Andre, still in the yard playing, started to go with her but she stopped and told him something. He stood in the rain, splattered with mud and his little shoulders slumped. Mrs Williams pointed to a big puddle and off he went, kicking his way through the water. She turned and headed for the barn, her skirt blowing sideways.

I had taken her for the kind of woman that got all lathered up and scared silly. Instead she went the other way and pulled a tight rein in on her feelings. As for me, I was pinned down with nerves. I stood on the veranda and everything I knew or had heard about big blows rushed through my mind. I was eight when the storm of '86 struck. It could have happened yesterday, it was that fresh in my mind. The gulf came through the passes at the sand hills but them hills slowed the water and kept it off the ridge. Things were different, though, for us close to the bayou. That water came out of its banks and marched its way to our house. When it got to the middle veranda step, Mama said it was time to clear out and go the mile down the island to my uncle Bumps' house. He lived on the ridge then. 'It ain't safe here,' she told Daddy. 'Three children, Frank. Even if they ain't babies, we have to think of them.' Daddy said the horses couldn't pull the wagon since the water was too deep and the ground was too mushy. 'We'll walk,' Mama said.

The water came to my waist. The day had turned dark, the wind fought us, the rain was needle sharp, and the current was so strong that Daddy had to carry me.

We nearly lost Wiley, I ain't never going to forget that. He was eleven and bean-pole thin. He stumbled; the current knocked him off his feet and carried him away. Mama screamed, and Daddy gave me to her. I wrapped my arms around her waist, both of us staggering, the water trying to take us, too. The stinging rain in my eyes, Wiley was nothing but a dark shape in the water. He kept trying to stop himself in the current, his arms going every which way, but the water was strong. Daddy and Frank T. went after him and the only thing that saved him was he caught hold of a branch on a salt cedar. Daddy got to him, and when we finally made our way to Uncle Bumps', Wiley fell down on the floor and went to sleep, he was that worn out. He didn't care that his hands were cut and bleeding, his arms and legs, too. He slept so hard that he didn't hear it when the wind lifted a corner of the roof and ripped part of it off. The next morning, the sun came out like nothing had happened. We went home, and the storm had taken some of our roof, too. Inside, the mud and sand were ankle deep on the floor. 'Would have been better off staying,' Daddy said, pointing to the brown line on the walls. 'Water didn't come but a foot inside the house.'

It happened different in the city. Hundreds of houses close to the beach were washed away. Folks were killed; roofs fell in and crushed them flat. Others were swept out into the gulf and never seen again.

Then there was the story that Mama's middle brother told. Before he married a woman from North Carolina and settled there, Uncle Ned was a sailor. When I was little, he stayed with us when he had shore leave. 'It's a wall of wind,' he said about hurricanes. 'A wall you can see coming from far off. The black clouds get to swirling and the air turns green. That wall pushes the waves and turns them the size of mountains.' I'd never seen a mountain but the way he said it made me clutch my elbows. 'And our schooner feeling like nothing but a scrap of wood,' he said.

I knew how to swim, and that was a comfort. Daddy had taught me. He believed anybody, even girls, that lived on an island should know something about how to save themselves if they ended up in the water. When I was seven, Mama skimmed me down to my underclothes and Daddy took me to the gulf. 'Paddle with your arms and kick your feet,' he said, and showed me how. 'Keep your head up and look over your shoulder. Watch for the wave coming up. If you get caught in a riptide, don't fight it. Let it carry you on down the beach. It'll run itself out; you'll be just fine.'

That wasn't always so. Oakley Hill, the first man I was to marry, drowned on a clear day, not a storm in sight. All it took was for him to get his feet tangled in rope while he trawled for shrimp. The rope was still wrapped around his ankles when he washed ashore. Nobody can say for sure but it was figured he lost his balance, hit his head, and fell overboard. The gulf didn't care one little bit that Oakley was a good man. Or that he was only nineteen. It took him like he didn't mean nothing to nobody.

Mrs Williams wouldn't know none of that, her not being here and thinking that an Ohio storm was as bad as it could get. But I knew better. Big blows didn't have laid-out plans; each one had a mind of its own. They came from the gulf and didn't stop until they hit land and killed people. And here we sat on a narrow bar of dirt and sand, water on all sides.

The corn pone was burning. I smelled it from the veranda; I'd forgotten all about it. That was what came from watching Mrs Williams as she made her way to the barn to tell Oscar about the water at the sand hills. I hurried inside. Smoke billowed out when I opened the oven door. I grabbed a pot holder and got them pans out quick as could be. But it was too late: the pones were black on the top. I tipped them onto cooling racks and covered them up with a towel. I'd feed them to the dogs when they'd cooled, nobody needed to see what I'd done. I stuck the pans into the wash basin to soak and went back out onto the veranda.

A little ways from the house, Andre poked at something in a puddle with a stick. As for Mrs Williams, she was at the barnyard gate, her closed umbrella under her arm so she could work the latch with both hands. The bottom part of her skirt was so wet it had stretched long and dragged around her feet. She opened the gate, then closed it behind her. She'd no sooner got the umbrella back up when it turned inside out and flew off, a white bowl-shaped thing with a long wood handle. It tumbled in the air, cleared the barn fence, bounced down, then flipped its way toward the sand hills where it landed in a pool of water. The wind to Mrs Williams' back, she nearly skipped across the barnyard. She took the plank walkway that sloped up to the barn door and I couldn't see her no more.

My mind was a jumble. There were things to do but I couldn't think what. I walked from one end of the veranda to the other, the rain splattering me and the bottoms of my stockings getting wet again. Inside the house, I peeled off my stockings and went from window to window and closed the ones where the rain blew in. I got a dish towel and mopped up water from the sills and floor. In Andre's room, the wind had blown his spare shirt and pants off the wall peg and onto the floor. I hung them up and they fell down again. This time it wasn't the wind; I'd closed the windows. It was the shake in my hands.

I should boil rice for noon dinner. I should call Andre in for his bath. I should bring in more firewood to keep it dry. I should fill the lamps with kerosene. I went out onto the veranda. Andre was squatted close to the ground, peering at something. Overhead, there were them fast-moving black clouds. At the sand hills, water kept coming through the passes, the thin pools of it spreading out and pushing inland, maybe a hundred feet from us.

Mrs Williams was on her way back to the house from the barn. Her hat was gone and her hair whipped around her face. I could tell she tried to hurry but them boots of mine slowed her down. She stumbled some, and one time she slipped, her feet churning on the muddy path, but she held on and kept going. And here I was, a tangled web of nerves.

'Miss Nan,' Andre hollered. He was wet down to the skin. His clothes were mashed flat, but he didn't care. He grinned as he pointed at something on the ground, then he hollered again. I shook my head: I couldn't hear him over the rain. With both hands, he picked up a turtle the size of a dinner plate and held it high.

'I see it,' I yelled back, but that mud turtle gave me a quivery feeling. It wasn't right. It belonged in the bayou, not in front of the house. The bayou was a mile from here and turtles, they weren't big walkers, not unless they were laying eggs and even then they didn't walk a mile. Not mud turtles.

'Look!' Andre hollered. He put it down, jumped to a nearby puddle and got himself another turtle, him grinning in the rain and me feeling slippery like the floor was tilted. Something bad was happening at the bayou, something more than it coming a little ways out of its banks.

The dogs were gone. That notion hit like a rock to the chest. I didn't know when I'd last seen them. They weren't playing with Andre; they'd run off. Critters knew: they sniffed the air, they felt things folks didn't. Dogs hid, and turtles showed up where they didn't belong.

I went inside and everything came at me: the gloom, the puny glow from the lamps, the closed windows, the heat, the laundry washtub and how the water in it sloshed from side to side, the floor that jittery from the wind.

I hurried back to Andre's bedroom, and my heart nearly quit. Out the rain-streaked windows, I saw what had carried the turtles. The back pasture was under water. Lapping water, rippling water, water that moved. Not rainwater. This was a living thing. It was the bayou, here, a stone's throw from the house.

'Miss Ogden.'

In the pasture, the bushy limbs of the salt cedar tussled in the wind. The lower branches dragged in the water. Little white-capped waves split as they rushed around clumps of bushes, just the tops of the plants showing. A fluttery feeling whooshed through me. Mama. Daddy. Our house by the bayou.

'Miss Ogden.'

It was Mrs Williams. She was in the doorway and before I knew it, I got myself to move, my bare feet hurrying. 'Andre,' I said.

'He's in the kitchen.'

My legs wobbled out from under me. Mrs Williams caught ahold of my arm. Water, all this water. Like in '86. Wiley in the current, Daddy and Frank T. going after him.

'Miss Ogden.' Mrs Williams' hand was tight on my arm. 'It's an overflow. You said it yourself. Five inches deep. Oscar measured it. Five inches. That's all.'

Andre's dogs gone. The bayou a mile out of its banks. Mrs Williams' hair undone and dripping wet. Nothing was where it should be; everything was in the wrong place.

'Look at me.' Mrs Williams' voice was sharp. Red spots flared on her cheeks. Them spots danced.

'Miss Ogden. Look at me.'

That voice of hers, it carried a slap, it made me do what she said. Her eyes were rings of blue, each ring a clearer blue than the last. Without a word she looked into me and saw how scared I was. Don't you go falling apart, her eyes said. Do not even think about it. An overflow. That's all.

Mrs Williams said, 'Oscar's hitching the wagon. He's going to get your mother and father and bring them here. It's safer on the ridge.'

Them words, they were another slap, but this time they

made me draw up my shoulders, they made me shake off her hand from my arm. We were island people; nobody told us what to do. Daddy built our house to hold up. He'd laid the wide studs in the walls crossways like how old-time ships were built. We were close to the bayou but the pilings were six feet high. If the bayou came inside, we'd go up in the loft. We didn't turn tail and leave the hog and chickens; we took care of our own. That was the lesson learned from the storm of '86. Oscar didn't know that, him not from here, him from Ohio. Daddy didn't need nobody to tell him what to do. If Daddy thought him and Mama needed to be on the ridge, they'd be here by now. If Daddy thought it was safe to stay home, it was.

I said, 'I'm going with Mr Williams. Mama and Daddy, they won't want to leave.' That was how I put it, the words just coming to me. I let her think I was riding with Oscar so I could talk them into coming back. But that wasn't so. Oscar was taking me home, and I was staying there. Us Ogdens, we were Texans. We didn't turn yellow and run.

Mud sucked at my boots, the rain was bitter sharp, and I had to walk to the barn with my head down and my eyes half closed. My bonnet was mushy, and my poncho was of no more account than that fancy coat of Mrs Williams' had been. There weren't no words for my shame, me getting so scared and her knowing it. Leastways I had found my grit; I wasn't scared no more. Up ahead, Oscar had driven the wagon out of the stable yard and was coming my way. When I met up with him, the horses all twitchy and rolling their eyes, I hollered up to Oscar and said how I had to come with him since talking Mama and Daddy into leaving wasn't going to be no easy thing.

'Climb on up,' he hollered back, and that was what I did, my conscience not overly prickly for telling him a half-truth. On the buckboard, I hunched down. The bottom of the floorboard was filled up with rain, but I put my feet flat in it. Beside me, rain ran from Oscar's wide-brim hat and down his waxed poncho. He had taken down the buckboard canopy; likely it had buckled and scared the horses. They were plenty skittish as it was, sidestepping like they wanted to break loose and run back to the stable, but Oscar wouldn't let them. He bore down and held on tight to the lines.

He kept that tight hold as we went by the house, Mrs Williams and Andre still on the veranda, her holding Andre's hand but leaning out against the railing. Oscar looked over me and up at her. This thing between them was its own kind of lightning; I felt it, her blue eyes seeing nothing but Oscar, and a wave of yearning coming from him. It was a powerful want for the other that no amount of water could dampen. It made me hunch down all the more, me witnessing something so naked, and then we were past the house.

Me and Oscar headed west down the island. We stayed on the ridge as long as we could, the horses splashing through pools of rainwater that were a few inches deep. I gripped the sideboard, me and him rocking against the other when the wheels fell into mushy spots. My thoughts skipped from the feel of Oscar beside me, to that wife of his, then to Andre and how he was likely scared. After that, I thought about my brothers in the city somewhere and how Mama and Daddy had to be bracing for the big blow. From time to time I lifted my head and tried to see, the rain making it hard. Up ahead but close to the sand hills, the two tall buildings of St. Mary's rose up in a fog of gray, and then I thought how it was a foolish thing to store orphans so close to the beach; they should be on the ridge. But the land had been given to the nuns and likely they didn't know all that much about big blows, them not born here. When we got closer to St. Mary's, I cupped my hands around my eyes and there it was, the gulf rushing under the buildings.

Seeing that brought a sharp pain to my insides. Them poor little orphans. And the nuns. They had to be scared to the bone. The buildings were on stilts, six feet up, and that should be plenty high. But the water was eating up the sand hill passes, widening them, the water coming like rivers. Them orphans would be all right, I told myself. The nuns talked directly to God, and God looked over every little sparrow. He wouldn't let nothing happen to them, not to little children that had already lost their mamas and daddies.

At the outbuilding, what the nuns called the barn though it was too small to be called such, water lapped against the lower part of the walls. A grown man, one of the caretakers likely, and two boys made their way to the outbuilding, their heads bent into the wind. The boys shuffled and that told me the water must be up to their knees. Beside me, Oscar strained forward.

'Should we stop?' I hollered. 'Help them?'

'On our way back,' he yelled. That was a poke to my conscience, but I didn't say nothing about me staying with Mama and Daddy. Oscar called out to the horses like they could hear him and he took up the lines, steering Maud and Mabel toward the right. Oscar had a time doing it; they didn't like it; we were leaving the high point on the ridge. The wind hit face on and with each step, the water got deeper and the soil turned mushier. Oscar gave them horses some slack, he let them toss their heads, but his knuckles were white, he held on that hard. This rain, it was like sewing needles coming at us and I wanted to close my eyes but didn't, not all the way. I kept my gaze fixed on the front legs of the horses, the water to their ankles, then over their ankles and riding up to their shins.

A little black kitten swept by. It was on a board, wet and crouched down, and I couldn't bring myself to watch. The horses kept stopping, the wagon hard to pull. Oscar called to them and they started up again, straining. The wind had gone cold, and my teeth chattered. I clamped my jaw tight but I couldn't get the shaking to quit. I nearly lost heart; I almost told Oscar to turn back, we were going to lose a wheel, this water was too strong. But Mama and Daddy weren't yellow; they weren't running away. Finally, I heard Oscar holler something and there, up ahead, was home.

It was the prettiest sight ever. Didn't matter there was water under the house, not one bit. It wasn't but to the third step, and Mama and Daddy were on the back veranda, both of them with a lantern held high. They'd been looking for me, I was sure of it. Likely they were looking for Frank T. and Wiley, too. Daddy took to waving Oscar off, his way of telling him not to come closer, it was too deep. Nobody had to tell the horses that. They'd come to a stop and nothing Oscar said or did could change their minds. Oscar took up waving to Daddy to come on, calling that he wanted to take Mama and Daddy to his house. 'We're dry,' Oscar hollered.

All that waving back and forth was foolishness. They were two stubborn men both trying to get the other to change his mind. I took off my boots and stuffed my stockings inside of

238

them. I tied the shoelaces together and slung them around my neck. I slid to the side of the wagon, my feet feeling for the wheel spoke, but Oscar grabbed hold of my arm. 'Got to get them,' he said. 'Take them back.'

'No,' I yelled. 'They won't leave. And I won't either. It'd take more than this to drive us out of our own home.'

I shook him off and then I was knee deep in rushing water. It was cold and muddy, and the ground was uneven and thick with tangled grass. Boards bumped against my legs, some of them painted, some fancy trim work, and I didn't want to think how any of it got here.

'I'm coming with you,' Oscar said, the wind biting the edges off his words.

'No, you ain't,' I said. 'Go home. You've done enough, your folks are waiting.' I hitched up my skirt, and just before I started to wade to the house, Oscar called out my name. Nan. Not Miss Ogden. Nan. Like what he called me before Bernadette died. Like how it was before we both had to step around the other, me thinking of the curse that hovered over me, and him just wanting to keep a distance. I looked up at him and real quick, I saw something in them green eyes of his. It wasn't like how he looked at Mrs Williams; it wasn't anything that strong. But I saw something.

'Nan,' Oscar said again. He said something else but only one word came through. 'Tomorrow.'

He nodded for me to go on, and that was what I did. I went home, Daddy taking the back steps, coming to help me. I plodded to meet him, stumbling as my skirt wrapped around my legs. Daddy stumbled, too, his arms going every which way. The ground was mushy and rough all at the same time, the long grass clutching my ankles. The force of the water was

239

as strong as a riptide. I took a few more steps, fell into a dip, and landed on my hands and knees.

Fear swelled. There was water in my mouth; the current was carrying me; I couldn't get up; the boots around my neck pulled me down. I grabbed ahold of a rooted clump of grass; that stopped my tumbling. I pushed myself up and stood, spitting and swatting the hair out of my eyes. I got Daddy back in my sights. I climbed my way out of the dip and kept on, hearing that word 'tomorrow'. Just before Daddy reached me, just before I took hold of his hand, I knew.

'Nan. See you tomorrow.' That was what Oscar said.

CHAPTER THIRTEEN

The Hurricane

Water rushed over the bottom veranda step.

'House is five feet up,' Oscar said on the day he brought me here. 'Never had a drop of floodwater inside.'

The waves thundered. Sea spray shot up over the tops of the sand hills, arching high, then raining down. Gulf water surged landward through the passes, carving and cutting, the sand hills crumbling and collapsing.

Currents crisscrossed and coursed over bushes and around the trees that Oscar called salt cedars. The barnyard fence had fallen. Rain poured from dark, swift clouds as though countless water buckets had been overturned. The horizon roiled with white-capped gray waves. The air whistled and swept the rain in sheets toward the gulf, the wind still coming from behind the house. I was on the front veranda by the door, and using a broom, I swatted at the frogs that leapt up the steps.

Oscar had been gone for two hours.

My clothes and face were wet from the rain spray that blew in from the sides of the veranda but I couldn't bear to be inside. The windows were closed and earlier, I had drawn the storm shutters. The house was a cave, dark, hot, and stuffy.

Unable to see out, I felt trapped and helpless. I labored to breathe, the walls pressing in around me. On the veranda, though, I could see the storm. Here, I could breathe even if the air was heavy with salt. Here, I looked into the shroud of wind-blown rain and watched for Oscar.

Two hours. Something must have happened to him. A wagon wheel had snapped, the horses had panicked. The wagon had overturned.

This morning when I'd gone to the barn to warn Oscar about the water coming through the sand hill passes, he'd been calm and reassuring. 'We're on the ridge,' he'd said. 'We're all right here. There's a little water in the back pasture, too. Just measured it. It's only five inches. That's all. We've had worse.' In the barn's dim light, the sheen of perspiration on his face glistened. He'd been pitching hay into what I thought might be a feed trough in one of the stalls. I was in the aisle, the stall railing between us. My skirt was muddy, and much of my hair had slipped loose from its pins and combs. The wind whined through the chinks in the walls. The cows were in the stalls, and the odors – dung, animals, my wet clothes – added to my ragged nerves.

Oscar reached over the railing and took my hand. 'I'm worried some about the Ogdens,' he said. 'Frank and Alice.' It was a moment before I realized these were Nan's father and mother. 'They could flood out; they're close to the bayou. They might need to get to the ridge. Wouldn't think much of it if Frank T. and Wiley were there to help. But they aren't and that leaves Frank and Alice stranded without their horses.' He paused. 'I'm going to get them and bring them here. I'll be gone an hour likely. An hour and a half at the most.'

I had been stunned into silence.

'You and Andre are plenty safe up here on the ridge,' Oscar went on to say, his fingers making circles on my palm. 'Wouldn't leave if I didn't think it. Wouldn't do it if you weren't who you are. You aren't the kind to let a storm scare you.'

He didn't know me, I thought now as I swept frogs off of the veranda. The water was halfway up the second step.

Mats of torn grass swirled past in the water, going toward the gulf, then coming back in the crossing currents. Everything that had been in the garbage heap in the back pasture had been carried off. Glass bottles and rusty pails bobbed and tumbled. Empty tin cans and wagon-wheel rims bumped up against bushes, catching in the branches and then breaking free. The crystal earrings must be somewhere in the water. The waves had uprooted the road that wound through the sand hills and its scattered planks rushed past the house. There were snakes, too, their yellow stripes rippling as they swam. Sleek, shiny rats clung to pieces of broken boards.

Five frogs, six, now seven. I swatted at them, their brown speckled bodies leaping away from me, some of them jumping back into the water. I refused to give in to my panic. I would not allow myself to think the unthinkable about Oscar. He was not hurt; he was not in trouble. Not Oscar.

The veranda floor vibrated from the wind. This must be what an earthquake felt like, I thought. Except earthquakes lasted seconds, not hours. It was one-thirty in the afternoon. The storm couldn't get any worse, I told myself. These massive waves, this unrelenting rain, this had to be the peak. And Oscar was somewhere out in the open.

Nine veranda steps, I thought. The water was only to the second one. I needed to keep my head. I could not allow myself to panic. The front door was held open with a door jamb and I looked into the house. I had lit every lamp and lantern but their narrow, jittering lights only deepened the shadows. Andre lay on the floor under the kitchen table, at last worn out from playing in the rain and from his fear of the storm. Three of the dogs, their heads raised, lay pressed close to him. The fourth one circled.

They had shown up just after Oscar and Nan rode past the house in the wagon. 'Daddy!' Andre had called. It was as though he noticed for the first time how dark the morning had turned. The wagon kept moving, Oscar's shoulders set as he gripped the lines to control the horses.

'Daddy!' Andre's cry was shrill with fear. The loose ends of Oscar's and Nan's ponchos beat and jerked in the wind. Rainwater filled the grooves in the mud made by the wagon wheels. Still wearing my soiled wet clothes, my hair blowing loose, I held Andre's hand and tried to get him into the house, but he bore down and made himself heavy. 'Daddy!' That was when the dogs loped up the steps and crowded around Andre, their fur soaked and muddy. The suddenness of their arrival distracted him. He patted them, his hands skimming their heads and backs, going from one to the next.

'Where'd you go?' he said to them. His voice trembled. 'I was looking for you. Why'd you hide?' Two of them were almost as tall as he, and their long pink tongues licked his tears. He swatted at the dogs but he grinned and I said nothing about filth or sanitation. I had turned back to watch the wagon, a blurring outline in the rain.

I coaxed Andre into the house with the promise of a teaspoon of honey. Another teaspoon convinced him to have his bath. He sat in the metal laundry washtub with his knees

244

up and his hands gripping the sides. I soaped a washcloth with the bar of Ivory and was all at once lightheaded, its cloying fragrance too strong in the closed house. Outside, the dogs scratched at the front door.

'Ma'am,' Andre said, his voice wobbling. It occurred to me that this was his name for me. 'When'll Daddy get home?'

'In a little while,' I said. I needed that to be true. For the first time in my life, another person was completely dependent on me. I had helped Andre get ready for bed before, but Oscar had always been nearby in the barn. In the kitchen with the storm all around us, Andre looked smaller and younger than before. His back was narrow, and his chest was thin. Everything about him was fragile: his collarbone, his wrists, each finger, the oval shape of his nails. Caring for Andre must have exhausted Oscar when Bernadette died. It was no wonder he turned to Nan. No wonder he never said the first word against her. She had watched over Andre; she had dressed and fed him. She must have held him when he cried for his mother.

On my knees, I bathed this small, frightened child who now had his hands over his ears. I talked above the whistling wind and cascading rain, trying to distract us both from the image of Oscar driving off into the storm. I said, 'In Dayton, where your father grew up, there are alleys between the back-yards of people's homes. Your grandfather once drove a wagon through those alleys with coal piled high in the bed. That coal kept families warm during the winter months.' Andre kept his eyes squeezed closed but I could tell he was listening. He had spread his fingers apart. 'Your grandfather's job was very impor-tant,' and as I said that, I wondered how I had not realized this before. I worked around Andre's fingers and washed his hair and his face. When he finally lowered his hands, I washed the small curves of each ear.

Something creaked, a long splintering moan. My pulse skipped. Andre whimpered, flinching.

I took a deep breath, willing my nerves to settle. 'The houses in Dayton have coal chutes,' I said. Andre peeked at me, then closed his eyes again. 'Those are tunnels, they're made of metal, and each house has a little door in a wall at the back. The tunnel goes down into the basement where the furnace is kept. Your grandfather shoveled coal from his wagon into the chutes. When he became ill, your father took his place.'

'He did?' Andre said, opening one eye.

'Most certainly. His family needed his help.'

And I did, too. If the wind worsened, if the water rose, if Oscar were hurt, if—

No, I told myself. Andre needed me to stay calm. As though he had read my thoughts, he was hunched over with both eyes closed and his hands again pressed against his ears.

I said, 'When your father delivered coal, his horses wore bells around their necks. They made a lively jangle as crisp as the January air. They announced your father's arrival, they lifted spirits.'

But perhaps not Oscar's. The constant jangle might have reminded him that he was fated to spend his life in back alleys, his spirits dulling with each passing year as coal dust settled in his lungs as it had settled in his father's. Those bells might have driven him to Texas, a place where no one knew him, a place where he could shape his own destiny.

Something thudded against the wall of the house. 'All clean,' I said, forcing a lilt in my tone. 'Let's get you dry.' I held up

246

a towel. 'I promise I won't look, don't worry.' I turned away while Andre dried himself and when he told me he was ready, I helped him dress, my fingers clumsy with the shirt and pant buttons. He flinched each time the wind's whistle turned sharp and stood as close to me as he could. Outside, the dogs still scratched the door. I said, 'Before your father took over the business, he attended Central High School. It was a big two-story brick building with tall arched windows.'

Andre clutched my hand as we went to the bedroom that I shared with Oscar. Between the two open wardrobe doors, I changed out of my soiled clothes while Andre stood on the other side of one of the doors, his small hand holding on to the edge so that I could see his fingers. The rain and wind were louder here, both pounding the back wall so hard that the crucifix over the bed was tilted at an odd angle.

'On winter mornings,' I said, 'your father arrived early to school.' This was a memory I had almost forgotten. 'The school principal depended on him. We all did. He lit the furnaces so that the classrooms were warm when classes began.'

I tied my hair with a green ribbon. I took Andre's hand and we went back to the kitchen. I said, 'Your father had to leave school when your grandfather was ill. But he was a good student.' I recalled an image of Oscar as a boy of fifteen or so. He had on a worn suit jacket but the knot in his tie was precise. Although his trousers were a little short, the creases were pressed. 'There was a ceremony at the end of the school year,' I said. 'The principal called your father to the stage and shook his hand. Your father excelled in mathematics and received a certificate of merit.'

Andre held on to my green skirt as I found oysters in the icebox and while I cut the blackened tops off the corn pones that were on the counter. I knew the water in the back pasture had concerned Nan but the burned corn pones shocked me. She did not make mistakes. She did everything with unquestioned authority. But not today.

I poured Andre's milk. The spout of the pitcher clattered against his canning jar. The wind howled in the chimney. I could bear anything if the wind would just stop shaking the house. Seated at the kitchen table, I raised my voice above the rain and the crash of the waves, and chanted the prayer that Oscar said at meals. 'In the name of the Father, and the Son, and the Holy Spirit.' My hands made the Catholic sign of the cross and Andre did the same. Anything to bring Oscar home, I thought. Anything to end this storm.

'Lakeside Park in Dayton had amusements during the summers,' I heard myself say while Andre had his lunch, a lunch that I could not eat. Beside me on the bench, Andre was so close that he was almost on my lap.

'The park was next to the Miami River, and my friends and I used to rent rowboats.' I put my arm around Andre. He slumped against me, his eyes heavy.

I spread the red blanket under the table for him, then scraped our dishes. 'There were concerts at Lakeside Park,' I told him. 'It might be a barbershop quartet, other times it could be a brass band with cornets, trombones, and tubas.' Andre lay on his side on the blanket and watched me with his thumb in his mouth, something I had not seen him do before.

'I used to see your father at the concerts. He was a handsome young man. All of my friends thought so.'

Andre kept his eyes open wide, fighting sleep. Near the table, the dirty bath water in the washtub sloshed from the wind's vibration in the floor. I had expected the vibration to upset Andre all the more but it seemed to calm him. I, though, could not bear the feel of it, or the sound of the rattling tub. I dragged it across the room and when I opened the front door so I could empty it, the dogs shot in and nearly knocked me down. They darted, sliding on the wood floor, their tails tucked as they sniffed the corners of the rooms, turning, circling, and thumping against the walls.

'Out,' I said. 'Out.' They ignored me. They found Andre and shook themselves. Dirty water flew in every direction and splattered Andre's clean clothes and face.

'Whoa, boys,' he said, sitting up now. 'Whoa, slow down.' Their wet smell filled the house. One of the dogs pawed him, and another one jumped up on the table bench, then back down. 'Sit, Tracker,' Andre said. 'Everybody sit. Be good, be good.'

I heard the plea in his voice. He expected me to turn them out into the storm. I knew little about dogs, but I could see that these were frightened. They trembled and cowed every time the house popped. I told Andre they might stay and that had made him smile.

Now, I waited on the veranda for Oscar, my nerves humming. The water was halfway up the third step.

The barn was an island in a sea of water, and the weather vane on the roof had blown off. Shallow rippling waves crested and broke over the collapsed outhouse. Far beyond the sand hills, shelves of dark clouds rolled.

Oscar had left us to fend for ourselves. The water was rising. The rain was a thousand waterfalls, and the house made noises that I couldn't identify. If something happened, if I needed help, I wouldn't know where to go. I didn't know where the Ogdens lived. Or any of the people who had come to the dance.

They all must be somewhere. But from here, there was only the faint outline of the orphanage farther down the beach. To get to St. Mary's, I'd have to carry Andre. He wouldn't be able to walk. The wind was too strong, and the water flowed too quickly for a five-year-old.

'You and Andre are plenty safe up here on the ridge,' Oscar had said.

He was wrong. The ridge was a myth. The island was flat and flooded.

Driftwood from the beach banged against the steps. I needed a plan; I needed to do something. This waiting was unbearable; my nerves were faltering. Rain spray blew in, gritty with sand. A shadow down the island caught my attention. Patches of shadow darkened the terrain everywhere but this one moved. It was coming this way. Through the heavy rain, I kept my gaze fixed on it, afraid that it would disappear if I looked away. I waited, straining, my eyes aching. Time slowed, the shadow stopping, then starting again.

Two horses. No wagon, just horses.

The broom slipped from my hands and clattered to the floor. I hurried inside. The dogs leapt to their feet. I picked up a lantern from the parlor. Back on the veranda, frogs jumping out of my way, I held it high. My hair blew in the wind, and the globe rattled and the flame flickered.

Horses. But not alone. Someone rode one of them. Oscar.

There was the press of his wet poncho against me, his kiss, and our arms around one another. Rain gusted onto the veranda and it didn't matter. Oscar was home. He was safe. We were all safe. We held each other, the storm momentarily forgotten, relief and joy coursing through me.

'Cathy,' Oscar said into my ear, 'I'm sorry. Didn't think it would flood. I'm so sorry. I never would have left if I'd thought we'd flood.'

'You're home,' I said.

'I don't understand it,' he said. 'The wind's coming from the mainland. But this gulf water here, pushing up on the ridge. It doesn't make sense.'

'You're safe,' I said. 'That's all that matters.'

'The Ogdens wouldn't leave. And neither would Nan. I left them there, Cathy. I left them and the water was high. It's like nothing I've seen before. Had to leave the wagon at St. Mary's. The wheels kept getting stuck and I couldn't drive the horses any harder. I asked the sisters what I could do for them, but Sister Camillus told me to get on home. God was watching the children, she said. She had them singing hymns. She told them they had to practice for Mass tomorrow.'

He'd been at the orphanage, I thought. While I had been nearly frantic about him, waiting, the water rising, he had taken the time to stop there.

Oscar's tone shifted, urgent now. 'Listen. You must listen to me.' He pulled away from me. 'This flood coming from the gulf,' he said. 'If the saltwater gets in our wells, the livestock could die of thirst. But it might not be too late. The kitchen pump, Cathy. Test the water for salt. If it's still fresh, fill every pot, every bucket, even the tub. I'll be doing the same at the barn.' His face was pale and drawn, and the scar along his jaw looked more jagged than before. 'I need you to do this,' he said. 'Do you understand?'

Fresh water. And not just for the livestock. It was for all of us. 'Yes,' I said.

'All right then,' he said. He looked over toward the barn.

Worry creased his forehead. Oscar turned back to me, and for a moment the tension in his face eased. He said, 'We might get a little roughed up, but just you wait and see. We'll get through this.'

I took his hand and gave it a little squeeze. He nodded, and without another word, he turned and went down the steps. He untied the horses from the veranda rail and left, the water to his calves as he led them to the barn. They pranced, twitched, and jerked, but he wouldn't let them bolt. Oscar was home.

The water in the kitchen was lukewarm and cloudy, but free of salt. I gathered up pans and buckets, rolled my sleeves above my elbows, and began to fill them. 'Your father's home; he's in the barn,' I said to Andre when the pump's squeak awakened him. Beside him, the dogs panted and beads of spittle dripped from their tongues.

'Your father needs you to keep me company,' I said before Andre could begin to cry. His face was tight with fear. The rain on the roof almost drowned out the sharp whistle of the wind now. 'Stand right here, beside me,' I said. 'Now tell me about your dogs. Such unusual names. Bear, for instance. However did you think of that?'

These were questions meant to distract. Mr Brand, my music teacher from Cincinnati, used this trick to calm my nerves before piano recitals. 'Your family's cottage,' he'd say while I waited offstage. 'How long is the train trip from Dayton to Lake Erie? How many stops?'

I pumped water and asked Andre about the cats in the barn. Did they have names? Did they bother the cows? He held on to my skirt and his answers were short but he didn't

252

cry. What color do you like best? Your favorite thing to do? Play with your dogs? Or dig for buried treasure? I strained to hear him above the roar of the pounding waves. From time to time, I ran my fingers under the pump water and tasted for traces of salt. The water still fresh, I kept on, the joints in my fingers stiffening and my arms and shoulders throbbing.

Twice, Oscar came to the veranda with empty milk containers for me to fill. 'Sit down,' I said each time. 'For a minute. A cup of coffee at the least.'

'Can't,' he said both times, his hand on my bare forearm. 'I'll have that coffee later. Keep it hot on the stove,' and then he was down the steps and on his way back to the barn.

I worked, the squeak in the pump the music of fresh water. I stopped once to take off my corset, my need to breathe a far greater concern than appearances. Later, I stopped to look outside through the open door. Waves battered the sand hills but the water had stopped rising. It was still at the third step. A good sign, I told myself. The storm wouldn't go on much longer; the wind couldn't get any stronger. Surely the day was almost over, it was dark as dusk but when I looked at the clock on the mantle, it was only a few minutes past four.

I filled the tub in the washroom, bucket by bucket. The air was laden with salt, and my clothes were wet with perspiration. Two of the dogs were nowhere to be seen, but I didn't question Andre about them. He sat on the floor by the cistern with the brown dog hunched beside him. The yellow dog was behind the tub, shivering. Blisters formed on my palms, and spasms pinched the muscles in my back. The work was exhausting, and a week ago, I would have been shocked to think of myself engaged in common labor with my hair loose around my shoulders and my blouse unbuttoned nearly to my bosom. But for the first time since I'd left the ensemble in Philadelphia, I had a purpose. I was necessary. I was doing something for Oscar and for Andre.

'When is your birthday?' I said to Andre.

'December.'

'And your father's?'

'I don't know.'

Nor did I, I realized with a start. 'We'll ask him,' I said. 'When all this work is finished, when the storm has ended. You must help me to remember. Now then, when is Thanksgiving?'

'When it's not so hot.'

I ran pump water over my fingers. 'Which month?' I said. I tasted the water and if Andre answered, I didn't hear him. I tasted my fingers again. Salt. The well was flooded.

Wind blasted through the propped-open front door. Oscar's newspapers flew. One of my bookends on the parlor table fell, then my books, small explosions as they hit the floor. The lamps blew out. I stood stunned at the kitchen counter, my skirt flapping around my legs as Andre clutched at them. I heard Oscar call to me; then he was inside, pushing the door closed. Rainwater streamed from his poncho, and his trousers were muddy and soaked. He latched the door and dragged a table bench in front of it to keep it from tearing off its hinges.

'It's here,' he said. 'Wind's turned and is coming from the gulf.' I couldn't grasp his meaning. Or the suddenness of the change, the wind beating against the front of the house. Everything shook: the floor, the house, and me.

Oscar went to the back veranda to look at the storm. I pushed against my panic. 'Stay with me,' I told Andre. 'Hold

254

on to my skirt and help me light the lamps.' The lantern on the kitchen counter was still lit and slivers of daylight came in around the frame of the rattling door. I found the matches on the cupboard shelf. They were damp from the air, and bent and broke when I tried to strike them. The one lantern would have to suffice. As though it were important, I began to pick up the scattered newspapers, my hands fluttering and moving too quickly. The glass of milk that I had poured a few minutes ago for Andre rattled on the counter. So did the panes in the windows.

Something banged hard against the front wall. 'My goodness,' I said to Andre, trying to control the tremor in my voice. 'The wind certainly does not blow like this in Ohio but if it should, it'd bring a blizzard of snow. And wouldn't that be exciting?' He stared up at me, his eyes too wide.

I felt sure that I looked the same when Oscar came into the kitchen and said he needed to go to the barn. He stood close to me with Andre between us, clinging to his legs. Oscar's hold on my arms was firm. 'Water's coming up fast, it's in the barn,' he said, his voice raised above the storm. 'Got to get the horses out. And the cows. It's their only chance. They'll panic in their stalls. They'll try to climb out; they'll get tangled in the rails. They could kill themselves.'

'No,' I said. 'Don't leave.'

'You'll be all right,' he said. 'If the wind gets worse or water comes in, get in the attic's stairwell. It's the safest place. If you have to, go up to the attic. I'll find you, don't worry about me. But don't latch the back door.'

'Water in the house?' I said. 'Was that what you said?'

'It's just a plan. That's all. If something happens.'

'Oscar. Don't go. Please. Don't go.'

255

'They're our livelihood.'

'This water. You said it yourself. It's rising. You could—'

'They'll panic. I can't do that to them.'

Every part of me shook.

'I'll be back before you know it.'

He'd risk his life for animals. 'I'm begging you,' I said.

'I have to. I won't let them suffer. I can't live with that.'

Guilt. I knew something about that. I touched Oscar's cheek. He put his hand on top of mine and with that, my panic eased. Beneath my fingertips, the stubble of his beard was rough and it was once again last Monday. He and I stood in the tide, our bare feet sinking into the eroding sand. I was off balance, the water pushing and pulling, but he held me steady.

'Go,' I said. 'Quickly. So you can hurry back.'

Oscar kissed me and left.

The four horses were the first to come out of the barn. They sidestepped down the ramp with their heads and tails raised. In the barnyard, the water was high on their legs. They lunged and thrashed, and turned in circles as if looking for escape from the storm. One of them bucked and kicked. Another horse reared up and pawed at the gusting wind and rain.

I watched from the back veranda where the house sheltered Andre and me from the brunt of the wind. Rain, cold and sharp, blew in from the sides. I kept my hands on the top of Andre's head as he cried into my skirt. The late afternoon light was an eerie gray tinged with pink. Broken boards planed over the surface of the floodwaters. Roof shingles spun in the air, and tree leaves swirled like snow. I swayed from side to side as though I rocked Andre in my arms. I had held him for

256

a few minutes but had bowed from his weight. I knew I should take him inside. He shouldn't be a part of any of this. But I had to watch. I could not let Oscar do this alone.

He came out of the barn, and I strained to see what he carried in his hands. A pitchfork, I thought. In his other hand, he carried what I thought was a feed sack. Walking backwards down the ramp, he shook the feed sack and a cow came out of the barn and followed him down the ramp. Then another cow came out, and the next, and the next. In the barnyard now, more cows behind him, Oscar plunged the pitchfork into the ground to steady himself as he shuffled and stumbled in the water. It was well over his knees and nearby, the four horses lunged, trying to bolt, but the water slowed them.

The wind tore a cupola off of the barn roof; it tumbled and flipped in the air. A horse fell onto its front knees, got up, and reared. In the barnyard, the cows milled, their tails whipping over their backs. Oscar dropped the feed sack, went up the ramp, and closed the barn door. He had gotten them out; he had done all that he could.

Through the driving rain, I watched each plunge of the pitchfork as he made his way toward us. The waves were higher, cresting and breaking. He fell and went under; terror shot through me. I cried out to him. He came back up and stumbled on, the water now to the tops of his legs. He fell again. A current carried him by a few yards. He steadied himself with the pitchfork and plunged his way back. I prayed, 'Our Father who art in heaven.' Andre held tighter to me. My hand on his head so that I could keep him from watching, I leaned toward Oscar and urged him on with each plunge of the pitchfork, with each small step. He was almost halfway home. The water was to his chest now, and the waves were white-capped.

257

A milk container crashed against the veranda. I flinched. My eyes closed only for an instant but it was long enough to lose sight of Oscar.

I searched for him, calling. I found him. He was caught in a current. His head was just above the water. He struggled, trying to catch a branch, a board, anything, but the waves carried Oscar toward the bayou, farther and farther away. He went under, came up floundering. A wave crested and broke. He disappeared. I held my breath, the wind shrieking. He didn't come back up.

I tried to hurry to the back steps, desperate to do something, to help Oscar, to find him, but Andre was clasped to my legs. I couldn't leave him, I didn't know how to swim, and the waves were so high. Oscar would tell me, No, stay with Andre.

The rain blew in, stinging. I strained, looking and praying. Please God. Let Oscar be all right. Take care of him, please. I told myself that Oscar had come back up but it was me; I hadn't been able to see him. Not in this light, not with this dense gray rain. He was all right; Oscar was strong.

'Ma'am,' Andre yelled, climbing up my legs. 'Help me!' Water rushed around our feet. The veranda was flooding.

I held Andre in the narrow stairwell that led to the attic. I rocked him as the wind struck the house and windows shattered. 'It's all right,' I said when the water drove us from the third step to the fifth. 'We're safe here,' I said when something slammed against the house, and the plaster fell in chunks from the stairwell walls. 'Just a summer storm,' I said each time the house cracked, the wood splintering. 'Daddy's taking care of the cows,' I told him when he called for Oscar. When

I could no longer hold on to these half-truths, I sang to Andre. The lyrics came in fragments, words I had not thought about in years.

'Amazing Grace, how sweet the sound,
That saved a wretch like me.'

It was a hymn from my childhood. 'The troops sang it before battles,' my father had told me. 'Yankees and Rebels, it didn't matter. We all sang it.'

'I once was lost, but now am found,
Was blind, but now I see.'

I sang for Andre; I sang for Oscar. He had disappeared but only from my sight. I told myself that he had found refuge in a tree. Or he had caught hold of a board or driftwood, the water was full of them.

Something in the attic screeched, ripping, then crashed. 'Ma'am,' Andre said, his voice trembling. 'Ma'am.'

''Twas Grace that taught my heart to fear,
And Grace my fears relieved.'

I had scorned Oscar's religion but now I needed it to keep him safe. A man who prayed before meals, who went to Sunday Mass, and who had a crucifix over his bed could not be forgotten by God. I had snatched up that crucifix before coming into the stairwell. It had fallen and was submerged in the layer of water that covered the bedroom floor. The sight of that terrified me. Rushing, Andre holding on to my skirt, I'd emptied

259

a hatbox, tossing the hat. It meant nothing to me. I put the crucifix in the hatbox and then I searched through the wardrobe, my thoughts jerky. I found Oscar's box with the inlaid W, his pocket watch, and the letters he had written to me. In Andre's bedroom, I filled the hatbox with his crucifix, the white rosary beads, and the photograph of Oscar and Bernadette. In the parlor, I got Oscar's book about the stars. The water to Andre's knees, I'd carried the hatbox into the stairwell with us.

Now I rocked Andre. The wind was a frenzied scream of terror.

> *'How precious did that Grace appear,*
> *The hour I first believed.'*

The water might have carried Oscar to the Ogdens'. The idea of it lifted me; I clung to it as Andre clung to me. I had never been there, but I pictured Oscar with Nan, Frank T., Wiley, and their parents, Frank and Alice. They were all in a stairwell. Oscar argued that he had to get home, but the others talked him out of it. 'No, sir, none of that,' Nan said. 'Won't have it. It ain't safe.'

Stay where you are, I thought. But, Oscar, if you're close, come home, come home.

Water slapped against the lower steps in the stairwell. Glass shattered. 'Daddy,' Andre said, the word a whimper.

> *'Through many dangers, toils, and snares,*
> *I have already come.'*

The dogs were in the attic, and I thought I heard them whimper as well. They had run up the stairs as soon as I'd

260

opened the door to the stairwell. Before that, the water had driven the two out from under Andre's bed where they'd been hiding. The other two left the washroom and they all paced, frantic, jumping up onto the beds, the chairs, trying to get out of the water. I sang for them, too, these friends of Andre, these animals that had frightened me when I first arrived. That was before I knew true fear, a fear that at first numbed my senses and then heightened each one so that the splintering of the house was deafening, the smell of salt was suffocating, and the beat of each wave against the stilts ricocheted in the stairwell.

'Tis Grace that brought me safe thus far,
And Grace will lead me home.'

The air hummed. In the attic, pieces of the roof tore, long painful screeches. Rain and wind tunneled through the stairwell. The door at the foot had flown open long ago and had stayed open, the water trapping it. Andre shook. I huddled over him. No one could survive this storm out in the open. No one.

'He will my shield and portion be,
As long as life endures.'

On and on the storm raged, once seeming to pause for a few minutes only to unleash a fury that was more vicious than before. How much longer before the flood rushed up the steps? Before the stilts broke? Before my heart shattered into count-less pieces, the image of Oscar caught in the current imprinted in my mind?

*

Something changed. The storm still pounded, but the sound was different. The shrieking and the howling had lessened. I listened, waiting. The rain swept in gusts but there were pauses between the gusts now, each pause lasting longer than the one before.

A patch of light flickered on the stairwell wall, then disappeared. I held Andre and waited for the next terror.

Rain pummeled the house, then tapered and stopped. The light returned. It wavered and brightened. A signal, I thought. From heaven. Or from hell.

'Ma'am?' Andre said, pointing at it.

'The moon,' I said. I didn't know where those words came from but as soon as I said them, I realized they were true. The moon. It shone through the broken roof at the top of the stairwell.

The water at the foot of the steps gurgled as if a plug had been pulled in a drain. It was retreating, I thought, receding as quickly as it had appeared.

A gust slammed against the house. The walls shuddered. But not like before. Nothing was like before.

'It's over,' I said finally. 'It's over.'

CHAPTER FOURTEEN

Wiley

Three nights ago, Oscar took me outside to see the night sky. 'Moon's working its way to full,' he had said. Now, in the stairwell, that same moon guided Andre and me as we went from the fifth step to the fourth. We held hands, his so small in mine.

'Go slowly,' I said.

'I am.'

'Whisper, please.'

I felt his nod.

Everything – the house, my courage – felt precarious. A sudden movement or a raised voice, I felt sure, could cause the house to rock and slide from its stilts. I was afraid to move; I kept the palm of my free hand pressed against the wall. I was like a woman who had been suddenly blinded, unsure of what was before me.

We continued down to the third step. I could not begin to guess how long the storm had lasted. It felt like days, but it might have only been hours. Nor did I know how long we had waited in the stairwell once its fury had passed. Oscar considered it the safest part of the house, and I would have stayed there until daylight. But once I said that the storm was over, Andre begged for water. 'My mouth,' he kept saying. 'It's dried up. I'm thirsty. And hungry.'

The second step. Andre sucked in his breath. The step was gritty with dirt. My fingertips clutched the wall for balance. Not dirt, I realized. Sand. 'From the flood,' I whispered as if Andre had asked. I gave his hand a quick squeeze of reassurance but I was sure of nothing.

We took the next step down, and then the last one. Our feet sank into ankle-deep mud. 'Ohhhh,' Andre said.

The house creaked; something groaned. We froze. Water dripped somewhere, plopping and pinging. The creaking stopped. The moon was out, I told myself. The worst of the storm was over. The house was settling back into place. It would not collapse.

I began to breathe. 'We're all right,' I said, my voice low. 'We are?'

'Yes.'

'But, ma'am. This mud. What's it doing here?'

'Whisper. Please.' Then, 'The flood carried it in.'

'Why?'

'I don't know.' I looked over my shoulder and into the stairwell, the moonlight faint on the wall. The one safe place, I thought. It was only a few steps away.

We inched into the parlor. The wet sandy mud crunched beneath our feet and seeped into my shoes between the soles and the leather. It was cold, and my stockings were quickly soaked. Before us, the house was filled with shadowy shapes. The two chairs in the parlor were overturned. The upright piano was in the middle of the room.

'Where'd the door go?' Andre said. His words boomed and

echoed. I tightened my grasp on his hand. The front door had blown off, leaving a dark, gaping hole.

We were exposed and defenseless. Anything – snakes and rats – could come inside. The line between us and nature had crumbled. What once had been outside was now in the house. Mud. Sand. And water. It leaked from the parlor ceiling, plopping and splattering.

We took a few more steps, both of us shuffling in the dark and unsteady in the thick mud. We tripped over the door that was prone on the floor. In the moonlight, the mud glittered. Shards of glass, I realized. The storm shutters were broken and the windowpanes had shattered inward.

Andre stumbled, kicking something. He bent over, pulling my hand. 'Look,' he said. 'Daddy's shaving mug. It's on the floor. Why? What's it doing here?'

'Andre. Please. Lower your voice.'

'But why's it here? Nobody's allowed to touch it. Only Daddy. Mama gave it to him. For Christmas. Who did this?'

'Please. Talk softly. No one did anything. It fell. The water must have carried it. We'll put it back.'

I picked it up, a gift from Oscar's first wife but now in my hands. Mud slid from it. The soap inside of the mug had been hollowed out so that only a thin rim of it was along the sides. I held it to my nose. It smelled of fish, seaweed, and dank mud, and I felt the sudden need to sit down and cry.

'Ma'am?' Andre pushed against me. I took his hand and we walked on, tripping over unseen objects. The sandy mud sucked and pulled at our shoes. The table bench that Oscar had pushed against the front door was on its side. The piano bench was upside down by the roll-top desk. The icebox was face down on the floor. The stove was angled away from the

265

wall as though someone had picked up one end and moved it. Some of the buckets that I had labored to fill with water had fallen onto the floor and were on their sides.

'I want my house back,' Andre said. 'The way it was.'

'Oh, Andre,' I said.

'Where's Daddy? Why isn't he here? And where are my dogs?'

Oscar. I saw him in the barnyard, the water rising and the horses rearing.

I put Oscar's shaving mug on the kitchen table and said, 'The dogs are in the attic. They'll come down when they're ready. And your father . . .' I stopped. During the storm, Andre had called for Oscar, and I'd told him that Oscar was helping the cows and horses. My words had not consoled him. He continued to ask for his father, and in turn I sang to him, the only thing I knew to do to comfort him.

'I want to go to the barn,' Andre said. 'You said Daddy's there. Why won't he come home?'

Oscar in the water, the waves crashing over him.

'Why?' Andre said. 'Why won't Daddy come home?'

Oscar swept away, disappearing from my sight.

Andre pulled my hand. 'Why?' he said.

He was five, too old and too bright to be easily fooled. I had been younger than he when my infant brother died. No one said a word to me; the baby simply disappeared. When I asked my father what had happened or why my mother stayed in bed, he did not answer my questions. Instead, he sent me to my room and told me to be quiet and to behave. To this day, I recalled how bewildered and frightened I had been.

I cupped Andre's face in my hands. 'Your father isn't in

the barn. He had been but then he left to come home. But something must have happened, and I don't know where your father is. I wish I did, but I don't. So we'll have to wait and see.'

'Something happened? To Daddy?'

'I'm not sure. But, Andre, I'm here. You aren't alone.' I stroked his cheeks with my thumbs. I couldn't read his eyes in the dark, and I was glad that he couldn't read mine. 'Do you understand?' I said.

He shook his head.

'Nor do I. But here's what I do know. You're thirsty and hungry. Let's see what we can do about that. How would that be?'

He didn't say anything.

I said, 'Things will be better in the morning.'

'They will?'

'Yes,' and I wanted that to be true.

I tried to lift the icebox from the floor, but it was waterlogged and I couldn't raise it more than a few inches. I fumbled in the dark and managed to put together a meal of canned peaches and water from one of the buckets that was on the table. Andre and I sat on a bench and faced the dark hole in the wall so that I could keep watch. We drank the water quickly, both of us parched. Andre asked for more. 'Just a little,' I said, my own mouth still dry. There were only five buckets.

When we finished the peaches, I took him to my bedroom and using as little water as possible, I washed his face, hands, and legs. I put him in one of Oscar's shirts; his nightshirt was a muddy heap on his bedroom floor. Andre was limp with fatigue, and his chin nodded close to his chest. Floodwater had come partway up the bed but the surface of the feather mattress was dry enough. 'I'm right here,' I said to him as I helped him into my bed. 'I won't leave you.' He mumbled something. By the wardrobe, I took off my soiled clothes, wiped my face and hands, and put on a clean shirtwaist and petticoat. I closed the bedroom door as though that would shelter us from all harm. I longed for another drink of water but instead, I lay down beside Andre, my arm around him. The mosquito netting was gone and above us, the torn cloth in the canopy seemed to float in the wind, sweeping over us.

'Hail Mary, full of Grace,' I said as I held Andre close. This was his prayer before bedtime. 'The Lord is with thee.' I could not remember the rest of the words. 'Do you know the next part?' I said. He didn't say anything; he was falling asleep. I started the prayer again but said only the first two lines, over and again until his breathing settled into the soft, shallow rise and fall of sleep.

Throughout the house, rainwater dripped from leaks in the ceiling and splattered into the mud. Oscar, I thought. Where are you? I closed my eyes, but I kept seeing him floundering in the waves. My heart racing, I sat up, then put on my shoes, and went out onto the back veranda.

The wicker chairs were in pieces, and above, the clouds were thin and shredded. The night sky glimmered white under the full moon. The land was patched with its light, and there were ponds of standing water. The wind was still strong, but it came from the gulf and the breeze was light at the back of the house. I looked for signs of life and listened for a voice that was stronger than the wind and the crash of the waves. If Oscar had found shelter at the Ogdens' or at other neighbors', he'd be on his way home. He must be frantic with worry about us.

Nothing could keep him from getting home as soon as he could. Unless he were injured, suffering, and alone in the dark.

The storm had been vicious and cruel. Anyone small or weak could have been hurt. Or worse. But not Oscar; he'd be home by daylight. If he wasn't, I'd summon help. I'd find the Ogdens or other neighbors, and we'd search for him.

The moon went behind the clouds, and rain showers came and went. Something pressed against my skirt, frightening me. It was one of the dogs, then all four were on the veranda. Their panting was labored, and listening to them made me thirsty. So little water, I thought. I had to make it last. Oscar, though, would be home in the morning, and he'd know what to do. At this moment these dogs were perhaps as parched as I. They were Andre's pets, his friends, and I couldn't let anything happen to them. Andre had been through enough.

I went inside and poured water into the two bowls that Andre and I had used for our peaches. A few days ago I would have been appalled at the lack of sanitation but there was nothing sanitary about the storm. The dogs crowded around the bowls and licked them dry. I filled them again. Listening to the dogs as they lapped the water made me all the thirstier. Only five buckets, I reminded myself. And the water in the bathtub and in the cistern.

I went back out onto the veranda. When my legs began to tremble with fatigue, I came inside, sat on the edge of the bed, and took off my shoes. I lay down beside Andre and curled around him.

I awoke with a start. For an instant, I was lost: the torn canopy overhead, the dank earthy smell of mud, and Andre beside me, stirring. Daylight showed through the broken storm shutters, and the memory of the storm returned. Outside, the dogs barked and yipped. From a distance, someone shouted, calling.

Oscar. Joy drove me to my feet, the cold mud on the floor momentarily stunning me. Barefoot, I hurried, slipping, to the back veranda. Oscar was midway between the house and the bayou, on foot and skirting around a pond of standing water. The dogs circled him, their tails wagging. I waved and went to the back steps. The veranda bounced as though the stilts had come loose, and all at once, my joy buckled and collapsed.

This wasn't Oscar. He wasn't tall enough, and his gait was wrong.

'It's Mr Wiley,' Andre said. I hadn't heard him come outside. Wearing Oscar's worn blue shirt, he looked all the smaller. He said, 'Mr Wiley's walking. He don't like to walk, not if he can hitch up a wagon. Or ride a horse.'

Wiley Ogden. The skin below my left eye twitched. I touched it. It wouldn't stop.

'Mr Wiley!' Andre shouted. 'How come you're walking?'

Wiley put his hand to his ear.

'He can't hear you,' I said. Andre looked up at me and there was Oscar in the shape of his jaw and in his eyebrows. 'Stay with me,' I said. I took his hand, the image of Oscar in the water so vivid that it was as though it were happening again before my eyes.

'Something's wrong with the cows,' Andre said. 'They look funny.'

The grass in the back pasture was flattened with mud. A shovel near the foot of the stairs lay abandoned and farther away, a wheelbarrow was upright as if waiting for someone to push it back to the barn. In places, boards were piled in heaps, and pieces of cloth caught in crushed bushes fluttered in the wind. Steel milk canisters were strewn in every direction and throughout the pasture, cows and horses lay on their sides.

Andre said, 'That one over there, see her? Her neck is twisted funny.'

Wiley was hatless and even from this distance I was able to see that his pale forehead was drawn with concern. There was something else about him, a sense of reluctance perhaps, his pace slowing as he looked up at us. Wiley had news about Oscar, I thought. Bad news.

'Why's her neck like that?' Andre said.

It was morning, overcast and gray but daylight. It was windy but the storm was over. Oscar should be home. A suffocating pain gripped my heart.

'Why?' Andre said.

'She's not well,' I heard myself say. 'Something happened to her.'

'She's sick? Is that what you mean? They're all sick?'

'Yes.'

'Over there, by that big puddle of water,' Andre said, pointing to one of the horses. 'That looks like Maud. Her leg is bent wrong. It's sticking up in the air.'

Wiley quickened his stride, and as he came closer, I saw his alarm. His glances darted from the barn to us, then past the house toward the shoreline, skimming the land before returning to us. 'Mrs Williams,' he called. 'Andre. You all right? Everybody there all right? Everybody?'

'Mr Wiley,' Andre shouted. 'The cows and Maud aren't right. They ain't moving.'

'They *aren't* moving,' I said, my words hollow and flat.

'I know. It's all wrong.'

I pressed my hand against my breastbone to ease the suffocating pain. I had been certain that Oscar had been swept to the Ogdens'. I had pictured him safe in their stairwell. I had convinced myself of this; I needed it to be true. But Wiley, here and alone, and his question – 'Everybody?' – meant only one thing. He knew nothing about Oscar.

Wiley's upper lip was split in the middle and crusted with blood. One of his eyes was swollen and bruised. His trousers were torn at the knees, and the buttons were missing from his shirt. He couldn't meet my eyes when I told him Oscar wasn't home, the three of us on the back veranda and Andre holding his hand. Wiley's gaze jittered from my bare feet to the bayou and then toward the barn, taking in its collapsed front wall, the piles of boards, and the overturned water trough. My words were edged with a tremor, an undercurrent of panic ready to surface. I said only what was necessary: Oscar had let the cows and horses out of the barn, and the water was swift and deep. I couldn't say more. Andre had acquired a puzzled, troubled look, and kept looking off at the pasture. I felt myself teetering toward despair, a dangerous bottomless place. To describe Oscar in the water, the waves and his struggle, to say any of that out loud was to relive those moments again.

'We'll find him,' Wiley said. 'And Frank T.'

'Frank T.?'

'Me and him was in the city,' Wiley said. His words lisped and there was a tremor in his voice, too. 'We was delivering milk, doing it quick. Him on his route, me on mine. Water came up, it was fast, I've never seen nothing like it. It came to the necks of Blaze and Mike. My horses. I looked for Frank T., couldn't find him nowhere. I had to ride out the storm

272

with the Browns on Broadway. When the water went down, I headed for home. On foot.'

'How come?' Andre said. 'What happened to Blaze and Mike?'

He shook the question off.

My throat tightened. Frank T. The man who had strutted when we danced together at the pavilion, the brother who Nan scolded every time he spoke to me.

'Parts of Galveston are gone,' Wiley said. An odd flatness had crept into his eyes and it was in his voice, too.

'Pardon?' I said.

'Blocks of it gone. The ones close to the beach.'

Andre said, 'Gone where?'

'Washed away.'

'Dear Lord,' I said. I couldn't imagine it; it wasn't possible. 'Are you sure?'

'Plenty.'

'Buildings? Is that what you mean? Homes? Gone?'

'It ain't good.'

A storm powerful enough to destroy houses, and Oscar had been in the water. My panic bubbled; I pushed it down. 'Your family?' I said. 'Other than Frank T.?'

'They're all right.'

'Thank God.'

'Yes, ma'am.' His voice shook. He swallowed. 'We'll find them. Frank T. and Oscar. Me and Daddy, we'll get the neighbors to help.'

A search party. I turned toward the pasture and looked for signs of life, trying to see past the dead cows and horses. Their positions were grotesque, their necks and legs bent and twisted. The cows' udders looked even more swollen than before.

'They could be hurt,' Wiley said. 'Broke legs.'

'Hurt,' I said. It was an instant before I realized he referred to Oscar and Frank T. 'Yes,' I said. 'I agree.' My hopes rose. They were injured and waiting for help. Oscar was injured but alive.

'Mrs Williams,' Wiley said. He cocked his head toward Andre, whose eyes were glassy. 'It could be a while. You and Andre, you best come on home with me. Wait with Mama and Nan.' His gaze slid over me and I saw myself as he did. I was disheveled, barefoot with mud to my ankles. My hair was tangled and loose, and I wore only my shirtwaist and petticoat.

He said, 'Ain't good for you to be here. Not right now.'

'Mr Ogden, no,' I said. 'I can't leave. Oscar could be on his way home this very minute. If he got here only to find an empty house, he'd be frantic.'

'But—'

'If you could take Andre, I'd be for ever grateful. He needs breakfast.' My words were rushed, the undercurrent of panic rising. I willed myself to slow down. 'You see,' I said, 'the icebox fell over and is filled with seawater. And yesterday, I had not thought to get the sacks of flour up off of the floor. Even if I had, I'm not a cook. But your sister is. And your mother. Please take Andre. He's better off there for now. But I need to stay here and wait for Oscar.'

'Oscar ain't going to like it, me going off without you.'

'I'll tell him that I insisted.'

A tired smile showed at the corners of Wiley's mouth.

'Thank you,' I said. I whisked Andre to his room to help him get dressed. I sorted through his clothes but he had so few and everything was wet and muddy. Finally I found a shirt

274

and short pants that would have to do. I got him out of Oscar's shirt and into his own. I said, 'Miss Nan will be so very pleased to see you.'

He didn't say anything: his teeth chattered too hard. He was cold with fear, I thought. Wiley and I had said too much about Oscar. I rubbed his arms and told him that things would get better.

'When?' he said.

'By tomorrow all of your clothes will be dry.' I forced a smile but Andre's eyes were flat. I fastened the buttons on his short pants; I put his stockings on him, then laced his muddy boots. I tried to smooth his cowlick with my fingers, but it had a will of its own. From the front of the house, I heard Wiley move the furniture back into place. The parlor chairs thumped as he righted them. So did the icebox and the stove. The upright was more difficult. I heard his groans as he pushed it back against the wall. When Andre was as present-able as I could manage, we went to the back veranda where Wiley met us. There, he pointed toward the bayou and to the west.

'We're that way, if you need us,' he said. A small grove of trees, or what was left of them, marked the Ogden home. I crouched and embraced Andre and as I did, he put his arms around my neck and his cheek to mine. Fighting sudden tears, I kissed him and his kiss in return was loud and sweet. 'You're a brave young man,' I whispered. 'I'm proud of you.'

'You are?'

'Immensely.' I tightened my embrace, then released him and said, 'Now mind your manners and listen to Mr Wiley and Miss Nan. And to Mr and Mrs Ogden. I'll see you soon.'

I smiled for Andre but he didn't notice. He looked up at

Wiley, and in his eyes, a small spark of excitement flickered. Going to the Ogdens' was a special treat, I realized.

Wiley nodded his goodbye to me. At the foot of the stairs where the dogs waited, he hoisted Andre to his shoulders so that Andre's legs straddled either side of his head.

Without a look back, they all headed toward the bayou. Wiley avoided the low places filled with standing water and picked his way past the cows and horses, turning his shoulders to shield Andre from the sight. He called to the dogs, his tone sharp when they showed too much interest in the carcasses. Once, I heard Andre call to them too, his voice shrill as if he were upset.

I expected to feel a measure of relief. Caring for Andre and the need to stay calm in his presence was exhausting. It was true that there was very little food, but that was an excuse. I needed time to myself without him clutching me and asking questions about Oscar. I needed silence. Or so I had thought. Now, as Wiley walked farther away with Andre on his shoulders, a profound sense of emptiness came over me. I had never felt more alone.

CHAPTER FIFTEEN

The Truth

Everything would be better once Oscar was home, I told myself. In the kitchen, I struck match after match, each one so soft from the sultry air that they bent and broke. At last, one of the matches sputtered and then flared long enough for me to light the oven. When I was sure that the fire would hold, I put a pot of water on the stove to heat. Oscar could be cut and bruised, but he'd be home at any minute.

I went to the bedroom and looked out the back window. Oscar was nowhere in sight. Rainwater leaked from the ceiling and splattered in the mud as I dressed and tied my hair with a ribbon. There was still no sign of Oscar. I straightened the damp bed linens the best that I could, the house settling, popping and creaking. Wiley and his father, I reminded myself, will find him. They'll bring him home, and I'll take care of him. I gathered towels and the bar of Ivory soap from the washroom and put them on the dressing table in our bedroom. Come home, Oscar. Please.

I went to the front veranda to look for him, mud clinging to my shoes. My breath caught; I backed into the doorway. The east end of the veranda dangled as though unattached to the stilts. The railing and the steps were gone, sheared off. In front of the house, a misshapen mattress was in a pond of standing water. Part of a picket fence was caught in the bushes, and a rowboat was beached on the scrubby land.

The gulf churned; the white-capped waves rolled and crashed. Channels of pooled water sliced the beach, and piles of rubble had washed up along the tide line. The tide, I thought. It was visible from the veranda. I rubbed my temples. The sand hills were gone.

And St. Mary's. I couldn't find it. It was missing. That couldn't be, I told myself. Two large wood buildings did not simply vanish. It was my nerves; I was imagining things. I needed food and rest. I was on the verge of collapse. I closed my eyes, then looked again. The place where the orphanage had been was swept clean.

The nuns who had danced at the pavilion. The children who chased one another, Andre, too, all of them darting around tables. The three boys who helped Oscar on Sundays.

Inside the house, something clinked and clattered. 'Who's there?' I called, turning.

It was the pot on the stove. It rocked, clattering, the water boiling. I started to pick it up, then let go, the handles burning my hands. I found two dish towels and using them as potholders, I moved it off the burner. The clinking stopped.

None of this was happening, I thought. Oscar couldn't be missing; the orphanage could not have disappeared. I turned away from the stove and as I did, I saw the house as I had not before. Dishes, pans, sheet music, and my books were strewn on the mud-covered floor. Overhead, the ceiling was splintered with cracks and bowed as if heavy with water. Stains darkened the walls, the plaster already peeling. A line of dirt rimmed the lower parts of the walls.

The watermark, I realized. From the flood.

While Andre and I had found shelter in the stairwell, St. Mary's had fallen. While I sang to Andre, the children and the nuns must have begged for help, reaching for one another, crying out as water rushed. And Oscar. He might have cried out too.

No. He was all right. And perhaps the nuns and orphans were too. They could have escaped before the storm destroyed the buildings; they could have clung to boards. But the little ones? The ones who were Andre's age, or younger?

I sank down onto a bench, each drop of water that dripped from the ceiling loud in my ears, the crashing waves at the gulf even louder. For some reason, this small house had stood. For some reason, Andre and I had been spared. For some reason, Oscar had been caught in a wave.

Why?

So I could understand how very dear he was to me, I realized. So the three of us could start over when he returned, so we could rebuild. Because he will come home, I was sure of it. We'd begin again. But not here in Galveston; I would never go through another hurricane again. Never. We'd go inland to Houston. Oscar could start a dairy there. I'd give piano lessons and every penny would go toward making a new home. It'd be difficult but we had one another. We'd do it together. First, though, Oscar must come home.

I hurried down the hallway to our bedroom, then to the back veranda. Still nothing. Stay calm, I told myself. Make a plan. Do something for Oscar, something more than boiling water. I looked toward the place in the pasture where I'd last seen him. I'd go there, I decided. Then I'd go directly to the bayou where surely he waited for help.

The stairs shook beneath my feet as I went down them. The wind caught my skirt, and I battered away strands of hair that gathered at the corners of my mouth. The ground was boggy with wet sand, and littered with broken boards, pieces of dishes and teacups, a doll, and a shattered gilt-framed mirror. I stopped to gather up the hem of my skirt so that I could walk faster and as I did, I was struck with a new fear.

If Oscar came home while I was gone, he'd find the house empty. He'd be beside himself with worry.

I'd leave him a note. I turned back toward the house. *Dearest,* I imagined myself writing. *Should you find this, do not worry. Andre and I are safe. I am looking for you but will be home soon.*

In the bedroom now, I found the box of stationery that I had stored in the bottom of the wardrobe. It was waterlogged and ruined. My fountain pen was gritty with mud but the ink bottle was still capped. I took it and the pen, and went to the parlor, a path now forming in the mud. I searched through the roll-top desk in the parlor, drips from the ceiling splattering my shirtwaist and face. All I needed was paper, even a scrap, so I could write my note and resume my search for Oscar.

There were only black leather-bound record-keeping books. I fanned through one, looking for a blank sheet but the pages were filled with Oscar's postings about money earned and money spent. I glanced toward the clock on the mantle. Two minutes past six. For a moment, I was unsure if it was morning or evening. I looked again at the clock. The pendulum had blown off. The clock had stopped. It had to be late morning if not early afternoon. The storm had been over for hours. Oscar was somewhere, waiting, injured and needing help.

He could be dead.

No, I told myself. No. Find a piece of paper and write a note. Then look for him and bring him home.

I pulled out another record-keeping book and as I did, a balled-up sheet of paper tumbled out from the back of the desk. I took it, stepped away from the leak in the ceiling, and worked at the paper. It was deeply creased and I smoothed the corners with my thumbs. It was a letter – *Dear Oscar*. There was handwriting on both sides of the sheet but it was blank at the bottom half of one side. It was enough space for me to write a note. I'd leave it on the kitchen table for Oscar to see.

Then I saw the closure. *Your loving sister, Vivian Boehmer.*

I turned it over. It was dated August 17, 1900. Two weeks before our marriage. Oscar's sister. Someone who had heard the rumors about me.

I crumpled the letter, squeezing it tight. As Oscar must have done, I thought. Something in the letter must have upset him. Or angered him. I jammed it into the back of the desk.

Tear out a page from a record-keeping book, I told myself. Write the note and search for Oscar. Find him and bring him home. That was all that mattered. Yet, it was the letter that I took out from the desk. I had to know what his sister had told him.

August 17, 1900

Dear Oscar,

I trust that you and my little nephew are well. All is well here.

281

I write this in a hurry because I want to put it in the after-noon post. Your letter came this morning and I wish I could say I am happy for you, but I cannot. Dear Brother, please do not marry her. There is so much talk about her and the things people say are shocking.

Oscar knew. I burned with shame.

It pains me to tell you but you must know the truth. She has disgraced herself. Respectable people will not let her in their homes. Even her mother will not. That is what people say.

I should stop reading; I'd read enough. But I had to finish it. I felt sure that Oscar had.

I will spare you the ugly things people have said. But I will say that her actions have broken the heart of a woman who has two children. And this woman is a cripple.

Bands of pain squeezed my heart.

Please do not marry her. I beg you, dear Oscar. I know you are lonely and miss Bernadette. But please do not do this.

> *Your loving sister,*
> *Vivian Boehmer*

Oscar knew.

The letter slipped from my hands. He must have been furious when he read it. I had deceived him. He might have written to me. *I will not Marry You, Miss Wainwright. I know the*

Truth about You. If he had, the letter would have arrived too late. I would have already left Dayton and been on my way to Galveston. For some reason, he went ahead and married me. Was it because he saw how very desperate I was? That I had no place else to go? Had he married me out of pity?

I looked at my wedding band, its gold bright and unmarred. Not pity, I thought. Oscar cared for me as no other man ever had. Knowing the truth about me, he took me as I was. He hadn't complained when I was cold and withdrawn; he didn't belittle me when I made mistakes with Andre. Instead, Oscar kept a firm hold on me, understanding that without him, I was lost.

I had to find him. I had to apologize for deceiving him. I had to make amends, set things straight. From this moment on, there would be only the truth.

The back veranda steps creaked and rattled as I went down them. The mud in the pasture was slippery, and the sole on my right shoe had come loose at the toe. The watery soft ground dipped in places, and I tripped over clumps of uprooted grass. In my mind, Oscar's hand was on my elbow, leading me toward the place where I had last seen him.

Yesterday, when the water came into the house, I had scooped up my letters from Oscar, the ones he had written when he first came to Texas, and put them in the hatbox. His letters had been with me during the storm just as they had been with me when I moved to Oberlin, to Philadelphia, back to Dayton, and finally to Galveston.

Tears filled my eyes. Andre, I thought. He had held my hand when we had left the stairwell, trusting me to keep him safe. After I found Oscar, I'd bring Andre home. Oscar will want that; I wanted that, too.

I blotted the tears with my fingers and all at once, I gagged, sickened by the stench of a nearby cow.

My hand over my nose, I hurried on. Debris lay everywhere in the flattened grass: milk canisters, driftwood, and the headboard from someone's bed. A piece of white cloth was tangled in the branches of a salt cedar tree, and farther on, a washtub was in the middle of a shallow pond. In the distance, someone – a woman – was coming my way. Nan Ogden. Or her mother. My pulse quickened all the more. There might be news about Oscar.

I waved to catch her attention, and as I did, I heard again his words: You do things right. He'd held on to that belief even after he knew the truth. I shook my head. Not me, I thought. You, Oscar. You're the one who does things right.

'Mrs Williams,' the woman called.

I waved again, then stumbled, tripping over a board. It shifted, exposing a snake. It coiled, the long brown body with black patches taut as a spring. Its head held high, its dark eyes stared into mine. The rattle was crisp and loud. I took a step away. The boggy ground dipped; I slipped and fell onto my hands and knees. The snake reared its head back, the tongue flickering. It darted forward and struck my left hand.

I couldn't get up. The loose sole of my shoe was caught in my hem. The snake coiled again, then darted. It struck my wrist. Somehow I got myself up on my feet. I backed away as it slithered off in the grass.

Pain shot through my hand and wrist. Dizzy from it, I held my arm to my chest, the pain deepening with each footstep as I tried to get farther from the snake, afraid that it might return to bite again.

'Mrs Williams,' the woman said, 'What's the matter? What're you doing out here?'

It was Nan Ogden. I expected her gray eyes to be critical and her mouth to be tight with disapproval. I had turned Andre over to her instead of caring for him myself. Instead, there was concern. I held out my left hand. The wounds bled and the skin around them was red. 'A snake,' I said.

'What kind?'

'I don't know.'

'Did it rattle?'

I nodded, too frightened to speak now.

'Oh good Lord, let's get you inside. How many times did it bite?'

Her face swam before me. A rattlesnake. My arm tingled, and I was suddenly down on the marshy ground, water seeping into my skirt. I blinked to bring Nan back into focus.

'Mrs Williams, stand up.' She got behind me and tried to lift me. Pain stabbed my left arm and streaked up my neck and into my jaw. I heard myself moan.

'Have to get you home,' Nan said. 'But you have to help. Can't do it by myself.'

My legs were sprawled out before me. A rattlesnake. Two bites. My teeth chattered, the cold water from the ground seeming to creep into my skin.

I gritted my teeth to stop the chattering. 'Oscar,' I said. 'Has there been any word of him?'

'Now you stand up. You hear me? I know all kinds of people that have been snakebit and they've walked home with no complaint. So get up. Now.'

She heaved me to my feet. Spots danced before my eyes. 'You can lean on me,' she said. 'Never said you couldn't. Lift your foot. Now the other.' She turned me around so that we faced the house. It was far away and seemed to float on top of the stilts.

'Is Andre all right?' I said.

'He's with Mama. Now walk, Mrs Williams. Walk.'

'I'm not going to die, am I?'

'For pity's sake, put some starch in your legs. I can't hold you up much longer. Now walk. One foot in front of the other.'

I willed myself to do as Nan said. I'll be fine, I told myself, the tingling in my arm now a burn. I had to be fine. Oscar and I had so much to do.

'Have you heard anything?' I said. 'About Oscar?'

'Walk, Mrs Williams. I can't carry you. You ain't as light as you look.'

I tried to shift my weight off of Nan. I can do this, I told myself. But my chest was so tight, my lungs squeezed as though crushed.

On and on we walked, the rusty sound of my breathing loud in my ears. Blood ran from the bites. My skirt was smeared with it; Nan's was too. My eyes kept closing; I fought to keep them open. The stench of the cow was again overpowering and I was all at once gagging, sick, Nan holding me.

'Don't you give up,' she said, wiping my chin with her fingers. 'Won't have it.'

I will not die, I told myself. Oscar needs me. Andre does too.

'We're almost there,' Nan said. 'All you've got to do is get up these steps.'

'What did you say about Andre?'

'I said he's with Mama. Now you've got to help me get you up the steps. Come on now, you can do it.'

The steps were so high, too high, but her grasp on my waist was firm. 'A few more,' she said. 'You're doing good.' We stumbled against one another; pain ricocheted through my arm.

'Now the veranda, almost there.'

'Miss Ogden, I'm concerned about Oscar.'

'You're slopping your words. Good Lord, this bed is a pretty sight even if all this mud ain't. Here now, turn around so I can get you in and tucked up.'

'My skirt,' I said.

'What?'

'The hem. It's filthy. And all the blood.'

'It don't matter.'

'It does matter.' My voice was shrill. 'The bed needs to be clean. For Oscar. He's hurt.' I started to reach around to the buttons at the back of my skirt. Pain tore through me.

'Mrs Williams, let me help you with that. Here.' She took my good hand. 'Hold on to the bed post. You ain't altogether steady.'

I wrapped my fingers around the post as she worked at the skirt buttons. Nearby, the tattered ends of the torn canopy over the bed rose and fell in the breeze, and the wardrobe seemed to be at a peculiar slant. 'You're quite sure that Andre is all right?' I said.

'He's with Mama. Like I said.' My skirt slipped off of my hips and onto the muddy floor. 'Now sit on the bed so you won't trip.'

She steadied me as I sat and then she unbuttoned my shoes and got me into the bed. My arm was sticky and hot. I shook; everything now so cold. Nan held up my wounded arm and pulled the quilt to my chin. Tears sprang to my ears. I squeezed them away. 'I'm worried about Oscar,' I said.

She didn't say anything.

'He let the cows and the horses out of the barn and the water carried him away.'

'I wish you'd stop all this talking. You're shaking bad and I need to clean your arm.' She paused. 'And don't you worry, no good comes from that. Mr Williams, well, he knows how to swim: Daddy showed him. Likely he's on his way home, could be he's helping somebody out. You know how he is. Can't turn his back on nobody.'

She dabbed at the wounds with a piece of cloth. I bit my lip to keep from crying out. When the pain subsided a little, I said, 'Oscar's helping someone? Was that what you said?'

Nan mumbled something, then said, 'I need to wash this.' She turned away and went toward the dressing table.

'But he's on his way home?'

Her back to me, she stopped, her shoulders drawing up. Her form blurred and there were two of her. I blinked, and Nan was again one person who now stood over me. 'Mrs Williams,' she said. 'That man of yours.' She put her hand on my cheek. Her touch was light and cool. She glanced down at my arm and then she looked into my eyes. 'He told you he'd get on home? After he saw to the cows? And the horses? Was that what he said?'

I nodded.

'Have you ever known Oscar Williams to let a person down?'

The boy who had attended my recitals. The one person who responded to my letters this spring. The man who knew the truth but believed me to be a better woman than I was. 'No,' I said. 'Never.'

'Well, then.'

Yes, I thought, now seeing an image of Oscar. He was on the platform at Union Station. He wore his suit and he held his pocket watch, checking the time, waiting for me.

I closed my eyes and gave in to the pain.

CHAPTER SIXTEEN

The House

It was a sorrowful time; there wasn't no other way to put it. What the storm did to us was cruel, and I won't never forget it. Or forgive it. The storm did what it wanted and then blew itself out, leaving us to try to put things right. But some things can't be put right.

Like St. Mary's, the orphanage. I couldn't keep from thinking about it when I walked through Oscar's back pasture a little while ago, stepping around the piles of black ashes and charred bones of the cows and horses. There weren't words for what happened at the orphanage. Them poor little children. I didn't like thinking how scared they likely were when the waves mashed the sand hills and flooded both buildings. The nuns had taken the orphans to the boys' dormitory, thinking it was the safer of the two. That was what Bill Murney said when Daddy found him wandering by the bayou wearing nothing but a tattered pair of pants. He was one of the orphans that helped out at the dairy on Sundays. When the water came in the dormitory, Bill said, the nuns herded everybody to the second floor. They all took up praying but God didn't pay them no mind. The roof blew off and the walls caved in, crushing them. What the wind didn't do, the water did. The whole place washed away.

Maybe if the nuns had taken off them headpieces that covered most of their faces or if they'd shucked the heavy rosary beads they wore around their waists, they might have had a chance. But they wouldn't have no part of doing that. Leastways that was what Bill told us. 'I caught ahold of a board,' he said, him glassy-eyed, and his hands and feet cut and bleeding. 'Caught ahold of my brother, too. Him and me washed into a tree, don't know how we got there. I held on to him the best I could, I did, that tree thrashing. But then a big wave hit us, bigger than the others.' He looked at us then. 'Have you all seen Joe anywhere?'

I could hardly think about it, him being in a tree during a big blow. Out of all them nuns and those children, only three orphans lived, Bill being one of them. But not Joe. We didn't find him. We didn't find James either, the red-headed foundling that worked at the dairy too.

It'd been two weeks and two days since the big blow but time didn't heal, not one bit. I don't know who came up with that notion but it was flat-out wrong. It was work that pulled a person through bad times. Even sorrowful work like what I did now, shoveling dried mud out of Oscar's house. There was nothing easy about this work, the mud breaking off in sheets and turning to powdery dirt. And there was nothing easy about being here today. I hadn't been back since Mrs Williams was snakebit. But this morning, I woke up ready. 'The house needs seeing to,' I told Mama. 'If you can spare me.'

I dumped the dried mud with pieces of window glass in it over the side of the back veranda. I hadn't figured on shoveling mud, but when I walked up from the pasture, there was a shovel close to the back steps. It was like Bernadette had left it there for me. 'Ahhh, Nan,' I could hear her say. 'I knew you'd be the one to take care of my house.'

I worked and as long as I kept moving, I was all right. My mind on work, I didn't have to think about the mattress in the bedroom that was stained with blood. When my hands were busy, I didn't think about all the dead people that washed up in the bayou by our house, and how they were swelled up and most of them stripped naked. The wind ripped off their clothes, that was what Daddy figured. As long as I stayed busy I didn't have to think what Daddy and Wiley had to do with them poor dead people.

The shovel scraped the parlor floor and it hurt me to mark up the wood, but we'd had to do the same in our house; there wasn't no other way. Oscar's house stank bad from all this mud that had footprints in it going every which way. Some of them prints were mine, and the narrow ones were Mrs Williams'. I figured the big ones were Wiley's, and I knew the little footprints were Andre's. Tracks were here too, and not all of them were the dogs'. 'Coons and 'possums had been inside; likely they'd climbed up the stilts looking for food. The front door needed to be boarded up, same for the windows. There wasn't nothing I could do about that, not today, so I kept on trying to get the dried-up mud out of the house, sorrow wrapped around my heart and me fighting it.

That wasn't all I fought. When I'd first come into the house, the door that went to the attic stairwell was open. It bothered me and I couldn't say why, other than it was one more thing that wasn't right. I started to close it, the dried mud sticking to it, and when I did, I saw something halfway up the stairs. A hatbox. Of all things. There was no counting for the peculiar things the storm had done, but that hatbox, I knew, hadn't been carried there by the water. Mrs Williams, I thought. She'd saved one of her fancy hats. If that wasn't like her, I didn't know what was.

But when I opened it, there wasn't a hat in it but other things – the crucifixes, letters, and Oscar's wood box with the *W* on the lid. I closed the hatbox quick. It was like looking at Mrs Williams' fear when the water came in, Oscar gone, and her gathering what had to be saved. Me and Mama had done the same. We'd filled a wood crate with the family Bible that nobody could read, a few photographs, my fiddle and bow, Daddy's deed to our land, and money. The dollar coin that Oscar gave me the night of the dance was some of that money. I'd carried the crate up into the attic, the water on my heels. I was plenty scared, I don't mind saying. Anybody would be.

I put the hatbox on the kitchen table, telling myself that it wasn't for me to look at the things inside it. If this storm had taught me anything it was this: once it was over, keep your eyes closed. And if you have to keep your eyes open, don't let your mind think.

I should have worn blinders when I went to the city last Sunday. I had felt a powerful need for church so I'd made the walk. We were down to just one horse, that being Jim Bowie, and Daddy said he needed a rest. Wiley had ridden Jim every day since the big blow, bringing home food supplies that came by boat from Houston. So I walked to the city, getting closer to the sooty smoke from all the fires in Galveston. I tried not to think about what those fires were burning but I knew. The stink told me.

There was another stink in the city. Lime. Houston sent it

293

by the barrel, and people in the city covered the streets with it. It was supposed to ward off sickness, and if there was one thing we didn't need, it was sick people. When I finally got to our Baptist church, the one on the west side of town, the roof was mostly gone but that didn't stop the preacher. He talked about courage, about doing the best that you could, and how there was no need to wonder why the storm took some but not us. 'Remember the dead,' he preached. The pulpit had fallen over and busted so he had to stand in front of us like a regular person. The church was filled, us all sitting shoulder to shoulder on benches that were warped from being under water.

'Mourn the dead,' the preacher said. 'But take care of the living.'

His words shored me up but what I saw in the city made me sorry I'd come. There was block after block of uprooted houses lying on their sides with caved-in walls. The floodwater had carried some of the houses away from their lots and when that happened, they'd plowed into other houses and knocked them down. Then there were the places near City Cemetery where there'd been houses, but now they were gone, not a thing left. And that cemetery. I didn't want to think about how the coffins came out of the ground and washed away. I didn't look to see if that had happened to Bernadette's grave; I couldn't bring myself to. It was bad enough seeing the long rows of rubble in the city that were as high as two-story houses. It was sorrowful enough that dead people were still being found under all of that.

There were carcasses, too. Horses, dogs, and cats, all of them bloated and stinking. After church, when I was leaving, I saw something I won't never forget. An overturned piano was pushed up by a dead horse on top of a heap of wood, and under the piano, a hand stuck out. A man's hand. I looked long enough to see if I knew it but I couldn't tell. The skin, gray, was starting to fall off of the bones.

In the kitchen, I moved one of the benches so I could shovel where it'd been. A pen and bottle of ink were on the table, and that was another peculiar thing. It was like Mrs Williams had been fixing to write something after the storm. But that didn't make sense, not even for her. Nobody would sit down and scratch out a few words, not when people were missing and needed looking for. But then, there was no making sense of a lot of things. Like the sand hills. They were gone and without them there wasn't nothing between the beach and the land. Everything ran together, all flat. The gulf was flat, too, not a wave nowhere. It looked like it couldn't hurt a fly.

I took the buckets that were on the floor and stacked them on the back veranda. The buckets could be washed out and used again. Most things couldn't. We had to start over with next to nothing. Other than a cup and a platter, all of Mama's dishes broke. Somebody's skiff landed on our front veranda but Daddy's was still missing. Oscar's traveled clear from the bayou and was sitting not more than a few yards in front of his house. Our hog drowned but we saved four of the piglets. One of the hens lived; it rode out the storm on a crossbeam in the attic. The other hens and the rooster had gone into the attic too, but they'd died. 'Their hearts likely gave out,' Daddy said about them. 'They'd been that scared.'

Back inside again, I took up shoveling. Something sparkling in the mud caught my eye. I bent down and picked it out with my fingers. It was a black bead made of glass. It made me think of them fancy dangling earrings of Mrs Williams' but this couldn't be hers. This bead was by itself; it didn't look to be part of anything. I rubbed it on my sleeve, then held it up. It was pretty how it caught the light, turning red and purple and blue. If there was ever a time I needed something pretty, it was now. I put it in my apron pocket.

The shovel blade hit something. I stopped and pulled out a plate that was buried. I took it outside and put it by the buckets. It could be used once it was washed. Daddy and Wiley had dug a new well, and the water was fresh enough. But nobody had done that at Oscar's. Wasn't no need to, not right now anyway.

I took up the shovel again, then stopped. There was a crumpled piece of paper on the floor by the icebox. Of all things. Dry, too, not falling apart like Mrs Williams' sheet music that must have blown around during the storm, me finding bits and pieces of it in the mud. I smoothed out the paper. It looked like a letter, the way it started out with a short line of words and ended the same way on the back side. The writing slanted hard to the right, and there were blots of ink in places. This didn't look like Mrs Williams' handwriting, least I didn't think so. I'd seen the letters that she'd written to Oscar this spring and summer, not that I'd been prying. Oscar had left them in his writing desk and the desk needed dusting.

I put the letter under the ink bottle. An orphanage washed away, but not a letter. Nothing about the storm made sense. Like Frank T. He was dead. There was no other way to put it. I'd tried to put it other ways – he was gone, he was in heaven – but that didn't change the hurt. It didn't change how much I missed him.

Wiley found him three days after the storm and we patched the story together. When the water came up in the city, Frank

T. had hightailed it for Maggie Mandora's house on the west side. That was what Maggie's brother, Mark, told Wiley. Their house took up shaking and a wall fell in, then the roof did, too. Mark was tossed through a hole and out into the water. The only thing that saved him was a table he caught hold of. He hung on to that and fought for his life in the dark, waves crashing over him, all that rain, the wind, and him carried off to the gulf. When the water started to go down, he was swept back and landed near his house. Except he didn't know it. He was in a state of bewilderment. Those were his words. All around him, there was nothing but rubble and pieces of houses. It was a day later before he recognized the heap that had been his home.

Frank T. didn't die alone and that made me feel some better. A person took her comfort where she could, that was another thing this storm taught me. When Wiley, Daddy, and Mark Mandora dug him out, he was hunched over Maggie like he'd tried to spare her. That made me sorry I had snapped at him for mooning over Mrs Williams. In the end, Frank T. showed what Maggie meant to him, and she would have known that. Wiley and Daddy brought Frank T. home so we could bury him right. He was a few hundred yards east of Oscar's house. 'I want him on the ridge,' Mama had said. 'It's the best place,' and that time, Daddy didn't say different.

We buried Maggie and her folks there, too. We couldn't burn them, not like Daddy and Wiley had to do to the ones that had been in the bayou. There'd been people washed up on the beach, too, and Daddy and Wiley couldn't build coffins fast enough; there wasn't enough planed lumber. So Daddy and Wiley hauled the dead inland as far as they could, Jim Bowie being the only horse to pull the wagon. I didn't ask nothing about it; I didn't want to know. But I saw the fires. Smelled them, too.

Thousands dead, that was what people at church said. Maybe six thousand, maybe more. But I wasn't going to think about that.

I needed to leave the hatbox alone, too. There was nothing but fresh hurt inside of that thing. Like seeing the crucifixes before I closed it. That surprised me plenty, Mrs Williams saving them. I'd seen how she'd reared back the first time Oscar said the Catholic prayer at dinner. I'd seen how she'd froze up at the pavilion when Oscar brought the nuns to her so they could meet her.

Oscar. Just saying his name made my heart knot up tight as a fist. He was dead.

There, I'd said it. Not 'he's missing', not 'he'll be home anytime'. Dead. It'd been two weeks and two days, and there hadn't been a word about him. We don't know what had happened to him other than what Mrs Williams saw. After looking for him for five days, Wiley went to the morgue in the city and when he got home, his eyes all red, he said, 'He ain't there. That's all I'm going to say; don't ask me nothing about it.'

If somebody had found Oscar, he was too far gone to be recognized and there weren't words for that kind of sorrow. Oscar deserved a burial. He should be on the ridge. The notion that he'd been in one of them fires made my heart ache so hard that I believed I'd be the next to die.

Like now. All this work that needed doing, but here I sat at Oscar's kitchen table because my knees were wobbling and my sorrow was bigger than me. When Wiley brought Andre home right after the storm and told us how Oscar had let the horses and cows out, how Mrs Williams said she hadn't seen him since, well, I couldn't let myself think about him. Or about Frank T. Instead, I lit into Wiley.

'You left her by herself?' I'd said. 'To wait alone? And her having nobody here, no kin? You did that?'

Wiley hung his head with shame. I got Andre settled as best I could with Mama, and left home to sit with Mrs Williams.

I found her in the pasture. She had been snakebit two times, and the venom was strong, that rattler stirred up bad from the storm. She wasn't the only one that got bit after the storm, that was what Wiley said. Rattlers were everywhere – up in trees, inside of people's houses, even in attics.

Leastways I got her to the house, I got her in her bed. I cleaned the bites the best I could, but her arm was streaked red and her breathing was ragged. She got worse and worse sweating, and her arm swelled big. 'You're doing good,' I told her. 'All this sweating, you're getting the venom out.' But I knew better and so did she. She started saying things about Oscar, how the waves carried him off, how she'd never told him what he meant to her, and how he'd saved her life.

That last part didn't make sense to me, but I was sweating myself, trying to save her, trying to cool her fever, trying to mop up the blood pouring from them bites. She told me that Andre saved her too, but if she died, she wanted me to look after him. 'Take care of Andre. You love him.' Them were her very words. I told her to quit talking, I was doing all I could for her. Her breathing got bad; she was fighting hard for air, gasping and gulping. She closed her eyes and then the rattle in her breathing stopped. 'I won't have it,' I told her. 'Don't you give up,' but she was dead.

One more person gone. And not from the storm but from a snake. That wasn't right, living through a big blow only to be took by a rattler. I'd sat on the bed holding her good hand and nearly bawled from the notion of it. Then, I washed her face and combed her hair. If I hadn't, it would have hurt her bad to see how she'd looked, all slick with sweat and her face gray.

But this hatbox. The things in it were Andre's now. I should see what was in it before I handed it over to him.

I opened it. Letters. Some were old, the envelopes yellowing, and others were newer. I saw Oscar's handwriting on a fair number of them. His penmanship was plain and made me think of how words looked in the newspapers, even and just right. But it was the other envelopes that I kept looking at. Some had the same slanted handwriting as the letter I'd found on the floor. Others were more upright. Oscar's family, I thought. His kin up there in Ohio.

Mrs Williams might have told me to take care of Andre, but that didn't make him mine. I wasn't kin. Oscar's mama and daddy were dead, but there were others. A sister and two brothers, all of them married and living in Ohio. Bernadette had told me.

I knew what I should do. I should take the letters to someone that could read. A year ago that would have been Bernadette. Two weeks and three days ago, it would have been the nuns at St. Mary's. Now I'd have to ask one of the neighbors to read them. If they came from Oscar's family, someone should write to them and tell them about Oscar and Mrs Williams. And about Andre.

They'd want him. He was all they had left of Oscar. Oscar's people would come for Andre and take him up North. They'd sell Oscar's land and I'd never see Andre again.

I put the letters back in the hatbox right quick. I wasn't going to think about none of that. Not today. Andre had nightmares; every day he asked for Oscar, crying. He even asked for Mrs Williams, calling her ma'am. I knew because it was me tending him, it was me rocking him. Not strangers up there in Ohio.

Work, I told myself. Put your mind to your work. I did, the raspy scrape of the blade grating some on my nerves. But marked-up floors was nothing, not when laid side by side with the notion of shipping Andre to people that didn't know one bitty thing about him.

I carried the shovel outside and hurled the dirt over the side of the veranda. I should tear them letters up and throw them away. Or burn them. No one would know. Even Mama hadn't said anything about finding Andre's kin. Nobody had. Likely nobody could take the notion of losing one more person.

I went back inside. Bigger things than letters had been lost; bigger things had been burned. A week ago, Everett Calloum, one of the neighbors, took up the chore of burning the carcasses of Oscar's cows and horses. The flood had taken his wife and their two little children, and he was in a bad way. 'Ain't ready to fix the house,' he'd told Daddy. 'Don't know if I ever will. But I'm wanting to do something powerful.' So Everett piled wood around and over Oscar's horses and cows, and set them on fire.

If there was one thing I was glad about, it was that Oscar wasn't here to see none of that. Leastways, four of the cows survived the storm; we don't know how. We found them roaming around, nicked with cuts.

But burning letters, that was something else. These weren't mine. And they could be from Andre's kin.

I looked again in the hatbox. Oscar's pocket watch was in it, so was his book about the stars. The polished wood box with the *W* was a wedding present; Bernadette had showed it to me. She had nearly busted with pride. 'From Oscar's family,' she told me. 'His sister and brothers. Think of it, Nan. Me, with hardly nobody and now I have Oscar and all his kin.'

Likely they were worried. People at church said the whole world was worried about Galveston and that relief money was coming in by the bucket from places as far away as England. They said Clara Barton, an important lady that knew the president of the United States, had come to Galveston to lend a hand. If people like her and people on the other side of the ocean knew about the storm, then people up in Ohio did too. Oscar's kin could come looking; Mrs Williams' could too. Hers didn't count, though. The way I saw it, they didn't have a claim on Andre.

It'd take some doing for Oscar's people to get here. The train trestles and the wagon bridge that crossed the bay had blown out. The only way to get here was by boat. For now, anyway. People said the trestles would be built again. Galveston wasn't finished, they said. 'Galveston will be better than ever,' the preacher on Sunday had said. 'Put your minds to that. And your shoulders.' Maybe that was so but as long as the trestles and the wagon bridge were down, Oscar's kin would have a mighty rough time getting here. It could be months before the trains ran again, maybe years.

The wood box with the *W* belonged to Andre now. It'd be good for him to have it. I opened it to make sure it didn't hold something he shouldn't see. There was a folded paper with a seal, like Daddy's land deed, and another paper with fancy writing. That was the one I studied. I didn't care nothing about reading but I knew months and numbers. August 30, 1900. That was the day Oscar married Mrs Williams.

Bernadette's wedding band was in Oscar's box, too. I purely missed her. Then I thought of Mrs Williams' band. She'd been buried on the ridge wearing it, not a scratch on it. 'Andre should have it,' Mama had said. But there was no getting the band off. Her hand was too swelled up.

I didn't count the bundle of paper money that was in Oscar's wood box; it wasn't mine. But there was plenty. More than enough to send Andre to Ohio.

Or it could be used to fix up Oscar's house and barn. For Andre. For when he was older. There were four cows; that was a start. Wiley could teach him to be a dairy farmer. Oscar would want that, so would Bernadette. Mrs Williams might have other notions, her being her. But she'd turned Andre over to me; she wanted him with me.

Mrs Williams. Catherine. I missed her too, even if I didn't like her all that much. I'd never been around nobody like her, a woman that didn't know one little thing about cooking or keeping a house. Her prissy ways and her fancy talk were something to behold. In the end, though, she'd done right for Andre. She took him into the stairwell and sang to him. Andre told us that.

I walked over to her piano and raised the cover over the keys. Just that quick, I heard that tune she'd played, the one that pulled Oscar away from the barn and to the house, the tune that laid bare what he meant to me. It was about the moonlight. I wasn't ever going to forget that music; each note was deep and pretty and sorrowful all at the same time. Neither was I going to forget how Mrs Williams looked at Oscar and

303

how he looked at her, the yearning between them a want that didn't leave room for nobody else.

I figured they were together now, Bernadette too. I didn't know how that would work out, but I never could figure how heaven worked. But they were up there, all three of them, Bernadette singing her swamp songs while Mrs Williams patted her mouth with her napkin but tapped her toe, wearing her shoes that were the color of butter. And Oscar, he was in the middle, with his easy smile, his broad hands with the little scars on the backs, and his way of taking care of others like it gave him pleasure.

That man. For a year I took care of him. I cooked and cleaned, and did his laundry. I helped to raise his son. But Oscar had never been mine.

My eyes watered up. He'd died taking care of his horses and cows. He couldn't let them suffer, not Oscar. I should let his kin up there in Ohio know that. I should let them know that Andre was all right, that he was being seen to. I should get somebody to write to them.

My tears were overflowing now, and I didn't do nothing to stop them. There was no one to see; there was no one to know. There was only the Gulf of Mexico, outside the window but off a good ways and shining in the sun. I didn't blame it for what happened. Not overly. It was the big blow that I mostly blamed, that wall of wind that came for us. I'd never forgive it. Never.

Thinking that stopped my tears. I mopped my face with my apron and as I did, I turned from the piano. Out the window, a line of pelicans floated in the sky, riding a current, their wings wide open. It came to me that these were the first I'd seen since the storm. But there they were, gliding along like nobody had died, like nobody's heart was in a state of bewilderment.

I went to the doorway and watched them birds drift over to where St. Mary's had been, some of them flapping their wings once in a while as they went down the island. I counted them; I did it for Oscar. He was partial to pelicans.

Oscar left his home up North and made this island his home. Andre was born here; he was a Texan. Taking that little boy away from his roots, the one place he knew, doing that would be as mean as the storm had been. And them dogs of his, Andre could barely let them out of his sight. If Oscar were here, he'd say this island was Andre's home. Bernadette would too. But it was Mrs Williams, she was the one that did say it. She fixed them blue eyes on me and told me what to do. 'Take care of Andre. You love him.'

I went back inside and picked up the shovel. Them letters in the hatbox were for another day. They were for the day when Andre's nightmares stopped, when things were better. Mama and me would talk it over then. I'd take home the book about the stars, Oscar's watch, the crucifixes, and the wood box with the *W* and all that was in it. Those were Andre's. But not the letters. Those belonged to his daddy. They weren't for others to read. They were going in the hatbox and the hatbox was going up to the attic even if the roof had holes. Same for the letter I'd found on the floor by the icebox, the letter that was crumpled and ripped in the middle. Whatever was in them letters could wait.

If someone should come looking for Andre, well, I'd think about that then. Today, there was enough sorrow. Today, Andre was mine. Mrs Williams made it so.

I picked up her books that were on the floor. They were

warped, and the pages were brittle and stained. Novels, she'd called them. I'd take them home for Andre; he should have something of hers. She'd like that, I figured. She was partial to fancy words and likely these books were full of them.

In the parlor, I shoveled dried mud, the raspy scrape of the blade not working on me like it had. It was the sound of work; it was me getting a start on this house, making it better. It was me doing it for Andre.

Author's Note

On the morning of Saturday, September 8, 1900, Galvestonians woke to cloudy skies, rain squalls, and high tides.
The local office of the US Weather Bureau had received cables
that a disturbance was in the gulf, and hurricane flags were
raised in the city. Accustomed to tropical storms, most residents went about the day as usual. Men reported to work,
women tended to household chores, and children and tourists
went to the beach to watch crashing waves slowly destroy the
Pagoda and Murdock's bathhouses. By noon, water was several feet deep in the streets but that didn't stop people from
attending business lunches at hotel dining rooms. Soon after,
though, the sky darkened, the wind increased, and rising water
rushed through the streets.

The 1900 Galveston storm was the worst US natural
disaster in the twentieth century. The city, population 37,789,
was submerged in 8 to 15 feet of water, and prior to the wind
destroying the Weather Bureau's anemometer, the last
recorded wind velocity was 84 miles per hour. It is speculated
that during the height of the storm the winds ranged from
120 to 150 miles per hour. Historians estimate that over 6,000

people were killed in the city and that another 1,000 perished on the rest of the island. On the mainland, the death toll was approximately 1,000.

The Promise is a work of fiction but I tried to keep the depiction of the island, the sequence of the storm, and the aftermath grounded in fact as much as possible. A great deal has been written about the city of Galveston but very little about the people who lived outside of the city limits. Historical sources indicate that some of these residents were dairy farmers, cattle ranchers, and fishermen. It is my belief that they and their families were keenly aware of the weather, and that they knew something bigger than a tropical storm brewed in the gulf. However, even this awareness could not save all of them. Entire families drowned and many were never found.

St. Mary's Orphan Asylum did exist and at the time of the storm, it housed about ninety-three children, ten nuns, and several workmen. Sister Camillus and William and Joseph Murney were actual people. The orphanage disappeared during the storm, and William Murney was one of only three survivors.

Galvestonians began to rebuild even as funeral pyres burned. West Bay was eventually dredged, and the sand was used to raise the city. A seawall was built along the beach and continues to protect the city. However, Galveston lost its foothold as one of the most important seaports in America and its fortunes declined.

Gulf coast Texans have not forgotten the 1900 Galveston storm. All other hurricanes are compared to it, and Galvestonians point with pride to the buildings that survived. The building that once was the Central Hotel, the place where Catherine and Oscar began their marriage, still stands.

*

For readers who would like to read more about the storm, I suggest the following books:

Through a Night of Horrors edited by Casey Edward Greene and Shelly Henley Kelly, 2000; *A Weekend in September* by John Edward Weems, 1957; *Galveston and the 1900 Storm* by Patricia Bellis Bixel and Elizabeth Hayes Turner, 2000; and *Isaac's Storm* by Erik Larson, 1999.

Acknowledgments

I am indebted to Rob, my husband, for keeping me on track; to Judithe Little, Leah Lax, Anne Sloan, Lois F. Stark, Julie C. Kemper, Pam Barton, and Bryan Jamison for their thorough readings and for pushing me to do my best; to Casey Edward Greene and Carol Woods, archivists at Galveston's Rosenberg Library, for their willingness to search through files and source documents for even the smallest of details; to John Sullivan, Galveston rancher, for his historical perspective and stories; and to the dedicated people at Houston's Inprint and San Antonio's Gemini Ink for their ongoing support of writers.

I owe many thanks to Maria Rejt and Sophie Orme, Mantle editors extraordinaire, for knowing what to do to make the story shine; to Mary Chamberlain for her copy-editing skills; to Harriet Sanders for helping me cross the pond; to the entire staff at Pan Macmillan that rallies around each and every book; and to Margaret Halton who is always ready to stand by my side.

Thank you to Herman Graf and Jennifer McCartney, my editors at Skyhorse Publishing, for their belief in my work.

Lastly, my admiration and appreciation go to the people of Galveston. No matter what nature throws their way, they hunker down, then begin again.

The Promise

A Reader's Guide

In *The Promise*, critically acclaimed and award-winning novelist Weisgarber returns with a deeply moving story about the Galveston, Texas 1900 Storm, the worst natural disaster in the United States in the twentieth century. While there are accounts of what happened to the city of Galveston and its residents, little has been written about what happened to the families on the rural, isolated end of the island, something Weisgarber sought to remedy.

The story begins a few weeks before the storm and is told by two narrators. The first, Catherine Wainwright, is a concert pianist fleeing scandal and Ohio society by marrying Oscar Williams, a recently widowed dairy farmer who lives on the island. The second narrator is Nan Ogden, the local young woman Oscar hired to care for his home and small, grieving son, Andre.

Nan has grown attached to Oscar and Andre, and she struggles to accept Catherine in the household. As for Catherine, she is overwhelmed by her secrets, by motherhood, and by the rougher surroundings. But when the hurricane strikes, Catherine and Nan are tested as never before.

Discussion Questions

In the prologue, Nan Ogden makes a deathbed promise to her friend, Bernadette Williams. Is this promise fulfilled? Do other characters make promises?

The novel has two narrators, Nan Ogden and Catherine Williams. Nan was born and raised in Galveston while Catherine is new to the island. Is this Nan's story? Or Catherine's?

Catherine broke a social taboo by having an affair with a married man. If she did this today rather than in 1900, how might she be treated?

Texas has long been a place where people go to escape their pasts and to start anew. Was Oscar Williams able to break free from his past? Was Catherine?

Nan is also haunted by the past. Not only did she make a promise to Bernadette, but she believes she's a curse to men. Discuss the turning point(s) where she realizes she's ready to look to the future.

Oscar has a five-year-old son, Andre. How does Andre influence the story?

Music is featured throughout the book and both Catherine and Nan are musicians. What is the significance of the selected songs and the classical pieces?

Oscar admires pelicans and counts them as they skim along the beach. What does this say about his character? What is the meaning of the pelicans in the prologue and in the last chapter?

Child-rearing practices were different in 1900 than they are today. How does Nan's approach to mothering differ from Catherine's? Who is the better mother?

Discuss the roles of the men in *The Promise* and their relationships with their children.

Oscar has been described as a man who honors his commitments. He's also been described as someone who rescues people such as Catherine and Bernadette. Is this his undoing?

During the storm, Catherine tells Andre about her girlhood memories of Oscar. What is the significance of these memories?

Most readers are aware a hurricane will hit Galveston. What were your expectations about the storm? How did you expect the novel to end?

314

A Conversation with Ann Weisgarber

You divide your time between Sugar Land, Texas, and Galveston, Texas. Was this story personal for you? Have you experienced a hurricane?
Galveston is dear to me, and I wrote much of *The Promise* there. I admire the residents who make this barrier island their home. It's an iffy proposition since its location makes it prone to storms. I've been through several hurricanes but never on Galveston. That's the last place I want to be during a storm.

Our most recent hurricane was Ike in 2008. About four days before landfall, we prepared our beach house for the storm. We emptied the refrigerator, took pictures down from the walls, turned off the water and electricity, and secured the metal storm shutters over the windows and doors. The mayor of Galveston issued a mandatory evacuation, and we rode out the storm in Sugar Land, seventy miles inland.

It was frightening. Like in *The Promise*, the air hummed and the house made eerie sounds as the wind and rain battered it. We lost electricity but we had a hand-crank radio for news reports. Communication from Galveston went down during the storm so we didn't know how the island was faring.

It took a beating. People died, some disappeared, homes and businesses were flooded with up to eight feet of saltwater, and beach houses were

315

swept away. Ironically, our beach house fared better than our Sugar Land house which had roof and floor damage. In Galveston, electricity, water, and telephone services were out for weeks. It was said that Galveston would not recover but those reports didn't take into account the feisty nature of Galvestonians. The rebuilding began immediately. That's the history of Galveston.

Why did you write The Promise?
I felt an obligation to remember the people who lived on the rural, isolated end of Galveston Island during 1900 when the hurricane struck. Much has been written about the storm's impact on the city of Galveston, but the dairy farmers, ranchers, fishermen and their families have been overlooked. That's an injustice and I wrote the novel to remember them.

I'd like to add that people who are born on the island are called BOIs. They count the generations of their families, and it's a tremendous point of pride to be able to say they are seven- or six- or five-generation BOI. They don't give up when times are tough. Their attitude is the inspiration for Nan Ogden, one of the narrators in *The Promise.*

Where did you let the research leave off and the fiction begin?
This is a great question since I can get so wrapped in the research that it's hard to stop. To avoid that, I begin with the writing and when I need answers for a particular scene, I stop and do research. An example is the hotel where Catherine, one of the narrators in *The Promise*, stays when she arrives in Galveston. I searched through a book that lists Galveston's historic buildings to find hotels that existed during 1900. Then I looked for one that was respectable but reasonably priced. I found the Central Hotel which was a few blocks from the train station. That made me think about how painful it would be for Catherine to hear trains leaving the island when she longed to return to her former life in Ohio. The hotel's location let me add a layer of meaning that I hadn't originally anticipated.

Some authors say they don't read fiction while writing. Is that true for you?
Reading is part of my life and I'd be miserable if I stopped. Apart from

reading for pleasure, I read novels that relate to my writing project. Since *The Promise* explores social rules, I reread Kate Chopin's *The Awakening* to help me understand the pressures women faced during the turn of the 20th Century. W. Somerset Maugham's *The Painted Veil* sat on my desk during the early drafts. His character, Kitty, has an affair, and so does my Catherine character. Ellen Feldman's *Scottsboro* was also on hand. Her character, Ruby, has a rural, unschooled voice similar to Nan in *The Promise*. Whenever I got stuck, I reread chapters from these novels.

In both of your novels you tap into history that is not well known. How do you see the stories that others miss?
Ideas hit me when I'm in isolated landscapes. I'm drawn to those places and admire the people who first settled in these inhospitable places. Their lives often had spells of drama – floods, droughts, kidnappings, murders – but since they didn't live close to cities, they weren't headline news. That bothers me since their stories are valuable. I find myself daydreaming about their lives and sometimes a story takes shape. It's a matter of listening to the landscape, reading historical records, and gathering the courage to ask people to share stories about their ancestors.